"How hungry are you?"

"For what?"

She started unbuttoning his shirt at the top, stopping to admire and touch the soft hair on his chest on the way to the bottom. When she reached the last one, she tugged the tail out from behind his belt, slipped her arms around his body, and laid her cheek against his chest.

"Let's make love and only use words when necessary," she whispered.

"Is that a pickup line?" he asked hoarsely.

"Is it working?"

Little gold flecks sparkled in her brown eyes. How was it that he'd never noticed that before?

"You are so beautiful." His tone said that he wanted her to believe him.

With a hop, her legs were suddenly wrapped around his waist, her body pressing against his zipper and making his erection ache. But he couldn't rush this. Tonight had to be special...

HOT COWBOY NIGHTS

A Lucky Penny Ranch Novel

CAROLYN BROWN

#2

FOREVER

NEW YORK   BOSTON

Copyright © 2016 by Carolyn Brown
Preview of *Merry Cowboy Christmas* © 2016 by Carolyn Brown

Cover illustration by Blake Morrow. Cover design by Elizabeth Turner.
Cover copyright © 2016 by Hachette Book Group, Inc.

Forever
Hachette Book Group
1290 Avenue of the Americas
New York, NY 10104

www.HachetteBookGroup.com

Printed in the United States of America

First edition: May 2016

10 9 8 7 6 5 4 3

OPM

Forever is an imprint of Grand Central Publishing.

The Forever name and logo are trademarks of Hachette Book Group, Inc.

The Hachette Speakers Bureau provides a wide range of authors for speaking events. To find out more, go to www.hachettespeakersbureau.com or call (866) 376-6591.

The publisher is not responsible for websites (or their content) that are not owned by the publisher.

ISBN 978-1-4555-3490-6 (reg.); 978-1-4555-6793-5 (Walmart); 978-1-4555-3492-0 (ebook)

ATTENTION CORPORATIONS AND ORGANIZATIONS:

Most Hachette Book Group books are available at quantity discounts with bulk purchase for educational, business, or sales promotional use. For information, please call or write:

Special Markets Department, Hachette Book Group
1290 Avenue of the Americas, New York, NY 10104
Telephone: 1-800-222-6747 Fax: 1-800-477-5925

To the Tishomingo High School
graduating class of 1966

Thanks for the memories!

Dear Readers,

I have to admit that I hated to write the last paragraph of *Hot Cowboy Nights*. Lizzy and I had gotten very well acquainted in *Wild Cowboy Ways* when I kept telling her that Mitch was not the man for her. She argued until I saw her turn blue in the face several times, but in the end of *Wild Cowboy Ways*, she understood that I wasn't just whistlin' "Dixie" in the wind. Mitch really wasn't the man for her. When that happened, she informed me that I had to tell her story next.

It all started when Toby took Lizzy in his arms for a dance at her sister's wedding. The rest, as they say, is history. I hope that you enjoy the new Lizzy with her sassy attitude and cowboy Toby Dawson with his pure hotness!

There are always so many folks who deserve more than a simple thank-you when a story goes from an idea to a finished book that you see on the shelves. I want to thank Grand Central and the Forever imprint again for buying this series. And my totally fantastic editor, Leah Hultenschmidt, for the friendship, the support, and for helping me create stronger stories...every single time! And many thanks to Erin Niumata, my agent who is always there for me. One more time, much love and thanks to my husband, Mr. B. It takes a special person to live with and understand an author, and he does a fine job of it.

Grab a glass of sweet tea, maybe in a mason jar, and settle down in a comfortable rocking chair and have a nice long visit with Toby and Lizzy as they tell you all about those hot cowboy nights.

Until next time, happy reading to all y'all!

Carolyn Brown

HOT
COWBOY
NIGHTS

CHAPTER ONE

Lizzy's plan was to sneak inside the house, up the stairs, and into her room. She could already feel the cool water from the shower, washing away the hot sex still lingering on her body.

Her plan did not work.

She hadn't even kicked her boots off in front of the hall tree when her sister Allie shot out of the kitchen, grabbed her by the hand, and tugged her in toward the table, where the man Lizzy'd been in bed with not thirty minutes ago stood and gave her a sly wink. Oh, my God, how could her mother—standing right there—not notice the sparks bouncing around the room? She was sure Allie's husband, Blake, also at the table, was picking up on something.

"Where have you been?" Allie accused. Lizzy braced herself. Allie never paused for breath when she got worked up. And sure enough she started talking faster than some auctioneers that Lizzy had heard.

"I've called a dozen times and we were ready to start up a search and rescue party to find you. Mama says you've been puttin' in too many hours at the store. You've got to get out of this depression, Lizzy. Mitch isn't worth it. He's a sorry son of a bitch, but don't let him ruin your life. It's been nearly six months since that bastard left for Mexico. In fact, tomorrow is June first, and I declare it the day that you are moving forward with your life." Allie paused to suck in some air and looked around at the other three people in the kitchen. "Okay, now that she's here, get out the ice cream, Mama, so we can tell y'all our news."

Lizzy pulled out a kitchen chair and melted into it. Droplets of water still hung from Toby's hair. So he'd had time for a shower before he'd been dragged across the fence to Lizzy and her mother's house. If she hadn't had to run by her feed store for a late delivery, she might have already had time to clean up, too. But Fate had not liked her in a very long time. She tried not to notice the way those droplets ran down his neck— exactly where her mouth had been less than an hour earlier. Or that sexy white scar on his face where a bull had gored him—her fingers itched to touch it again like she'd done so many times.

He gave her a wink, and she could scarcely believe the heat between them hadn't set the wallpaper on fire. A downright miracle.

Her mother, Katy, dipped ice cream into five bowls. These days she was less stressed, now that Granny was in a care facility in Wichita Falls that specialized in the treatment and care of folks with dementia and Alzheimer's.

Allie looked like she was about to explode with some kind of fabulous news. Her husband, Blake Dawson, had one of those smiles on his face that a dose of alum couldn't erase. And then there was Blake's brother, Toby, leaning against the wall, his rock-hard body sending waves of desire shooting through her body like blasts of lightning. It wasn't fair that he could stand there all calm and collected while butterflies fluttered around in her stomach. Sweet Jesus! Why did he have to be right there in the room with her so soon after they'd gotten all slick with sweat on that twin-size bed in the back room of her mama's convenience store?

Allie and Katy carried the ice cream to the table and as luck would have it, Toby sat beside Lizzy around the table made for four people. His thigh pressed against hers and she had trouble concentrating on the ice cream, the excitement in her sister's dark brown eyes, her brother-in-law's grin, or anything else.

"We had the ultrasound done yesterday, and it's a girl..." Allie reached for Blake's hand.

Katy's spoon hit the table with a thud.

Toby jumped up and hugged his brother across the table.

Lizzy felt as if someone sucked all the oxygen from her lungs and left her to smother to death in a grove of mesquite trees. It was exactly the vision she'd had for herself before her fiancé had run off with another woman.

"Oh, Allie, th-that's wonderful," Lizzy stammered.

Tears filled Lizzy's eyes. As happy as she was for her sister, she couldn't help feeling a stab of jealousy that Allie now had everything Lizzy ever wanted. Then guilt set in and the tears flowed down her cheeks even worse. How could she ever be jealous of her sister who only wanted the same things that Lizzy did? Poor Allie's ex-husband had lied to her and left her feeling like less of a woman because she couldn't have children. It had taken years for her to get over it, and now she'd finally found happiness with Blake in her life.

Lizzy pushed back her chair and rounded the table to hug her sister. "Have you thought of names?"

"We had three boy names picked out, but now we have to do some rethinking." Allie smiled.

Blake kissed her on the cheek and beamed.

A loud sob turned all their attention in that direction.

"Mama? Are you all right?" Allie asked.

Katy wiped at the tears with a paper towel. "I'm going to be a grandmother, and it's a girl. I wish your dad could have seen this day. He wanted grandchildren so badly."

"Don't cry, Mama. He knows and so does Granny even though her mind is gone. They both still know on some level." Allie reached over and squeezed her mother's hand. "I feel like I've been given miracles and magic. Blake and I are having a family and the doctor says there's no reason we can't have more children when we want them."

Miracles and magic. Those two words played in a continuous loop through Lizzy's mind as she dipped into her ice cream. That's exactly what Lizzy wanted, and she'd get neither if she kept fooling around with Toby Dawson.

Lightning zipped through the sky. Thunder sounded like it was rolling right over the top of Toby's travel trailer, and the heavy rain pounded on the metal roof, drowning out Blue's whimpering as the old Catahoula dog cowered beside his bed.

Toby laced his hands behind his head and tried to make sense of what he'd gotten himself into. He'd met Lizzy Logan back in the winter when he came to the Lucky Penny Ranch to visit Blake one weekend and wasn't real impressed with her. But then her fiancé broke up with her on the day of Blake and Allie's wedding and he'd felt sorry for the woman. So he asked her to dance. One thing had led to another, and by the time spring rolled around and he'd moved out to the Lucky Penny permanently, the two of them had just been waiting to combust. Now he and Lizzy were hot and heavy and out of hand, and he wasn't sure what to do about it. The sex was nothing but booty calls for him and rebound sex for her and it was getting damned awkward, so it was time to end the after-hour visits to the convenience store.

Ending the fling couldn't make things any weirder

than they were already. Sitting beside her at the table that night, pretending to be nothing more than acquaintances and knowing that they'd been between the sheets earlier was downright crazy. But he'd seen that yearning look in her eyes when Allie made the announcement about the baby. Lizzy was ready for a real relationship that led to the altar and then babies. Toby still had a lot of wild oats to sow, and just thinking of settling down with one woman made him shudder.

The travel trailer where he was living had a small sitting room and kitchen combination right inside the front door. The sofa made out into a bed that slept two people. A booth-type table could be lowered and cushions readjusted to sleep two more. The kitchen consisted of a single sink, microwave, two-burner cooktop, and a dorm-size refrigerator that was situated underneath part of the cabinets. Beyond that was a bedroom with a double bed that took up nearly all the room and a tiny bathroom with a shower, potty, and wall-hung sink.

In the beginning when he and his brother, Blake, and cousin, Jud, had pooled their money and bought the Lucky Penny, the plan had been that they would all live in the ranch house until such time as Jud and Toby could build a place of their own. But then Blake got married and that changed everything. There was still a room in the house that Toby could use, but newlyweds needed their privacy, and truth be told, so did he. Living with Blake would be one thing; living with a new sister-in-law was a whole different ball game.

Not that he didn't like Allie. No sir! She was an angel complete with a halo and wings, or maybe since she was a crackerjack carpenter, complete with a hammer and a buzz saw. She'd tamed his brother, who had the reputation for being the wildest cowboy in Texas, and that took someone with special powers for sure.

When the storm moved on, cow dog Blue scratched his ear and then headed toward the trap door in the floor beside the sofa and disappeared down under the trailer. The old boy didn't like being cooped up except when it thundered. He wasn't a bit afraid of a full-grown Angus bull, and between him and Shooter, Blake's dog, they could herd cattle with the best of the dogs in the state. But when it came to thunder, poor old Blue wanted to lie on the foot of Toby's bed until it ceased.

Toby heard a noise and thought that Blue had changed his mind and was on his way back inside, when suddenly a body appeared inside his bedroom door. Adrenaline pumped through his veins as he shot into a sitting position and wished to hell that he wasn't strip stark naked under the covers.

"Toby, are you asleep?" Lizzy whispered.

"Lizzy? Dammit! You scared me," he said. "I thought we agreed this was too close to the house for us to meet here."

She sat down on the edge of the bed. "We need to talk."

"Oh?" He switched on the reading lamp attached to the headboard. If there were four words a man ever dreaded more, he wasn't sure what they were. "About what?"

Her eyes locked with his, but she immediately blinked and looked away. "Toby, I'm not this person. Before you moved to Dry Creek, I was going to marry a preacher, for God's sake. I've never been a wild woman who fell into bed with a guy she'd just met."

"I know that you don't trust men after what Mitch did..."

She held up a palm. "It has nothing to do with trust. Mitch was a rotten apple down at the bottom of a barrel. That doesn't mean all the other apples have to be rotten. Some of them might taste real good, so it wouldn't be fair to judge them by the rotten one. Trust isn't an issue."

"Then what is it?"

"It's just...When Allie...What we're doing..." She took a deep breath. "Toby, we have to stop this. I want kids and maybe someday a place big enough they can have freedom to run and play. You are a player, a damn hot cowboy, but I know you aren't interested in settling down. So let's not waste each other's time."

"Blunt, aren't you?" He gently turned her chin so she was looking into his eyes. "Lizzy, I was well aware this was rebound sex from the first time." His mouth curved up in an enticing grin. "And I'm still happy to help you practice in the hot sex department until you find your Mr. Wonderful."

"You aren't even my type, but I'd be lying if I said it hasn't been fun."

"And you damn sure aren't mine," he said.

"What is your type?" she asked.

"No strings. Likes to party, drink beer, dance in old honky-tonks, and after my famous breakfast-after-sex the next morning, she goes on her way."

"Well, then I guess this is good-bye, Toby," she whispered.

"Can't be. We'll see each other every day probably."

"Then it's good-bye to the sex," she said.

He waggled his dark eyebrows. "Unless you want one more time to seal the deal."

She stood and moved to the door. "It sounds inviting, but if I fall into that bed with you tonight, my gut tells me we'll never end this."

"Hey, I told you what my type is, so before you go, tell me what you want in a man," he said.

She tucked a damp strand of hair back into her ponytail and pulled the hood of her sweatshirt up. "Someone who loves me for who I am, not what he wants to change me into, and someone who wants the same things I do. Who'd just as soon sit on the porch and hold hands as go dancing in a honky-tonk. And who wants a yard full of kids and who isn't afraid of hard work."

"I hope you find him," Toby said.

"Thanks for the good times, Toby." She paused. "You helped more than you know."

"Does that make me a therapist?" He didn't want her to go, but the thought of settling down put him in flight mode.

"Maybe it does." She smiled again. "See you Sunday after church. I guess dinner is at our place."

"Lizzy..." He swallowed hard. "Thanks for being honest with me."

She slipped out the door and Blue found his way back up through the trap door to stretch out on the rug in front of the bed. Toby shut his eyes, glad that she'd made the first step. God, he hated it when women cried, which was probably the reason he didn't let himself get roped into relationships. Toby Dawson was a player, plain and simple, and he had just dodged a bullet.

Lizzy let herself into the house quietly and went straight to her room. She heard the rattle of glass as her mother unloaded the dishwasher, but Lizzy didn't want to talk to or see anyone that night. Especially her mother. Mama would've immediately sniffed out the lie, and the house would have exploded if Lizzy had admitted that she'd been screwing around with Toby Dawson almost every day for three weeks.

It was nothing short of a miracle that they hadn't gotten caught.

Already the rumors were hovering like buzzards waiting for roadkill. From day one the Lucky Penny couldn't buy an ounce of good luck, and everything that happened on the ranch was fodder for the gossip mill. Half the folks in Dry Creek, Texas, were hoping that Blake and his family joined the long list of owners who failed at trying to make the Lucky Penny a profitable ranch. The other half was rooting for the three

Dawsons—Blake, Toby, and their cousin, Jud, who would be joining them in the fall.

Lizzy pulled off her boots, kicked them somewhere close to the closet door, and changed into a faded nightshirt that she pulled from last week's laundry still tossed in the rocking chair in the corner. Cleanliness was a virtue, according to the Good Book, but neatness was not mentioned. Unlike her sisters, Allie and Fiona, Lizzy must have been out chasing butterflies or playing with baby lambs when they passed out neatness because she didn't get a bit of it.

She fell back on the bed, legs dangling off the side and her head nowhere near a pillow. Staring at the ceiling with nothing but the small bedside lamp to light the room, she let the past run through her mind again for the hundredth time since Mitch had called to tell her he loved another woman. He and the preacher's daughter had decided to become missionaries, and he would preach at the little church they'd gone to Mexico to build.

Her world had shattered. And then Toby had taken her in his arms at Blake and Allie's wedding and she realized maybe all wasn't over for her after all. He'd charmed her and made her feel alive again—like a woman to be desired. It hadn't ended with the dance but they'd talked on the phone, exchanged text messages, and when he moved to town they were both primed and ready for a hot little affair. But that night when Allie told them she was having a girl, Lizzy knew it was time to end the secretive, wild nights.

Lizzy crawled under the covers and turned out the light.

So which was she? A sweet little preacher's-wife type who would let her husband lead her around by his every whim, like she'd been with Mitch? Or a brazen hussy, like the loose women who'd founded Audrey's Place, who took what she wanted from life and didn't have any regrets?

She'd far rather be the latter if she had to choose. She'd come out of the Mitch experience a stronger woman than ever, and she'd been honest when she told Toby that it hadn't made her shy away from guys in general. And it damn sure hadn't made her feel sorry for herself. It had taught her to be brutally honest and not let anyone try to change her into something she wasn't.

She picked up her phone to check for a sexy text message from Toby, but there was nothing. Nada. Nil. Zilch. Not a single missed message. Finally she wrote one to him: *Changed my mind. See you tomorrow at six at Mama's store.*

With one thumb on the DELETE button and the other on the SEND button, she sat there in the darkness, her body telling her to send the message and her heart telling her that she was in for misery if she didn't press DELETE.

CHAPTER TWO

June was coming in hot with the temperatures already in the eighties that morning. The cowbell hanging on the door of the Dry Creek Feed and Seed store had sounded loud and clear early the next morning, and a blast of hot air swept across the whole store.

Hot! That word reminded Lizzy of what she'd given up with Toby, and she blushed. She stretched the kinks from her neck and rounded the end of the display case where she'd been moving flower seeds to another part of the store. Thank God she'd not given in to the moment of weakness the night before. It had taken ten minutes before she finally pressed the DELETE button and tossed her phone to the recliner across the room.

If it was all the way on the other side of the room, she wouldn't be nearly so tempted to send Toby a message, or God forbid, call him. But that didn't mean she wasn't going to miss the calls, texts, and the sex. Maybe this whole thing with him was like craving alcohol. Too bad there weren't meetings in town that she could go to, but no one had thought to start up a therapy group for TDA—Toby Dawson Anonymous. Give it six months, though, and there might be enough women in the area to begin one.

The cowbell above the door into the feed store announced a customer, and Lizzy peeked around the corner of the aisle between two rows of shelves to see Lucy Hudson. At least it wasn't Toby. This was only day one of her resolution, and she wasn't ready to be alone with him just yet.

"Good morning, Lucy. What are you doing in town this morning?"

Lucy's jeans hung on her slim frame like a tow sack on a broom handle. Her long gray hair had been twisted up in a bun on top of her hair, but several wispy strands had escaped and stuck to her sweaty neck.

"I'm here to see if you still got that size small orange hooded jacket. Nadine said you put it on half price last week, and the zipper in mine done broke last week. I can put it up for another year." Lucy found the jacket and latched on to it. "You take this and put it on the counter so nobody else will come in here while I'm lookin' around and steal it out from under my nose."

"Yes, ma'am. I'll start a ticket and put it in a sack," Lizzy said.

Lucy kept going through the sales rack, one item at a time. "I'm supposed to get Herman a chain saw blade. He said you kept a note of what kind and size up under the counter."

Lizzy bagged the jacket and went to the aisle where she kept supplies for chain saws, chose the right blade, and was on her way to the checkout counter when the cowbell rang again. Truman O'Dell brought in a gust of hot air with him along with a sneeze that sounded like it came from a three-hundred-pound trucker rather than a skinny little fellow who wasn't much taller than Lizzy's five feet, five inches. He quickly jerked a red bandanna from the hip pocket of his bibbed overalls and held it against his face for the second sneeze. The paisley pattern didn't do much to muffle the sound, but it did seem to stop the attack.

"Damned old allergies. Hits me every year at this time," Truman said. "Mornin', Lucy. How's things at your place? Y'all's garden producin'?"

"Comin' right on. We got tomatoes and squash comin' out our ears. Can't seem to work fast enough to get everything frozen or canned. Y'all still runnin' produce down to Throckmorton to the farmers' market on Saturdays?" Lucy kept going through clothing racks without looking up.

"Yes, we are."

"If you got room, I could send some produce down there with you. You still chargin' ten percent for the extra stuff you take?"

Truman propped an elbow on the edge of the clothing rack. "Herman still cuttin' wood out there at the Lucky Penny?"

"Yes, he is. Long as Blake is willing to bulldoze it down, he'll be taking it to the wood yard. Could be we'll have another hard winter next year and we're gettin' a supply for then," Lucy answered.

"I don't agree with him helpin' them boys," Truman said.

"Don't reckon anybody that size can be called boys," Lucy answered. "And Herman likes Blake and Toby. Says they are hardworkin' cowboys who love the land and will take care of it."

"Summer is just about to get geared up, and I reckon they'll get tired of hard work when they have to sweat and fight every kind of varmint there is. Ain't no use in us folks that's been here all these years helpin' them clear the land," Truman said.

Lucy glared across the clothing at him. "So, are you sayin' that if my husband cuts wood on the Lucky Penny, wood that Blake and Toby are giving away for free when they clear the land, that you won't take my extra produce to the market?"

"That's what I'm sayin'." Truman nodded.

"Why are you being a horse's rear end about that ranch?" she asked. "It ain't nothing to you whether they make it work or not."

"I just think the folks around here need to be careful who they go openin' up their arms to is all. Why make a big show of welcomin' them boys to the community when they ain't goin' to stay?" Truman sniffed.

Lizzy grabbed a dusting rag and worked over every inch of the checkout counter and the cash register while she kept an ear tuned to the argument.

"That's a crock of horse crap. Maybe the folks who didn't stick with it would have if they'd have had some support. And you're still mad because you wanted to buy that place but you wanted it for nothing," Lucy said.

"Well," Truman huffed. "If they'd have kept their money in their pockets, I could have got that ranch for what I was willin' to give. I'm not about to support them and I'm not helping anyone who does."

"That's your choice, but I think you are a dang fool." Lucy carried several more orange jackets to the counter. "Lizzy, put these on my ticket. Herman and our sons will need new ones come fall for huntin' season, and this is a right good price."

"Can I help you with something, Truman?" Lizzy called out.

"I come to pay my last month's bill." He whipped out a roll of bills and removed the rubber band from them. "If there was another place to buy my feed, I wouldn't do business with you anymore, not since your sister married Blake Dawson."

"Truman O'Dell!" Lucy slapped him on the arm hard enough that he flinched. "Listen to your stupid mouth spoutin' off like that. God almighty, your daddy did business here with Lizzy's grandpa. Get that bug out of your butt before it eats holes in your gut and kills you graveyard dead."

Lizzy seethed inside but kept a sweet smile on her face. At least she hoped it was sweet because it sure felt like more of a grimace. "Let me ring up Lucy's purchases and then we'll square up your bill."

"That wasn't nice to hit me," Truman growled. "If you wasn't a woman, you wouldn't get away with that."

Lucy popped her veined hands on her skinny hip bones. "Truman O'Dell, if you want to hit me back you go right ahead, but I promise I will mop up Lizzy's floor with you if you do. I'm strong and I'm mean and Herman don't even cross me, so you ought to watch your mouth."

Lord, please let me grow up to be just like her. Lizzy sent up a silent prayer as she figured up Lucy's bill and laid out a ticket for her to sign. "I was going to knock those jackets down another twenty-five percent come Monday so I gave you a better price."

"Well, bless your heart, darlin'. See there, Truman, that's why you do business with the folks you know. They won't cheat you out of your boxer shorts." Lucy signed the ticket and carried her purchases outside. She headed off to the left instead of getting into her truck, which was parked in front of the feed and seed store. That meant she was going to Nadine's for a cup of coffee and to tell anyone who would listen about the argument she had with Truman.

Lizzy turned to Truman. "Now, let's see about that bill."

"Add a twenty-pound bag of seed potatoes to it. I always plant a later crop so we have potatoes up into the fall," he said.

She picked up the shoe box from under the counter, pulled out all his yellow copies, and added them up. The old folks didn't like the idea of a computerized bill and it made double work for her, but it made them happy. "Looks like you owe six hundred thirty dollars and fifty-five cents. I'll add in the seed potatoes now." She poked in several numbers on the cash register, fighting back the urge to charge double for the potatoes after what he said about Allie. "And that brings your total to six hundred forty-eight dollars and ninety cents."

He peeled seven hundred-dollar bills from the roll and laid them on the counter. "Your granddaddy would have thrown a fit about Allie marryin' up with that boy."

"My granddaddy has been dead for a long time," Lizzy said. "And Allie is my sister, so be careful what you say about her."

"Are you going to hit me, too?" Truman taunted.

"No, sir. My mama trained me up right. I wouldn't hit an elderly gentleman. But if you say too much about my sister, I might have to take the pistol out from under this counter and shoot an old fart in the leg." She laid his change on the counter. "There's fifty-one dollars and a dime and, Truman, if you don't want to do business with me, then don't."

He picked it up and marched out of the store without saying another word. Lizzy went back to her office and started to work on her computer. She'd barely gotten two bills entered when the phone rang, and since it was an old corded phone beside the cash register, she had to hustle to get to it.

"Hello," she said, wishing for caller ID.

"Lizzy Logan, did you threaten to shoot Truman?" Lucy asked.

"Yes, ma'am, I did. He was saying mean things about my sister," Lizzy answered. "How do you know that? He just left here five minutes ago."

"Bobby Ray is cutting wood out on the Lucky Penny today, so Truman called him and asked to speak to Herman to tattle on me and you both. Herman hates cell phones to begin with and he and Truman are crossways over everything, so he put him straight. Then Bobby Ray called Nadine to tell her and I'm sittin' right here in Nadine's café," Lucy said.

"It don't take things long to get around, does it? Maybe I shouldn't have said I'd shoot him, but I was really mad and he got all cocky and asked if I was going to hit him like you did," Lizzy said.

Lucy chuckled. "Hell, honey, only thing you did wrong was in givin' him a warnin'. Next time shoot first and ask questions later. I'll help you bury the body where not even the buzzards can find him."

The line went dead and Lizzy put the receiver back on the old black base. At first she giggled, then it grew to a side-splitting laughter that echoed off the walls of the feed store so loudly that she didn't even hear the cowbell ringing. She wasn't aware of a presence until she looked across the counter into Toby's steely blue eyes.

Her first thought was that she wished she'd put off having hot sex with him one more day, because a quickie in the office with the shades all pulled down would have been one sweet way to celebrate the whole morning. She blinked and looked away as the laughter dried up.

I have gone, she glanced at the clock on the counter, *fifteen hours and thirty minutes without sex with Toby Dawson. They say the first twenty-four hours are the hardest, so if I can resist that hot cowboy eight hours and thirty more minutes, the tough part will be behind me.*

"What's so funny?" he asked.

"You would have had to been here," she said. "God bless the women of Dry Creek."

"Oh, yeah?" Toby propped a hip on the counter. "I could use a good story this morning."

"It all started when this old guy said he wasn't going to take Lucy's produce to the farmers' market." Lizzy went on to tell the whole tale.

By the time she finished Toby was laughing even harder than she had.

"You should take these stories and do a gig as a comedian. You have a way with words and telling things that is a hell of a lot funnier than a lot of stand-up comedians I've heard," he said.

"Well!" She rolled her eyes and threw open her

arms. "Some people can tell a joke and some people can't."

The expression on her face made him laugh even harder.

"You, darlin', are a hoot."

"Too damn bad I'm not your type." She smiled.

"And too damn bad I'm not yours because I do like the way you make me laugh," Toby said. "But to get on with why I'm here, I need about a hundred fence posts and a couple of rolls of barbed wire delivered out to the Lucky Penny."

"Want to start a charge?" she asked.

One eyebrow slid up slightly. "I thought we had to pay cash if we were from the Lucky Penny."

"You did until my sister married your brother. Now if you and Blake want a charge account, I can set it up for you. Payment's due on the first of every month with a two percent finance charge if it's not paid by the tenth," she said.

He shook his head. "Why the change of heart?"

"Truman O'Dell made me mad this morning," she said honestly.

"Truman?" Toby asked.

Was he an old boyfriend? Or maybe a friend of her ex? Suddenly, Toby's curiosity was piqued beyond keeping quiet.

"Truman of the story I just told you," she answered. "He's the old guy. Not much taller than me and goes around looking like he kissed the south end of a north-bound heifer."

Toby chuckled. The woman did have a way with words.

"Oh, *that* Truman. I understand now."

"So do you want credit or not?" she asked.

"No, thank you. We like to use our business credit card. Keeps things simpler for our accountant at tax time. You do have our farm tax number, though, don't you?"

She nodded. "Blake gave it to me. So a hundred fence posts and two rolls of wire. You aren't working Allie too hard out there are you?"

"You kidding? Hard to keep her down. She's bedding and taping the Sheetrock that Blake and I hung in the kitchen today. But this evening we're running her out of the house while we paint it because the fumes aren't good for the baby. So she'll be over at your place until bedtime. Don't worry your pretty head about us doing anything that would harm Allie." He leaned over the counter to flirt and then remembered that the fling was over and straightened up quickly.

"Forgot there, didn't you? Once a bad boy, always a bad boy," Lizzy said.

The door opened and Sharlene Tucker pushed her way inside. If her skinny jeans had been any tighter they would have burst at the seams. Her blond hair was thrown up in a ratty ponytail, and her cowboy boots were scuffed at the toes.

Sharlene eyed Toby like a coyote going after a one-legged chicken. "I'm Sharlene Tucker. Got time for a cup of coffee down at Nadine's?"

Blake and Deke both had warned him about Sharlene and Mary Jo, but the strongest tip had been about Sharlene. She had been bragging that she would bed and wed Toby Dawson before the year was out since she'd missed out on doing the same thing with his brother, Blake.

"Thank you, but not today, Miz Sharlene, but it was nice meeting you. Good day, Lizzy. I'll look for that order sometime this afternoon, right?"

"Soon as my part-time guy gets here." She ran the card, rang up the bill, and pushed the receipt across the counter for him to sign.

Sharlene tilted her head to one side. "How about Sunday dinner? I've been out of pocket the last few weekends, but I'll be in church this week. Nadine makes a mean chicken fried steak on Sundays."

He shook his head and took a step back. "Got plans but thanks for the offer."

"With Deke? You can bring him along."

Deke was a lifelong friend of all the Logan women. He was Allie's right-hand man when it came to construction jobs, and his ranch was right next door to the Lucky Penny. Plus, he'd become Blake's friend the first week that he'd moved to the Lucky Penny and he was always, always ready for a good time. His taste in tall, loose-legged blondes ran the same as Toby's.

"No, not with Deke. Good day, Sharlene."

"Maybe another time." She smiled.

He tipped his hat toward both ladies and headed for the door.

"Dammit!" Sharlene slapped the countertop. "I'm not giving up, Lizzy."

Before Lizzy could answer, her phone buzzed. She pulled it out of her hip pocket, saw Toby's face on the screen, and answered it in her best business voice. "Yes, sir, did you forget something?"

"Is that woman still there?"

"Of course. Here she is." Lizzy handed the phone off to Sharlene.

CHAPTER THREE

I'm still mad at you," Toby said that Sunday afternoon as he, Blake, Allie, Katy, and Lizzy found seats at Nadine's. "I cannot believe you'd do that to me after all we had."

"Shhh!" Lizzy shushed him. "Someone will hear you. I figured if you had anything to say to Sharlene, you might as well say it to her yourself."

"She's stalking me now. I've gotten a dozen text messages and that many calls that I didn't answer. You gave her my cell phone number, didn't you?" Toby narrowed his eyes at Lizzy as they sat down in the last two chairs on the back row.

"You told me exactly what you are interested in, and she fits the bill to a tee," Lizzy said. "You should be thanking me for my help."

"I could wring your neck for your help," Toby said. "Tell me again why we're here."

"Nadine and a few other folks have decided to get up a homecoming combined with a big Fourth of July bash this year. It's to help entice folks into coming back for a visit and celebrate the town, I suppose," she whispered.

"Well, it looks like everyone in Dry Creek has turned out for it. This place is jam-packed. Oh, shit! There's Sharlene up there and she's staring right at me."

"It's love at first sight." Lizzy giggled.

"You are not funny," Toby said.

Nadine's café had opened back in February and already it was the central hub for everything from gossip to Sunday dinner in Dry Creek. It shared the block with the Dry Creek Convenience Store owned by Katy, which offered staples like milk and bread and had two gas pumps out front. Then two empty storefronts with dirty windows separated it from the Dry Creek Feed and Seed, which Lizzy ran, on the other end of the street.

That Sunday afternoon, the café had closed at two, right after the after-church dinner run, and reopened at three for a town meeting. Nadine provided coffee, sweet tea, and an assortment of homemade cookies on a table right inside the door. She and her two best friends, Sharlene and Mary Jo, sat in three chairs facing the crowd. At exactly three thirty, Nadine turned on the portable microphone and got the meeting started.

"All y'all know me but for the record, I'm Nadine and this meeting is about our first ever homecoming here in Dry Creek. I know we have the football home-coming at the school in the fall every year, but this is something different. We are putting out the word to everyone who has ever lived in Dry Creek to come home on the Saturday before July Fourth." She stopped and glanced over at the other two women. "Sitting up here with me are my two best friends, Mary Jo and Sharlene, and they've promised to help me with re-freshments here in the café for the whole day so folks will have a place to sit and visit." She turned and pointed to Mary Jo and Sharlene, and they both waved to the packed café.

"This whole idea came about when we were talking about how wonderful it would be if we could entice folks back to Dry Creek and maybe in the next few years, we'd have all the empty buildings filled up on Main Street again. Remember a great oak once started as a little old acorn and this idea might produce some-thing awesome. It could take a few years, but then an oak tree grows slowly. Do we have other volunteers for contributions?"

Toby raised his hand. "The Lucky Penny will pro-vide banners to stretch across Main Street on both ends announcing the homecoming. If we don't put a date on them, they could be used more than one year if this be-comes an annual affair."

If he had to attend because Blake, Allie, and Lizzy said so, then he'd at least show the people of Dry Creek that the cowboys on the Lucky Penny intended to be a part of the community.

Katy's hand shot up. "My store will foot the bill for an advertisement in the Throckmorton newspaper to run two weeks before the festival. Y'all be thinkin' about anything you want to add to it. Will there be a western theme where folks dress up or will it simply be a visiting and eating cookies day?"

Lucy Hudson stood up. "The ladies at the church will lay out a nice potluck noon meal for anyone who attends. That way Nadine won't have to try to cook and be a hostess, too. I'll head the committee and make it right with the preacher."

Sharlene reached for the microphone. "This is great. How about if we bill it as the past, present, and future of Dry Creek, Texas?"

"With prizes for the oldest person who attends and maybe the youngest," Herman said.

"And maybe a gift card to a nice restaurant for the family who attends with the most children," Lucy added.

"I'll supply balloons and a tank of helium if anyone wants to give them out to the kids," Lizzy said.

Mary Jo took the microphone. "I'll be glad to take care of the balloons right here in the store," she offered. "So if you'll bring them and the helium down here the day before, I'll have the ribbons cut and ready. And I'll head that committee and be sure the prizes are for gift cards to the three stores right here in Dry Creek so we can keep our money at home. Anyone who wants to donate anything from a dollar to a million." She hesitated while the chuckles faded. "Just give it to me. I'll write you a receipt and your name will be listed when we present the prizes."

"So we got a past and we're here in the present," Truman spoke up from a back corner. "Why would any of y'all think we have a future?"

Lizzy sat close enough to Toby that he leaned slightly and whispered right into her ear. "Who is that man?"

"That is Truman. Remember the story I told you? Don't pay any attention to him," Lizzy answered.

"Truman, we are hoping that with some hard work we can bring Dry Creek back to a prosperous little Texas town," Mary Jo said.

"You might as well scratch your fanny and wish for the moon. This whole thing will be a big bust just like these fool cowboys who think they can turn the Lucky Penny around," Truman said.

"Well, ain't you just a ray of sunshine and help?" Lucy said. "We've already got Mary Jo talking about putting in a beauty shop, and Sharlene is considering starting a day care center."

Nadine quickly took the microphone. "And that's all we've got right now, so y'all have some cookies and visit about this. We'll be putting things into the works right soon since we've got about three weeks to pull it together. But all three of us believe that we truly can bring Dry Creek back to a nice little town if we work at it...together." She pointed to the refreshment table. "And we can start by showing all the folks who've lived here that we are positive and that we are determined."

Allie started the applause but Toby noticed that Truman kept his arms folded over his skinny chest and glared at them from across the room.

Folks were still talking about the festival when Katy and Lizzy escaped out the front door. They were about to get in the car when they heard a horn honk, and Allie waved from halfway down the block.

"Hey, y'all come on over to the ranch and see my new kitchen. It's so pretty and shiny," she shouted.

"I've got to drive up to Wichita Falls and see Mama this afternoon. They need me to sign some more papers, and she's been whining for a chocolate pie so I'm taking her one," Katy said. "But Lizzy can go. If she can ride with you, it'll save me the trip of taking her home."

"What if I don't want to go?" Lizzy asked.

"You do, though, so don't argue about it. Get on down there and go with Allie. It's a fine day for a nice walk across the pasture when you want to go home," Katy answered.

"Thirty minutes. That is the limit of how long I'm staying. I've promised myself a long Sunday afternoon nap and then I'm reading that brand-new cowboy romance by Katie Lane," Lizzy said.

"That's up to you." Katy fastened her seat belt and backed out onto the street.

"Hey, Lizzy," Mary Jo hollered from the front of the café. "I need to tell you something quick before you get away."

Lizzy held up a finger to let Allie know she'd be a minute and waited for Mary Jo to catch up. The bright sun was hot on her cheeks and there wasn't a hint of a breeze, which in itself was about the norm for June in Dry Creek. Granny always said it was because it was so damn hot in the summer if the wind blew like it did the rest of the year, it would cook the skin right off of a person.

Mary Jo's high-heeled shoes made a tapping noise on the old wooden sidewalks as she made her way from the café to the front of the feed store. The closer she got, the more convinced Lizzy was that she was bringing bad news because she looked like someone had died.

"I thought you should know." She laid a hand on Lizzy's shoulder. "That Mitch and his new wife are going to be in the States over July Fourth. Bobby Ray told him about the festival even before we announced it today and he says since he preached at this church a few times it would be a great time to see everyone."

Bobby Ray, Nadine's husband, was friends with both her ex-fiancé, Mitch, and Allie's ex-husband, Riley. If Nadine didn't keep a solid thumb on him, he'd probably be as big of a jackass as both his friends, but she did a good job of reeling him in.

"It's a free country. I expect he can go wherever he wants. What we had is over and in the past."

"Well, if you need any of us, you call and we'll be there for you." Mary Jo hugged her briefly, whipped around, and headed back toward the café.

Lizzy wouldn't hold her breath waiting for Mary Jo or Sharlene or even Nadine to support her—especially Sharlene. That woman had Toby Dawson on the brain, and the only reason she'd help Lizzy out of any situation would be so she'd tell her about Toby.

Lizzy waited to feel anger, betrayal, or something, but nothing happened. She opened the back door of Blake's truck and crawled inside with Toby right beside her. Frankly, she really, really didn't care what all the gossips in town had to say about that, either.

"What was that all about?" Allie asked.

"Mitch and his new bride are planning to be at the festival here in town." She roped herself in with the seat belt.

"Don't let it get to you." One side of Allie's nose twitched in disgust. "After what he did to you, he shouldn't show his face in this town again."

"Frankly, my dear, I don't give a shit," Lizzy replied with a giggle at her Rhett Butler impression. "I'm over him."

Lizzy realized she didn't give a rat's ass if Mitch came to town or not, with or without his new wife. She'd burned that bridge and roasted virtual marshmallows in the fire.

"That's a few weeks from now. Maybe he'll change his mind." Allie peeked over the front seat.

"Things can change in a matter of seconds," Toby said.

Blake put the dual cab truck in reverse, backed out, and headed down the road a mile to the Lucky Penny.

"Hey, changing the subject here. Deke called and said he'd be at the house when we get there. He's bringing five big thick rib eye steaks to grill for supper."

Toby's hand covered Lizzy's but then he jerked it back. "You sure this isn't a problem?"

"I like steak and I like Deke's better than anyone's, so it's not a problem." She used both hands to smooth out the wrinkles from the peach-colored flippy skirt she'd worn to church that morning. She'd tucked a sleeveless western-cut shirt with lace insets down the front into the waistband.

"Hey, we should call Fiona and see if she can get away to come to the festival. We haven't seen her in months," Lizzy said, quickly changing the subject.

"Wouldn't that be great?" Allie clapped her hands. "Let's do it when we get home. We'll convince her to come home even if it's just for the weekend."

"So is Fiona married? I know she's your sister, but I haven't heard much about her," Toby asked.

"She's not your type, either," Lizzy said.

"Either?" Toby asked.

"Yes, either?" Allie twisted around in the seat again. "Who else are you talking about?"

"Sharlene." Lizzy covered her slip of the tongue quickly. "She's stalking Toby."

"For real?" Blake asked.

"And it's all Lizzy's fault. I called the store to ask her if Sharlene was still there so I'd know if it was safe to go to Nadine's for a cup of coffee without running into the woman. And Lizzy gave her the phone, so I had to talk to her and then Lizzy gave her my cell phone number," Toby said.

Allie giggled. "That's pretty mean, Lizzy."

"That's exactly what I said," Toby chimed in.

"It's not as mean as Mitch coming back to town and flaunting his new wife," Lizzy protested.

Blake parked in front of the house. "Let him come to town. After the stunt he pulled, he won't get a warm reception, believe me."

Allie unfastened her seat belt so she could turn around in the seat. "He won't have much of a backing from this family or from Nadine and her cronies. Nadine thinks Mama is a saint straight from the portals of heaven for letting her have that café building so cheap. And Sharlene and Mary Jo are both talking about putting in businesses in town, which means they'll have to deal with Mama, too. Mitch won't mess with those three, and I don't expect he'll get too warm a reception from Lucy Hudson, either, and everyone knows that if you are on Lucy's bad side, then it's bad news."

Deke met them on the porch and led the way into the house. Taller than the Dawson brothers, he was every bit as handsome with thick brown hair that he wore long enough to be sexy, hazel eyes, and broad shoulders. Women tended to flock to him like a moth to a burning candle. But taming Deke would be harder than training a Dawson cowboy to the halter. He was full of tough cowboy charm, and it would take a special woman to rope him and get him aimed toward the altar.

"Why the long faces? Did somebody die at that town meeting?" He yawned. "I would've gone but I had a wicked hangover. I knew redheads were firecrackers, but I had no idea she could drink me under the table."

Toby chuckled. "Got a hold of a wild one, did you?"

"Oh, man! Blake's hangover medicine even took a while to take effect. I'm going to make sweet tea. Who all wants a glass?" Deke asked. "I've got the steaks marinating in the refrigerator and I brought one of them cheesecakes from the store for dessert."

"There's a gallon jug already made up in the fridge," Allie said.

"I'd rather have a beer," Lizzy said.

Allie spun around to stare at her. "What did you say?"

Lizzy repeated it. "I want a beer."

Deke almost ran his glass over before he realized he needed to stop pouring. "Holy shit! What did happen at that town meeting? Saint Lizzy doesn't drink beer."

"Mitch is coming for the festival on July Fourth weekend. Lizzy says it doesn't bother her and I expect she's tired of talking about it," Allie said.

Toby twisted the top off two beers and handed one to Lizzy.

She guzzled down a third of it before coming up for air. "And he's bringing his new little wife and I *am* tired of talking about it. And if you call me Saint Lizzy again, I will hit you in the head with this beer bottle."

Deke bent over to drink the tea from his glass without picking it up. "Yes, ma'am. Does the new wife walk three steps behind him and one to the left like you did?"

"Hell if I know," Lizzy answered.

"Drinkin' and swearin'." He laughed. "Next thing you know she'll be putting out a red light on the porch over at Audrey's Place. I knew she'd never make a preacher's wife."

Lizzy turned up the beer bottle again. "Where does one buy a red lightbulb anyway? Oh, and Allie, this kitchen looks gorgeous. I love the color."

Allie draped an arm around her sister's shoulders. "Lean over here so I can at least smell the fumes off your beer. I miss being able to have one in the evenings. Sometimes sweet tea doesn't quite hit the spot."

Deke carried his tea to the living room and claimed the recliner. "What you need is a boyfriend, Lizzy. And I only say that because I love you like a sister."

Lizzy felt the dark look from Toby before she actually glanced that way and caught him staring at her, eyebrows knit together and jaw set. What was his problem? Deke could love her like a sister if he wanted to. That was none of Toby's business.

Lizzy plopped down on the end of the sofa closest to Deke. Toby's tall, sexy frame melted into the oversized wooden rocking chair. Blake and Allie cuddled up together on the other end of the sofa.

"Maybe," Blake said, "she could advertise in the Throckmorton newspaper for a boyfriend-for-a-day service. He could show up on a white horse wearing a white hat, and she could dress up like one of the former girls from Audrey's, and he could be her boyfriend while Mitch is here."

"This is not funny," Lizzy declared.

"It is a little bit," Deke told her.

"I could be your pretend boyfriend," Toby offered. "It would solve my Sharlene stalker problem if I had a girlfriend. I don't doubt for one minute that you are over that fool man, but honey, I'm in a world of hot water. If I had a steady girlfriend, I could get her off my back."

"And here I thought you were a big, strong cowboy who could take care of yourself." Lizzy's palms went a little clammy and her pulse jacked up a notch at the thought of snuggling up to Toby, of him throwing an arm around her—all those things that a boyfriend did to make a girl feel special. But sweet lord, could she handle it without falling right back into bed with him?

Blake chuckled. "I know Sharlene and believe me, Lizzy, when I say Toby needs you even if you don't need him. Do you want that hussy in your family? If she runs Toby to ground then she'll be Allie's sister-in-law and your shirttail kin."

"We can fake date until after the festival," Toby said. "Even if you are over Mitch, it will be good for him to see that you've moved on. After the festival you can break up with me. I can be heartbroken for a few weeks, which will mean I don't want to see anyone, and by then Sharlene will have moved on to someone else."

Deke ran a hand through his thick hair. "Are you crazy, Toby? That would mean no flirting, no fussing, and definitely no sneaking women into your trailer. Celibacy for about five whole weeks. Think about that."

Blake chuckled. "He couldn't do it."

Allie smiled. "But it'd be good for Mitch to see her with a tall, handsome rancher. Think about it, Lizzy. It would be like throwing him into hell."

Oh, sister, you don't know me anymore, Lizzy said to herself.

She searched her mind for a reason—any reason— why she couldn't agree to this crazy scheme, but imagining Mitch's expression when she introduced him to Toby was powerful motivation. She'd been strong enough to get over that sorry son of a bitch, but it would just reinforce the fact if she did have a new guy in her life, now wouldn't it? And after all, she did owe Toby since she'd given Sharlene his phone number without asking.

I am a strong woman. I can do this. I will not fall into bed with him. It will be totally pretend. Her chin went up a notch higher with each silent statement.

Finally, she nodded. "We can give it a shot. But ground rules must be laid down. I will sit beside you in church. I will go to dinner with you, but this will be in name only and not for real."

"Will you go honky-tonkin' with me?" he asked.

"Hell, yeah! That's what dating couples in this part of the world do, and then they go to church on Sunday to beg for forgiveness for what they did all weekend. But one beer is my limit and if you flirt with another woman while we are there, well, my fake temper is something no one wants to reckon with," she said.

Deke sighed. "I've lost my wingman until the middle of the summer. Anyone for a game of Monopoly?"

Lizzy shook her empty beer bottle at him again and shook her head emphatically. "God, I hated playing that boring game every Sunday with Mitch and his cousin Grady. I'd rather clean house than play Monopoly, and everyone knows how much I hate cleaning."

Allie kicked her on the hip. "You hypocrite. You made me play with y'all and acted like you loved every minute of it. What else did you hate?"

"Don't get me started. Get out the cards and let's play poker. I'm a bad girl, remember?" Lizzy grinned.

"Strip poker?" Toby asked.

"Not in your wildest dreams, cowboy."

CHAPTER FOUR

Sweat poured off Toby as he raised the post driver and slammed it down on the metal fence post. Blake wasn't far behind him with the barbed wire, stretching it as tight as fiddle strings. Toby was amazed at how much land Blake had cleared since he'd arrived at the Lucky Penny back in January. Forty acres was planted in alfalfa for winter hay and forty had beautiful grass growing for the cattle that Toby had brought with him when he moved to Dry Creek.

Now there was another forty cleared off and they were busy getting the new fence up around that. Herman Hudson and his sons' chain saws sounded in the distance as they cleaned up the piles of mesquite to get the lumber for their wood yard. A hot summer breeze fluttered the leaves on the mesquite forest still covering the almost twelve hundred acres of the Lucky Penny.

"You've been pretty quiet. Thinkin' about that deal you made with Lizzy?" Blake asked when they stopped for a break at noon on Monday. "Or were you picturing what it would've been like if Lizzy agreed to strip poker after all?"

"The way those girls played, they would've had us naked in no time." Toby chuckled.

"No kidding," Blake said. "Think you'll be able to handle her as a girlfriend?"

Sitting in the shade of the pickup truck and eating from a bag of barbecued potato chips, Toby shook his head. "It's only pretend. Just until I get Sharlene off my back."

"Oh, yeah?" Blake hooked a finger in the tab on top of a can of soda, ripped it open, and handed it to his brother. "She's tall, blond, and itchin' to get you into bed. So what's the big deal?"

"That girl is nothing but trouble. Once she gets her claws in, she's damn sure not going to let go." Toby drank heavily from the soda and set it down beside the truck tire. "Besides, this will force me to settle down at least until I get my toe in the door with the people like you did. It will be the longest damn few weeks of my life, but I'm a tough old cowboy. I can do the job."

"It's a hell of a long time, especially for you," Blake said.

"You don't think I can do it, do you?"

Blake removed the tab from another can and turned it up. "You haven't been celibate that long since you were sixteen."

"Guess we'll see what happens. You want to put some money on the deal?" Toby asked.

Blake shook his head. "Not on your life. If you don't keep the stray women out of your bed, Allie is going to shoot you for making her sister the laughingstock of the town again. If you do stay celibate, you're going to be an old bear and drive me insane. So, no, sir! I do not want to bet either way."

Toby finished the chips and tossed the empty bag into the back of the truck. "Are you happy? Really, really happy? Six months ago, you were the guy who was never going to settle down."

"And party every weekend until we got too old to two-step or drink whiskey or beer." Blake laughed. "Yes, Toby, I'm happy. I love Allie and I'm excited about the baby and this ranch. We're making a real home here. I can only hope someday you are as content as I am."

Toby stood and stretched, working the kinks from his back. "Don't put your hopes on the impossible, brother. Now, it's your turn to work up a sweat pounding those posts into the ground."

Blake popped him on the upper arm. "That's it. You ask a question and then change the subject to fencing?"

"I'm happy for you but I don't think there's a woman out there who could make me feel like you do. I'll just be the old uncle who spoils your kids. They'll love me more than you, especially the boys. I'll teach them to chase women and drink beer." Toby chuckled.

"Remember when you get a wild idea like that, just

exactly who their mama is." Blake picked up the post setter and headed toward the fence. "I love ranchin'. I'm so glad we bought this place."

"You love everything, brother. You're still on the honeymoon high," Toby said as he pulled on his tough leather gloves and got ready to string barbed wire.

Toby tried arguing with the voice in his head, but the damn thing always had a comeback so finally he let it have the last word. But all afternoon, he wondered about whether he was really wanting to have a fake relationship with Lizzy because of Sharlene, or if it was because he had been more than a little jealous when Deke said that about her needing a boyfriend.

By evening the parcel of land was cleared, plowed, and ready to plant. Blake had a heart like that now. Cleared of all the past right along with his wild ways. It was plowed and ready to raise children, be a good husband, and love Allie forever.

Toby thought about never flirting with a woman at a bar again and his heart almost stopped. No, sir! He was not ready to throw in the towel and sign his name on the dotted line of a marriage license. He was more than willing to give up his lifestyle for a little while, but knowing they were still there waiting for him—well, now that was another story altogether.

Then his mind drifted over to Lizzy. Her firm body next to his, her soft hands roaming over his chest, her lips on his, and suddenly the pressure behind his zipper started to increase. What in the hell was it about that woman that turned him on anyway? He'd been honest when he told her he wasn't the settling-down type, and she damn sure wouldn't want a womanizer like him. If she weren't so stubborn, he might've held out hope that he could get her to fall back into bed with him. But once she set her mind, wild bulls couldn't change it. That much he'd already figured out about her.

He sighed.

Deke was right. It was going to be one hell of a dry spell.

Of all the jobs that Lizzy did in her ranch supply store, cleaning was the one she hated the most. But there came a time when the store shelves had to be dusted or else a simple sneeze could turn the whole store into a fog. So that Wednesday afternoon, she set out to put things right. Armed with a dust rag, a can of sweet-smelling spray, and determination, she started at the back of the store with the notion of working her way to the front.

She'd gotten the bottom shelf of the first of six racks done when the cowbell rang. Rolling her eyes toward the ceiling, she mouthed, "Thank you!" to whatever deity sent someone to give her an excuse for a break.

"Lizzy, where are you?" a feminine voice called out.

"Be right there." Lizzy popped up on her feet from a sitting position and brushed the dust from the butt of her jeans with the palm of her hand. Leaving the cleaning behind, she hurried to the front of the store.

"Good morning," Mary Jo said as she waved. "Lucy told me that this sale rack of hooded sweatshirts was going on a bigger sale this week and I came by to see what was left."

"Seventy-five percent off for today only. Sizes are limited though. How are things coming along for the festival?" Lizzy hopped up to sit on the checkout counter and crossed her legs.

"It's gathering momentum. Everyone is talking about it, which is good because they'll spread the news and more people will attend. You've got all the sizes I need for my dad and brothers." She stopped and sucked in a lungful of air before she went on. "What was that all about Sunday? You got in the backseat of Blake's truck and his brother Toby was sitting beside you. Are y'all flirtin' or datin'? I heard he was a player. You might want to be careful with that one, Lizzy. Besides Sharlene has let it be known that she's got him staked out and you don't want to mess with her."

The cowbell rang and a blast of fresh air preceded Lucy Hudson into the store. "I came back for more of those jackets, Lizzy. I swear to God, Herman can wear one out every two weeks out there in the fields cuttin' wood so I'm going to stock up for winter. Mary Jo, you'd best not have bought the biggest ones or I'll have to fight you for them."

"No, ma'am, my family takes the smaller sizes. I see there's bigger sizes still here," Mary Jo said. "And Lizzy, you didn't answer me."

"About what? The fact that she got into the backseat with Toby Dawson on Sunday?" Lucy asked. "Might as well 'fess up, girl. If the whole town wasn't talkin' about this reunion thing, you and that hot cowboy would take the top billing."

Lizzy fidgeted with the mason jar of pens sitting on the counter. The door swung open again and she thought she'd been saved by the old proverbial bell. Then she looked up into Toby's steady blue eyes. His faded plaid shirt hung open, revealing what used to be a white tank top under it, but now it was dirty and wet with sweat. That lovely dark chest hair that she'd run her fingers through so many times was plastered to his chest. And right then he was even more sexy than when he was all slicked up for church on Sunday mornings.

"Good mornin', ladies." He tipped his hat toward Mary Jo and Lucy. "Lizzy, I've got my truck backed up to the back door. I need about five bags of fertilizer. I'll pay for them, get them loaded, and shut the big doors behind me when I leave."

She spun around on the counter and slid off on the other side. "You did say five bags, right?"

"Yep, I think that will do for what we're going to do today. Hey." He turned his head and winked just for her benefit. "We should be done by six. Want to ride down to Throckmorton with me and get some ice cream tonight?"

The crucial moment had arrived. Swim? Drown? Let Mitch breeze back into Dry Creek with everyone congratulating him on all his newfound love and missionary work while they felt sorry for her. Or jump right into the deep water and let everyone know that she was seeing Toby Dawson.

"I'd love to." She smiled, her hormones buzzing so loudly that she was amazed no one could hear them.

What I'd really like to do is find a hay barn between here and there and have another hot night with you. But that won't happen, so ice cream might be the next best thing.

"We've got that women's thing at the church tonight," Mary Jo said.

"And we can take care of it without Lizzy, I'm sure," Lucy said with a raised voice. "It's only a discussion about the potluck dinner. Lizzy, you are bringing two chocolate sheet cakes and a cherry pie. There, that's settled."

Toby handed her his charge card. "Pick you up at six thirty?"

The electricity that skipped from his hand to hers put pictures of his naked body in her mind. Why, oh why, had she ever started something with him to begin with?

"I'll be ready." She tallied up the bill, laid a copy for him to sign and his card on the counter. "We could go to Olney. It's closer."

Lucy piled six orange jackets on the counter. "And the ride is more romantic."

His eyes locked with hers. "You choose the road we take."

"Can't beat a deal like that, Lizzy." Lucy laughed.

Toby leaned across the counter and kissed her on the tip of the nose. "See you tonight."

She caught a whiff of the remnants of his shaving

lotion from that morning, a touch of bacon and coffee that he'd eaten for breakfast, combined with all that manly sweat. It turned her on like a hot water faucet.

The farce was set in motion now and by tonight it would be like a giant boulder gathering speed as it rolled down the side of a steep mountain. She stole glances of Toby heading toward the back door as she wrote up Lucy's ticket. That tight little swagger and knowing what it looked like without jeans covering his butt put two spots of high color in her cheeks.

"I'm worried about you, girl. Steam is going to come out Sharlene's ears. If I was you, I'd steer clear of her until she settles down. She missed out on Blake and she's had her heart set on Toby." Mary Jo pushed back a wayward strand of burgundy hair and unloaded her jackets onto the counter. She was a beauty operator and changed the style and color of her hair even more often than she changed her under britches.

Lizzy sacked Lucy's purchases. "Don't worry about me. I'm a big girl. I can take care of myself."

Liar, liar, pants on fire. Complete with an orchestra in the background, the lyrics of the old children's song played on a continuous loop through her mind.

"Going for ice cream doesn't mean she's going to marry the man, Mary Jo. But she does need to get some distance between her and Mitch before he comes back for the reunion," Lucy said.

"From a saint to a sinner." Mary Jo sighed. "But I got to admit, I'd rather be a sinner as a saint when I compare Mitch and Toby."

"I didn't ever believe that Mitch was a saint. And that cowboy might have one wing in the fire but that don't mean he's all the way into hell. Lizzy might turn him around the way Allie did his brother." Lucy signed the ticket and handed it to Lizzy. "I remember back nearly fifty years ago when I wanted to date a wild boy. His name was Herman Hudson and my mama almost had a heart attack over it. But I was in love with that blue-eyed boy and..." She hesitated and lowered her voice. "He might have gained sixty pounds and he might be old but them blue eyes can still make me want to haul him to the bedroom."

"Lucy!" Mary Jo covered her cheeks with her hands.

"Darlin', old don't mean dead," Lucy said. "And Lizzy, you have fun with that cowboy. He might not be settlin'-down material, but darlin', I'd bet my checkbook that he'll wash that sorry Mitch right out of your heart."

"News flash," Lizzy whispered. "Mitch is already gone from my heart."

"You know that. We know that. Now it's time for Mitch to know that." Lucy picked up her bags. "I'm on my way to Nadine's for a cup of coffee. You want me to hold off tellin' her the news till you get there, Mary Jo?"

Mary Jo nodded. "Thanks, Lucy. I want to see her face when she hears this and Sharlene is there." She pulled several bills from her purse and laid them on the counter. "You are playin' with fire, Lizzy. And that means you could get burned."

"Yep, but I reckon I've got whole shelves full of stuff that will cure burns on cattle, dogs, cats, and even hamsters in this store. It might work on a human," Lizzy teased.

Mary Jo stuffed the change from her purchases back into her purse. "He's only dating you because y'all are thrown together by family so much. He's a bad boy and you, darlin', are not a bad boy's type. Sharlene is but you are definitely not." She picked up her sack and left the store.

CHAPTER FIVE

Toby refilled his bowl with chili and added a layer of grated cheddar cheese on the top. Despite having known Lizzy in the most intimate ways possible during their hot and heavy fling, he was as nervous as he'd been on his first date back when he was sixteen.

Toby certainly had not expected to be tangled up in drama like this when he came to Dry Creek almost a month before. If anyone had told him that he would be taking Allie's sister on a fake date and he would not be chasing bar bunnies for at least five weeks, he would have had them committed. Yet here he was, doing just that.

"Are you sure about this? I've already had a dozen phone calls telling me that I'm insane for letting Lizzy go anywhere with you. After all, she was engaged and almost married to a preacher." Allie passed the corn bread around the table.

Deke took the plate from her and handed it off to Toby. "Sorry son of a bitch wasn't a preacher. He's a gold digger with a god complex. And Allie, if Lizzy wanted to date Toby as in the real sense of the word, there wouldn't be a damn thing anyone could do about it. She's even more headstrong than you are and that's saying a lot. So you ain't *lettin'* her do jack shit. She will do whatever she wants to do."

Blake took two pieces of the warm bread and crumbled it into his chili. "I'm speaking from experience here, brother. Getting close to a woman, no matter if it's real or not, can backfire."

Allie slapped Blake on the arm. "I wasn't pretending to like you."

"Yes, you were." Deke chuckled. "No, I take that back. You were pretending not to like him but we could all see that you did."

Allie's dark eyes sparkled when she looked at Blake. She was so damn much in love with Blake that it made Toby's heart yearn to have the same thing.

Whoa, cowboy! His inner voice made a screeching sound in his head as it hauled up on the reins. *You are not settlin' down material. You are going to be the old uncle that spoils your brothers' kids. The ones that are already here and Allie's baby, too, are going to love you like a grandpa. Slap that shit out of your head about wanting a wife and kids. That boring life ain't for you.*

He dipped into the chili and let the idea fade as quickly as it had appeared, nodding his head in agreement the whole time. The room had gone quiet and he noticed everyone staring at him.

"What? Do I have chili on my shirt?" he asked.

"You were fighting with yourself and you agreed with something," Deke said.

"It happens. I do it all the time." Allie smiled. "But back to this Lizzy thing. It's a good plan, but don't let it get plumb out of hand. I heard that Sharlene bragged that she's not giving up and that she'll knock Lizzy right out of the saddle before the festival."

Blake laid a hand over Allie's. "Darlin', you don't have to worry about Toby. He'll never settle down to one woman. If you have to fret, do it about Lizzy, not Toby. And he's handled overbearing Sharlene-types before."

"In those days he could love 'em and leave 'em, though. He didn't have to live in the same town with the woman," Deke said.

Toby was already tired of talking this situation to death. He wanted to finish his supper, take a shower, and go get Lizzy for their ice cream date. At least this business of a pseudo-girlfriend gave him an escape.

Deke pushed back his chair and carried his bowl to the sink. "Thanks for supper, guys. I've still got laundry to do over at my place and some chores to get done. I'll be gone for a couple of days starting tomorrow. Rodeos are getting geared up."

"Don't worry about anything. I'll take care of your

livestock and pets," Allie told him. "You'll be back Sunday with no hickeys, right?"

One corner of Deke's mouth curled in half a smile. "I'll be home real late Saturday night, maybe even up near daylight on Sunday. I'll see y'all in church but I don't make promises about hickeys. How 'bout you, Toby?"

Toby tightened his grip on the spoon to keep from touching the last fading mark Lizzy had put on his shoulder. Thank goodness his shirt covered it.

It wasn't a real date, but it felt so good that Lizzy put extra care into getting ready for it. It was the first time she'd been out since Mitch broke up with her almost five months ago, on the telephone for God's sake and on the day of her sister's wedding and on Valentine's Day to boot.

She showered, shaved her legs, washed her hair, and applied the whole regiment of makeup. She flipped through the hangers in her closet and chose her best pair of skinny jeans, topped off with an orange tank top. She thought about cowboy boots but the temperature was still in the nineties when she left work, so she picked out a strappy pair of sandals with a small heel.

Too antsy to sit in the living room and wait for the doorbell to ring, she opted to wait on the front porch swing. It had been painted four or five different colors down through the years, but Allie had stripped it down to the original oak wood the year before and applied several coats of varnish. The squeaky chains competed with sounds of singing birds, chirping crickets, and howling coyotes. Occasionally she heard a cow bawling from over on the Lucky Penny. The latter sounded out of place since there hadn't been livestock over there in at least two or three decades.

The noise of an approaching truck's engine filled the hot June night long before it appeared in the lane leading from the road up to Audrey's Place. The sinking sun cast its glow on the shiny black club cab truck as Toby parked outside the yard fence. He stepped out and shook the legs of his creased jeans over the tops of black boots that were almost as shiny as the truck. Every pearl snap on the plaid western shirt sparkled.

He looked so different from the dirty, sweaty cowboy who had appeared in her store earlier that day and yet, both versions were sexy as the devil. His jeans were low slung on his hips and hugged his butt just right. The shirt was a basic navy button down, worn loose over a Luke Bryan concert T-shirt. She couldn't see his eyes because of the sunglasses and the way his straw hat sat low on his forehead, but she could feel them assessing her from a distance—just like they did when he was propped up on an elbow after a bout of steamy sex on a twin-size bed. That sent a burst of desire surging through her body. She'd have to be very careful or she'd wind up losing control of her better judgment for sure.

He waved. "You aren't going to keep me waiting. I like that."

She stood up. "You aren't keeping me waiting, either. I like that."

"You'll have to show me the way to the ice cream place. I haven't been to Olney yet." He escorted her from porch to truck with his hand on her lower back. "We'd better make this look real in case there's anyone sitting in one of those scrub oak trees with binoculars."

"That was pretty slick of you to ask me right in front of Mary Jo and Lucy," she said.

"Did I do good?" He grinned.

"Oh, yeah. They're the best gossip spreaders in the whole town. I imagine that someone has already called Mitch by now, and I heard that Sharlene might put a contract out on me."

"Isn't Mitch in Mexico?" He opened the door for her.

She hoisted herself up into the passenger's seat. "News from here to anywhere in the world travels faster than a speeding bullet."

"I'll protect you, darlin'."

Lizzy giggled. "I can protect myself. It's you who has the problem. You might be a Dawson but that woman could eat you alive, cowboy."

"Blake managed to dodge her, and I'm tougher than he is," Toby countered.

"She's honed her skills in the past five months, darlin'. You ain't got a sinner's chance at the pearly gates," she told him. "Turn at the next corner. You have to drive a little slower on this route, but it's a nice ride at this time of year."

He backed the truck around and followed her instructions. "So tell me, Lizzy Logan, whatever made you go into the retail business for ranchers?"

"I inherited it. Granny and Grandpa had the business before I was even born. Grandpa died and Granny kept us kids so Mama and Daddy could work. He helped run the feed business and also did construction. Mama took over the convenience store. Allie followed Daddy around at construction sites, but I was never interested in hammers and nails and all that. I couldn't wait to get off the school bus and go to the feed store where Daddy always worked the last two hours of the day," she said. "By the time we were in high school, Allie was getting a paycheck from the construction business and I was pretty much running the store when I wasn't in school. After graduation, the guy who'd been minding it for us retired and I took over full time."

"You ever wish you'd gone to college or done something different?" Toby asked.

"Not one time."

"Then I have a hard personal question. What in the hell made you think you'd be happy married to someone who was probably going to insist that you stop working and be a full-time preacher's wife?" he asked.

The question wasn't one she hadn't asked herself those first few weeks after Mitch dumped her. Her job was a nine-to-five, six days a week, and pretty often if someone needed a bag of feed or some cattle medicine, she'd open up so they could get it after hours or on Sunday.

"That is definitely a hard question but I don't have to answer it because I didn't marry Mitch," she said.

"Hypothetically?" He pressured.

"I wanted to get away from the stigma of Audrey's Place so badly, Toby," she said softly. "Even all these decades later, it's still known as the old whorehouse. Growing up, it was hard."

"Why? It's colorful and it doesn't make *you* a whore."

"No but old rumors die hard in Dry Creek," she said.

He braked so suddenly that the truck tires spun gravel every which way. "Look! Over there up against the mesquite grove. See that big buck and all those does." His finger shot right under her nose.

Lizzy gasped at the serenity before her eyes. The buck with his head up, not a muscle moving; the does munching away on the grass, knowing they were protected and their babies wouldn't come to harm. "Look at the fawns," she whispered. "Aren't they the cutest things? Sometimes a deer or two comes right up close to the fence at the back side of our property. When we were little girls we used to take a pallet out there and watch for them in the late evening."

The buck eyed them warily without moving a muscle. The does continued eating the new spring grass, and the fawns romped around unafraid of the strange big black truck.

"He's protecting his family." Toby eased his foot from the brake and drove slower.

"My turn to ask questions," Lizzy said. "What makes

you think you'll be happy in Dry Creek? You are used to being close enough to all kinds of honky-tonks that you can party when you want. What happens when you get bored here?"

"I like to have a good time, Lizzy, but I love to ranch. It's always been my dream to buy one and build it from scratch. But land prices are high. When the Lucky Penny came up for sale and we found out if we pooled our money we could buy it without a loan, it was a dream come true. I'll be happy because ranchin' makes me happy," he said.

She pondered on that as they crossed the bridge and drove on in to Olney. Would she have found happiness if she did have to give up her store? Would she have simply settled into fitting into the mold that Mitch had carved out for her? When Toby parked in front of the Dairy Queen, she had the answers and they were both a loud hell no!

"Oh. My. God!" she muttered as he laced his fingers in hers and led her inside. "What is *she* doing here?"

"Who? I thought every woman in Dry Creek was at some church meeting tonight," Toby asked.

"Mitch's mother and her friends. I haven't seen her since Mitch and I broke up," Lizzy groaned.

"Get into character, darlin'," he whispered seductively, his warm breath creating delicious shivers up and down her spine. "We can sell this. I know we can."

"Well, hello, Elizabeth," Mitch's mother, Wanda, said.

"Elizabeth?" Toby chuckled.

"She hates my nickname," Lizzy whispered.

Wanda was an elegant woman in her cute little navy blue slacks and matching powder blue sweater set that matched her cold pale blue eyes. Her thick blond hair was styled in the latest feathered back cut and not one single strand was out of place.

"Hello, Wanda." Lizzy took three steps but didn't let go of Toby's hand. "I'd like you to meet my boyfriend, Toby Dawson. You may have heard that on Valentine's Day his brother Blake and my sister Allie were married."

"Oh, I do remember Valentine's Day very well. Poor Mitch was distraught but I told him he had to listen to God. I'm very sorry for the way things turned out with you two, but God knows best and I'm sure that you would have never been happy outside of Dry Creek, Elizabeth. And likewise, Mitch could have never ever lived or reached his potential in that ghost town. Besides that, I'm quite sure you understand that he needs a wife without a questionable background."

Wanda's pasted-on smile annoyed Lizzy so badly that she wanted to slap the shit out of the woman and then slap her again for calling her Elizabeth.

Wanda held out a limp hand bedecked with diamond rings on three fingers and nails that had been freshly done in a pale pink polish. "It's so nice to meet you. Was that Blake or Toby?"

He shook her hand and then dropped it. "Toby, ma'am. My pleasure. Now if you will excuse us, we're going to share a banana split to celebrate this lovely spring day."

"I'll tell Mitch that I saw you and met your new boyfriend, Elizabeth. I can't wait for him and his new bride to come home this summer. We're planning a big shower at the church for them. They've rented a lovely villa and they need things for it." Wanda waved as they walked away.

Lizzy wiggled her fingers in acknowledgment but didn't look back. "I bet his mother rented that villa and I bet she's soliciting churches for sponsorship for his mission work. And I bet dollars to cow patties that he will live like a king."

"Jealous?"

"No, I am not. I've got my store and the sexiest cowboy in the whole area for a boyfriend tonight." She smiled.

"Hey, Lizzy, where you been, girl?" the lady behind the counter asked. "I haven't seen you in weeks."

"Been busy. I want a banana split with whipped cream, nuts, and a cherry on the top of each dip," she said.

"And two spoons." Mitch reached for his wallet.

"Are you going to introduce me or just let me stand here drooling?" the cashier asked.

"I'm sorry. Wanda rattled me," Lizzy said honestly. "Toby, darlin', this is Cricket and, Cricket, this is my boyfriend, Toby." It was amazing how slick that word rolled off her tongue the second time she said it.

"Well, you lucky dog." Cricket smiled. "Y'all go on to that back booth and I'll bring the ice cream to you. That way Wanda can't even see you."

"Oh, no!" Toby laid his money on the counter. "We are going to sit right there by the window so we can watch the cars go by while we eat." He motioned to one not six feet from Wanda and her three friends.

"Brave soul!" Cricket giggled. "Brave, sexy, and smart. I like him, Lizzy. I'll have this ready in a few minutes."

Toby slid into the booth across from Lizzy and laid his cowboy hat beside him. When she was settled, he reached across the table, took both her hands in his, and gazed into her eyes. She leaned forward slightly and he could see two inches of cleavage along with the lacy edge of a black bra. "You are so beautiful tonight, but not as sexy as you were the last time I was in the store and you reached up on that high shelf. I bet you didn't know that your shirt rides up when you do that and shows an inch of your lower back."

"What are you doing?" Lizzy whispered.

He moved from his side of the booth to sit beside her. "This is much better and it will make sharing a banana split so much easier." He pushed her hair back behind her ear and kissed her on the earlobe as he murmured, "I'm making a believer out of that woman."

"Well, I'm sure glad that you think my bare skin is sexy." She giggled softly and played along. "What else do you like?"

"I like an independent woman who knows how to do something other than fry meat and raise kids."

Lizzy bit the inside of her lip to contain the laughter.

"Well, thank you, Toby. I don't think anyone has ever said romantic things like that to me before."

"Then you've been dating idiots," he said bluntly.

Lizzy could practically hear Wanda's heart palpitations. If the woman had a cardiac arrest and rolled out onto the floor, would it be a sin to wait until Lizzy finished her banana split to call 911?

Toby eased his arm around Lizzy's shoulders. "We've been doing some rough designs on the house I want to build on the Lucky Penny. Allie says she can take care of it for me. What she doesn't do, she'll contract out. If you were building a house, what would you want?"

Lizzy noticed that Toby had pitched his voice just loudly enough for anyone to hear.

Cricket brought their banana split, set it down, handed them each a plastic spoon, and then crossed the short distance to Wanda's table to ask if they needed refills on their coffee. All four nodded so she went back to get a full pot.

Toby picked up a cherry and held it out to Lizzy. She bit it from the stem and returned the favor by feeding him one of hers. Then they both dipped into the ice cream and started to eat.

"I would never want another house with a second floor if I was building." She raised her voice just enough that the old gals didn't have to fall out of the booth when they leaned over to hear what she said. "And the simpler the better, because I hate cleaning. I do like to cook and I don't mind laundry, but keeping things all beautifully neat is not my thing."

"I'm capable of cooking, but I don't enjoy it. I do like to clean because I'm the world's biggest neat freak. We might make a good pair, Miz Lizzy Logan," he said.

Wanda choked on her sip of coffee. It looked like she might need some CPR, and Lizzy was glad that she had no idea how to do it. Wanda finally got control of her breathing and took a sip of water before she and her cronies put their heads together and whispered like little girls on the playground.

"So a ranch house then? That's what Allie and I have been designing. Long, low, and with a big front porch with a swing where two people could sit and talk about their day. You could tell me how things went at the feed store and I could fill you in on all that went on at the Lucky Penny every evening," he said.

"Why, Toby Dawson, are you proposing to me?" she said in her best sweet Southern voice.

"No, ma'am. I am not! When and if I ever do that it will be in a romantic setting like out in a field of wild daisies with the sun setting over the horizon on the Lucky Penny." He kept eating ice cream as if they were discussing a herd of deer instead of proposals. "Tell me what else you'd do in a house? What kind of kitchen would you want?"

"Nothing big, but I would like a stove with six burners on the top and a double oven. And a window above the sink so I could see the baby calves playing out there beyond the yard fence." Lizzy knew their conversation was only pretend, but that was exactly what she really did want—when she found the right cowboy to trust with her heart.

She'd skipped supper, so she was hungry and she ate faster than she would normally, but Toby still beat her by two spoons full.

"Let's go home the longest way possible. We can get two cups of coffee to go and drive slow," he said.

"Sounds good to me." She nodded.

"And Saturday night I thought we might hit that little bar up near Wichita Falls and have a beer. Maybe dance a little leather off a pair of your pretty cowboy boots," he said on the way to the counter.

"I'll look forward to that the rest of the week. I haven't been dancing in months," she said.

With coffee in one hand, Lizzy waved at Wanda as Toby ushered her out the door and to his truck. Wanda's evil looks sliced through the air like a hot knife through butter. Lizzy wasn't certain if she really would be drinking beer and dancing on Saturday night, but knowing that Wanda would rush home and call Mitch to tell him put a smile on her face. Maybe this idea that had been hatched over the kitchen table at the Lucky Penny wasn't such a bad one after all.

"That was so much fun," Toby said.

"And if it had been real?" she asked.

"I don't usually build houses for my women on first dates." He grinned.

"What's your highest number?" She sipped her coffee.

"For what?"

"Dates? What's the cutoff number before you consider it getting too serious? Two, ten, twenty?"

His eyebrows drew down into a solid line. Didn't he know if he frowned longer than two minutes his face would freeze like that? If he didn't believe her, then Lizzy's granny would tell him. Irene might have forgotten most everything these days but she would remember that for sure.

"I dated a girl in high school for two weeks. Took her to my senior prom," he finally answered.

"So three or four real dates?"

"Two." He grimaced. "We went to the movies and to the prom."

"And since?"

"No more than three, tops. After that they start to get ideas about diamond rings and big white dresses. It's the dresses that give me the hives," he said. "And all that planning shit. My older brothers almost threw in the towel when it came to those wedding books. I wouldn't ever want to do that."

Lizzy filed that bit of information into the back of her mind. She'd had the wedding book and kept everything in it, from swatches of the ribbons she might or might not use for the bouquets, to pictures of boutonnières made with roses, gardenias, and even magnolia petals. She'd burned the thing in the fire pit in the backyard the night Mitch had broken up with her. She'd lost the deposit on her dress but nothing else had been ordered, thank goodness.

"I heard you had a wedding book," he said.

"I did but I will never have another one. It takes too much energy and time for all that," she said.

He drove up into the front yard and parked the truck. "I'll walk you to the door. I thought I saw a glint of binoculars over there to the east."

Her mother's car was parked beside his truck and the porch light burned brightly. He slung an arm around her shoulders and kept in step with her all the way to the door where he caged her with a hand on each side. She wanted nothing more than to curl up beside him in a cocoon of delicious foreplay followed by a round of that mind-numbing sex, but this wasn't real even if the kiss did leave her panting.

"I had a good time tonight, Lizzy. This fake dating is more fun than I thought it would be," he drawled.

His eyelids fluttered shut and she barely had time to moisten her lips before his lips claimed hers. Instinctively her hands went up to loop around his neck and she rolled up on her toes. There probably wasn't anyone over there in the trees, but she couldn't prove it because when he ended the kiss, there were glittery sparks everywhere.

CHAPTER SIX

When Lizzy opened the store on Thursday morning, there were more than a dozen women waiting to check out what was left on her sales racks or to buy something that they had to have before life could go on that day. Lucy Hudson led the pack of rumor-hungry women into the feed store and went straight to the checkout counter where she took up post.

"I'm here to protect you from the coyotes and wolves," she whispered to Lizzy.

"Thank you," Lizzy mouthed.

Dora June, Truman's wife, pretended to look through the round sales rack at the front of the store, but it didn't take her long to make her way to the counter. "Elizabeth Logan, I hear you were seen in public last night with that new cowboy who's at the Lucky Penny."

"And who told you such a thing?" Lizzy asked.

Dora June shook her finger at Lizzy. "You know exactly who told me. Mitch's mother was mortified."

Lizzy held her hands tightly behind her back to keep from grabbing that bony finger and giving it two or three twists to the left. "Why? Wanda was the one with the objection to Mitch marrying someone of questionable background. She was afraid that I might be too wild for her precious son. I would have expected her to be gloating because she was right."

Nadine, along with half a dozen other women, left the rack and gathered around the counter like heifers at feeding time. She caught Lizzy's eye and winked. "If I wasn't married, I'd give you a run for your money with Toby Dawson. He's the hottest thing I've seen in this part of the state in years and years. I'm dying to know if he kissed you and what it was like. Sharlene says to tell you that the race ain't done until there's rings and wedding bells involved."

Dora June's finger shot around so fast that it barely missed clipping Lucy's nose. "Lord have mercy, Nadine! Married women don't talk like that."

"Miz Dora June, darlin', when you are on a diet do you stop looking at all those lovely candy bars over at Katy's store? I don't think so. The rules say we can't touch or be touched. They don't say that we can't look." Nadine giggled.

Dora June pursed her thin mouth so tightly that it completely disappeared into the bed of wrinkles surrounding it. She sucked in enough air to push out her ample breasts a few more inches and narrowed her beady little eyes. "Elizabeth, I had high hopes for you," she said tersely.

"And those were?" Lizzy asked.

"That you would realize God had other plans for Mitch and that you would find another godly man." Dora June crossed her arms over her chest and tapped her foot on the wooden floor.

"All godly men are not trustworthy or exciting. We all found that out when Mitch pulled that stunt that he did," Lucy said quickly. "I heard you were discussing building a house with Toby. Just how fast is this train moving?"

Oh, Lucy, you have no idea where that train has already been, Lizzy said to herself. *Crazy how that we managed to sneak around for sex for three weeks and no one even suspected. But let me get in the truck with him and suddenly they assume we're heading for the altar. Well, they don't know Toby Dawson.*

"Well?" Dora June asked. "Are you going to answer Lucy's question or not?"

"I'm not sure. Can I wait until after Saturday night to answer that question? If you like I could stand up in church on Sunday morning and tell everyone so you don't have to make so many phone calls to repeat the gossip. I'm going dancing with him at a bar up near Wichita Falls and I'll know more after that," Lizzy answered.

"I was planning to go to that bar to celebrate this Saturday," Mary Jo said.

"What are you celebrating?" Lizzy asked.

Mary Jo shrugged. "Maybe that I've decided to be a blond this weekend with strawberry streaks. Maybe that I went twenty-four hours without chocolate. I celebrate something new every weekend."

Dora June rolled her eyes toward the ceiling. "Women these days..."

"What?" Lizzy asked. "Something wrong with having a little fun? I would appreciate it if you tell Wanda that if she wants to be right there for firsthand gossip, I'll save her a place at our table or beside us at the bar."

"Well, I never in all my life heard such insolence from you, Elizabeth. Your mama needs to give you a talkin' to. I can't believe she is going to let you go to a sinful place like that with that awful cowboy." Dora June spun around like an agile ballerina, but it took her three chins a while to catch up. They were still wiggling, trying to find their comfort zone under her bulldog cheeks, when she glared over her shoulder at Lizzy.

"I was thinkin' about askin' Mama to go with me. She hasn't been out dancin' since Daddy died," Lizzy called out.

"And you might do well to remember, Dora June, that Lizzy is not sixteen. Last time I checked she's past twenty-five and I reckon she can make up her own mind about where she goes and what cowboy she drags along behind her to buy the beer. And furthermore, she is Irene Miller's granddaughter. That alone says volumes about her determination and stubbornness." Lucy raised her voice.

All she got for an answer was the ring of a cowbell above the exit and the slamming of an old wooden door. The women were soon gone, leaving only Lucy and Nadine in the store.

"Lizzy, are you even aware that Deke has been in love with you for years. You'd do a hell of a lot better with him," Nadine whispered.

"Deke is Allie's best friend and like a brother to me. You're just trying to free up my man for Sharlene." Lizzy laughed. Deke, indeed! He'd never given any indication that he had feelings for her.

Before Nadine could say another word, a rooster crowed in Lucy's purse. She fetched her phone out, checked the caller ID, and put it back.

"I swear to God, Herman is right. Phones are the bane of society. The kids got me the damn thing so if I fall over with a heart attack when I'm feedin' cows or workin' in the garden I can hit that nine-one-one number and get some help, and now every time I turn around someone is callin'. Most days I want to throw it down the well. I leave it in the truck when Herman is home because he hates the thing worse than I do," she said.

"I started a wildfire with Dora June, didn't I?" Lizzy whispered. "But she made me so mad that I couldn't control my tongue, no matter how hard I tried."

"That's what happens when you get a good night kiss like you did," Lucy said.

"How did you know that?" Nadine asked. "I've been trying to find out all morning and no one knew."

"I have special powers," Lucy answered. "It's time for my morning coffee down at your café, but if Dora June comes back and starts her bullshit, Lizzy, you call me and I'll come runnin'."

Nadine shook her head and pursed her lips together. "Sharlene and Mary Jo are minding the café right now so I guess I'd best go with you, Lucy. You remember what I said about Deke, Lizzy."

She waved as the door shut behind her and suddenly there was nothing but quiet surrounding Lizzy. Holy smokin' crap! What had she done? She had made up her mind that morning on the way to work that she wouldn't go to the bar with Toby. If he wanted to go somewhere and eat and maybe catch a movie, she might be game. But the idea of a crowded bar with loud music didn't sound like her idea of a fun Saturday night.

"But I guess I will be going now," she muttered.

Lizzy picked up the romance novel she'd been reading along with a glass of sweet tea and carried them out to the porch. A slight breeze brought the smell of roses from the barbed wire fence separating the Lucky Penny from Audrey's Place. She set her tea on the table at the end of the porch swing before she sat down with her back against one end and her legs stretched out to the other. She opened the book and heard a vehicle coming down the lane at the same time. Allie had said she might come over after she finished the job she was doing for Nadine at the café, so she hurriedly read a few pages before she glanced up.

As usual her breath caught in her chest when Toby stepped out of the truck. He'd evidently come straight from the fields because his jeans were dusty, his white T-shirt sweat stained, and he had a day's growth of dark stubble. When she could breathe, she immediately thought of Allie. Oh, no! Had she had trouble with the pregnancy? Did they send Toby to bring bad news?

Toby removed his straw hat and sat down on the top step. "We need to talk."

"Is Allie all right?" Lizzy's voice was little more than a high-pitched squeak.

"Allie is making fried chicken right now and Blake is making biscuits. Want to come over for supper?"

"I've already eaten. Is that what you came to talk about?"

He shook his head. "No, it's not, Lizzy. I need to be up front and honest with you. I heard that those women practically hung you on a cross this morning and that you held your ground."

"Like I've said a thousand times, I can take care of myself, Toby."

"I like you, Lizzy. You are spunky and fun and I don't ever want to be dishonest with you. But I need to make sure you understand, I'm not the settlin' type," he said.

She picked up the glass of tea and handed it to him. "Since we've kissed and done even more than that, I don't suppose it will hurt to share a glass of tea and you look hot."

"Thank you." He took a large gulp and handed it back to her. "So knowing where we both stand, do you still want to go dancing Saturday night?"

"Guess we'd better or else Dora June wouldn't have a thing to talk about. If she couldn't gossip, she'd die and Mama would make me go to the funeral. I hate funerals so I guess we'll go dancing," she said, and smiled. "Toby, I'm not sneaking in on your blind side. This is a business deal. Can you believe that we didn't get caught or even suspected all those weeks and all I had to do was get into the truck with you last Sunday to set all this in motion?"

"Small towns!" He slapped his hat against his leg and dust flew. Then he stood and headed toward his truck. "See you Saturday night. Seven thirty all right?"

"I'll be ready." She picked up the tea and downed the rest of it before coming up for air. It did absolutely nothing to cool the desire running hot through her body. She'd thought Toby was the sexiest man in the state of Texas before, but seeing him all sweaty and dirty again got her hormones swirling.

On Friday morning she wasn't a bit surprised to see Lucy, Dora June, and three other ladies waiting in their parked vehicles outside her store. She waved at them and opened the door with the ancient key that her grandpa had used.

She flipped on the lights and adjusted the thermostat,

went to her office to take the day's start-up money from the safe, and noticed that all five women had gathered 'round her checkout counter. The sorry hussies could at least try to find something on the sale rack, couldn't they?

She busied herself with loading the cash register with bills and change from the bag. "What can I do for you girls today?"

"We've had an executive committee meeting at the church," Dora June said in her most authoritative tone.

"Whoa! Hold your horses," Lucy protested loudly. "I'm not here with this bunch of self-righteous women, Lizzy. I came to stand in your corner."

"You aren't part of the ladies' executive committee at church anyway," Dora June said.

"No and I don't want to be if you're going to play God and meddle where you ain't got no business," Lucy said.

"Spit it out. What have you ladies decided? Are you going with me to the honky-tonk to be sure I don't get too drunk to drive home?" Lizzy asked.

Martha and Ruby sputtered so badly that Lizzy thought she should rustle up a couple of bibs to keep them from spitting all over the fronts of their shirts. Henrietta, the fourth woman, gave Lizzy a severe dose of stink eye, meant to fry her on the spot.

"Don't you get sassy with me, young lady!" Dora June's famous finger waggled in front of Lizzy's face. "We are here to tell you that we've canceled your membership to the Ladies Auxiliary. You are not welcome at the meetings and you will not be a voting member anymore."

"All because I went for ice cream with Toby? Or is there another reason?" Lizzy asked.

"We should have done this back when Allie was all but living with Blake. We know what went on in that house. She was caught in there wearing nothing but his robe that one evening and we know when that baby is due and they sure won't be married nine months, either." Dora June's voice lowered like she was saying dirty words. "And we ain't puttin' up with it a second time. Fool me once, shame on you. Fool me twice, means we got our heads in the sand. The world is going to hell in a handbasket, but we aim to protect the integrity of our organization."

"We had high hopes for you." Ruby sighed. "Even after Mitch didn't marry you because of … well, you know … we hoped you would settle down with another preacher."

Lizzy could feel the steamy heat of anger whooshing through her ears. She wondered for a split second if it was visible as it shot from the sides of her head or if it really made a whistling noise like a freight train.

"And Mama?" Lizzy asked. "Y'all going to throw her to the curb? What about Allie? She married the father of her baby. Y'all going to take her down to the river and drown her sorry butt for sinning or just haul her out in the middle of the road and stone her to death?"

"The only thing your mama has done wrong is failing to control two of her daughters. We can't punish her for your sins," Henrietta answered.

"I expect one of you better get ready to put on the president's crown because Katy won't stand for this crap," Lucy said.

"Are you going to ban me from church, too?" Lizzy grinned.

"No, there is a possibility that you might see the error of your ways, repent, and still yet find a godly man to take care of you," Martha answered.

"Mitch broke me from looking for another godly man, Dora June. All I'm doing is dating Toby. Allie married his brother so are you going to tell my sister that she's been excommunicated from our community church or shall I? She's working down at Nadine's today, building shelving in her pantry, but I can sure tell her if you don't want to," Lizzy said coldly.

"We are going there next," Ruby said.

"Sweet Jesus!" Lizzy said from clenched teeth. "There's more adultery going on in Dry Creek than in a soap opera and lots of pure old hot sex without the benefit of a marriage license. I'm surprised y'all got enough women to even keep your self-righteous club going."

"Me, too," Lucy piped up. "From the looks of things, I'd say there's barely enough even now to put on a funeral dinner."

"You best be careful, Lucy Hudson," Dora June said tersely. "We'll be leaving now."

Lucy slipped back between the display shelves and

pulled the phone from her pocket, called Katy, and told her to hang a sign on the door and meet her at Nadine's in five minutes. "I'm going with you." Lizzy could not believe this was happening in the modern world.

They paraded down the old wooden sidewalk, heads held high and determination on their faces. Mary Jo greeted the church ladies with a smile until she saw Lucy and Lizzy right behind them and Katy bringing up the rear.

"Something going on here?" she asked.

"Where is Allie? We've come to talk to her," Dora June said loudly.

"Hey, Allie, you've got company," Mary Jo yelled loudly.

Wearing cargo pants and a faded orange T-shirt, work boots, and carrying a hammer, Allie peeked over the top of the swinging doors into the kitchen. "What's going on? Y'all need to put your name on the list for a job?"

Dora June took a step forward and delivered the news. The wide grin that spread across Allie's face told Lizzy that her sister wasn't going to deliver a speech hot enough to melt the paint right off the wall, or throw the hammer at Dora June's head, either. Lizzy sighed. It wasn't fair for them to get away with this whole thing without a single black eye, even if they were old women set in their ways.

Allie nodded curtly. "Well, thank you so much for that. Now I don't have to make up excuses not to come to the meetings every week, and I can stay home with my wild cowboy and do things that would make your eyes roll around in your heads. I'm going back to work. Y'all have a right nice day." Allie disappeared into the back room again.

"You have decided what about my girls?" Katy stepped out of the shadows. Her tone was colder than water dripping off icicles, and if that wasn't steam blowing out her mother's ears, Lizzy would clean the house for six months without a single whiny word.

Martha tilted her head up. "It has nothing to do with you. When they get grown, we realize we can't control them but they do have to be accountable for their sins."

Before Katy could form a sentence, Toby swaggered into the café. His faded blue T-shirt that advertised a rodeo from three years before stretched across his broad chest and his worn work jeans that perfectly hugged his butt.

"Hey, Lizzy, I need a few more fence posts. I thought the store opened at eight," he said.

"It does and I'm on my way back over there right now. You can walk with me. Want Nadine to pour us up a cup of coffee or a sweet tea to go?"

Martha sighed.

Dora June gasped.

Henrietta and Ruby glanced his way and then looked up at the ceiling. Maybe they were praying that he'd drop dead right there between table number four and the checkout counter. If so, God wasn't listening that day.

"Your biggest takeout cup of sweet tea would be

great, Nadine. Tearing up that mesquite is thirsty work, and Herman is getting ahead of us." Toby threw an arm around Lizzy's shoulders and pulled her close.

"Back to my girls." Katy glared at all four women.

"You heard us," Ruby said.

"One of those cowboys over at the Lucky Penny is my son-in-law. The other is dating my daughter, so consider this a verbal resignation from my post as president. I will bring all the books to church on Sunday and y'all can do whatever you want. I will not be a part of this ugliness," Katy said.

"What is going on here?" Toby whispered.

"They're ousting me and Allie from their ladies' group at church and Mama just resigned. They know they've stepped in it because Mama does a hell of a lot for the church," she said.

"You don't need to do that," Ruby said.

"It's done." Katy held up a palm to stop any more comments. "I'm going back to work like Allie did. See you at lunchtime, Lizzy. Don't work too hard, Toby."

"Because of me and Blake?" Toby asked.

"Yes, it is." Dora June took a step forward. "We thought you'd give up and be gone by now. You all have reputations that preceded you into our community. It does look like y'all might succeed at the Lucky Penny. But it is our business who is allowed into our church organization."

Lucy got between Toby and Dora June. She shook her head slowly from side to side as if she couldn't believe what the woman had said. "Y'all need to pull

your heads out of your asses and use them for thinkin'
rather than condemnation. It's going to take five of you
to do Katy's job at the church, not to mention what all
she gives in money to keep the church going."

Nadine handed Lizzy two tall take-out cups of sweet
tea. "These are on the house, Lizzy. I'm so sorry about
all this."

"Not me. It gives me more time to spend with Toby.
Y'all all have a great day, now. Lucy, are you coming
with us?"

"No, I'm stayin' right here. I'm not nearly finished
with what I got to say."

Toby waited until they were out on the sidewalk
to explode. "That is the most asinine thing I've ever
heard. This isn't the cave days. I'm glad we're out
of there before them old gals start pullin' hair and
scratchin' at each other's eyes. That was even worse
than some bar fights I've seen. You sure you want to go
on with this?"

"More than ever. Those old hens are not about to tell
me what I can or cannot do with my life. Let them stew.
If they sit in hot water long enough, it might even soften
them up a little bit. Let's go get those fence posts."

Big black storm clouds gathered in the southwest, blot-
ting out the sun on their journey up tornado alley. The
radio weatherman said that the temperatures would
drop slightly by midnight because of the rain blowing
in but that by morning it would all be over and the sun
would be out again.

Lizzy had gotten out of her truck and was on the first porch step when she noticed Toby sitting on the swing, a beer in his hand and another one opened and sitting on the table beside him.

"Thought you might like something cold this evening. It looks like rain and feels like a tornado even though we are supposed to be past that season," he said.

She sat down on the swing beside him and took the extra beer from his hand. While the first cold sip slid down her throat, she kicked off her boots and drew her legs up on the swing. Toby picked up her feet and spun her around so that they were laying in his lap. With cold hands he massaged her right foot, his fingertips digging into all the right places to make her groan.

"Feel good?" he asked.

"You can't imagine. You have until midnight to stop."

He chuckled. "Why midnight?"

"Because from then until daylight you can work on the other foot."

"Equal time, huh?" He started on the left foot.

This time the coolness from holding the beer bottle had disappeared and his hands were warm. It did not take away from the floating sensation one bit.

"Why don't you give up ranching and do this or have sex for a living? You could make lots more money," she teased.

"I like sex and I really like having you for a friend, but ranching is my first love. That's why most women don't really want to settle with me. They'd always take second place," he answered. "Besides I don't reckon that Dry Creek would appreciate a male whorehouse over on the Lucky Penny."

She giggled, then laughed and then guffawed until tears rolled and she got a case of hiccups. "We'd make a good pair, then, for sure. Me with my hooker genes. You with your magic hands and…" She paused and blushed.

"And?" he asked.

"Your fantastic bedroom skills." She finished but the crimson in her cheeks deepened.

"Why, Lizzy Logan, you are blushing."

She took a long gulp of the beer and was happier than she'd ever been that things had not worked out with Mitch. She'd missed having a beer occasionally, and besides Mitch had never rubbed her feet or taken her to the heights that Toby did in the bedroom.

"I should be going," he said. "Blake is cooking tonight. You want to come over? I'll tell him to bring an extra one."

"Thanks but no thanks. I'll grab something here so I can have more time to get all prettied up for my date with my boyfriend." She batted her long eyelashes at him.

"Don't forget to eat something. Drinking on an empty stomach is not a good thing." He eased out from under her feet, finished off his beer, and set the empty bottle on the table. Then he bent forward at the waist and brushed a kiss across her lips. "That's for the imaginary guy wearing camouflage up in the tree—the one who spreads the gossip. Good night, Lizzy."

She downed the rest of the beer, but it didn't do much in the way of cooling off her steamy hot lips. It was only a sweet kiss, but it brought back memories of blistering hot sex when their bodies were bathed in sweat. When she went into the house, she headed straight for the bathroom and a cold shower.

Half an hour later she emerged with a towel around her body and another one wrapped turban-style around her hair to find her mother sitting on the top step of the staircase with a glass in her hand.

"Mama, is that whiskey?" Lizzy asked.

"Jack Daniel's to be exact, and I needed it after that crap Dora June and her evil minions pulled today. People kept coming in the store, including the preacher, trying to talk me out of resigning. But it is done and I'm not undoing it. I'd quit the church and go to one in Throckmorton but that would make them too happy. Want a shot?" Katy held up a square bottle with a black label.

"I had a beer with Toby before I came in the house." Lizzy went on to tell her the details of what had been going on for the past two days.

"I like Toby. I do. I'm glad this isn't real between y'all, though. Talk about awkward among all the family if you let this build into something and then it ended," Katy said.

"I know, Mama." Lizzy sat down beside her mother and took one tiny sip of the whiskey. "That tastes like heaven from a bottle. So did the beer. Are you still angry?" Lizzy asked.

"Not angry. Madder'n hell's blazes." Katy took another sip. Her dark hair was frosted these days with wisps of white, but her smooth complexion was something that twenty-year-old women would die for. She'd gone from a size ten back before her husband died to a fourteen, but hey, the tabloids said that curvy women were the *in thing* these days.

"Want to go dancin' with me and Toby tomorrow night?" Lizzy treated herself to another small sip right from the bottle. It was silky warmth, not totally unlike the afterglow after sex with Toby.

"Hell, no! I'm going to Wichita Falls to dinner with my old friends, Janie and Trudy. Janie is getting a divorce and we are going to cheer her up," Katy answered.

"Good grief! Hasn't she been married a long time? And you haven't talked about them in years."

"She's been married thirty years just like me and your daddy would have been this year if he'd lived. I was her bridesmaid and she was mine. And we kind of lost touch, but Trudy called this evening and I'm going up there to see them."

Lizzy eyed the whiskey bottle but didn't touch it. "I thought Trudy moved off somewhere. Didn't we get Christmas cards from her from Oregon?"

"That's right. She's been married three times but she's been divorced from the last one for six years. We're going to catch up tomorrow night. Maybe they can spend that reunion weekend with us. I hope Fiona can come home for the festival. Seems like a year since last Christmas when we saw her."

Lizzy held the towel tightly and stood up. "I'm glad you are reuniting with Janie and Trudy, Mama. Friends are important. And we can gang up on Fiona when we talk to her. I don't reckon we'll have to talk too long and hard when we tell her that Mitch will be here. She's been achin' to tell him off ever since he broke it off with me."

"I hope she listens to you. And darlin' daughter, you are so right about friends, but they'll never be as important as family," Katy said.

CHAPTER SEVEN

Lizzy slid a Travis Tritt CD in the player to get her in the mood for the evening. She dressed in a pair of low-slung tight jeans with rhinestones on the hip pockets and a form-fitting western-cut shirt of black lace insets on the back yoke. Then she pulled on her oldest, most comfortable dress boots.

As she brushed her dishwater blond curls out, Travis sang a song about it being a great day to be alive. The lyrics said that there were hard times in the neighborhood and that sometimes it was lonely.

Travis was preaching to the choir if he was singing just for Lizzy. There were definitely hard times in the neighborhood and she did get lonely. But tough times came and went, and that night she had somewhere to go and a handsome cowboy to dance with her. Plus there had been no bitchy women in her store today. So this day, as Mary Jo had said, was a day to celebrate and it was a great day to be alive.

The music continued to play as she left the room and headed down the stairs. One song ended and before another began, the empty house echoed the sound of her boots on the wooden steps. Lizzy had discovered that she didn't like living in the big house with no sisters. They might fight and argue with each other, but she missed having someone around other than her mother.

She'd been a senior in high school when Allie's two-year marriage came apart at the seams. Fiona had been a sophomore and suddenly all three girls were back in the house again. Fiona left to go to college two years later, and that left two sisters. But now it was only Lizzy and she had found out pretty quick she wasn't cut out to be an only child.

Sitting on the bottom step, Lizzy listened wistfully as every other song Travis sang spoke to her heart. The last song was still playing when the doorbell rang. She opened the door and Toby came right inside, took her in his arms, and started a fast swing dance right there in the foyer. All thoughts of Lizzy's past disappeared as he smoothly twisted her in circles and deftly brought her back to his chest in perfect time with the music.

When the song ended, he kissed her on the forehead. "Darlin', any woman who can dance like that was not cut out to be a preacher's wife. And may I say that you are absolutely stunning tonight. Maybe I should go on back to the trailer and get my pistol to keep the other cowboys away from my girlfriend."

"Don't bother. There's a little derringer in my purse and yes, I have a concealed permit and yes, I do know how to shoot the thing," she said.

"She dances and she knows how to shoot. My kind of woman." He draped an arm loosely around her shoulders and kept in step with her from house to truck.

"I thought your kind of woman was tall, blond, blue eyed, and ready to fall into bed with no questions asked." She tossed her purse on the console and fastened her seat belt. Of all things, the radio was playing one of Travis Tritt's songs right then, too. Was it an omen?

"Well, there is that, but I do like a woman who is light on her feet and who knows her way around a pistol. Plus one who knows how many rolls of barbed wire it takes to fence in forty acres." He drove to the end of the lane and stopped. "Long way or short-cuts?"

"Back farm roads can get us there quicker." She pointed to the left.

"And?" He made a left-hand turn.

"The roads aren't as good as the highway, but it does cut off a few miles," she answered.

She felt his eyes on her, and like always before it created an antsy feeling deep down inside.

"What?" she asked.

"What what?" he threw back.

"You are looking at me with questions in your eyes. What is it?"

He turned the radio off. "You told me that you want what Allie has with Blake. I was wondering what kind of guy would be so lucky as to have you in his life?"

"I do believe I answered this question the night we decided not to continue with that fling. I don't want anyone who tries to change me to fit inside his neat little wife mold and who tells me what to do, what to eat, and how to dress. And I will never let another man win at Monopoly, if I ever play that boring game again." She stopped and took a breath. "Mitch pouted when he lost, so I got real good at losing."

"Holy shit!" Toby covered her hand with his. "You must've really wanted to be married."

"I've had a while to analyze my actions. What I wanted was for folks to see me as a preacher's wife, not as someone who came from Audrey's Place. I've always hated that," she said.

He squeezed gently. "Why? I told you before that what your ancestors did or didn't do doesn't affect you."

"But it does," she whispered. "I was a sophomore in high school when a really popular boy from Throckmorton asked me out on a date. We met at a countywide Future Farmers of America conference. To make a long story short, he'd heard of Audrey's and when he couldn't talk or force me into the backseat because of course anyone at an old brothel had to put out, didn't they...he took me home and spread it around that we'd had sex. So yes, it does affect me."

"That sorry kid should have been strung up from the nearest scrub oak tree with a length of rusty barbed wire," Toby said through clenched teeth.

"Oh, really? Were you different from that at sixteen?"

Toby put both hands on the steering wheel. "My hormones were raging at that age but if I'd bragged like he did, my daddy would have taken me to the woodshed. And believe me, even at that age, I did not like trips to that place."

"Pretty tough with the whippings, was he?" Lizzy asked.

"Never laid a hand on me, not once. Mama swatted my butt on occasion but not Daddy. I would have rather taken a whipping as listened to the lectures that got dealt out in the woodshed or know that I'd disappointed him. I have no doubt that damaging a lady's reputation would have been just cause for both." Toby turned the radio back on.

For the next thirty minutes every damn song that played on the radio spoke to Lizzy in some form or another. When Blake Shelton sang, "Goodbye Time," it reminded her again that it was time to let the past go and embrace the future.

A big neon sign above a rustic-looking building let Lizzy know they had arrived at the Rusty Spur. If the parking lot was any indication, the place was packed that Saturday night. As they walked hand-in-hand toward the place, she hoped it wasn't filled with people from Dry Creek.

"What are you thinking right now?" Toby asked.

"Hoping that Mitch's mama or Dora June isn't here," she said honestly.

Toby's laughter rang out above the noise of the live band. "If they are, I'll make sure to save one dance apiece for them."

When he opened the door, a fog of smoke and cool air flowed out to meet them and dozens of loud conversations added to the racket of the music. Lizzy had not expected the primal emotion that flowed through her veins. She felt like a wild animal that had been set free from a cage to prowl in its natural habitat. She sucked in the smoke, wanted a beer, and had the urge to dance, pressed up to Toby so close that light couldn't find its way between them.

She might have been engaged to a preacher, but she was out with a prophet because he'd said she wasn't cut out to be a preacher's wife. And he was so right!

Toby tucked her elbow into his hand. "I see two bar stools at the end."

She nodded and wove her way through the crowd, willing no one to claim the spots before they got there because she really did want a drink. She and Toby had settled on the tall stools before they noticed Deke sitting right beside them.

"Well, hello, Lizzy! Imagine finding you really here. Even with all the gossip spreading around town, I didn't think you'd really come along with Toby," he said.

"Call the folks who write the *Guinness Book* and all

the newspapers in Texas. Surely it will make the ten-o'clock news if they hurry," she said.

"What are y'all drinkin'? I'll buy the first round just to soften up her sass, Toby," Deke said.

Lizzy had planned on nursing one beer all evening, but Deke's smartass remark was nothing short of a challenge. "I'll have a double shot of Jack Daniel's on the rocks."

"I suppose that means I'm the designated driver tonight, so I'll just have a beer. Coors, long neck, please," Toby said.

"Are you saying I can't hold my liquor?" She took the first sip of the whiskey and enjoyed the taste and the way it warmed her mouth. Not totally unlike a hot and heavy kiss from Toby. Oh, those were the glorious days. Sex with no strings and no one had any idea what they were doing.

"I'm saying that the night is young and one of us has to drive back to Dry Creek," Toby answered.

Deke held up both palms. "Don't look at me. I'm here to have a good time and I've already spotted a lady that I plan to sweet-talk into keeping my bed warm tonight so don't plan on me driving you two drunks home."

"Wouldn't think of spoilin' your Saturday night. If you would be a sweet guy and warn me if you see Mitch's mama lurkin' around I would appreciate it. I'll buy her a drink if she shows up," Lizzy said.

"She's not half done with the drink and she's already drunk. Talkin' about Mitch's mama comin' to a bar proves my point. That woman would rather pick the white tops off chicken shit in the moonlight as come to a honky-tonk. If she shows up I'm for sure calling the television stations." Deke disappeared into the smoky fog.

Toby leaned over so she could hear him above the din. The warmth of his breath combined with the whiskey sent sweet little shivers up and down her spine.

"Are you feelin' totally out of place? We can leave anytime you want."

She shook her head emphatically. "Crazy thing is that I feel right at home. Give me time to finish this drink and then I want to dance."

"I've got a request for a Billy Currington song," the lead singer said from the corner of the room where the stage had been set up. The band broke into a good two-steppin' song, "People Are Crazy." Toby held his hand out to Lizzy. She threw back the rest of her drink and slapped her hand into his. He led her to the middle of the dance floor. She wrapped her arms around his neck and he rested his on the middle of her back. If anyone was spying on them, there would be no doubt that they were a couple.

"And one more request from Billy and then we'll move on to someone else," the singer said, and the first sounds of "Must Be Doin' Somethin' Right." Lizzy leaned back enough to look up at Toby. In her head she could see the video of Billy Currington on the beach wearing wet jeans, no shoes, and with his shirt unbuttoned to reveal a broad muscular chest. It might have been the whiskey blurring her vision, but right then Toby Dawson looked a hell of a lot like Billy, down to those clear blue eyes and that wide kissable mouth.

"Ready to sit one out?" Toby asked when the singer started singing a Blake Shelton song that called for a country waltz.

"Not yet. I like this song. Who are you when I'm not lookin', Toby Dawson?" She asked the same question that the song title did. "What secrets are you hiding?"

"I believe you know me pretty damn well." Toby kissed her on the top of her head. "Who are you when I'm not lookin', Lizzy Logan?"

"Well, I paint my toenails in the summer because I wear sandals. I don't throw things, but I do carry a grudge for a long time. I fight with my sisters, but I'll tear into anyone who says a bad word about either of them. I like my work and I do slide down the hall in my socks, like the song says. Sometimes I cuss, especially when I'm mad. Other than that, I expect you know me about as well as anyone," she said.

"I know the hotter'n hell Lizzy in the bedroom, but I've got a feeling that if we are friends for fifty years, there will be some secrets I never find out," he said.

"I hope so." She laid her head back on his chest and followed his smooth steps.

"Oh. My. God." Lizzy leaned her head back. "Toby, why did you let me drink so much? I'm floating like an angel. I think I'm having an out of body experience."

"You, darlin', are drunk."

The idea of being drunk was so funny that she giggled. "I can't be drunk. I only had half a bottle of Jack and we danced it out of my system. I'm not wasted."

The dash clock had to be wrong. There was no way it was two o'clock in the morning. Lizzy had never stayed out that late in her life, not even when it was a girls' night out with her sisters.

"Hey, Toby, do you reckon God uses Christmas tree hangers to keep those stars up there in the sky?" In her head the words were spoken clear as a sunny day, but her ears heard several of them slur.

"That would explain it for sure," he said with a chuckle.

"I liked drinkin' and dancin'. Can we do it again? Why don't you stop right here in the church parking lot and we can finish off the evening with some scalding-hot sex? That backseat looks every bit as big as the bed in the back of Mama's store."

"I'd better get you on home tonight, darlin'. Remember, we decided that part of our business was over," he said.

"Well, shit!" Her eyes fluttered shut and she dreamed of Toby lying on the beach with sand on his chest. Like in the Billy Currington video, he was curled around her, his finger tracing the outline of her belly button.

Sunlight poured into her bedroom window when she awoke on Sunday morning. Disoriented, with the radio

playing loudly right beside her head, she couldn't figure out where she was or how she got there. Then it all
came back in a rush and she shoved a pillow over her
aching head. Holding it down with one hand, she let
the other one travel from her shirt to her jeans.

At least she was dressed even if her boots had been
kicked off, but how in the hell had she gotten home?
She remembered something about God and the stars
and then nothing except...

"Sweet Jesus!"

"Yes, he is sweet," Allie said from the doorway.

She peeked out from the edge of the pillow with
one eye. "Toby brought me up the stairs slung over his
shoulder like a bag of chicken feed. I thought it was
funny because..." She clamped her mouth shut.

"Because that put your lips right on his cute little
ass? I'm here with the hangover cure. Sit up. At least
you got to dance and have a good time. I was in
Granny's closet with nothing but memories," Allie
said.

Lizzy eased to a sitting position without opening her
eyes. "God, my head hurts. What is this hangover cure?
I'm never doin' this again."

"First, a tablespoon of honey. Then Mama is bringing up two scrambled eggs and a piece of toast. After
that you get a cup of hot black coffee, followed by a
banana and a shower," Allie said. "Open your mouth.
Honey is coming your way."

"I hate honey and I feel like I licked the bottom of
an ash tray," she said.

The spoon touched her lips and instinctively her mouth opened. "I'm never getting drunk again. One shot or one beer and then it will be club soda or plain water. I can't eat eggs, Allie. I can't. I'm not going to church, either. Tell Mama that I'm sick."

"Mama knows you've got a hangover and you are definitely going to church. Are you going to let Dora June get ahead of you and are you going to let Lucy down? You will eat the eggs. Believe me, sister, it's not as tough as the banana to get down."

"Who died and made you a damn doctor?" Lizzy fussed.

"Blake taught me that this works. And I declared I'd never get drunk again, too. Remember when I wrecked my truck and spent the night over at the Lucky Penny because I was so damn drunk on whiskey and tequila? Us Logan girls were not made for hangovers. At least you are waking up fully dressed." Allie sat down on the edge of the bed.

Lizzy's hand covered her mouth. "Don't wiggle the bed. I'll upchuck the honey if you do. Did you really wake up naked?"

"I don't kiss and tell." Allie laughed. "But darlin', everything those old hens tossed me out of the ladies' club for doing? Well, I did them and enjoyed the hell out of every minute."

"Eggs and toast," Katy said from the doorway. "What were you drinkin'?"

"Jack on the rocks. Deke said I couldn't hold my liquor and I was showing him that I could. How'd you know to bring over this remedy stuff, Allie?" Lizzy asked. "And Allie, has Deke been in love with me forever?"

"Hell, no! What made you ask that stupid question? We are like sisters to him." Allie patted her on the shoulder. "Toby left a note on the counter telling me you would need the hangover cure."

"If it works, then God bless Toby. If it doesn't and I puke I may need a sharpened shovel to bury him." Lizzy snarled at the plate of eggs and toast. "Do I have to?"

"I can feed you," Allie said.

Lizzy picked up the fork and forced the eggs and toast down, bite by bite. "What's next? Greasy sausage gravy?"

"Hot coffee." Katy put the cup in her hand and sat down on the other side of the bed. "At least you are dressed and in bed alone. That's a good sign."

It was on the tip of Lizzy's tongue to say that it wasn't her idea to come home fully dressed, but she filled her mouth with hot coffee so she'd keep quiet. She and Toby were friends, not lovers, not anymore.

Blake, Allie, Deke, and Toby were lined up on the pew when Katy and Lizzy arrived at church that morning. Toby moved out into the aisle and Katy settled in beside Deke. Lizzy sat down beside her mother and Toby took the end of the pew. The moment he sat down, he reached for her hand, holding it on his thigh.

"You might want to take off the sunglasses." He

knew exactly how she felt because he'd been there many times on Sunday morning. His grandpa used to say that he sowed his wild oats on Saturday night and attended church on Sunday morning to pray for a crop failure. Grandpa might have been making a joke, but in Toby's case, it was the absolute gospel truth.

She whipped off the glasses and dropped them in her purse. Even with her eyes still glazed slightly, she was so damn cute that he wanted to kiss her right there on the back pew of the church. Settling down might not be in his future, but he did enjoy having a pretty woman beside him.

"Did the cure work?" he whispered.

"It's much better. Sharlene is shooting dirty looks across the aisle at me, though," Lizzy whispered.

"By the time services are over, you'll feel almost normal, and darlin', Sharlene Tucker can't hold a candle to you when it comes to determination or beauty," he said.

"I appreciate that but her looks would fry the wings off an angel. And is that business about a hangover the voice of experience?" she asked.

"Yes, ma'am." He squeezed her hand gently.

The music director said the congregation would sing "I'll Fly Away." She tensed when the lady at the piano hit the keys for the prelude. Then tears started to flow and drip off her cheeks to spot the light brown shirt she wore with a pretty knee-length floral skirt.

"What is it?" He brought a snow-white handkerchief from his pocket and handed it to her.

"Granny liked this song. She sang it real loud while we sang something altogether different more than one time," she explained.

He put his arm around her shoulders and hugged her close to his side. "Why don't we go up to Wichita Falls this afternoon and see her? Would that help?"

She nodded. "I'd like that."

"What's her favorite food? We'll stop at a grocery store and take her something."

She dabbed at her eyes. "White powdered doughnuts and cherry pie."

Toby got that antsy, itchy feeling that said someone was staring at him. Without moving his head, he scanned the room, finally coming to rest on Dora June's accusatory glare. He shot his sexiest wink all the way across the church at the woman. She whipped around in her seat so fast that she probably had trouble focusing for several minutes.

He didn't listen to one thing the preacher said but rather sat there and let his thoughts wander. True, he'd never had a good friend like Lizzy. His friends and buddies had been guys. Some were fishing buddies; some were rodeo buddies; and some were party buddies. Maybe the protective feeling he had toward her was the way he would have felt toward a sister.

Whoa there, hoss! The voice in his head yelled so loud that it startled him. *You don't kiss your sister or dance with her plastered up to your body. And you damn sure don't spend three weeks of scorching hot nights with her.*

Okay, then. It had to be the friend thing since it definitely was not sister feelings. He'd have to ask Blake if he and Allie started off as friends. No, he couldn't do that or Blake would know.

Know what? the voice asked in a soft whisper.

I don't know, he argued. *That's what I'm trying to figure out.*

"I'm going to ask Deke to deliver the benediction for us this morning," the preacher said.

Toby was glad he'd been thinking with his eyes open. Poor old Deke wasn't sure what was going on when Blake flipped him on the back of the head.

"Benediction," Blake said in a loud whisper.

Deke hopped up to his feet, bowed his head, and managed to thank God for the day and the church service. Then everyone said, "Amen," and the quiet disappeared into a buzz of conversation. Most of it, from the way everyone was looking toward the Logan pew, was centered around Lizzy and Toby.

"I'm so glad that you and Lizzy are in a relationship even if it isn't real," Blake said out the side of his mouth. "It sure takes the pressure off me and Allie for a while."

"Glad to be of help. We're going to Wichita Falls to see her granny. Y'all want to go with us?" Toby asked.

Truman O'Dell pushed through the crowded church and stopped in front of Lizzy. "I heard where you were last night and what you were doing. I guess Mitch was right in finding another woman. You sure ain't no preacher's wife and you've proven it."

"That is enough, sir," Toby said.

"Yes, it is." Katy laid a hand on Truman's shoulder. "You have no idea what happened in Lizzy's life and you won't judge her. Don't talk to my girls like that again or you'll answer to me."

"I've said my piece." Truman marched out of the church without even shaking the preacher's hand.

They found Granny sitting in her room watching episodes of *The Golden Girls*. While they waited in the door she fussed at Rose for being so stupid and told Blanche she was too damn old to be flirting with those young men. Then she noticed them and clapped her hands.

"Lizzy, you've come to visit and brought a new boyfriend. Thank God! I thought you might moon around and never get over Mitch. What's in the bag?" Irene asked.

"Granny, this is Toby. Remember meeting him? He's Blake's brother," Lizzy said.

"Well, come on in and drag up a chair. How's Allie? Is the baby here yet?"

Lizzy situated her chair as close to her grandmother as she could get, and Toby sat across the room. "No, not until fall, Granny."

"I forget, you know," she whispered. "What did you bring me?"

"Powdered sugar doughnuts and a couple of those fried cherry pies from the deli in the grocery store. Which one do you want first?" Lizzy pulled them from the brown paper bag. "And a bag of miniature candy bars to put in your drawer."

"I'll hide them real good. The people in this prison steal candy," she whispered.

"Granny, this is not a prison," Lizzy said.

"Window won't raise up. Doors are locked. It's fancy, but it's a prison," Granny argued. "When are you and this fine-lookin' young man gettin' married? Can I wear red to this one? I hated that blue dress you had picked out for me to wear to the last one. I was glad that son of a bitch broke up with you because I didn't have to wear that dress." She opened the bag of small doughnuts and stuffed two into her mouth.

"We sang 'I'll Fly Away' in church this morning," Lizzy said.

Irene swallowed the doughnuts, sucked down part of a glass of water through a straw, and started the old hymn in a high clear soprano voice. Lizzy could have kissed Toby when he joined in with his deep voice. She harmonized with them and Irene smiled through the whole song.

"Now I've been to church." She clapped her hands again. "Who is this young man again?"

"Toby Dawson," Lizzy said.

"Katy, darlin', you know you shouldn't bring him here. You are engaged to someone else."

Just like that Granny had left the present and was back to that time when Katy was preparing for her wedding to Lizzy's father. "I won't tell your daddy, but tell me this is a friend and not that awful boy from the Lucky Penny."

Lizzy leaned closer to her grandmother and laid her head on her shoulder. "He's the music director at the church and we thought you might like to sing some songs today so I brought him with me."

Irene broke out into "I'll Fly Away" again with Toby and Lizzy singing right along with her for a second time. When they'd finished she brought out three doughnuts and ate them slowly.

"Katy, I'm really getting sleepy. It was fun going to choir practice with you and this young preacher, but it's time for you to go now so I can take a nap. Maybe later we'll work on your wedding dress," she said.

"I'd like that. I'm going to set your doughnuts and pies right here on the bedside table and your candy is in your top drawer," Lizzy said.

"Good girl." Irene curled up on her bed.

Lizzy pulled a throw over her, kissed her on the forehead, and nodded at Toby. She'd planned to spend the whole afternoon with her grandmother and almost cried when Irene recognized her. But she'd have to be happy with a few minutes of real time when she could get it.

She made it to the door when Irene called out. "Lizzy, darlin', I like your boyfriend. Give Allie a kiss for me. And tell Dora June that she can kiss my ass."

Lizzy started back into the room but before she got to the bed, Irene was snoring.

"How did she know about Dora June?" she wondered aloud as she and Toby made their way back up the hall to the lobby.

"Your mama probably told her when she stopped by to see her and told her everything that had happened," Toby answered. "It's a lovely day. Let's get an ice cream cone and go to the park."

One of the attendants punched in the code to open the door. "We love Miz Irene in here. She's a hoot no matter what world she is in."

"We appreciate y'all taking such good care of her," Lizzy said as she and Toby stepped outside. "It's going to rain. I can smell it in the air."

"Then we'd best get our ice cream and go to the park before it starts. I'm having a double dip of pecans, pralines, and cream. What are you getting?"

"That sounds good." She smiled. "Thank you for singing with her."

"My pleasure," Toby said. "Guess you were right. Here comes the rain." He slammed the door as the first raindrops hit the windshield with a force usually reserved for sleet or hail. "Ice cream at the drive-through window and a slow ride home? I won't say a bad word about this rain because we need it so badly."

"And then maybe a movie with Allie and Blake? Nothing better than cuddling up and watching a movie on a rainy day," she suggested.

"Sounds like a plan. Those two do love movies," he said, and chuckled.

"No, they like cuddling on the sofa. The movies are an excuse and gives them something to talk about while they are in each other's arms," she told him. "That's the kind of relationship I want someday."

"That's love for sure. Never thought I'd see Blake settle down to one woman or be still and watch movies. He always wanted to be outside or else at a bar chasing women."

"Never thought I'd see Allie trust any man again after Riley."

"They got the miracle, didn't they?" Toby started the engine. "But it would have been nice if they'd left some of the magic for the rest of us."

"Oh, hush! You've already said you aren't the settling type. You can't have wings and roots both, cowboy."

"She can shoot. She speaks her mind. She can dance and she is a prophet. And she is so right. I can't have it both ways so I'm taking the wings. I can put down roots in Dry Creek, but I don't ever intend to put them down when it comes to matters of my heart." He laughed. "Still, you are a remarkable woman, Lizzy Logan."

CHAPTER EIGHT

Lizzy's grandfather had started the Dry Creek Feed and Seed in what was now the front part of the store. In those days he kept a supply of cattle and chicken feed on one side of the store and pig food, along with seeds of all kinds and plants in the spring on the other side. The cashier's counter was always right in the middle so he could see every which way, and a few shelves lined the outer edges. He'd sold a limited supply of do-it-yourself vet supplies and cattle medicines, and since there was a hardware store on the other side of the street, he had not offered things like extension cords, chain saw blades, or nails and screws.

Nowadays the store was a combination of hardware and feed store and the actual feed had moved to the back, a room her father had framed in and covered with corrugated sheet metal. It wasn't heated or cooled, but the space served its purpose. Sacks of cattle, hog, and chicken feed were stacked neatly on one side of the big barnlike enclosure. The rest of the area was taken up with fence posts and rolls of barbed wire. A big over-head garage door let the ranchers back their trucks up close to load whatever they wanted. The smaller door that opened into the store used to be the outside en-trance. And during the evolution of the store, Lizzy had put in a few racks of clothing, mainly jeans, western shirts, and hunting clothes, but these days it took on the look of an old-time general store more than just a feed and seed place.

Lizzy stood in the middle of the back room and took stock of what she needed to order that Tuesday morn-ing. She started humming as she wrote numbers on the order pad.

She was in such a good mood when she finished the job that she did several steps of a line dance to the tune of "Footloose" that was playing on the radio. When the song ended, she called the distributor and put in her order, then two-stepped with a broom all the way to her office to Luke Bryan's song, "Kick the Dust Up."

She swirled the broom around once more and stood it in the corner. "Well, by golly, some things never change, do they, Luke?" she said as she listened to the lyrics talking about the life of a rancher working all week and then turning a cornfield into a party.

She sighed as she remembered the concert shirt that

Toby wore to the bar. It had been a hell of a lot more fun dancing with Toby than it was with a broom.

The cowbell rang loudly and Toby rushed inside and motioned for her to join him. He looked absolutely frantic so she hurried out into the store, heart pumping double time and hands going clammy. Every single time anyone in the family had a look like that on their face, she immediately worried about Allie's pregnancy.

"Why aren't you answering your phone?" he yelled across the store.

She jerked it out of her hip pocket and held it up. "It needs charging."

"What about the store phone?"

She reached the front desk and picked it up. "It's not working. It was a few minutes ago. I called in some orders. What's going on? Is it Allie?"

"No, it's a tornado. It whipped through Throckmorton a few minutes ago and tore up a couple of barns. It's still on the ground and coming toward us. Allie was having a fit about you and her mama. I just warned Katy and she said her cellar is full. There were a dozen people in the store and they are already in the cellar." He talked fast, his eyes darting around the store.

"My cellar door is under a hatch in the back room. Come on." She jogged to the door with him right behind her. The big overhead doors were open and the view offered that slightly green sky color that preceded a tornado. The eerie still feeling in the air made the hair on her neck stand straight up.

"Where is it, Lizzy?" Toby's voice sounded as if it was coming from a vacuum.

She kicked a bag of feed to one side and grabbed an iron ring on the floor. One second the wind was stone-cold still, the next it sounded like a freight train in the distance and a roll of barbed wire tumbled across the floor.

"I've got to shut the overhead doors, Toby."

He took the ring from her hand and opened the hatch, shaking his head the whole time. "You don't have time. Just get down in the cellar."

"You have to throw the bolt once it's shut. I haven't been down here since before Daddy died." Her hand closed around an old wooden thread spool when she reached up. When she pulled it, a bulb hanging in the middle of the cellar lit the room long enough to let her find the matches to light the oil lamp sitting on a dusty orange crate. Once they had a dim light from that, she pulled the string again, turning the bulb off.

"Why did you do that?" Toby eased his tall frame down into a metal folding chair.

"Because it's what Daddy told me to do if I had to come down here. I didn't ask why," she said.

The cellar was exactly like she remembered. Two folding chairs and an olive green military cot filled up the six-by-eight-foot space. Even through the thick concrete walls, the noise above them sounded like two semi-trucks had smashed together.

The crashing sound of metal against metal made her jump back as a length of barbed wire dangled down from the air vent. Toby grabbed her, sat down with a thud on one of the chairs, and hugged her tightly against his chest.

"Don't touch that thing. Lightning might have electrified it," he said above the din.

"I wasn't going to," she gasped. "My store is blowing away, isn't it?"

The next crash sounded like monsters were beating on the hatch door with hammers. She flipped around and buried her face in his chest. "I'm not going to have a thing left. We'll be lucky if they get us out from under the rubble."

"Blake and Deke will rescue us. Don't worry about that or the store. That's why you have insurance," Toby said.

One minute Toby and Lizzy were yelling as loud as they did in the bar. The next everything went so quiet that they could have heard another spider inching its way up the concrete walls. Lizzy shivered and his arms tightened.

"It's over, isn't it? Just like that, it's over," she whispered.

"I think so. I'll unbolt the hatch and see if I can push it open."

She didn't want to see the damage and she damn sure did not want to leave the security of his lap. "Hold me one more minute, Toby. I don't want to face what's out there when we go out."

He kissed her on the top of her head and then the rain started—hard, driving rain that dripped off the end of the barbed wire hanging through the vent, making a puddle on the floor. Hail followed, beating against the hatch door. The wind roared angrily through Dry Creek as if showing the tornado who was the real boss.

"Sounds like you might have lost the roof to your feed shed," he said.

"I'll be grateful if that's all," she murmured.

Lizzy hated cellars or any small, enclosed spaces for that matter. Thinking about crawling under a house like Allie did gave her an acute case of hives. But she felt safe and secure in the tiny underground space with Toby's arms around her. Someday in the distant future she wanted a man like Toby who would...

Whoa, girl! The voice in her head made a screeching sound like tires leaving twenty feet of rubber on a dry pavement. *You are the one who broke this thing off with him because it was only sex. Now you are letting thoughts of a future with him into your head? There is no future with Toby.*

She frowned and argued with the voice. *I said like Toby, not Toby. One with strong arms and who will hold me when I'm afraid and not belittle me.*

Why had she ever had that mindless fling with him anyway? It had ruined any chance that they might have of anything beyond friendship or this new fake relationship they'd entered into. She liked him. There, she'd admitted it. She liked Toby Dawson as a man, as a friend, and as a pseudo-boyfriend. And there was a tiny little bit of her heart that really would like for him to be more. But it would never happen, because she'd destroyed any hope with a three-week sex fling.

She stood up and started up the narrow stairs. "I'll help you. Maybe whatever we heard fall on the hatch blew off and with two of us pushing against the wind, we can open it."

"You made of salt or sugar, either one?" He grinned.

"Not this old feed store woman." She smiled back at him.

Together they pushed against the flat door but it did not budge a quarter of an inch. Lizzy took a step back and slapped the concrete. "Aggravating son of a bitch."

Toby took a deep breath and gave it all he had but nothing, nada, zilch.

"If cussin' won't work, do you think sweet-talkin' might?" she asked, and then groaned. "What if we have to stay down here for hours? No food, no potty."

He pointed to the vent. "We've got water and air and trust me, as soon as Allie and Blake can get here, they will get us out."

"Oh, no!" The cellar walls started closing in on Lizzy. She sat down and put her head between her knees. "Oh, Toby, I've been selfish. I wasn't thinkin' of anyone but me. What if Allie and Blake are..." She could barely think the words much less say them out loud.

"Lizzy, Lizzy, are y'all okay? Is Toby with you? Did he make it to the store in time to get underground?" The barbed wire went up as Allie's voice came down through the vent and filled the room.

"Allie! We're fine," Lizzy yelled. "What's on the hatch door?"

"Half of your back room," Allie said. "Tell Toby that the tornado didn't touch down on the Lucky Penny. Looks like your place is all that got hit here in town. Mama and her customers are fine and Audrey's Place lost a few shingles in the wind but it's still standing."

"The rest of my store?" Lizzy asked.

"Got a hole in the roof but I threw a trash can under it to catch the water. We can fix it soon as the rain stops. Blake and Deke are working on getting the lumber off the door. Sit tight. We'll have you out soon. I'm going inside out of the rain," Allie said.

Katy's voice was the next one that came down the vent. "Allie said you were okay but I have to hear it for myself."

"We're fine, Mama," Lizzy said.

"Good, then I'll go on inside and help Allie mop up the floor where the roof leaked. Blake is hooking a chain up to his truck to drag part of a ceiling truss off the hatch," Katy said. "Lord, this rain is cold. I'm going inside now that I know you are okay."

"Well, shit!" Lizzy murmured.

"Cussin' again?" Toby sat down on the same chair and patted his lap.

"Yes, I am." She ignored his lap and sat down on the bottom step. With the adrenaline still rushing through her veins she sure didn't need to feel his body that close to hers.

"Shhh, what if someone still has an ear to that vent?"

Something rattled across the pipe in the ceiling, and all kinds of splintered wood came down with the rain to splash in the puddle on the floor.

"I shouldn't be cussin' or complainin'. At least the feed truck doesn't come until tomorrow and the back room had very little stock in it," she said.

Toby grinned. "You are a good, positive woman, Lizzy."

"I hope so," she said. But Toby didn't want a good, positive woman to settle down with. Hell, he didn't want to settle with any woman, and she wanted what Allie had so that left a gap between them as wide as the Grand-damn-Canyon.

"Lizzy, I've been thinking..." He hesitated.

She looked up into his blue eyes. "About?"

The hatch popped open.

Light, rain, and voices filled the whole cellar.

"Come on up out of there and let's get in out of this miserable rain. It's trickling down my back and it's cold as ice," Deke hollered.

"Don't forget to blow out the lamp. We'll put a chunk of wood over the vent pipe so it won't leak and you can get the cleanup done later," Blake said.

Thirty more seconds! Why couldn't they have waited another half a minute to raise the hatch? Then Toby might have finished his sentence. Now Lizzy would never know what he'd been thinking about.

Lizzy wasn't prepared for the sight before her eyes as they climbed out of the hatch. It looked like a bomb had gone off all around her. Feed sacks must have been sucked up and then tossed back to land in among all the debris, because wet corn and cattle feed crunched her feet as she hurried through the door into the rest of the store.

Allie threw the mop on the floor and raced across the room to hug her sister in a fierce embrace. "I've never been so worried about you in my life. I couldn't get you on your cell phone and then the store phone gave a busy signal. Right after that it went dead, too. None of us have cell service, electricity, or phones right now but we're lucky to be alive."

Lizzy returned the hug. "I was afraid you and Blake would be blown away. There's no cellar on the ranch. We've got to put one in, Allie. We can put it right outside the back door and extend the porch roof out over it."

Blake removed his slicker and hung it on a nail right inside the door. "Next thing on the list, I promise. But we could see the tail of that thing and tell it was going to bypass us and Audrey's Place."

"You never know about a tornado. It can turn on a dime." Deke hung his slicker beside Blake's and shook the water from his light brown hair. "That feels like winter rain, not summer."

"It's comin' off hail." Katy picked up Allie's mop and went to work on the rest of the floor. "Would you look at that?" She pointed to the hole in the ceiling at the bright sunshine pouring in.

"Looks like the rain is over," Blake said.

"Well, shit!" Deke said. "If we would have waited

thirty more minutes we could have rescued you two without having to do it under water."

"Allie, you're going to have to let me go. I drank a whole pot of coffee before this thing hit and I've got to go to the restroom." Lizzy pushed away from her sister and practically ran the whole way through her office to the small restroom.

She was just reaching for the toilet paper when something furry touched her foot. She wasn't sure how she got from a sitting position to standing on the toilet seat with her eyes closed, but she managed it without breaking a leg. Her jeans might still have been around her knees, but her boots were planted as firmly on that toilet as if someone had super-glued them there.

Lizzy hated mice with a passion. A spider, she could handle. A snake, she could kill with a hoe or a pistol. But a damn mouse was only slightly smaller than a full-grown gorilla and it roared like a lion.

Keeping her eyes closed tightly, she pulled her pants up, zipped and buttoned them, and then fastened her belt. Maybe the mouse would be gone now.

One eyelid barely opened and she held her breath, almighty glad that she'd at least finished her business before having her soul scared from her body. Her heart pumped double time as she scanned the floor from potty to door and saw nothing. Then a movement in her peripheral vision snapped the one open eye shut again. She'd seen enough to know the creature was black and furry and it had a tail. Should she yell at Toby to come save her?

Hell, no, don't do that. He thinks you're tough as nails. Don't ruin that by letting him know you are afraid of a little old mouse.

If she stepped down really fast and grabbed the door handle, she could be out of the tiny bathroom in no more than three seconds.

But what if I step on it and it gets mouse on my boots? What then? These are my favorite work boots and if there are mouse guts on the sole, I'll have to throw them away.

If she reached forward she could open the door, bail off the potty in one long jump, and then slam the door shut. That was the plan until she heard a squeaking noise to her left and she opened both eyes before she thought.

"What the hell?" She eased down off the potty. A black and white cat with three little yellow kittens pawing at her belly was curled up tightly in the corner of the bathroom behind a small cabinet. "Where did you come from? We must have left the door open when we ran to the cellar. Are you wild?" She gingerly touched the cat on the head and she started to purr.

"Lizzy, are you all right in there?" Allie knocked.

"Shhh!" She put a finger to her lips and eased the door open. "Come and see what came lookin' for refuge from the storm."

Allie put the lid down on the potty and sat down. "Can I pet her?"

Lizzy nodded. "She's friendly."

Lizzy had been offered cats from every rancher in

the county to keep the mice away from the feed sacks. She always refused, telling them that she'd buried too many cats as a child to want to go through the pain of losing one as an adult. The real reason was that she hated any form of rodents, from field mice to rats, and cats often left dead ones as presents. In Lizzy's books, dead ones were just about as wicked as live ones. But this little family needed her and that made a difference.

"What's going on in there?" Katy peeked in.

"Lizzy has a cat and what looks like three, no four, kittens. There's a little black head down there under that fat yellow one," Allie said. "Either the tornado dropped it or it came looking for a safe place to get out of the storm."

Toby's blue eyes showed up over the top of Katy's head.

"Most feed stores have at least one cat."

"I never wanted one but I think I'll keep this family," Lizzy said.

"Good for you, sister. Now, Blake, either take me home or take me to Nadine's café. I'm starving."

"Home it is. Nadine won't have any electricity. At least we can rustle up food at our house," Blake said.

Lizzy left her new family of cats and stepped out of the bathroom. "Give me time to open a can of food for my new mama cat and fix up a litter pan and I'll be right with y'all. No electricity means I can't do a bit of business here right now. I'm going home with you, Allie, if there's food involved."

"Me, too," Katy said. "What are you cooking, Blake?"

"There's a pot of chili ready to be heated up. Allie has been craving it for a week so I made a big batch." He slipped his arm around Allie's waist. "And Allie made a cherry cobbler this morning."

"When we get done, I'll get up on that roof and stretch some plastic over that leak until the insurance adjustor comes. Then we'll fix it for you," Allie said.

Deke shook his head. "You will not be getting up on any roof. Not until after this baby is born. I'll take care of it for Lizzy. Won't take but an hour at the most."

"I'm pregnant, not dead," Allie protested.

"And let's keep you that way," Blake said.

CHAPTER NINE

The electricity came back on in town at two o'clock that afternoon. It was hard to believe that not three hours before, a tornado had ripped through Throckmorton County, leaving trees uprooted, barn roofs gone, sheet metal wrapped around trees. The mesquite trees looked like a bunch of pranksters had toilet-papered half the county, but in reality it was wet shredded paper from businesses on south of Throckmorton that had gotten hit harder than Dry Creek.

"I've never seen mesquite look like that," Lizzy said as Deke drove them all back to town. "All the leaves have been stripped off the limbs and replaced with paper. It's kind of eerie."

"I saw it once or twice down around Muenster," Toby said.

He'd had more than two hours to think about that comment he'd been about to make in the cellar and had changed his mind about voicing it. The hatch had opened at the exact right moment to keep him from saying anything more. Granny Dawson used to say that sometimes fate stepped in to help us out when we're about to make a big, big mistake.

Why would he ever even think about asking Lizzy to change their relationship status from fake to real? He chalked it up to simple adrenaline from the tornado. Thank God, Allie and Blake had shown up when they did or he'd be doing some fancy back-stepping.

He tapped out the beat of an old Conway Twitty song playing on the classic radio station. The lyrics talked about the games people play when they broke each other's hearts.

"We're playing a game like he's talking about, aren't we?" Lizzy asked.

"And doing a fine job, but there won't be broken hearts at the end of our game, will there?" he answered.

She shook her head. "We knew going into this, both with the fling and with the relationship we're in, what we were doing."

"And now we've got a request for another Conway song today," the radio announcer said.

Lizzy moved her shoulders to the beat of the music.

"What are you thinkin' about?" Toby figured she was thinking about the night they'd gone to the bar. It had been the first date he could remember actually relaxing and enjoying himself instead of worrying about what lines it would take to get a woman into bed. Not that he'd ever had to work too hard at that.

"Tight-fittin' jeans, just like Conway is singing about. I was remembering all the beer that we went through at the bar that night... well, maybe not beer for me but shots of Jack Daniel's. I didn't marry money like he's singing about, but I almost married a preacher, which is just as bad. I loved the feeling in that bar, Toby. I liked the noise and the dancing."

"And the hangover?" Even when she was drunk off her ass he didn't feel like a seductive player just waiting to get all hot and dirty between the sheets.

"Taught me a hell of a lesson that I won't need to repeat," she said with a smile.

"And now you are back in your world and I'm in mine, like Conway says, but I won't forget the fun we had that night, Lizzy." The feel of her in his arms. The joy of making her laugh. Despite their differences, it was so easy to just let go and enjoy himself around her. Yes, he'd remember that night for a long time.

"Me, either," she said.

Toby had to force himself back to the reality that she was looking for a lot more than he was willing to give, no matter how much fun they had together. Lizzy was a good woman and he hoped all her dreams came true, but the very thought of settling down, of being a father—well, bring on his usual pickup lines and morning-after breakfasts for nameless women.

* * *

Lizzy bailed out of her truck before Toby had time to come around and open the door for her. She caught the keys when he tossed them over the hood toward her and opened up the store and flipped on the lights. That was the moment that the whole experience hit her full force. She'd been so grateful to be alive that the logistics didn't surface until she saw the trash can sitting in the middle of the store and remembered the destruction in the back room.

Where was she going to put her feed and barbed wire when the new order came in? There were lots of empty stores in town. Katy owned four of them but she'd already leased the café to Nadine and had promised two of the others to Sharlene and Mary Jo. The last one was the old hotel across the street and down the block from the feed store.

What Lizzy really needed was the empty store right next to hers. It had been a grocery store at one time and had a big storage room in the back that would be perfect, but Truman O'Dell owned the building. She might as well wish for hell to freeze over or for Toby Dawson to change his type from a leggy blue-eyed Barbie to a dishwater blond with brown eyes and a curvy body. Neither one was likely to happen.

Toby crossed his arms over his chest and studied the situation with her. "Okay, the way I see it for the short term is this, Lizzy. I'll put the idea out there and you think about it until your orders come in. We've got an empty barn on the ranch and whatever you've got coming in to restock what blew away can go out there. You can write folks up a ticket here and they can bring it out to the ranch where I'll make sure they get what they bought all loaded up."

The first lick of the nail gun snapping down the plastic tarp on the roof above her made her jump and brought her new cat out from the office. Toby picked her up and held her close to his chest.

"Poor mama cat," he crooned. "Did that mean old storm scare you or were you hiding those babies out there in the back room? I bet that's the real story. You had those babies back in a corner and brought them inside when we left the door open."

Lizzy had been shifting the trash can, with a couple of gallons of water in it, to one side, but she stopped long enough to rub the cat's ears. "You did good, mama cat. Taking those babies to a room in the center of the place was smart. It's what I would have done with my babies if I couldn't get down inside a cellar."

All that talk about babies sent another streak of shivers down Toby's backbone. He shifted the cat over into Lizzy's arms and changed the subject. "So what about putting the feed out at the Lucky Penny until you can get your storage room rebuilt?"

"I'd like to have the store right next door, but Truman owns it," she said.

"That most likely means that you won't ever get your hands on it. Sounds like Deke is about done up there, so I'll take this out back and dump it for you." He picked up the heavy trash can like it weighed nothing.

The store phone rang and Lizzy set the cat down on the checkout counter. She promptly jumped down, picked something up in her mouth, and with one leap she was back with a dead mouse, which she deposited beside the phone and purred loudly. There was no way Lizzy was answering the phone with a dead mouse laying right beside it.

"Looks like she brought you a present. Think it would offend her if I took it away?" Toby chuckled.

Lizzy took two steps back and wrapped her arms around her waist. "I don't care if it hurts her little feline feelings. That right there is the number one reason I've never had a store cat. I absolutely hate mice—dead or alive."

Toby picked up the vicious creature by the tail and slung it out the back door, then went straight to the bathroom to wash his hands. She picked up a spray bottle of disinfectant cleaner and wiped down the whole counter with the cat right behind her, leaving paw prints everywhere before the cleaner had time to dry. Lizzy's cell phone rang and she recognized the tune so she answered without even looking at the ID.

"Hello, Allie," she said. "This cat brought a mouse and put it right by my cash register."

"She's showing you that she appreciates you letting her live in your store," Allie said. "I called the store phone. Was the mouse close to it? Is that why you didn't pick up?"

"Yes, it is. Do you need something?" Lizzy asked.

"Well, that was abrupt," Allie answered.

"I'm sorry." Lizzy rolled her eyes toward the ceiling in time to see another wet spot not two feet from the actual hole. "I think I may need a whole new roof and the back room will have to be rebuilt and I'm stressing out, Allie."

"Okay, settle down. I've already called the lumberyard and gotten my estimates for repairs. Deke has promised to give me a couple of weeks' work so we should have the roof fixed and the back room rebuilt within a week," Allie said.

"Blake is going to let you put a roof on?" Lizzy asked.

"My marriage contract doesn't say a damn word about being submissive. It does say love and respect."

"Whoa, sister!" Lizzy held up her free hand defensively. "If you want to put a roof on my store and build a new storage room out back, I'm not saying another word."

"Good. That is settled. Toby already talked to Blake about putting your supplies out here until we get finished. Two miles for a vendor to bring the stuff or for your customers to get feed and wire and posts is a hell of a lot closer than having to drive all the way to Throckmorton or Olney."

"Thanks, Allie. I appreciate that." Lizzy dropped her hand. "We should know something by the end of the week about the insurance, and then you can get started on your part of the job. I feel better already."

When she hung up and turned around, Toby was right behind her, cat in his arms again. "Blake isn't going to let her fix a roof and rebuild that room for you, is he?"

"We Logans aren't delicate flowers. We're tough as cow tongue cactus. I'm not arguing with her and if you and Blake are smart, you won't either. Deke will do the heavy lifting, trust me. He loves her," Lizzy said.

Toby's phone buzzed and he set the cat on the counter so he could check the message. A broad smile covered his face and he shoved it back in his pocket without replying. "At least she's tame and she's a mouser."

"Are we talking about my new cat, Miz Stormy, or the woman on the phone?" Lizzy asked, and immediately wished she could cram the words back in her mouth.

"Miz Stormy? Name fits her well. As for the other, what makes you think it was a woman?"

"You would have answered it if it had been family." No way was she telling him that she'd guessed it was a woman by the smile that the message created. She'd been right in breaking off the fling with him; Toby was probably never going to be ready for the things she wanted in life.

"Yes, it was a woman. Why? You jealous?" he teased. "It's nothing I'm going to answer," he added quickly. "I can't be talking to other women when we're dating."

"Fake dating," Lizzy reminded him, steeling herself. She was so not jealous. Not the least little bit.

"Even so"—he took a step closer—"I'm not a cheater. Fake or otherwise."

Lizzy tried not to get dizzy looking up into his blue

eyes. It was hard not to be mesmerized. It took everything she had not to push herself to her tiptoes and bring her lips to his.

He placed his hands on her shoulders and dropped a kiss on her forehead. "So you're naming her Stormy?"

She swallowed hard and nodded. Clearly he hadn't felt the intensity of the moment the same way she had.

He ran his hand down the length of the cat from ears to the tail. "Sounds fitting. Should have been your name."

"You don't like Lizzy?"

"I love your name, but Stormy fits your attitude better."

The cowbell sounded above the door but Lizzy didn't move an inch. Unreal or not, she needed to convince folks that what she and Toby had was genuine. Besides, she admitted to herself, she liked being close to him.

Lizzy looked over Toby's shoulder and asked, "What can I do for you, Truman?"

"I came to tell you not to ask me for the use of my store building and to buy a new hammer. Tornado made off with my best hammer I had to leave out in the yard when me and Dora June made a run for the cellar. Left the drill layin' right there and took the hammer."

"Did I ask for the use of your store building?" Lizzy moved away from Toby so she could see the man better.

"No, but you were going to and I wanted to tell you right away not to even ask."

"Well, that's right neighborly of you," she said sarcastically. "But you are smack out of luck. I don't have a hammer to sell you."

"You are just like your crazy old grandma," Truman said.

"Thank you."

Truman pointed at a shelf with hammers of several different sizes and weights. "And what is that?"

"Those have all been asked for from folks who need to get some work done on their places. I have a salesman coming in a few days. Check back with me then and, Truman, don't talk about my granny again or call her crazy. And one more thing before you drive on down to Throckmorton to buy a hammer, I don't want or need your store. I'm storing my supplies out at the Lucky Penny." She paused long enough to enjoy the look on his face. "If you will need any wire, posts, or feed this next month, you might want to pick that up while you are in Throckmorton since I heard you wouldn't be caught dead on the Lucky Penny."

Truman shook his finger under her nose. "You will pay for this, Lizzy. God spoke this morning when he blew away part of your store."

She stood up straight and rounded the counter. "What did he do to your place? Other than take your hammer?"

"Blew off a roof, stole one of my goats, and broke the window above Dora June's kitchen sink." Truman started toward the door.

"Maybe God is mad at you for being so hateful, Truman. Ever think of that?" Lizzy said.

"Or maybe all of it is what they call a natural disaster," Toby said.

"Hey, what's going on in here? I heard you got a little damage out at your place, Truman." Deke pushed his way into the store. "Got that tarp up there real good, Lizzy, and I done told Allie, I'll help her fix your place up better than new."

"Truman lost his hammer in the tornado but Lizzy doesn't have any left to sell." Toby winked.

"But…" Deke glanced back at the shelf.

"Every one of them is already spoken for." Toby smiled.

"Guess the tornado must've liked the taste of hammers and twisted-up metal." Deke nodded.

"You are all a bunch of smartass kids." Truman slammed the door behind him as he left.

"Been a long time since I've been called a kid," Deke said.

"But not a smartass?" Lizzy spun around, lost her balance, and fell into Toby's chest. His arms closed around her and he buried his face in her hair. His warm breath making its way down to her scalp created pictures in her imagination that would never be anything but illusive visions.

"Y'all don't have to do stunts like that in front of me." Deke picked up the cat and rubbed her ears. "I know you're not for real. I'll take this girl home with me if you don't want her."

"Lizzy's named the cat so I don't reckon she'll let you have her now." Toby took a step back.

"Stormy. That's her name," Lizzy said.

"Fittin' name but I want her and the kittens for my barn if you change your mind." Deke handed the cat off to Lizzy. "You ready to get back to work, Toby? You got mesquite to plow down and I've got wood to cut if I'm going to take a few weeks off and help Allie."

Stormy cuddled right into Lizzy's arms. "You didn't get any damage at all, Deke?"

"Not a bit, but I'm livin' right," he teased.

CHAPTER TEN

Every song on the radio reminded Toby in some way of Lizzy that Saturday morning when he settled into the dozer seat and started pushing mesquite trees up out of the wet earth. It had been four days since the tornado stripped them of their leaves, but they still had paper stuck firmly to their limber branches.

It was hot work, and by midmorning sweat had soaked through his shirt, plastering it to his body. The sun was almost straight up when he geared down and braked. He reached down to the floorboard and opened a small cooler, took out a fistful of ice, and rubbed it across his forehead, letting the cold water mix with the hot sweat as it ran down his cheeks and dripped onto his chest. He settled his hat on the steering wheel and scooped up a double handful of chilly water and hurriedly dumped it on the top of his head.

"Ahhh," he murmured.

Josh Turner's song, "Why Don't We Just Dance," started up as Toby settled the hat back on his wet hair. He kept time with his shoulders and sang along with the lyrics. He chuckled when the lyrics said that the whole world had gone crazy. That was damn sure the story of his life, but by the middle of July, it would go back to normal.

Right now he had a job to do and then he was picking Lizzy up for dinner at six o'clock. Thinking about seeing her again brought back memories of those nights he'd spent with her in the back room of her mama's convenience store. Imagining her soft skin and those gorgeous breasts made his mouth go dry. Without stopping the dozer, he pulled a bottle of cold water from the cooler and nearly drank the whole thing in one guzzle, unsure what was making him hotter: the midday sun or his thoughts of those sweaty nights with Lizzy.

Lizzy was in a horrible mood that Saturday night. She had dealt, finally, with the insurance company, and the work to repair the store could begin on Monday. Allie and Deke had set aside time to get it done, barring bad weather. Folks might not pray for a tornado, but they did for rain at least twice a day and three times on Sunday, and either storms or rain could slow down the work.

She dressed in jeans, a plaid pearl snap shirt, and her most comfortable boots, the ones she'd gone dancing in the week before. She brushed out her hair and thought about the curling iron but, hey, this wasn't a real date. Why do the whole nine yards? They could each take a book, go to the banks of the river, and sit in the bed of his truck and read until time to come home. As long as he picked her up at about the right time and gave her a good night kiss on the porch before he left, the gossipmongers would be satisfied.

"Damn it, this whole play-dating thing is so childish that he should be picking me up in a little red wagon and taking me up the lane to get a snow cone." She fussed at her reflection in the mirror.

The doorbell rang and she picked up her purse. Toby was braced against the doorjamb when she opened the old-fashioned screen door and stepped out onto the porch. Sweet Lord! He looked like sex on a stick in that plaid shirt that stretched across his chest and tucked into his trim waist behind a big silver belt buckle. His blue eyes never left hers and—well, merciful heavens—all that sweltering heat would convince anyone that they were seriously dating. A soft breeze delivered his aftershave right to her nose. The scent was something clean and fresh like a hot summer night with a hint of musk in the air after a warm rain.

"I'm leaving, Mama. See you tomorrow morning," she called over her shoulder, amazed that her voice sounded even semi-normal.

"So you are planning to stay out all night?" Toby wiggled his eyebrows, his eyes dancing with mischief.

"No, Mama won't be home until midnight. She and her two friends are going to dinner and then to a late movie. I'll be snoring long before she gets home," Lizzy said.

"Where to?" Toby ushered her out to the truck.

"I don't care if it's a Dairy Queen cheeseburger. Matter of fact that sounds delicious, but the closest one is in Olney and you know what happened when we went there. The next one is up in Seymour and that's forty miles from here," she said.

"Sounds good to me. You navigate and I'll drive," he said.

"I'm hungry so we'll take the shortcut. It's back roads but very little traffic."

He nodded when she told him which way to turn, and they made it to the Dairy Queen in thirty-eight minutes. She'd kept count of the words he'd said during that time and it was far less than a word a minute. This fake shit wasn't worth a damn when it came right down to it.

He parked at the edge of the parking lot and when he opened the door for her, she caught a whiff of something floral.

"Honeysuckle." He sniffed the air.

"I'm going to plant it when I get my own place. I love that smell and the vines are pretty three seasons out of the year," she said, and smiled.

Well, hell's bells on a snake oil wagon! If he'd known honeysuckle could turn her pretty lips into a smile, he would have found a whole fistful and brought them to her. "Oh, yeah, and what else are you going to do to your own place? I figured you'd be content to live at Audrey's Place forever."

She shook her head. "That's home and I will most likely end up living there because of default. Fiona is married and living in Houston. She has no desire to ever come home. Allie is settling in real well over on y'all's ranch, and she won't come back to Audrey's now that she's got a home with Blake."

The scent of burgers, fries, and taco seasonings met them when they were inside the place. "But it's not what you wanted, is it?"

"No, looks like they've got a special on tacos. Now I don't know what I want. I've been craving a big juicy bacon cheeseburger, but those tacos sure smell good," she said.

They lined up behind an elderly couple who couldn't make up their minds between chicken sandwiches or shrimp baskets. Toby used the time to ask her again what she'd have if she could build anything.

"I always thought I'd start with a trailer house. When I was a kid I went over onto the Lucky Penny property to the east of us and discovered this really old water well. I used to dream that someday I would own that little bit of acreage and would put a trailer on it that was all mine and use that well for the water. Then when I got it paid for I would build a house and sell the trailer to Fiona," she said. "But that was a ten-year-old little girl's dream as she laid on her back and looked up past the mesquite and cow tongue cactus at the clouds in the sky."

"Why wouldn't you sell it to Allie?" he asked.

"When I was ten, I did not like my older sister. She was bossy."

Toby laughed so loud that the elderly couple turned around.

"I'm sorry," he said.

"Never apologize for humor," the lady said. "It's what makes life worth living."

"What is so funny?" Lizzy whispered.

"I hated my older brothers and even my cousin Jud when I was ten years old, too. They were full of themselves and bossy as hell," he said.

"So we were in the same boat. You had a bossy cousin and brothers. I had sisters," she said. "Any chance you want to sell five acres of your ranch to me? The five over beside that old water well?"

"Hell, no! We're going to need that well water for our cattle tanks. In a few weeks we'll be beggin' for rain to irrigate the fields."

"What can I get you?" the teenager behind the counter asked when the elderly couple took a table number and moved on. "Tonight's special is tacos or taco salad."

They ordered and the lady set the disposable cups on the counter. Lizzy handed one to Toby and headed straight back to the fountain machine to fill hers with Diet Coke. He followed her and stuck his under the ice dispenser and then the spigot on the big metal sweet tea container.

"We could have gone somewhere else, but I thought you liked tacos," he said.

"I'm in a pissy mood, Toby. When I get like this I eat too much and then feel guilty and it puts me in a worse mood. We could take our food to go and drive back home. Granny called this my Jesus mood and you shouldn't have to put up with it," she said honestly.

"Jesus mood?" One eyebrow shot up.

She slid into the nearest booth. "Even Jesus couldn't live with me when I get like this."

He sat across from her instead of beside her. "We might as well eat here because I'm in the same mood. Just never heard it called that before." He removed his cowboy hat, laid it to the side, and combed his dark hair back with his fingertips.

"What's your problem?" she asked.

"If I knew that, I could talk myself out of whatever it is." He knew exactly what his problem was, and it was sitting across the table from him. "And yours?"

Lizzy shrugged. "Tornadoes, insurance adjustors, a sister who scares the hell out of me when she talks about roofing my whole shop, a mother who's making friends and leaving me alone, and a granny who doesn't know me most of the time. Take your choice."

She was lying but she wasn't going to admit that her problem was Toby Dawson and that when his knee touched hers every so often, it reminded her too damn clearly of how much she'd enjoyed those sizzling nights she'd spent with him.

The waitress brought their food on a tray. Lizzy removed the paper from a taco and added a healthy dose of Louisiana hot sauce from the bottle on the table.

Toby peeled the paper back from his burger and bit into it. "Like your tacos with a little fire, do you?"

Tacos weren't the only thing Lizzy liked served hot. She hadn't known it until she met Toby, and going back to anything less would be dull as...well, as dull as Mitch. There she'd said it, or rather thought it. Mitch was dull, both in the bedroom and outside of it. Naturally, he'd come out on the short end of the stick when compared to someone like Toby, so she wasn't being fair. But then Mitch hadn't been fair, either, when he broke up with her on the phone on the day of her sister's wedding.

"So hot you can't speak?" Toby asked.

"Not nearly that hot," she answered.

The only thing that hot had been sex with Toby, and anything with that much heat couldn't last longer than a few weeks. Like a flash in a pan it would burn itself out, and all that would remain would be two people that were totally unsuited to each other.

"Thoughts?" he asked.

"I'm glad Wanda isn't here. This taco has flat out put me in a good mood and I'd hate to lose it because of her." Maybe it wasn't what she'd been thinking about but it was the truth. "And I think my eyes were bigger than my stomach, so I'll be taking my burger home for a midnight snack."

"I'd forgotten how big one of these things are, too. My tacos will go out of here in a take-out sack rather than my stomach." He grinned. "I'll have them for breakfast. And, Lizzy, don't let that woman or all the gossip get under your skin. Be yourself and tell anyone who doesn't like it to go to hell."

"Practice what you preach," she shot back at him.

"What is that supposed to mean?"

"Exactly what it says. You've had this reputation that you work hard to live up to, but down deep in your heart, you're not happy with it. How old are you?" Lizzy asked.

"Twenty-seven," he answered gruffly.

"Each year you'll get older and the bar bunnies will get younger. Think about that. The ones you'll be chasing when you are forty are playing with Barbie dolls today," she said.

He took a long drink of his sweet tea. "That was mean."

"That, darlin', was the truth. You don't fit into that mold any more than I fit into one with preacher's wife engraved on the outside."

He laid the burger down and his blue eyes locked with her brown ones, searching her soul. "Go on," he whispered.

"Nothing to go on about. I would have been miserable."

"And you think I'm not happy with my lifestyle? That I'm miserable?" he asked.

"Fake girlfriend's opinions don't amount to a damn."

"Lizzy, you are my friend. So tell me why you think I'm miserable," he pressed.

She carefully undid her second taco and was a lot less generous with the hot sauce that time. "First, you tell me why you think I don't fit in the mold Mitch tried to put me in."

"I know you, Lizzy. I know you like burgers and tacos and that you are a no-fuss type of woman. That's why I brought you here instead of some fancy restaurant where we'd have a five-course meal and it would take three hours to get through it. I know you like your work and that you love Dry Creek and you'd be miserable outside of it. Mitch was trying to change you into a different Lizzy Logan, one that he wanted. Now you tell me why I don't like my fancy-free lifestyle. You didn't stay in your mold long enough to get it warm. I've been in mine more than a decade." He picked up her cup and carried them to the fountain machine for a refill. "It was Diet Coke, right?"

She nodded. "Yes, but this time I want sweet tea, please."

He set both cups of tea on the table and slid back into the booth. "I've been in my mold so long that I'm real warm and comfortable in it. No matter what people think or say, I'm not sure I want to move over to something else. It would be like changing beds. The old one has lumps and dips and maybe the springs even poke me once in a while. But a new one would take weeks, maybe years, to get used to."

"That's your decision. I like my new bed, and the more time goes by the better I like it. But remember that you can stop this anytime you want and crawl right back into your comfortable rut that is so warm and cozy. We don't have to keep up this charade a day longer than you want to," Lizzy said.

She'd never seen a man chew as slowly as Toby did on that last bite of burger. Evidently he needed a long time to think about her suggestion. It would free him to chase his bar bimbos on the weekends instead of eating burgers and tacos with her, a plain old Dairy Queen.

His phone buzzed and he pulled it out of his pocket, checked the message, and put it back.

"Another woman trying to chase down a morning-after breakfast?" she asked.

He nodded and picked up his tea. It buzzed again before he could even take a drink. Pulling it out again, he rolled his sexy blue eyes toward the ceiling and sighed. "Sharlene, this time! I thought she'd quit when she found out that we are seeing each other. If you're game we might need to stretch this out past July Fourth. That woman is relentless. And she's supposed to be your friend?"

"She usually gets what she wants." Lizzy smiled for the first time.

"Then we are still a couple. Church tomorrow morning on the Logan pew?"

"You got it!" Lizzy nodded.

CHAPTER ELEVEN

Could we turn off the air conditioner and roll down the windows?" Lizzy asked when they'd left town and were on their way home.

"Are you cold?" Toby asked.

"No, I just love the smell of the night air after a rain."

He flipped a switch on the dashboard and hit the buttons to roll down both their windows. "There's something about the scent of damp earth that words can't describe," he said.

"I've always loved it." Lizzy put a hand out the window as if she was trying to catch the aroma to take home with her.

"If a tornado would be a little more selective and take out only cactus and mesquite, folks might start petitioning God to send a tornado more often," he said.

Lizzy pointed to a twisted piece of metal bent around like a big oversized pretzel. "That is a cell tower. I wonder..." She fished around in her purse until she found her phone. "Nope, no service. I bet we don't have any from here to home."

Toby was looking right at the moon when he heard what sounded like the crack of a shotgun nearby. Then the steering wheel took on a mind of its own and no matter which way he turned it, nothing happened. Lizzy squealed when the truck veered off the road and started a vertical decline right down into a ditch, coming to a stop only when it hit a good sturdy fence post. Two airbags filled the cab of the truck, and the hiss of the radiator blowing steam, plus an angry old Angus bull's bawling, drowned out the crickets and tree frogs.

Lizzy pushed at the airbag and unfastened her seat belt. "Are you alive?" she asked.

"Yes," he said hoarsely. "Don't put your feet on the ground. Unless I was seeing things, we're sitting in about a foot of water, nose down into a creek with a high muddy bank on both sides of us."

He fought with the bag, opened his door, and stepped out onto the running board, which was a mere two inches above the stagnant water. "We aren't getting out of here until someone comes along and sees us, Lizzy. We've gone through a guardrail and it's at least fifteen or twenty feet up to the road, and the rain has turned it into nothing but a slippery mess of red clay. I don't think we can get out without a rope or someone's help."

She crawled over the front seat into the back, away from the air bag.

He followed her example. "Are you sure you aren't hurt? You didn't hit your head or get whiplash?"

"I'm fine, Toby, but who shot at us?" she asked.

"It was a blowout. If we hadn't slowed down to look at that twisted cell phone tower, we would have rolled and probably been upside down with water up to our noses or higher."

"So there is a silver lining in this dark cloud? Looks like we slid right into Miller's Creek."

"Much traffic going through here at this time of night?" he asked.

"We can only hope," she said.

His long legs were not made for a cramped backseat and he couldn't get comfortable. He groaned and flattened out a palm over his chest. Lizzy moved from the corner where she'd hugged up to the door to give him more room.

"Please tell me you aren't having a heart attack."

"I'm not having a heart attack," he answered with a chuckle. "You okay?"

"It scared me, but it was like slow motion and I knew we weren't going to roll when we started to slide. Ouch!" she exclaimed as her knee bumped her chest.

"Seat belt, right?" he asked.

"We'll both have a bruise, but we could have gotten bloody noses from the bags so we're lucky. This is going to make for some cramped quarters. Let's go to the bed of the truck."

"It's sitting at a pretty good angle," he said, "and we'd have to crawl over the side. Getting there wouldn't be nearly the problem as getting back if we don't like it. But I do have a blanket stashed in the toolbox back there."

"Anything is better than this," she said. "Let's give it a try. If I don't like it, I'll wade down this creek and find a way out of here."

"You're taking this well," he said.

"It's not raining. It's a fairly nice night. We've got a burger and four tacos plus tea if we're brave enough to trust our bladders. It could be a hell of a lot worse." She paused for a breath and winced at the pain in her shoulder from the seat belt. "How many women have been on that blanket in your toolbox?"

"None," he answered quickly. "Not a single one because it's a brand-new one, but we will definitely not talk about the one that it replaced. Are you ready to try this acrobatic act?"

"The front seats are full of air bags. You couldn't cuss a cat in this backseat without getting a hair in your mouth or scratched all to the devil, so it's either that or walk home with wet feet." She picked up the brown bag with their food and tried to open the door, but it was jammed. "Looks like you are going first and I'll climb out on that side."

He pushed against the door but it didn't budge. "And we will be using the windows because my door isn't opening, either. Dammit! I liked this truck."

"It might not be totaled," she said.

"It's eight years old, which means it probably is, but it's paid for and I wanted to be on my feet before I had to buy another one."

Lizzy pushed the button to roll down her window and nothing happened. "Are the keys still in the ignition?"

He bent at the waist, leaned over the seat as far as possible, and tried to start the engine. Like the windows, not a damn thing happened. The only thing left was to push the bags out of the way, go out the front doors, and crawl over into the bed of the truck.

"My side board is underwater," she said. "So I'll have to follow you out your side. Here, take the food bags and flip them over into the truck bed. We may be glad to have them if we aren't found by breakfast time." She flipped a leg over the seat and used her boot to stomp the air bag into submission.

The truck had created a dam with water rising up level with the running board and still climbing. When Toby stepped out, his foot slipped. Grabbing the top of the truck, he let out a string of swear words that made an old bull over there on the other side of the embankment throw back his head and bellow.

"Guess he's a preacher." Lizzy laughed.

"It's not funny." Toby inched his way up the slick surface until he could ease a leg over into the bed of the truck. But the whole vehicle was nose down on a fairly steep incline so he didn't have anything steady to step into. Finally, with a leap, he landed on his butt with a thud, his boots coming to rest only a few inches from the bag with the food in it. God help him if he smashed her burger. She'd been a good sport, but after a night in the sloped back of a truck and no breakfast, she would have every right to turn into a shrew.

Lizzy had never been graceful. Fiona could scramble up a tree like a monkey and Allie could maneuver around on an uneven rooftop as if she was walking on flat ground. But not Lizzy. She tripped over air and she could never get a toehold on even the rough bark of a small mesquite tree.

She slung a foot out and hugged the top of the truck like it was a long-lost cousin. One step at a time, she made her way to the back where Toby held a hand out to her. She reached for it, and the slick soles of her boots gave way on the wet metal. She felt herself falling sideways and then boom; she was over the side of the truck and lying flat on top of Toby, her lungs deflated and gasping for air.

"Welcome to my club house," Toby gasped.

She rolled to the side, her head a good foot higher than her boots that were braced against the toolbox down by the truck's cab. "I wonder," she inhaled deeply, "how that window got," another quick intake of breath, "cracked." She pointed to the spiderweb that started in the middle of the window and inched its way out to every corner.

"Looks like a rock flew up when the tire blew out," he said.

"Or a twenty-two bullet?"

"Lizzy, don't see ghosts or villains where they don't exist. Truman is the only person I know of that would try to run us off by shooting at our tires, and he's so old he probably goes to sleep with the chickens." Toby was still flat on his back, staring at the sky.

"I hope you are right because if he did do this I'm going to pray that God kills all of his goats," Lizzy said. "Where is that blanket? We can use it for a pillow."

The toolbox popped right open and he brought out a zippered bag with a thick red blanket in it. In a few minutes they were side-by-side, bodies touching and sharing a rolled-up blanket for a pillow.

"Why did you have this tucked away in a toolbox?" she asked.

"My mama gave it to me for Christmas and I forgot to put it in the trailer when I moved up here. She found it just as I was about to leave, and I put it in the toolbox because there wasn't any room in the truck. Fate blessed us, I guess." He slipped an arm under her and pulled her closely to his side. "If we don't huddle up, the pillow will be too small for us both to use."

Lizzy had a choice. Either be able to sleep but wake up with a sore neck, or lay awake wanting what she knew she couldn't have but at least be semi-comfortable. She chose to stay cuddled up next to him. His big strong body made her forget all about the fact that they were trapped in a deep ravine with milk chocolate–colored water flowing all around them. Strong arms held her close and his chest made a wonderful pillow. She wiggled in a little closer into his warmth, feeling safe and happy as she drifted off to sleep.

The sun was peeking over the eastern horizon when she awoke the next morning, surprised that she'd slept with no hint of dreams. "Hey, anybody in there?" A deep voice yelled at the same time a rock hit the side of the truck. "If y'all is alive, raise up and answer me."

Lizzy braced herself, peeked over the truck bed at an elderly man squatting on the other side of a barbed wire fence at the other edge of the gully. "We're fine. Do you have a phone?"

"Back at the house. This gall-durned thing the kids bought me to carry around in my pocket ain't worth a damn since the tornado swept through here. Want me to call someone for you?" The man was a short little fellow with a crop of curly gray hair and deep wrinkles. "Good thing y'all didn't try to wade that water to find help. I ain't never seen Miller Creek rushin' like that. You would have drowned for sure if you'd tried to follow the creek, and there ain't no way you could have scaled them banks, muddy as they are."

Lizzy nodded. "I figured that much. We sure would appreciate it if you'd make a call for us."

Toby sat up and waved at the guy. "Please get in touch with Blake Dawson at the Lucky Penny Ranch. Got something to write with?"

"Sure I do. Never leave the house without a pencil and some paper these days or I forget what it is I'm supposed to do. Wife says the whiskey has eat my brain up. Don't know if she is right, but it was good whiskey so I ain't complainin'." He took a stubby pencil and a small notepad from the bibbed pocket of his overalls.

Toby gave him the number. "Thank you so much. We really appreciate your help. I don't think we can get out of here on our own."

"You're right welcome, young man, and you're right. You got to have some help. My tractor is down or I'd drive it around and see if I could pull you up." He wrote down the number and shoved the notepad back into his pocket. "I heard tell that half a dozen septic tanks up the road is overflowed with all the rain we got and that's what you are sittin' in. So y'all just sit real tight and I'll call this here number for you." He slapped the bull on the butt, got on a four–wheeler, and disappeared down a path.

"Good mornin'," Toby said. "Ready for my morning-after breakfast?"

"Allie told me about that little send-off that you do for the women you pick up. Is that to appease your conscience? Give them something since they gave you something?" she asked.

"Share something with them because we shared something is the way I like to think of it." He raked his fingers through his hair but it didn't downplay his sexiness; if anything the dark stubble on his face, the sleep still in his eyes, and the wrinkled clothes made him even hotter.

"Changing subject here," she said. "How long do you think it will be before Blake gets here?"

"Depends on whether our new forgetful friend remembers that he has a phone number or if his wife finds it when she empties his pockets to wash those overalls next week," Toby answered. "I'll share my tacos for breakfast since I can't make biscuits and sausage gravy for you."

"They've been sitting out all night. They're probably soggy and we'll get sick if we eat them anyway. I'll wait until we get home to eat. Besides now that the rancher told us where part of that water is coming from, it smells bad."

She changed her mind when he removed the paper wrapper from the taco and the morning breeze wafted the taco aroma straight to her nose. "Give me one of those things. I'd rather spend a day in the bathroom with food poisoning as starve to death. At least it will give me strength to walk home this morning."

"The aroma of what we're surrounded by…" he started.

She put a finger over his lips. "I'm pretending it's the bull over there in the pasture that I smell."

He grinned. "Two for you and two for me and then we can share your burger, right?"

"Just give me my tacos and you can have the burger if you like soggy lettuce and buns." She reached out her hand and he put two tacos in it.

The shell was soft and the filling wasn't the best, but the only thing that would taste better was a cup of hot black coffee. Thinking about liquid of any kind made her bladder feel like an overripe watermelon about to explode, so she pushed that idea to the back of her mind.

Toby polished off his second taco and reached for the hamburger. "Now that it's daylight and we can see better, we might try to scale the muddy embankment. We'll get muddy and if we lose our foothold, we'll wind up in that filthy water. If someone isn't here in an hour, I'll take the rope that's in the toolbox and give it my best shot."

"Rope?" she asked.

"If I can make it to the top, then I'll throw the rope down and you can use it to climb up."

He started to tear the sandwich in half but she shook her head. "You can have it all. It won't be long until I won't need a rope; I'll scramble up over that wet mud like a mountain goat."

He chuckled. "I'm going to sit right here and watch your cute little butt wiggle its way up that muddy mess."

They could hear a vehicle approaching for several seconds before it was right overhead and then the squeal of brakes. "Hey, y'all all right down there? Need some help?" a woman's voice yelled down.

"We're fine but we don't have phone service. Would you make a call for us?" Toby cupped his hands over his mouth and hollered.

"Sure I will. Soon as I get to the church over in Dry Creek. They've got a phone there. What number do I call?"

"Henrietta, is that you?" Lizzy shouted.

"Yes, it is. Oh, my goodness! Lizzy Logan?" The truck door slammed and Henrietta peered down over the edge. "Is that Toby Dawson with you? How long have you been down there?"

"Yes, it is and we had a blowout last night. We had to spend the night here because we can't climb up and the ditch is full of nasty water. Please call my sister at the Lucky Penny," Lizzy said.

"Sorry, darlin'. I cannot call her, or your mama, or Dora June will get really mad at me." She eyed the red blanket and narrowed her eyes at Lizzy. "Too bad you were keepin' company with that man or I might have helped you. Don't suppose you are goin' to make it to church, are you?"

"Not unless you make a phone call," Lizzy said.

"Come on, Miz Henrietta. Think of the Good Samaritan in the Bible. Are you going to pass on the other side and leave us down here to die or are you going to have the right spirit about this?" Toby asked.

"You can't sweet-talk me, Mr. Dawson. Let this be a lesson to you, Lizzy." Henrietta disappeared. The truck engine started back up and the rattle of tires on a country road faded until nothing but the sounds of a spring morning were heard in the bed of the wrecked truck.

"She won't help us, but I bet she tells everyone she meets about this," Lizzy fumed.

"You can bank on that. Reckon your mama is going to bring a shotgun and make me marry you since we've slept together now?" he asked.

"I can't imagine you married to anyone, with or without a shotgun to convince you." She was amazed at the sad look that flitted across his face before he looked away.

"Your reputation says that you've served up lots of morning-after breakfasts. What would you do if someone came up pregnant with your child?"

Toby hesitated a moment. "I don't know. Are you telling me something or is this hypothetical?"

She put up a hand. "Purely hypothetical. I'm not pregnant and if I was, I wouldn't marry you."

"Why?" He looked as if someone had hit him in the head with a hammer.

"Because you would only be marrying me because of the pregnancy. You've already stated that you don't want that lifestyle, so we'd both be miserable. I want a husband who can't wait to get home to me in the evenings, not one who can't wait to get away from me. A baby wouldn't change what you or I either one want."

"Pretty blunt aren't you?"

"I tried that submissive crap. It didn't work for me," she said.

Another vehicle passed but it didn't slow down.

"Third time is the charm," Toby said. "Want to make a bet about how long it takes that third one to get here?"

"Sure. Ten bucks says that Farmer Forgetful remembers to tell his wife about those stupid kids sitting in shit creek, and Blake and Allie are here within thirty minutes," she said.

"I bet Henrietta gets a dose of guilty conscience and calls them from the church. If you win, we'll try this date again only at a nicer restaurant and somewhere that does not have a gully like this on the road going there. If you win." He tapped his chin and grinned.

"I will not go to bed with you if I win," she said.

"I wasn't going to suggest that. You have to cook supper for me at Audrey's Place."

She stuck out her hand and they shook on it.

Ten minutes later they heard a vehicle on the road. Lizzy held her breath until it stopped and then a voice squealed. She looked up and saw Allie peering down over the edge of the road into the ditch.

"Man, are we glad to see you," Lizzy said.

Blake's face appeared next to Allie's. "Are either of you hurt?"

"We've got a couple of seat belt bruises that will be tender for a few days, but no broken bones or blood," Toby answered.

"That's good. Allie was about to have a heart attack the whole way here," Blake said. "I brought chains but there ain't no way we're going to get that up out of there without a winch and a tractor. We'll get y'all out and then we'll bring back what we need to get the truck home," Blake said. "Reckon the best way to do this is to throw a chain down and then haul you up with the truck."

"Whatever you think," Lizzy said.

"Okay then. I'll hook things up and Allie can ease the truck down the road while I help get y'all up over this mess. If you'd been a mile or two down the road, you would have been on flat land."

In a few minutes the chain dropped smack into the bed of the truck and Lizzy got a hold with both hands. He motioned with his arm and she started up, digging her toes into the bank for traction and praying that she didn't wet her pants.

Blake held up a fist toward his truck moving very slowly down the road and extended her his other hand as soon as she cleared the top. "I got you. Go on and get in the truck with Allie and I'll get my brother up out of there. What happened anyway?"

"Blowout is what Toby thinks."

As luck would have it the other side of the road was as flat as a pancake with lots of bushes and mesquite trees. If a different tire had blown, they would have plowed down a few trees and cactus but would have probably been able to back the truck out, put on a spare, and limp home.

"You okay?" Allie yelled as she backed the truck up.

"I'm fine but..." Lizzy headed for the nearest place to hide behind a big clump of green broom weed and jerked her jeans down. She was almighty glad for the Dairy Queen napkin from her shirt pocket that she'd squirreled away when she finished her tacos. When she stood and zipped her jeans she took a step backward into a fresh pile of coyote crap. She groaned and trotted through the weeds, past a big cactus and to the truck.

"Feel better?" Allie grinned from the driver's window.

Lizzy looked down at her stinky boot. "Much better but this is not my lucky day."

"Move it out," Blake yelled.

Allie eased the truck down the road at a snail's pace.

Lizzy waited until the vehicle came to a stop and then carefully pulled off her boots. She tossed them into the bed before she got into the backseat and then she remembered her purse was in Toby's wrecked truck.

"My purse!" she moaned.

"Will be fine until we can get back. It's got a moat around it on three sides and a mountain on the other. I don't think anyone is brave enough to go searching through things. Are you sure you are okay? I see a bruise on your forehead," Allie said. "How long were you down there? The old guy who called said he had no idea if you'd been there an hour or two days."

"From about nine last night until right now."

Allie looked in the rearview mirror. "Without a bathroom?"

Lizzy caught her eye and nodded. "And it was not pleasant. Henrietta came by and wouldn't even take the number to call you."

"That's what happens when you don't abide by the church ladies' rules." Allie started forward a few feet at a time until she could see Toby standing on the road. "Looks like y'all took out a section of guardrail. The guys can call the county yard tomorrow and report the damage. But we might want to send some red bandannas to mark the place so folks will know it's a dangerous area."

Lizzy laid her head back on the seat. "It's going to be a mess."

"Gossip or fixing Toby's truck?"

"Both. The radiator most likely is blown. A rock hit the back window and it's cracked all to hell, and neither of the back doors will open. The front is filled with air bags and no telling what all that water has done to the undercarriage. As old as the truck is I imagine that it is totaled. And the gossip? It'll be a nightmare." Lizzy groaned.

"Look on the bright side. Everyone will know that you aren't wallowing in misery after the Mitch ordeal, and what a story to tell your kids someday," Allie said. "So now that you've slept with Toby, what's your opinion of him?"

"I didn't sleep with him," Lizzy protested.

"Oh, really?" Allie turned around in the seat. "Did you stay awake all night?"

"I mean I didn't have sex with him." It wasn't a lie. She had not had sex with him last night, and they weren't talking about the previous times.

"Does he snore? Does he wake up in a good mood or all grouchy? Was he nice to you and let you have your share of that red blanket? And where did it come from anyway?" Allie bombarded her with questions.

"No, he does not snore. He woke up in a good mood. The blanket was a gift from his mama that he shoved into the toolbox because his backseat was full," Lizzy answered.

Allie's phone flew over the seat and landed in

Lizzy's lap. "Text Mama right now. She needs to know what's going on before Henrietta and Dora June start spreading the news soon as the benediction is over."

"Did you see that tower? We don't have service here," Lizzy said. "If we'd had any at all, I would have called or texted you last night."

"Well, keep the phone and as soon as that no service thing shuts off, you get in touch with Mama," Allie said.

The door opened and Toby settled into the seat beside her and fastened his seat belt.

"Don't reckon there is a place to buy a cup of coffee between here and home is there?" he asked.

"No, but the pot is full and we'll be home in fifteen minutes," Blake answered.

"You can drop me off first, right?" Lizzy asked.

"No, you can go home with me," Allie answered. "I'm making Sunday dinner and Mama will be there soon as church is over."

"I need a shower."

"Take one at our place and borrow some of my clothes."

Toby's hand covered hers. Words were not needed. He was as relieved as she was to get out of that damn ravine. She looped her little finger over his and squeezed. He smiled but didn't open his eyes.

Elizabeth Jane Logan had been baptized when she was ten years old. The preacher said that when her head went under the water and he said the words that she would come up a new creature without sin and with a holy spirit. At that age, she expected to rise up with at least a slightly visible halo or maybe the sprouting of some wings, but the only thing different was that her hair was wet. That and the fact that she hadn't taken time to dry off completely with that hand-size towel they'd given her and her underpants stuck to her butt all during church services that Sunday evening.

She thought of that day as she slid down the back of the claw-foot tub in Allie's bathroom, getting her hair wet and holding her breath. If she stayed under long enough, would a new improved Lizzy arise when she surfaced?

Pushing against the tub with her feet and pulling on the sides, she brought herself up out of the water and waited. She didn't expect a halo but it would be nice to have something after that night down there in a ditch. She brushed the water from her eyes and opened them. Peace settled over like she hadn't known in months.

Lizzy might not have a halo but the very last smidgen of Mitch's betrayal was gone. In that moment, it wasn't words but honesty when she said she was finished with that man and the past. The smile that covered her face and the pure joy of no baggage hanging on her heart; well, it damn near made her gravitate to the ceiling. She wanted to hug herself and hang on to the feeling inside as long as possible.

"Hot damn!" she muttered. "I can cuss and I can have a beer and I can do whatever I want. And if I want to have sex I can do that, too. I'm going to love this new Lizzy. If the rest of the world doesn't, then bring out the fish heads."

It was one of her granny's sayings when someone was being a complete jerk. "Screw 'em and feed 'em fish heads," she'd say. Then after a while she would remark, "Way these fools are acting, I feel a night for boiled fish heads is comin' on."

"But not today. Today is not a day for fish heads. It's a day to rejoice and be glad." She stood up and shook out two towels. One went around her head, turban-style; the other made a wrap for her body. When she was completely dry, she zipped the worn chenille robe up from the bottom. Her underwear and bra should be in the dryer by now and she could fit into a pair of Allie's yoga pants and a T-shirt even though she was a couple of inches taller than her sister and a few pounds heavier.

She met Allie coming up the hall with a pair of socks, clean bra, and panties folded on top of an outfit.

"These should make you feel like a brand-new woman," Allie said. "You already smell better. You can borrow a pair of my rubber boots to wear home. I'm not cleaning the crap off yours for you, not unless you want to clean up the floor or porch when I upchuck. I didn't have morning sickness that first trimester, but just yesterday scents have started to make my stomach do flips."

Lizzy took the clothing from her sister. "Please don't tell me you can't stand to smell food."

"Mostly anything spicy like chili and it's always been my favorite." Allie sighed.

"Oh, no!" Lizzy hugged her. "Remember when Lucy's daughter-in-law was pregnant and she couldn't stand to even smell fish cooking? Granny told her it was because her baby hated fish and sure enough that kid has never liked any kind, not even deep-fried catfish."

"I don't care if the baby doesn't like chili when it gets here, just so long as it doesn't ruin my love for it. No beer. No chili. This little girl may be an only child." Allie smiled.

Lizzy gave Allie a quick hug and went back into the bathroom. "I'm going to get dressed and then I'll help you with dinner. What are we having?"

"Fried chicken, Blake's favorite," Allie answered. "Sweet tea is made and coffeepot is full when you get dressed."

Lizzy left the robe on the hook where she'd found it and smiled when she pulled on her hip-hugging panties because her fanny was fully dry. No sticking to the kitchen chair while she was enjoying her sister's scrumptious fried chicken.

She had finished brushing her hair when someone knocked on the bathroom door. She slung it open to find Toby standing there, mud covering him from the hips down and splattered all over his shirt. He must've taken his boots off at the door because the only clean thing on him was a pair of snow-white socks that looked as out of place as a string of pearls around a sow's neck.

"I believe I'm next in line," he said.

"You look like you ought to be," she agreed.

"Blake's gone out to the trailer to get me some clean clothes. Don't suppose you'd want to stay long enough to scrub my back for me, would you?"

Lizzy might have had a wonderful experience when she rose up from the bathwater, but it damn sure hadn't set her free enough to do what Toby asked. She shook her head and smiled. "This is not a real relationship, darlin'."

"I'd be willin' to turn it into a real one for a good woman to give me a bath." His eyes glittered.

She reached up and traced the scar on his cheek and then patted him on the chest. "I'd be willin' to change it from fake to real for a few more nights in the back room at Mama's store, but we agreed not to do that anymore, didn't we?" She stepped around him, careful not to get too close to all that mud.

"We might change our minds."

She looked back over her shoulder. "Not today."

The wonderful smell of hot rolls baking in the oven filled the kitchen. And the sizzle of chicken frying in a big cast-iron skillet made Lizzy's stomach start to grumble. The tacos she'd had that morning had long since been digested and there was no way a day-old greasy taco could measure up to Allie's chicken even on a good day.

Lizzy leaned against the doorjamb and smiled. With one hand, Blake was stirring the green beans and the other was massaging Allie's back. She'd seen him do those little endearing things for her for months now, but Lizzy never got tired of watching them together. It was those things that made a lasting marriage, not a few hot nights of sex, and she yearned for that kind of real, honest to god, relationship in her own life.

Blake laid the spoon to one side and moved over a step so that he was right behind Allie. He slipped his arms around her midsection and splayed his hands out over her rounded belly. When the baby kicked him, they both laughed.

"What can I do to help?" Lizzy asked.

Blake looked back over his shoulder. "I was about to set the table so you can come over here and help Allie. The potatoes are about done so they'll need to be mashed. And the green beans need about five more minutes."

It didn't take Lizzy long to pad across the floor in her bare feet and pick up the wooden spoon. "Lord, that chicken smells good. I can use the same batter mix that you do and mine never comes out as good."

"It's all about the temperature of the grease. Too hot cooks the outside and leaves the inside either raw or tough. Not hot enough gives you a soggy crust instead of a crispy one. I talked to Fiona last night, and she said she'd walk up here barefoot and naked for a fried chicken dinner. I promised her one if she'd come home for the reunion thing on the Fourth," Allie said.

"And is she bringing Paul? I can't see that preppy guy walking from the bedroom to the bathroom in his bare feet," Lizzy said.

"No, she said she'd come by herself if she can wrangle the time away at all," Allie answered, and lowered her voice. "I'm kind of glad. We haven't been around her husband very often but he makes me nervous."

"Really? Why?"

"He's got shifty eyes."

Allie nodded. "I kinda got those vibes, too. I wonder if he's faithful?"

"I hope so. Fiona might not live here but she's got a temper. She'd kill him and the woman without batting an eye."

"Goes with her red hair," Lizzy said. "Potatoes are done."

"Mixer is under the bar. Put a whole stick of real butter in them and use canned milk," Allie said. "Another reason I want Fiona to come home is that this thing with the church has made Mama sad. I think all her girls together will help."

"Fiona?" Toby said as he crossed the floor and poured himself a cup of coffee. "Is she definitely coming for the July Fourth homecoming?"

"Don't know," Lizzy said. "But we're hoping so."

"Hoping what?" Katy came through the kitchen door.

"That Fiona comes home for the hoop-la," Allie said.

"I'm going to send her a plane ticket that is nonrefundable or changeable," Katy said. "It's guilting her, but I really don't care. I want to see her."

With all three women working together and Blake

setting the table, it wasn't but a few minutes until they had sat down to eat. Lizzy noticed that Blake reached under the table and held Allie's hand while he said grace and then leaned over and kissed her on the cheek when he finished. The ache in Lizzy's soul deepened—surely there was a man somewhere out there that would love her like that, and after the festival she intended to start looking.

"So what's the news on the war front about your daughter getting stuck in a gully with one of these Dawson cowboys?" Allie asked as she passed the platter of chicken to her mother.

"It's not good." Katy smiled. "Truman thinks I should shoot both Blake and Toby. Dora June is convinced that she's made the right decision about the ladies' club. But I don't give a damn what any of them think. It's not a bit of their business."

"Hear! Hear!" Toby raised his tea glass.

"And how did your evening go, Mama?" Lizzy asked.

"Absolutely wonderful. We ate at this amazing little Italian place, went back to Trudy's for coffee, and wound up talking until after midnight. The three of us have a friendship that endures time, separation, and life. We've been apart for years and years, but when we are together, it's like we just saw each other yesterday. And to make the whole evening even better, I went by and saw Mama, and she was lucid," Katy said. "Pass me those green beans. I sent them on without putting any on my plate."

Lizzy picked up a chicken leg and bit into it. It was every bit as good as always, but as wonderful as it tasted, it didn't compare to the fullness in her heart right then with her family around her. This was what she wanted and she was not settling for anything less.

CHAPTER TWELVE

On Monday morning, Toby restacked the feed sacks that had been shoved to the side so the last customer could get at the chicken scratch while he waited on the barbed wire and fence post deliveryman to arrive. It wouldn't be long until all of these supplies would be moved back to the feed store, but for now, Toby was determined to keep things neat and in order. Blue chased a squirrel out the back door and trotted back with a smile on his face. Shooter glanced over at him as if telling him not to waste his energy on squirrels on a hot day like this.

"Good boy." Toby patted his head. "I know you and Shooter will take good care of this barn and keep those pesky squirrels away from the feed sacks. I'm glad y'all are good friends. Dogs and cowboys, they need friends in this world."

His phone buzzed and he fished it out of his shirt pocket. The text, from Lizzy, said that two different customers were on the way to pick up merchandise. The first one had paid for three rolls of barbed wire and twenty fence posts. The second one would be picking up chicken feed. She sent over copies of the sales so he would know exactly how much and what to let them have.

Three trucks rolled up at the same time and Blue scrambled to his feet to go welcome them. Something about the way he ambled outside, eager to make new friends, gave Toby an idea. Later, he would wonder what circular path had taken him from the dog going out to meet the visitors to the end of the road that put the smile on his face.

"There is more than one way to diffuse a bomb," Toby said.

"Hey, Toby," Wallace Jones said, waving. "I'm here for three bags of chicken scratch. Lizzy said she'd send you a message. I heard y'all got stuck in a ditch and had to spend the night out there."

"It's all the women in Dry Creek have talked about," Lester Wilson said. "I swear they've talked it damn near to death. I heard that you had a devil of a time haulin' your truck up out of the ditch. Is it going to be fixable?"

"It's totaled for sure. The insurance company will come out and make the final decision but I'm not holding out a bit of hope," Toby said. "I'll help you load up the bags, Wallace, and then we'll get to the barbed wire and posts, Lester. Looks like you're going to have to wait until the delivery guy unloads to get your full order. Lots of folks puttin' in new fence this time of year and stock got down low this week, but give this feller a few minutes and we'll get you fixed right up."

"No problem." Lester sat down in a rusty old metal chair. "I heard that Henrietta wouldn't help y'all because the way the church women has set their heels against Allie and Lizzy Logan bein' in their club thing. Crazy old farts. Ain't a one of them wearin' halos."

"Well"—Toby winked at Lester—"Henrietta said she wouldn't make a phone call for us, but Blake and Allie showed up pretty quick after she left. Don't go spreadin' that around, because I wouldn't want to get her in trouble with the ladies' group. We were so happy that someone called Blake that we sure wouldn't want to stir anything up. I hear that she and Irene Miller, Lizzy's grandma, were real good friends back before Granny got dementia. Maybe she felt beholden to Lizzy because of that."

Constant scraping noise combined with the loud music playing on the roof of the store made Lizzy nervous as a hooker in a church revival. Stormy curled around her four kittens in her new laundry basket bed behind the checkout counter as if she had no fears at all. Nothing bothered the cat, but then she'd carried her babies to safety in the midst of a hell of a storm. Shingles coming down off the roof and Conway Twitty singing so loud that the folks down at Nadine's could hear it wouldn't faze Stormy.

Lizzy was busy moving all the sales merchandise onto a smaller rack and marking them down to eighty percent off, when Dora June and Ruby pushed their way into the store. Up on the roof Conway was belting out "Goodbye Time." Lizzy wished that she could wave at the two old gals and tell them good-bye without having to talk to them.

Rumors had covered the town worse than all that paper stuck to the trees, but Lizzy pasted on her best smile and pointed at the rack of sweatshirts, western shirts, and hoodies. "Y'all should take a look at this. It'll go fast at this price."

Ruby hitched up her jeans and sniffed the air dramatically. "We're not here to shop."

Had Stormy passed gas again? It sure looked like Ruby had smelled something horrible. Maybe the cat food caused flatulence. She made a mental note to check the effects of the stuff. It could be that, after a diet of mice and whatever she could scrounge up in the alleys, the cat couldn't tolerate that high-dollar canned food.

"We're here for a straight answer. Did Henrietta break her vow and make a phone call for you?" Dora June glared at Lizzy.

"What makes you think that she did?"

"We heard some news to that effect," Ruby said.

"And if she did?"

Dora June crossed her arms over her chest and

glared at Lizzy. "Then we will excommunicate her from the ladies' group."

"Shit. Whatever happened to spreading Christian kindness? We were stuck down there in a ditch. She showed up and we asked for help. Why would you treat your good friend like that? Y'all have all three been friends for years and were friends with my granny before her mind got bad. I can't believe the way you are acting. Before long there won't be enough women to make up a club. Come on, lay down your heavy burden of hate and stop this shit," Lizzy said.

"Did Henrietta call Blake?" Dora June asked again, this time through clenched teeth.

"I was not in the car with Henrietta. What she did or did not do is between her and God and really not a damn bit of your business." Lizzy picked up the black kitten and held it close to her chest. It stared up at her with bright blue eyes and purred when she started to pet it.

"I hate cats," Ruby said.

"I love them," Lizzy said coldly.

"That's all you're going to tell us about Henrietta?" Dora June snapped.

"That's all I can tell you. If she was a Good Samaritan, I hope God puts an extra jewel in her crown. If she didn't call, then that's on her. If y'all want to throw her out of the ladies' group, then tell her she's welcome at Audrey's on Wednesday nights for supper. That way she won't be lonely while y'all are down at the church getting your weekly dose of self-righteousness."

Dora June shook her finger at Lizzy. "You are an abomination unto the Lord."

"Maybe so but I'll talk to him tonight about it and we'll work out my problems. I don't need your help, but I did need Henrietta's yesterday morning. And if she made a simple call, then I'll be glad to thank her." Lizzy put the kitten in the basket with the others. When she straightened up the women were on their way out the door and Blake Shelton's voice singing, "I Still Got a Finger," filtered down through the hole in the roof.

Lizzy shook her fanny to the beat of the music and held her hands above her head to keep from using her tallest finger to show Dora June and Ruby what she thought of them. After all, they had been her grandmother's friends and she should respect that part of their past. Besides, there was hope that they would see the light at the end of the tunnel before the train hit them head on.

"This music is pretty dang good," she told Stormy. "Nothing against Conway. He's a king in my books, but I do love some Blake Shelton."

When the song ended, she slipped out the back door and walked all the way to the other side of the alley so she could see what was going on up there on the roof. She was amazed at the sight. It looked like a whole crew of gangly monkeys crawling around on her roof. No wonder it was so noisy inside the store.

"What do you think?" Allie climbed down the ladder with a nail gun in her hand.

"I think you'll have it done today at that rate. Where'd those kids come from?"

"Deke rounded up a dozen of them to help take care of this job and the one I've got lined up next," Allie said.

"And that would be Herman's new hay barn, right?"

Allie put the tool away in the back of her truck and pulled out another one. "Battery needs recharging. I'll take it into the store and plug it up soon as I take this one up to Deke. And yes, it is Herman's new barn. That's all I've got on the docket right now so after that's done I'm going to start on my own house. It needs painting on the outside and some wood replaced around a few windows."

"I won't worry so much about you since you've got help. Come on in the shop. Deke can run the crew and we'll have a soda. You can play with the kittens and..." Lizzy paused.

"And what?" Allie eyed her.

"I need to talk and I'm scared."

Allie yelled up from the bottom of the ladder. "Deke, send one of the boys down to get this. I'm going into the store for a little while."

He gave her a thumbs-up sign and tapped a kid on the shoulder.

Allie looped her arm in Lizzy's and together they tiptoed around the debris and twisted metal still lying everywhere between the alley and the store. "It looks like to me, if the tornado wanted to chew all this up, it could take it to a landfill somewhere and spit it out.

Doesn't seem fair that it tears it up and leaves it layin' right here. Please tell me you haven't been talking to Mitch and y'all are getting back together."

"He's married," Lizzy said.

"No, he's not. He will be over July Fourth weekend but not yet. He and that woman aren't really married yet. Lucy told me that she won't marry him until her daddy can perform the ceremony and her mama can be at the wedding. Mitch's mama spread that rumor about him getting married so folks wouldn't think he and that woman were living together."

Lizzy went straight to her office, opened the refrigerator, and took out two cans of soda. She ran one over her forehead before she carried them to the counter where Allie sat on the floor with all four kittens in her lap.

"Are you sure?" Lizzy asked. "Which one is a rumor and which is truth?"

"I'm sure. Wanda couldn't bear the idea of them living down there together in that villa, so she and Mitch cooked up the story that they were already married. The people in that area think that they were married when they arrived." She jerked the tab off the top of the soda can and took a long drink. "But they're really planning a ceremony with only family when they fly in for that weekend. Then Sunday the church is cooking up a reception and shower. In between, they will be here in Dry Creek for our festival."

"A lie like that is starting off a ministry on a sour note if you ask me, which no one did, but Mitch isn't even a blip on my radar anymore." Lizzy touched her soda can to Allie's in a toast. "May they be happy, wealthy, and in love all their married life."

"Well, that's real generous of you considering what he put you through. So if that's not why you are scared, then what is? If it's me on the roof, I'm not even big enough to be off balance yet, Lizzy. And I'm not stopping what I do because I love my work. I'd go crazy without it."

Lizzy sat down in the floor beside the laundry basket and rubbed Stormy's fur. "I worry about you but I understand. I wouldn't know what to do with myself with this store."

Why couldn't God have shared the need to vent, to talk matter of the heart to death, to take hours to make a decision, and then change their minds with the male species? Why did he have to put the entire burden of all that upon the female gender? Add in the inability to get the words formed so they wouldn't sound so silly with the absolute need to say them, and dammit, life was not fair.

"Spit it out," Allie said.

"I really, really like Toby."

There she'd said it, but she already wished she could cram the words back into her mouth. It didn't bring a bit of relief.

"I know," Allie said softly.

"How?"

"The way your eyes yearn for him when he's anywhere around or when his name is mentioned. I did the same thing with Blake, but it's not the same for you and Toby, Lizzy."

"Why?"

Allie put the kittens back into the basket where they began to bite at anything that moved, whether it was their tails or their littermates. "I was a long time out of my relationship with Riley. Blake and I were pretty much on the same page about what we wanted in the long picture. He was wild but down deep he wanted to settle down. Toby is a player, plain and simple. It's not that he won't settle down with one woman. It's more that he can't."

"Then you are saying a pretend relationship is the best I can hope for?"

Allie nodded. "Deke will settle before Toby. Do you see that ever happening?"

Lizzy opened her mouth to disagree but snapped it shut before she blurted out the whole story about the fling they'd had and the very real flirting that had gone on in the bathroom door the day before. Allie was right and Lizzy knew she should listen to her older sister for once.

"They'll sell snow cones in hell before Deke quits his way of life. There's not a woman alive who could drag him to the altar. Not even with a loaded shotgun." Lizzy laughed and changed the subject. "The way those kids are working, the roof is going to be done by quittin' time."

Allie sipped at her soda. "And I'm willin' to sit right here and let them finish it."

"Hiring all that help sure cuts into your profit." Lizzy tossed her empty can into the trash can. It made a loud clanging noise when it hit bottom, and all four kittens buried their little faces into their mama's belly.

"Reminds me of three little girls who always hung on their mama's apron strings when they were scared." Lizzy laughed.

"Or their granny's," Allie agreed. "Maybe you've got three sisters and a brother in that basket."

"Yep, Allie, Lizzy, Fiona, and Deke. I should name them that if there's three girls and a boy. I never can tell if they are boys or girls. Check for me. You've always been good at that."

Allie picked up each kitten and flipped it over on its belly. "You've got a boy here with this yellow one and here's another boy and yep, all the yellow ones are boy kitties. Let me look at the black one."

Fiona handed over the ball of fur and Allie turned it over. "A girl. Poor little thing will have to contend with three mean old brothers. Are you naming her Fiona?"

Lizzy nodded. "She'll have to have a good strong name. I'll call her Fefe for short. Help me name the boys."

"Let's give them our favorite cowboys' names," Allie said.

"Raylan is that cocky little guy who hisses when you pick him up." Lizzy laughed.

"And this fat feller is Hoss from Bonanza," Allie said.

"Only one left? Think we ought to name him Duke?" Lizzy asked.

"Perfect. We've got Hoss, Raylan, Duke, and Fiona to keep them all on their toes. I miss her so much. I want three daughters so my girls will have sisters like we've always had," Allie said.

"I thought this was going to be an only child because she's made you nauseous when you smell chili." Lizzy picked up Hoss and buried her nose in his thick yellow fur.

"Oh, no, never. This baby will need a sister to help her name her kittens and to confide in when she likes a boy." Allie grinned.

Rich aromas of chocolate mixed with barbecue met Toby when he entered the house through the back door that evening. Big black clouds hovered down in the southwest, but the sky didn't have that eerie quiet feeling that preceded a tornado. He felt good about the day's work. Perhaps clearing land wasn't as exciting as his days on the rodeo circuit, but he loved seeing the results. With the cash he'd earned in those four years of chasing the rodeo around the country he'd been able to buy the High Roller ranch down in Muenster. It had been nothing but weeds, cow tongue cactus, and mesquite, but he'd put a lot of hard work into it and now it was a prosperous ranch that had brought in enough money to more than pay for his third of the Lucky Penny.

"Please tell me that is your famous pulled-pork barbecue." He clamped a hand on Blake's shoulder. "And do I smell chocolate cake? Lord, I think even this old scar on my face is aching tonight. I feel like I'm looking eighty in the eye rather than thirty."

"Twenty-seven is not close to looking thirty in the eye, but I do not doubt for one minute that you have aches and pains from your rodeo days," Blake said. "It's time for you to settle down."

"Not yet, brother. Maybe after I'm thirty, but definitely not now. This damn celibacy thing is teaching me right quick that I was born to raise hell not kids," Toby said. "I do smell chocolate, right?" He changed the subject.

"It's Mama's sheet cake recipe," Allie said. "We'll eat it warm with a scoop of ice cream on top for dessert."

"Now this is the life. Comin' back to good home-cooked food after a day out there clearing land and listenin' to country music with old Blue perched up there in the seat with me. How's the roofin' business, Allie?" Toby went to the sink and washed his hands. "I'll set the table. My mouth is watering just thinking about pulled pork sandwiches and fried potatoes."

"You see fried potatoes?" Blake asked.

"Please tell me you've got them in the oven keeping warm."

"Cake is in the oven, but the potatoes are in the microwave," Allie said. "And to answer your question, those boys have got the roof on the store. Deke is a slave driver. He swears we'll have Lizzy's back room done by Thursday at quittin' time so the kids can have a three-day weekend to waste their money."

"I remember those days very well," Toby said. "We couldn't wait to get old enough to take our money to the bar, could we, Blake?"

"I'm glad I'm past that time in my life." Blake brushed a kiss across Allie's lips as he carried the potatoes to the table.

Toby beat down the streak of jealousy. It wasn't the first time in his life that Toby had been jealous of his older brother, Blake. But it had been a long time since the green-eyed monster had hit him as hard as it did that evening.

Can't have your cake and eat it, too.

"What's on your mind?" Blake touched him on the shoulder.

"Arguing with myself," Toby answered honestly.

"You know what Jerry Clower said about that. When you start arguing with what you know is right, you're about to mess up real bad. What's the problem?"

"Something I have to work out for myself."

Blake pulled out a chair for Allie. "Been where you are. It's miserable. Don't want to go back there. Let's have some supper. Things always look better with a full stomach."

"You got that right and I'm starving," Toby said with a nod, avoiding what he couldn't come to terms with...not yet.

* * *

Roast, simmered all day with potatoes and carrots in the slow cooker, was one of Lizzy's favorite meals. Katy had also made one of her famous sheet cakes for dessert to top off the meal. When they sat down to eat, Lizzy's urge to bare her soul to her mother was almost more than she could stand. But how did a daughter describe how hot those sexy nights were without burning herself up in embarrassment?

"Janie and Trudy and I are planning a little trip this next weekend," Katy said. "We're going to fly out of Dallas on Friday night to Las Vegas and we'll come home Sunday evening. Sharlene is going to mind the store for me on Saturday."

"Good for you."

"It still feels strange, going places. Even up to Wichita Falls to the movies with Janie and Trudy. Your dad and I were tied down to the businesses all our lives, and then after he died, your grandmother needed us. I would have done things different if I had them to do over again. We would have taken vacations with you girls even if it was only short ones to the beach," Katy said.

"We had lots of vacations, Mama. Don't tell me your mind is slipping like Granny's. They may have only lasted a day, but Sunday was family day. Remember all those summer days we spent at the lake on Sunday afternoons or how about Christmas when we all went together to stomp around in the mesquite looking for the right tree to drag home? We had fifty-two of those days a year. Do you realize that's more than a six-week vacation if you stacked them all up together?"

Katy brushed away a tear. "Thank you, Lizzy."

"Mama, there's no regrets in this corner for the way we were raised and I don't reckon you'd get any complaints out of Fiona or Allie, either. So go have fun with your friends, and good luck at the blackjack table." Lizzy winked.

Fiona!

She hurried through her supper and said she was going up to take a long, hot bath and then watch some television in her room. No lie there. She was going to do both but not until after she'd talked to her sister.

Lizzy was antsy by the time she finished dessert. Could she really confide in anyone and could she trust her youngest sister to keep her secret? Her bedroom was a complete mess, as usual. Clothing strung everywhere and dust all over her dresser. The floor hadn't been vacuumed in two weeks because when it had been her turn to clean the house last week, she'd rushed through it and ignored her room.

"This is a teenager's room, not a grown woman's who owns a business," she fussed as she started cleaning. "Granny said lots of problems could be solved with good hard work. Let's see if she's right. Maybe I won't need to call Fiona after all."

Sweat streamed down her neck and through the valley between her breasts. She tugged at the wet band of her bra and kept on working until the room was neater than those times when it was Allie's turn to do the house cleaning. "Take that, Alora Raine Logan Dawson," she said as she sank into the rocking chair to catch her breath.

Trouble was she didn't feel a damn bit better than she did when she started. A spotless room that took two whole hours to put to rights didn't erase the feeling that she needed to talk to her sister.

The phone was in her hand when it rang, and it startled her so badly that she threw it across the room. It bounced in the middle of her bed and landed on the pillows. She left the rocker and snatched it, saw that the call was from Fiona, counted that as an omen, and hit the TALK button.

"Fiona! I'm so glad you called. How are things in Houston? God, I miss you. Please tell me you are coming home this month. You really need to meet Blake and Toby and see Allie at least once while she is pregnant and I'm about to lay a guilt trip on you so get ready for it—Granny don't have many good days anymore so you need to come home and see her." Lizzy rattled on and on.

"I talked to Allie and she said that she hired a crew to get your roof done and Herman's barn built. Okay, okay! Mama is sending plane tickets and has rented a car for me so I'll be there. But it'll only be from Friday evening until Sunday. I can't be away from work any longer than that and I miss you, too. Now tell me what else is going on? I hear you've got kittens and one is named for me."

"Yes, four of them. Their mama is Stormy and the

babies are Raylan, Duke, and Hoss, and the one little black lady is Fefe. She's my favorite because she's so sassy. But I've got a big problem and Mama and Allie are too close..." She paused.

"Toby Dawson," Fiona said.

"What did Allie tell you?"

"Just that you liked him a lot and that she discouraged you and I should do the same if you brought up the subject," Fiona answered. "How bad is it?"

Lizzy sat down on the edge of the bed, then remembered how sweaty she was and moved to the rocking chair. "I cleaned my room and it's spotless. Clothes hung up. No dust, not even on the window blinds, and shoes are in neat rows. Does that tell you anything?"

"Holy hell! What have you done that warranted that punishment?"

"Are you sitting down and how much time do you have?"

"I am now and I don't have to be at work until three tomorrow," Fiona said.

"Okay, here goes." Lizzy started with that evening when she was watching the store for her mother. Business had been slow at the feed store and Katy had to go to Wichita Falls to sign more papers for Granny's care, so Lizzy put a sign on the door and went down to the convenience store for the last hour of the workday.

Toby had come in for a couple of pounds of bologna. Blue, as well as Blake's dog, Shooter, liked a piece of bologna as a treat in the evenings. One thing led to another and after she locked the store, they wound up on the cot in the back room. Since she had the key to her mother's store, it was the perfect spot for three weeks of the hottest sex in all of Dry Creek's history.

She went on to tell the rest of the story. "And now we're in this fake relationship. Toby is in it because he wants the people in Dry Creek to see him as a respectable citizen and not the player he is and because Sharlene is stalking him and he gets text messages and probably phone calls from women all the time and he needs a pretend girlfriend. I'm still not totally sure why I'm in it. I'm over Mitch even though some folks don't think I am. Like I told Toby, one bad apple does not mean we have to throw out the whole crop."

"And you've gone and fallen for him?" Fiona said.

"I wouldn't go that far, but I do like him a lot."

"You need a counselor. You've been hurt and . . ."

Lizzy laughed sarcastically. "Oh, sure. I'll rush right down to Dr. Know Yourself Better on Main Street in Dry Creek and make an appointment tomorrow morning. And don't tell me to talk to the preacher. I can't tell him all this stuff."

"Not the preacher. God no! I meant a real licensed counselor like I saw."

Suddenly, the line went so quiet that Lizzy held it out to see if she'd lost the connection.

"When did you see a therapist?" Lizzy asked.

"I'll keep your secret if you keep mine," Fiona said.

"Deal."

"I've been divorced for over a year and it was a

messy one. I'd signed a pre-nup so all he had to give me was ten thousand dollars. Lawyers' fees for the divorce cut that down considerably and when I went looking for a job, his firm had blackballed me. I'm working in a little coffee shop. Meet your sister, the barista, who is now Fiona Catherine Logan again," she said in a rush. "God, that feels good to tell you, but you can't tell Mama or she will worry. I make enough to get by, but I did lose my car. I've got an old pickup truck that manages to get me to work and back to my efficiency apartment, so I'm good. Don't tell Mama, but I'm so tickled to get that plane ticket and the rental car so I can come see y'all. I've been so homesick lately."

"Holy shit!"

Fiona giggled. "Back in the winter you weren't cussin'. Maybe this Toby is a bad influence on you in more ways than one."

"Come home, Fiona. You can put in an office here as a tax consultant and accountant with your education. I can't believe that you got kicked out of the law firm. You were the best damn accountant they had. Most folks even thought you were a lawyer." Lizzy shook her head to get rid of the image of her perfect sister pouring coffee for folks.

It didn't work.

Fiona, the smart sister who'd gone to college. Fiona, the neat sister whose room always looked like it came out of a picture book. Fiona, the pretty redhead who had turned the heads of all the cowboys in Dry Creek. The vision of Fiona, wearing an apron and her pretty red hair in a ponytail sticking out the back of a ball cap, wouldn't go away.

"I'm okay, Lizzy. For real, I'm okay. It will blow over and everyone will forget and a new firm will come to town and I'll get a good job again. The counseling helped me tremendously. I wish you could go for a few sessions," she said.

"You be my counselor. What should I do first?" Lizzy asked.

"Face your feelings. Scream. Yell. Cry. Then decide what you want and go get it. I could only afford a few sessions but basically that's what I got out of it. I wanted to stay here so that's what I did. I do not ever want to live in Dry Creek again, period, end of story."

"I've already faced my feelings. What happened with Mitch was as much my fault as his," Lizzy admitted. "I should've broken it off with him long before."

"That's good. I could see that you were changing yourself to meet his standards. I did the same thing with Paul and when I got tired of being the person he wanted and went back to being myself, he hated the small-town woman he'd married. So he found himself another woman that he should've married in the first place," she answered. "So you really feel like you have closure on the Mitch issue?"

"Definitely," Lizzy said firmly. "Do you have that yet with Paul?"

"I do. Last week he came into the coffee shop and I realized how much better off I am without his egotistical attitude ruling every day of my life," she said.

"How long was it until you got to that place?"

"More than a year."

"You always were a slow learner," Lizzy teased.

"You are going to see Toby tonight, aren't you?"

"What makes you ask that question out of the clear blue sky?" Lizzy asked.

"All I can say is be careful, sister. Now pinky-swear that you won't tattle on me."

Lizzy held up her smallest finger and crooked it around an imaginary one. "I pinky-swear and cross my heart and all that shit. Love you, Fiona," Lizzy's voice squeaked out around the lump in her throat. "And miss you."

"Right back atcha."

CHAPTER THIRTEEN

Toby popped out an old green webbed lawn chair and sat down with Blue right beside him. He rubbed Blue's ears with one hand and held a glass of sweating iced tea in the other. His phone rang and he answered it after he'd checked the picture to be sure it wasn't Sharlene.

"Hello, darlin'," he said in his sexiest drawl.

"Don't you 'hello, darlin'" me, Toby Dawson. You promised you'd call and it's been two months. I've sent you dozens of texts and went back to the bar where we met every weekend. Where in the hell are you?" Teresa asked.

Thank goodness her name had come on the phone with her picture or he would have had no idea who he was talking to. "Well, sweetheart, it's like this. I moved out of the area. Bought a little chunk of land

and haven't had time to go back to our favorite bar. But I might come home for a visit in a few weeks, so don't give up on me."

"Never." She giggled. "The sex was that good but so was the breakfast afterwards."

"Well, I'm right glad that you have such good memories." He said the right words, but his heart wasn't in it. He would have rather been bantering with Lizzy. "Got to go, but you keep a watch out for me and we might have another weekend like the last one."

Blue's tail thumped against the ground and a coyote howled in the distance. The dog backed his ears and growled down deep in his throat, warning those varmints to keep their distance.

Toby made up his mind that the next day he would buy a donkey. A pack of coyotes could bring down a heifer. One or two could drag off a newborn calf. He should have brought his old donkey, Lucifer, with him to the Lucky Penny, but Toby couldn't bear to take him away from his surroundings. Even with his advanced age, Lucifer could stomp a coyote to death if he thought for one second the varmint was coming after a calf in his pasture.

Toby set the tea down on the ground and started walking slowly, thinking about all the changes he wanted to make to the place, the cattle he planned to breed and raise there, and the future for him, his cousin, and his brother. He came to the fence separating the Lucky Penny from the property on Audrey's Place and sat down on a flat rock. Blue plopped down on the ground and tucked his nose under his paw. The high wind that had accompanied the tornado had blown some of the petals from the red roses from the tangled mass on the barbed wire. But there were enough blossoms left to permeate the air with their scent.

All thoughts of a donkey vanished. The roses reminded him of Lizzy. She was beautiful and yet tough enough to endure a tornado, just like those beautiful roses. His eyes shifted to all the wildflowers dotting the distance from him to the fence, and that made him think of the fierceness of her feelings for her family and loved ones. Wind, rain, hot broiling sun, or drought couldn't kill out those wildflowers any more than anything could ever get between Lizzy and someone that she truly loved.

Lizzy paced the floor after she finished talking to Fiona. The room got smaller and smaller and the walls began to move toward the center. She jerked on her work boots and started outside, meeting her mother halfway down the stairs.

"Where are you off to?" Katy asked.

"I can't remember if I fed Stormy, so I'm going to take a drive, feed the cat, and clear my head," she answered.

"Got something stuck in there like Toby Dawson?" Katy asked.

One of Lizzy's shoulders lifted in a shrug. "Maybe so."

Katy patted her on the shoulder. "Pet Stormy for me.

She's a good cat. Now that your grandmother isn't living here we could bring her home if you want. She was so allergic to anything that had to do with cats and she didn't like dogs, so you kids couldn't have pets in the house."

"If she doesn't adapt to the store we will." She had to get out of the house, away from the confinement so she could think. Once she was outside in the fresh air with no walls around her, she took a deep breath and sat down on the swing. A coyote howled off to the south and another one answered from somewhere over near the old well on the other side of the Lucky Penny. Hopefully, they weren't planning to meet in the middle and have one of Toby's new calves for supper that night.

He needed a couple of donkeys to keep the cattle safe. Coyotes and wild animals had ruled the Lucky Penny for years. They had no idea that whatever was on the ranch wasn't fair game. But a donkey or a couple of them would keep the coyotes at bay for sure. She should tell him tonight before he lost a baby calf.

She popped up off the swing with a purpose and jogged out across the yard, jumped the rail fence by putting a hand on the top rail and bailing over it like a kid, and then slowed her pace to a fast walk toward the fence separating the two places.

The waning moon gave enough light that she could see well enough without a flashlight. Good thing since she'd left her purse sitting on the swing and the tiny light attached to her key chain was the only one she owned. The coyote sounded closer that time so she hurried.

"You cannot pull a donkey out of thin air just by putting some extra giddy-up in your step. Blue won't let a coyote get a calf tonight and neither will Shooter." She fussed out loud.

"No they won't," Toby said from the other side of the fence.

Her hand flew to her chest and her lungs deflated. It took a full five seconds before she remembered to inhale and when she did, all she could smell was roses. "Dammit! You startled me so bad my heart nearly stopped."

"Maybe it was trying to pull a donkey out of thin air," Toby teased.

"What are you doing over there anyway?" She leaned on a crooked wooden fence post.

"Thinkin' about asking Herman or Deke where I could buy a couple of donkeys to keep those pesky coyotes away from my cattle," he answered.

She sat down on the green grass. "Herman has donkeys for sale sometimes. When he or his kids get too many they sell a few off. You'd have to ask him, but if he's not getting rid of any, then Deke will know someone. The coyotes aren't the only predators on your ranch, Toby. We've seen bobcats although I don't think they'd bother your cattle but the mountain lions might."

"Maybe I'd better buy more than two then," he said. "I'm glad you thought of donkeys when you heard the coyotes singing tonight, Lizzy. I wanted to talk to you but I didn't have the courage to climb over this fence and knock on your door."

"Why?" Lizzy asked. Less than a foot of space and a barbed wire fence separated them but with the fence between them it seemed like a mile.

"It involves a whole new scene for me. I don't know how to date so I'm not sure how to go about any of this," he said.

Her chest tightened. "You've been doing a pretty good job of practicin'."

Was he about to tell her that he'd found a woman he wanted to see and that this artificial thing between them was over? Bad timing was a bigger bitch than karma.

"Ah, that was nothing but showin' off. It's real dating that scares the bejesus right out of me. Never was any good at it," he admitted.

"Bullshit!" Lizzy said. "You are a player. You know all the moves."

"Yes, I am. Yes, I do. But that's the game of take a woman home, take her to bed, feed her breakfast, kiss her good-bye, and start a new game the next week. Dating and getting to really know a woman is a different game. Kind of like the difference in Monopoly and Texas Hold 'Em."

"You mean one is exciting and the other is boring. I wouldn't want to be the Monopoly lady then," she said.

"Nothing boring about you, Lizzy Logan," he said, and chuckled. "Will you go on a date with me Friday night? A real date, not a pretend one? I'll probably be so clumsy that you won't go out with me a second time, but please say yes."

"Where are we going? Bar? Ice cream?"

"Is that a yes?" He slipped his hand under the barbed wire and laced his fingers with hers.

"It's a yes, but I don't know if I'm ready to tell our relatives that this has turned from fake to real," she said.

He squeezed her hand gently. "I agree and don't expect too much from me here at first. I'm new at this."

"This new Lizzy Logan is pretty new at it, too. The old one was busy trying to be something she wasn't. This new one is going to be herself, so you might not want to ask her out on a second real date," she said. "Just one thing before we get out the chisel and set this in that rock you are sitting on right now and be honest with me. Is this one of your pickup lines?"

He shook his head. "No, ma'am. I have not asked a woman on a date since my senior year in high school. I asked Betsy Dulaney to the prom and the night was a disaster. From then on I honed my player skills and to hell with dating."

"What changed your mind?" she asked.

"Promise you won't laugh," he whispered.

A warm breeze kicked up under her hair and kissed that soft spot on her neck right below her ear. It wasn't hard to imagine that it was his whisper that caused it or to embrace the feeling that it evoked.

"I promise," she said softly.

He removed his cowboy hat and laid it in his lap. "I do not believe in voodoo or spirits or any of that hocus-pocus crap. But I got a feeling this evening as Blue and I were sitting out behind my trailer that something is missing in me."

"I know the feeling."

His face was half in shadows and half dimly lit by the moon, creating an air of mystery about him. There was a dark side that had honed the craft of a player, but there was a light side that wanted so badly to open up his heart. One side would win and like the story Granny told about the wolf and the baby rabbit. The side that got fed would emerge the winner. The one that he starved would eventually fade away into the dust of the history books.

"What time should I be ready and what should I wear?" she asked.

"Something very comfortable. Jeans will be fine."

"Really? Then I take it we are not going to one of those fancy restaurants where it takes all evening to eat a meal?"

"No, ma'am," he answered.

"Where are we going?"

"It's a surprise but we might be late getting back home."

She drew her knees up to her chin, pulled her hand free, and wrapped her arms around her legs. "Mama is leaving Friday and won't be home until Sunday. I don't have to worry about anyone comin' to look for us. Sure you don't want to tell me what this date involves?"

"No, I want it to be perfect enough that you'll say you want to go out with me again," he answered. "And to do that it has to be a surprise. I will pick you up at seven."

"Okay." She tried to ignore the jitters, but it wasn't possible. She had just agreed to go on a real date with Toby that did not involve sex or a breakfast afterward. Her heart rate jacked up a notch or two at the idea, and she couldn't help but smile.

He bounced up on his feet, grabbed his hat before it hit the ground, put a hand on a fence post, and cleared the barbed wire like an expert high jumper. "I'll walk you back to your house. Wouldn't look too good if that imaginary man with the binoculars in the tree saw us going our own way. By morning it would be all over Dry Creek that we'd had a fight and broken up and we couldn't go on our real date without everyone knowing."

With his hat settled on his head, he threw an arm around her shoulders and kept pace with her all the way to the yard fence, where he opened the gate for her. "I swear I caught a faint glimpse of a flash over there to the east."

"It was probably a fallen star," she said.

He started humming the old song by that name, coming in with parts of lines as he remembered them. When the lyrics said that she was a fallen star, he drew her close and danced with her on the green lawn. He sang a line when it said that she must have strayed from the Milky Way and went back to humming as he waltzed her around the yard under the stars and moon.

There wasn't a person over there in the fork of an old scrub oak tree but in case there was, she moved in closer to Toby to give them a good show. The gossip vines would not wither up and die in Dry Creek that week, for sure.

He stopped humming, bent her backward, and gave her a real Hollywood kiss. When he righted her, she was totally breathless and the stars were spinning blurs in the sky.

"Wow!" she said.

"Did you recognize the song?" he asked.

She leaned on him for support until the world was set upright again. "Granny had it on a vinyl record with Jimmy Newman singing and played it all the time when I was a little girl. She said that it was hers and Grandpa's song. I remember the singer because I thought Newman was a strange name."

He smiled down at her. "You are amazing because not many people of our generation even know that song! And that's not a line, either. I'll see you tomorrow probably but definitely on Friday. Good night, Lizzy."

She sat down on the swing until her heart stopped thumping around, threatening to bust the straps on her bra. What kind of date was he thinking about?

She picked up her purse and smiled all the way to her bedroom. This was a real honest-to-God date, and she had several days to be excited about it.

CHAPTER FOURTEEN

Elbows on the checkout counter, chin resting in her hands, Lizzy tried to figure out where Toby was taking her on their first real date. Since he'd said jeans would be fine, maybe it was fishing. She loved to sit on the riverbank under the moonlight and fish. If he'd tell her, then she could offer to pack a cooler full of food and beer.

Stormy hopped out of the basket, leaving her four squirmy babies behind to tumble around and fight with each other. Lizzy absentmindedly rubbed Stormy's fur from nose to tail. Maybe it was a movie he'd picked out to watch in his trailer. Lizzy's eyes popped wide open. That would mean the bed would be within falling-down distance, and under those circumstances she might start up the old fling again.

The cowbell above the door sounded and she

jumped as if she'd been caught strip stark naked in the bed with Toby. In one leap the cat went from the counter to the floor and into the basket to protect her babies.

"Good morning, Dora June. What can I do for you this fine Tuesday?" Lizzy fanned her face with a catalog that had come in the mail that day. "Kinda warm, isn't it? I forgot to adjust the thermostat this morning." Anything to explain away the high color burning her cheeks.

"Feels pretty good to me. Wait until August when it really gets hot, then you'll need that air conditioner for sure. What is that horrible noise out back?"

Lizzy laid the book aside. "Allie and her crew have started putting up the studs." Crap! The word *stud* brought up another picture that turned her face crimson again. There in her mind, in living color, was Toby, bare-chested with only a sheet covering his lower half. He was propped up on an elbow and his blue eyes were locked with hers. "For the new back room," she stammered.

"She has no business doing construction work in her condition," Dora June hissed. "When I was expecting," she whispered the word, "we stayed out of the public eye as much as possible and that last six weeks, wild horses couldn't have even hauled us to church."

"Times change. What can I do for you today?" Lizzy asked.

"For starters you could stop seeing that man you spent the night with on Saturday night." Dora June's nose tilted up so high that if the roof had still been leaking, she might've drowned. She was, after all, standing right under the place where the water streamed down. "I was your grandmother's friend and she is not able in her present state of mind to advise you, so I feel it my God-given duty to help you see things right."

"And that would be to not see Toby anymore, right?" Lizzy asked.

"I'm glad you see the light." Dora June nodded several times, all of her chins in agreement.

"Miz Dora June, I am way past needing my granny or you to steer me right in the ways of love, politics, or religion. I have no intentions of breaking up with Toby. And besides, if Granny was in her right mind, she'd fall in love with Toby. She'd tell me to follow my heart and not let anyone tell me it was wrong." Lizzy picked up the catalog again.

Dora June leaned over the counter and sniffed loudly. "Have you been drinkin'?"

Lizzy dropped the magazine and it landed on the floor beside the basket of cats. "Why would you suggest such a thing?"

"Your face is beet red. You've been drinkin' or else you've got unholy thoughts in your head about that wild cowboy, girl. Nothing else could make them cheeks that red. In either case you'd better be careful. If you are drinkin', then stop right now." Dora June straightened up. "I don't smell no liquor."

"Must be wicked, sexy thoughts about what I'd do

with Toby Dawson if I could just peel those jeans off his body and jump his bones, then." Lizzy leaned forward and whispered. "To tell the truth, I've got a bottle of Jack Daniel's in my office and a couple of red plastic cups. You want to have a little nip with me? That's why I keep peppermints on the counter in the bowl." Lizzy winked. "Folks think it's for the kids but it sure covers up the smell of whiskey on my breath. You couldn't even detect it, could you?"

"Well, I never," Dora June huffed. "No, I don't want to drink with you and I think it's a cryin' shame that you've gone so far backward from that sweet girl who was going to be a preacher's wife."

"Don't blame me for Mitch's sins," Lizzy said coldly.

Allie pushed through the back door and closed it behind her. "Hey, I'm taking a break and thought we might get something to drink in your office. Oh, hello, Dora June. What brings you to town this fine spring morning?"

"I'm going home to pray for you girls. Since Irene was put away up there in that glorified nursing home, the whole bunch of you." She threw up a palm, shut her eyes, and shivered. "Y'all have gone over the edge. This one talking about…about…"

"Hot cowboy sex that gets you all sweaty?" Lizzy finished the sentence for her.

"Edge of what?" Allie asked.

"The edge of morality. Pregnant and right out in public doing a man's work. Drinking? Irene would be ashamed. I'm going to gather up the ladies from the church and we're going to have a prayer vigil for you."

"I thought we'd been excommunicated from your ladies' group," Allie said.

"We pray for all sinners," Dora June mumbled on her way to the door. She was still shaking her head when the cowbell announced that she had left.

"What caused all that? I only wanted a soda from your refrigerator," Allie said.

Lizzy led the way to the office where she sank down into her chair. "It's a long story. Help yourself to a soda and pull up a chair. I'll tell you the rest while you take a break."

Allie came close to spewing soda pop right out her nose several times during the story, which Lizzy embellished with hand movements and different voices.

"Lord, Lizzy, you sound enough like her that you could call Truman and he wouldn't know that he wasn't talking to his wife." Allie hiccupped.

"And then you came in and asked for a drink. It was the icing on the cupcake." Lizzy laughed with her sister. "Tomorrow we will both be drunks. You'll have a baby addicted to alcohol and you and Mama will be looking for rehab centers to put me in. And I'm sure," Lizzy went on, "that all of this will be blamed on those sexy Dawson cowboys. I can't wait until Jud gets here in the fall. That will give the rumors about time to die down, and his arrival can start a whole new bunch."

The laughter stopped and Allie's face turned serious. "You aren't in love with Toby, are you?"

"The townspeople don't know that. They think we are a hot little item, remember," Lizzy quickly covered her tracks.

"Don't you wish that they'd leave us alone and pray for someone else for a change?" Allie sighed.

Lizzy left the chair, rounded the desk, and hugged her sister. "It will burn itself out pretty soon and they'll move on. When they see that these Dawson cowboys are going to turn that ranch into a fine place they'll gag on their words, and how much whiskey they think we drink won't even be worth mentioning."

"I hope it happens real soon," Allie said.

On Wednesday morning Toby and Blue settled into the truck, put in an Alan Jackson CD, and drove out to the back pasture. Today he and Blake were going to work cattle. Castrate the bull calves, vaccinate them all, and check them over good to make sure they were healthy.

Blake was standing beside a couple four-wheelers when Toby got to the pasture. Not a cow or calf was in sight, but he did hear a calf bawling off to the left where they were all probably either belly deep in the farm pond or else bunched up together under the shade of a scrub oak tree.

"There's one old cow that produces good-size calves, but she's wild as hell and she usually throws that DNA right over into her calves. Crawl on one of these things and we'll go round up as many as we can into the corral," Blake said.

"Come on, Blue. It's time to run some of that

bologna fat off your ribs," Toby said as he settled down into the seat of the four-wheeler. "I like horses better for this," he yelled over the noise of the engine.

"Me, too, and maybe next year we'll have a few but today, this is what we have," Blake said. He made a clucking noise with his tongue and Shooter took off toward the mesquite.

The cows came right along to the corral with the calves, meandering around the mesquite like they had all day to go nowhere. But the guys didn't rush them. A stampede might cause them to veer off to either side and refuse to go into the corral at all.

By midmorning the job of separating the calves from their mamas had started. That was where the muscle work came in and the sweating really started. Toby got a hand around one little bull calf and led him to the round pen with no problem, but the minute he started bawling for his mama, the others got the message loud and clear and they huddled up in the far corner.

Blake nodded and got out his kit containing the vaccines. "Bring her on in the chute and down to the head gate and let's get her shots so she can get back with her mama. Soon as you see what cow she goes with, we'll pop an ear tag in her ear. Bulls can go from there to the table to get their rings."

Toby started the black calf toward the chute leading to the head gate, but the feisty animal turned at the last minute and made a beeline back toward her mama on the other side of the fence. Blue steered her away and back toward Toby, but when she saw him, she put her head down and ran right at him. When she was close enough he reached down and scooped her up into his arms.

"Shit!" he groaned. "You weigh a ton already."

"Fine-lookin' calf there." Blake laughed.

"You try carryin' her to the chute and then tell me how fine she is." Toby set her down and she took off like greased lightning toward the other end. Blake waited until she was almost to the end and opened the gate enough she could get her head through it, then clamped it shut.

"I'll get both her shots while you go get another one. And Toby, you don't have to carry them all like babies," Blake teased.

Toby's arms were aching by noon. He hadn't had to carry another one, but wrestling calves all morning let him remember exactly how many times he'd been bucked off of two tons of raging bull and exactly what bones he'd landed on. They had half the herd done, which meant they should be done by suppertime.

When the hot broiling sun was straight up in the sky, they took a break to eat dinner. They grabbed a sack lunch out of Toby's truck and sat down on the ground on the shady side of the pickup, two paper bags in their laps and a gallon of sweet tea between them.

"I'd about as soon have a nap as eat," Toby said.

"It's all that fake dating that's wearing you out." Blake laughed. "Settle down like I have and you'll have more energy to use for ranchin'."

"I ain't ready for that." Toby reached into the sack and pulled out a thick ham and cheese sandwich. "I might bitch and gripe when I have to manhandle calves, but I love this job, brother."

"Me, too," Blake said.

"You think that marriage has helped you understand womenfolk?" Toby asked.

"Hell no! Sometimes I wonder why God couldn't have given Mama and Daddy a daughter. Boys need a sister so they'll get some inkling of the way a female's brain works."

"You got that right. Maybe that's why us Dawsons are so wild. We don't have a lot of girls in the family. I could use a sister."

"You can talk to Allie," Blake said. "Or if it's about Lizzy, maybe you'd better call up Josie, but then she'll tell her brother and then Jud will tell me and I'll have to tell Allie because we don't keep secrets. So you might as well spit out what's on your mind rather than going through all that shit."

A mosquito made several buzzes around his ear before he located it and swatted it mid-air as it made a dive for Blue's ear. With mosquitoes as big as buzzards, maybe he shouldn't plan something outside for this big date with Lizzy, and yet the picture in his mind kept centering on a secluded area with just the two of them on a blanket on the ground with a picnic basket in front of them.

That's when he remembered that his mother always lit citronella candles when they were outside in the summertime. Lizzy had them at the store but it would ruin the surprise if he walked in and asked for candles. He could make a trip to Throckmorton or maybe over to Olney or...he grinned...Deke could buy them for him and he could repay him.

The whole date started with candles so exactly how many did he need? Enough to outline a blanket on the ground? Only a couple? He decided on a dozen of the ones in pint-size mason jars.

He had a blanket and one dozen candles. Now what did he do with them and where did he put them?

"You got quiet all of a sudden," Blake said.

"Just thinkin' about how buyin' this ranch turned our lives around," Toby said.

"It sure did do that." Blake nodded. "And since I love my wife so much, I'm right glad for the changes it's brought about."

Toby's phone buzzed. He laid his sandwich to the side and read the sexy text from one of his previous women. Any other time he would have shot a message right back—and it would have been so hot that the woman on the other end would have been panting when she finished it. But not today.

"Sharlene?" Blake asked.

"No, she hasn't called in..."

The phone buzzed again before he could even finish his sentence. Another woman and this time the text was accompanied by a picture of her in a sexy night-gown on satin sheets. She had a come-hither look in her eyes and was blowing kisses toward him.

"Holy hell, Toby, who is that?" Blake asked.

"One of those lovely ladies that I've made breakfast for in the past." Toby smiled.

"Miss those days?"

"Not when I'm this tired."

At quitting time on Thursday, Deke popped into the store. "Allie has gone home and the boys are cleaning up the rest of the mess back there. Y'all can haul your supplies back in from the Lucky Penny over the weekend. We've worked like termites, but it's all done."

"I can't believe it." Lizzy made her way to the back of the store. "It's amazing what you and these guys have all accomplished. And Deke, thank you for all you did to make sure Allie..." she paused.

Deke laid a hand on her shoulder. "I love her, too. And I'll take care of her. Don't you worry your head none about that. You and Allie can settle up financially, but right now I'm taking all these boys out to the ranch so she can write them a paycheck. Oh, and I need a case of twelve of those citronella candles that keep the mosquitoes away."

"They're on the bottom shelf at the back. You plannin' on sitting out a lot this summer, are you?" she asked.

"I want to be ready. Never know when a pretty girl will want to spend some time outside under the stars rather than under the fan above my bed." He chuckled.

"Put them on your bill?" she asked.

"No, I got cash. Can't hardly classify them as a farm expense on my taxes," he answered.

Lizzy rang up the total and Deke paid her with two twenty-dollar bills. He put the change in his shirt pocket and carried the box out the front door. "Hey, don't forget to lock up that new overhead door." He stopped and turned back around. "I told the boys to leave it up when they got all done. And we moved the light switch over a foot so be prepared for that change. Other than that, it's all the same as it was."

"Thanks again, Deke," she called out.

She made sure everything was locked up tight, that Stormy was fed and the kittens were all given equal petting time, and closed up shop at five fifteen. Katy had offered to pick up takeout from Nadine's that evening for supper because she had to pack for her Vegas trip and wanted Lizzy to help her.

Lizzy was glad to have something to do to take her mind off the next night. She'd been to bed with Toby numerous times. They'd shared dozens of kisses that came close to melting her insides with the fake dating thing. The whole town knew they were a couple these days, but this was the first time they were really going out together.

She'd never been so nervous about anything in her life. Not when she went out with Mitch the first time. Not even when she dated those other two guys she'd had brief relationships with. So what did it all mean? That she was playing with fire and was sure to get burned? Or that she was doing the right thing in spite of all the advice she'd been given against it?

CHAPTER FIFTEEN

Friday night was hot so Lizzy opted for a pair of jean shorts, a pastel plaid shirt, and sandals for her date. Surely that wasn't too casual since he'd said she could wear jeans. She pulled her hair up away from her face and clamped it with a big clip, slapped on a minimum of makeup, and hoped that wherever they were going food was involved.

Nervousness made her hungry and right then she could have eaten half an Angus steer and polished off a couple of apple pies—with ice cream on top! Purse slung over her shoulder, she was on her way to the porch swing when she heard the crunch of tires on the gravel lane.

Her stomach knotted up and her palms went clammy. But it was a false alarm. Katy pulled up into the driveway, parked her vehicle, and waved. "We made last-minute changes. We are meeting here and all going down to Dallas in one vehicle. Janie and Trudy will be here in about five minutes. They're coming down the back roads from Seymour."

If Lizzy could have kicked Madam Fate right square in the shins she would have done so and enjoyed every second of it, even if it broke her toes. Now all those women who hadn't seen her since she was a little girl would arrive at the same time Toby did. Dammit! Dammit! Dammit! The words kept repeating themselves.

Be nice or she'll figure that something is going on.

"Want a glass of sweet tea?" Lizzy asked.

"Not now. I'd have to stop at every bathroom from here to Dallas if I drank tea. I thought you and Toby were going dancing or out to eat tonight." Katy sat down on the swing and eyed Lizzy from sandals to hair.

"We are going out, but it's casual. Are you playing slots or poker this weekend?" Lizzy changed the subject.

"Slots. I've got a set amount that I plan to spend tonight, tomorrow, and Sunday morning before we leave. I'll stretch it out and make it last all weekend. We are going to see a show tomorrow night and, Lizzy, I'm so excited I can hardly sit still. But another part of me is worried that something will happen while I'm gone. If they call about your grandmother, you get in touch with me immediately." Katy finally took a breath. "I've taken care of her so long that I feel guilty taking the weekend for something other than going to see her."

Lizzy patted her mother's hand. "Mama, most of the time she doesn't know us anyway, but if it will make you feel better, I'll go see her Sunday after church. Or I'll go see her instead of church."

Katy smiled. "Church first and then go see her. That helps my feelings a lot, Lizzy. Even if she doesn't recognize us, I don't want her to go two weeks with no one dropping by."

"I'll see if Allie wants to go with me and we'll make a girls' day of it." Lizzy withdrew her hand and set the swing in motion with her foot.

"Allie and Blake left this evening to go to his folks' place in Muenster. They'll be gone until Sunday night. It was spur of the moment. Toby said he'd hold down the fort so they could get away for the weekend."

Lizzy sucked in a double lungful of air and let it out in a rush. "That means I'm going to church with no support group. Dora June and her little buddies will slice me up and feed me to the buzzards."

"Why?" Katy narrowed her eyes.

Lizzy gave her the short version of what had happened in the store that day. When she finished, Katy's mouth was set in a firm line and her perfectly arched brows drawn down into a frown.

"That which does not kill us," she said.

"After Sunday I should be able to bench-press a John Deere tractor. I hear the parade turning off the main road." Lizzy pointed.

Katy stood up and waved two vans into parking spaces beside her car. "Thank you again, Lizzy, for taking care of things."

"Is this Lizzy or Allie?" Trudy yelled as she opened the yard fence and made her way to the porch. Tall, thin, and with gorgeous blond hair cut in a feathered back style, Trudy looked at least ten years younger than her age.

Lizzy left the swing behind and extended her hand. "Thank you. I'm Lizzy."

"Bullshit, girl! I want a hug." Trudy smelled like expensive perfume.

"And Lizzy is the middle girl, right?" Janie came up behind Trudy.

"Yes, I am. Allie is the oldest and Fiona is the youngest."

"Well, I'm glad to see one of Katy's girls." Janie's thick gray hair brushed against her chin and bangs touched arched brows over brilliant blue eyes. The total opposite of Trudy, she was short and slightly overweight. "Now come here and give your long lost Aunt Janie a hug."

Her back was to the road but Lizzy heard the truck, loud and clear, coming up the lane. In five more minutes they would have been on their way to Dallas and now they'd stick around to meet Toby. All three of the older women turned around to watch Toby get out of his truck, shake the legs of his jeans down over his boot tops, and swagger up to the porch.

"Oh. My. God." Trudy fanned herself with her hand.

"That is sex on a stick. If only I was thirty years younger and had a hell of a lot more energy."

"Honey, I'd have to get me some of that Viagra for women to keep up with that," Janie whispered.

Toby tipped his straw hat as he started up the porch steps. "Ladies?"

"Toby, these are my friends, Trudy and Janie. Girls, this is Toby Dawson, the cowboy Lizzy is dating." Katy made introductions. "Remember I told you about him." She winked broadly.

Toby bent at the waist and kissed first Trudy's hand and then Janie's. "Pleasure to meet you lovely ladies."

"Sweet Jesus! You need to keep this one for real not pretend. And if you don't want him call me. I won't even mind if they make me wear a sign around my neck with *cougar* written on it," Trudy said.

"I'm not going to wash my hand until we get to Vegas. I know that kiss is going to be my good luck charm and I'm going to win a bunch of money right off the bat," Janie said.

"Y'all have a lovely time," Toby drawled.

"And where are you going tonight?" Katy asked.

"Cinderella and I are going to the ball. If she loses a glass slipper, I will bring it by tomorrow." He smiled.

Lizzy fell in love at that moment. She might not be in love when morning came because she'd proven that falling in love didn't mean staying in love. But at that very moment on a Friday in June, she loved Toby Dawson.

"I'll fight you for him," Janie teased Trudy. "You've

already had three and I only had one. I deserve him more than you."

"Y'all are making Lizzy blush," Katy scolded. "Let's move our things into Trudy's van. If we get to the airport early, we might have time for a margarita before we have to board."

Toby pulled Lizzy close to his side with an arm around her shoulders, and they waved from the porch until the van was out of sight. He rested his chin on her head and inhaled.

"I love whatever perfume or shampoo you use and, Miz Lizzy Logan, you are gorgeous this evening."

"Thank you," she whispered. "You handled them well so thank you for that, too."

"The ladies love attention." He kissed her on the forehead. "You might want to change your shoes into your oldest boots, and you won't need that purse over there on the porch."

"Where exactly are we going?"

"Hiking at first," he answered.

"Give me five minutes. Do I need longer pants?" she asked.

"No those sexy little things will work just fine."

Toby sat down in the swing, tilted his hat over his eyes, and crossed his long legs at the ankle. He'd worked hard to make the evening special and he hoped that no coyotes or raccoons had made off with the picnic basket, because he was really hungry. If anyone would have told him six months ago that he'd be interested in a short, curvy woman with dirty blond hair and brown eyes, he'd have thought they'd lost their minds.

And yet, here he was.

The door closed and he straightened up, resettled his hat, and grinned. She was the cutest thing ever in those cowboy boots worn down at the heels and denim shorts. His heart kicked in an extra beat when he took her hand in his and led the way off the porch.

She started toward his truck but he shook his head. "Not that way, darlin'. Our hiking begins right here."

"Is there food involved? I'm so hungry, I could eat a bear," she said.

He opened the back gate for her. "Trust me, darlin'. I asked you out so I've got everything covered. It's only about fifteen minutes of hiking."

"What is that?" She pointed. "Holy smoke, Toby, you have cleared a path through the mesquite for us. When did you do this? I didn't even hear the dozer this close to the house."

He stopped at the edge of the heavy mesquite, whipped off his hat, and did a bow. "It's not as smooth as I would have liked, but we can pretend that it's the yellow brick road. I know I'm getting all kinds of fairy tales mixed up. Boys aren't much for those things, but I've had to learn when my oldest two brothers got married and brought a couple of girl-type babies into the family that was previously all boys. So this is the yellow brick road that takes Cinderella to the ball. It may look like nothing but a swath through the mesquite, but tonight it is the entrance to the magical forest."

He shortened his step to make it easier for her, but she quickly proved she was no stranger to rough ground. "And, darlin', you were at work in the daylight hours when I cleared out the mesquite to make us a fairy-tale road."

Most women, especially those in his past, would have whined from the first step. Not Lizzy. Her body language said that it was an adventure for her, not something to endure until she could get back to the party.

"Sleeping Beauty." She stepped in a rut and lost her grip on his hand.

His arms went around her waist and held her tightly to his chest to keep her from falling. "Yes, you are a beauty and I reckon we could sleep." He could feel her racing heart keeping time with his.

Half her face was darkened by shadows, but moon-light lit the other part. It might take a lifetime, but someday he wanted to be the cowboy that lit up both sides when he kissed her.

She rolled up on her toes and the tip of her tongue moistened her lips. Heavy lashes fanned across her cheeks as her eyes fluttered shut. Arms snaked up around his neck and fingers splayed through the back of his hair. Then his lips were on hers and all the fairy tales in the world couldn't describe the way he felt.

Men weren't supposed to go all tingly and mushy when they kissed a woman. Toby could testify from past experience that cowboys got aroused, loved the chase, and enjoyed kissing a woman. But this business with Lizzy tugged at something inside his heart as well as behind his zipper.

"I believe"—she panted when the kiss ended—"that Sleeping Beauty has been awakened."

"I remember that story now." He wrapped an arm around her waist and took a step. "Does that make me a prince? I always thought I was just an old cowboy."

"Depends on whether it works again." She fell right in beside him. "Oh, no! I see a flame. Is the pasture on fire? I left my phone in my purse." She whipped around to run back toward the house.

He scooped her up in his arms. "It's not a fire. It's part of the surprise."

She wiggled. "Then put me down, Prince Charming, so I can go see it."

Lizzy had been skeptical as well as hungry when they started down the pathway that he'd evidently cleared in the past couple of days. It hadn't been there before and the ground was still rough from where the mesquite had been ripped out of the ground and pushed to one side or the other.

Dates involved going out to dinner, maybe a movie, or dancing at a honky-tonk. Hiking through thick mesquite to a place where firelight flickered in the distance had certainly never been one of her past dates. Excitement replaced skepticism and she was eager to see what he'd planned.

Sure, he would have eventually cleared the trees off the land to make room for pastures and cattle, but he'd done all this especially for her for only one evening. It was enough to render her speechless, and Lizzy Logan hadn't been in that position very often in her lifetime.

A red bandanna appeared out of nowhere. "After we make this turn, you'll be able to see the surprise but I want to keep it secret a little longer. Trust me?"

She nodded and he blindfolded her. Taking both her hands in his, he walked backward and led her. She hadn't hesitated about the blindfold, but now all those stories about that book and movie, *Fifty Shades of Grey*, flashed through her mind. She hadn't read the book or seen the movie, but with all the hoopla in every magazine at the time, it wasn't difficult to imagine what all it involved. If whips or leather came out, she would be nothing but a blur as she made her way back to the house.

"Stand right here," he whispered.

Without sight, all her other senses became heightened. The frogs, crickets, and a lonely old owl joined with a howling coyote. A soft breeze fluttered the mesquite leaves around her, adding a crispy sound to the wild animal concert. There was something else, a crackling sound much too faint to be wood burning.

The aroma of freshly turned earth and Toby's shaving lotion blended together to tease her sense of smell. She inhaled and caught a whiff of something familiar. Citronella. The date involved candles in the middle of a forest of mesquite trees.

She'd never noticed how rough or big his hands were until she couldn't see them anymore. They'd reached out to her when she'd come close to falling. They'd roamed her body on those hot nights they'd shared. But right then, she recognized the intense comfort in knowing they would protect her.

His lips closed on hers and he teased her mouth open with his tongue. She tasted sweet tea and excitement as her knees went more than a little weak. Sometime during the scorching-hot kiss she felt the blindfold disappear, but even after Toby took a step back, she kept her eyes closed.

"Open your eyes," he drawled.

She obeyed and gasped. To most women it would have been nothing more than a cleared patch in the middle of a bunch of small, gnarly trees, but to Lizzy it was enchanting. She stood beneath an archway formed of uprooted branches piled and stuck together, wide enough for two people to walk under if they stayed close together. On the other side a spot had been cleared with the old well in the northeast corner and a patchwork quilt on the other side.

Thick branches covered with green leaves entangled from one tree to the next, forming walls for a room with the sky for a roof. Two candles were on top of the board covering the well. Ten others surrounded the blanket. Throw pillows had been tossed about randomly on the quilt, but right there in the middle of it was a huge picnic basket. She didn't know such things existed outside of romance books and movies.

The work. The planning. The whole ball of wax. This had been done for her.

"This is amazing," she whispered. "It's a perfect first date."

Bless his heart.

His face clearly showed relief, which meant he not only went to a lot of work, he was worried that she would think it was silly or stupid. She took a step forward, put both hands on his chest, and rolled up on her toes. His lips met hers in a soft, sweet kiss that told her how vulnerable he really was. The brass and show of the hottest cowboy in Texas was only surface. The real Toby Dawson was holding her in a clearing with a blanket on the ground.

"Hungry?" he asked when the kiss broke.

"Starving. I hope there's food in that basket."

He smiled and the stars dimmed. "Yes, ma'am. Fried chicken, potato salad, dinner rolls, and fried okra, and over there by the well in a cooler, there is a six-pack of beer iced down."

"I really do feel like Cinderella," she said as her eyes met his.

The flicker of a dozen jar candles reflected his happiness. "I'm so glad that you like it. I wanted to spend time with you, not with the families, not in a café or a bar. Deke bought the candles for me but he doesn't have any idea about this." He picked up her hands and led her to the blanket. "I was afraid it would look like a redneck harem."

"Oh, no! It is an enchanted fairy tale." She kicked off her boots and walked to the middle of the quilt in her bare feet.

He carried the cooler to the edge of the quilt, re-moved his boots, and sat down beside the basket. "Come and sit in front of me."

She eased down and crossed her legs Indian-style, her knees touching his. He opened the basket, drawing out two china plates, flatware, and blue bandannas to use for napkins. Next he took out an aluminum pan full of fried chicken, a bowl of potato salad, and one of fried okra. He leaned forward, cupped her face in his hands, and kissed her on the tip of her nose.

"I've said it before but you really are an amazing woman, Lizzy."

"Right now I'm a hungry woman, Toby."

"And a very honest one."

He brought out two bottles of beer, twisted the cap off the first one, and handed it to her. She took a sip and propped it in the corner of the empty basket. He did the same, setting his right beside hers.

"You like legs?" she asked.

"On you, yes. On a chicken, I prefer wings and breasts."

She picked up both legs with her fingers. "Then we are going to get along just fine."

"Potato salad?" He held the bowl out to her. "I have to admit, this all came from Nadine's. I didn't have time to build an enchanted forest and cook, too. I told her the truth, though."

Lizzy was glad she hadn't taken a bite of food be-cause she would have choked on it. "You didn't?" she gasped.

"Yes, I did. I told her that Allie and Blake were going north for the weekend and that I didn't want to cook. She laughed and said that if Deke was coming over for supper I might not have enough, and she talked me into buying an apple pie for dessert. It wouldn't fit into the basket so it's setting on the top of the well."

"Apple pie is my favorite." Lizzy bit into the fried chicken leg.

In spite of the vow she'd made not to think about Mitch or the times they'd had together, a memory popped into her head. The whole family was gathered around the table and Katy had made a cherry and an apple pie. Lizzy had looked forward to having a piece of that apple pie all morning but then when it was time for dessert, Mitch had said that the pie was too fattening and that they'd both have to watch their desserts or they'd be big as circus clowns. Then he'd thrown an arm around her and had led to the living room to set up a Monopoly game. Looking back it had not been an arm of love but a controlling one.

And here was a man who told her that she was amazing, beautiful, and bought a whole apple pie for them to share. How could she not compare?

"You are pretty quiet. What are you thinking about?" Toby asked her.

It was on the tip of her tongue to say something about apple pie, but in a real relationship, two people had to build a foundation and the first stone in it was honesty. "Do you really want to know or should we talk about our favorite desserts?"

"I want to know," he answered.

She told him, keeping the story straight and the emotion out of her voice. "And I did what my mama says I'm never to do and that's compare two people."

"And?" Toby raised a dark eyebrow.

"And I'm real glad I'm sitting in this wonderful place with you and that I can eat all of that apple pie I want." She smiled and it felt good.

The whole atmosphere, even the howling coyotes and the screeching locusts, had the ring of right to it that evening.

"Me, too," he said. "Ten-question time while we eat. I'll ask one, then you can and we have to answer honestly. I'll go first. What is your favorite food, other than apple pie for dessert?"

"Steak, medium rare. And apple is just my favorite pie. My favorite dessert is Mama's chocolate sheet cake when it's still warm with a scoop of ice cream on the top," she said.

"You can't ask me the same question because my answer will be the same as yours. I love a good beefsteak cooked the same way you do. And I'd never had that chocolate sheet cake until Allie made it, and it's my new favorite dessert."

She scooped up a forkful of potato salad and chewed slowly while she organized her ten questions from least to most important. "Okay, then favorite song?"

"By whom? My favorite two-steppin' song is different than my favorite shower song or my favorite church song. So which one?" he asked.

"All time. Any artist. Any genre?"

"That would be 'I'll Fly Away' because when we sang it with your granny, it lifted my heart. Her face was so content that day, and the way the sun filtered through the window onto your face made you look like an angel," he answered. "And that sounds like a bunch of bullshit, but the song has come back to me several times and I always get a vision of you two. It was like seeing the past and the future right there in the room with me," he answered. "My turn and I'll ask you the same question. What's your favorite song?"

She was glad she had popped three small pieces of okra in her mouth. After his comments, she had trouble thinking about anything other than how sweet and sensitive he was once she'd gotten past that outer tough layer.

"My favorite song is the old one by Garth called 'The Dance,'" she said. "It not only tells the story of an incident but also of life. Every dance we take leads us up to the last one we enjoy before we die, and if we miss one, then we aren't the same people."

"So that means that all our past forms us into who we are today, right?" Toby asked.

"I think it does. The pain and the joys intermingled together," she answered. "Your turn."

"Flowers? What's your favorite flowers?" He picked up the second chicken breast and bit into it.

"Any kind of wildflower, but I'm real partial to those wild roses that grow on the fences and bloom all summer. I'm an outdoor person, Toby. I own and manage

a store, but when my workday is done I like to be outside. Since you are a rough and tough cowboy I won't
ask you about flowers."

"Daffodils," he said quickly. "I love those little yellow flowers that say spring is on the way. Winter is
over and it's time to plant. Time to think of a fall har-
vest. Time for new baby calves to be born. Daffodils
remind me of all that. Your favorite color?"

"Blue, the color of your eyes and the summer sky
after a hard rain when the clouds pass on by and the
sun comes out. Yours?"

"Green, not dark or olive green but the color of new
winter wheat as it comes up through the dirt. Thank you
for saying that about my eyes. I've always thought they
looked a bit out of place with my dark hair. I'm the only
blue-eyed Dawson in the family. Blake's are green and
Jud's are brown. What about your favorite movie?"

She picked up the beer and took a long gulp. "You
promise not to laugh."

"Cross my heart. What is it? *Steel Magnolias* or *Little Mermaid*?"

She shook her head. "How'd you come up with
those two?"

"My sisters-in-law and my mother love the first one.
My nieces like the last one. I've sat through both more
times than I can count on my fingers and toes."

"*Dirty Dancing*," she said quickly.

"I would have never guessed that one."

"It tells a story of never giving up and not letting
anyone put you down," she said.

"I've never seen it. Maybe sometime we'll watch it together?" He stacked all their dirty dishes into a plastic bag and put them inside the basket with the leftovers and then brought the pie to the quilt.

She looked around for plates and he held up two clean spoons.

"We'll eat it right out of the pie pan. My favorite all-time movie is *The Cowboy Way*."

"Haven't seen it."

"That's two date nights, then." He dipped into the middle of the pie and held the spoon out to her.

"Mmmm," she mumbled around the taste of cinnamon and apples. "Nadine does have a way with an apple pie. Let's save the other five questions for another night and stretch out on these pillows when we get done. I love this place, Toby, but you already know that. I could lie on my back and watch the stars for hours."

Toby shoved the basket off to one side and arranged the pillows behind him. "There's going to be another night, then?"

"Darlin', you did too much work here for this to be a one-night-stand place. Next time I'll bring the dinner and the beer."

He had a couple of more bites of the pie and then stretched out on the quilt, his head on the pillows. "You sure it won't get to be old hat and boring? The first time is exciting but after a while ..." He let the sentence hang.

"If it gets boring, we'll know what we have is a flash

in the pan. If it continues to be as exciting as tonight, then we'll know it's genuine." She set the pie inside the basket on top of the leftover fried chicken before following his lead. Back on the quilt, hands laced over her full stomach, head on the pillows, eyes looking straight ahead at the stars.

He reached across the six inches separating them and took her hand in his. Fingers laced together, they watched the sky, each in their own comfort zone of thoughts and memories until a bright, shiny star danced across the sky, leaving a long tail of brilliance behind it.

"A falling star!" she said. "That was the brightest, prettiest one I've ever seen. We get to make a wish."

"One wish that we have to agree on or one each?" He let go of her hand and rolled up on an elbow.

"There was one star so we have to agree." She gazed up into his eyes.

"Then my wish is that this is not a flash in the pan and that it is genuine." He bent enough that his lips met hers in a sweet gentle kiss.

Even that set her hormones into a loud whine begging for more, crying out to her to strip out of all her clothing and be damned to any mosquitoes that braved the citronella to get at her bare-assed skin.

"I think." She rolled to the side so that she was facing him. Now their faces were so close that if she squinted his eyes were out of focus. "That we can agree on that wish."

"Good. Now let me hold you and let's enjoy being together."

No sex? Sleep?

"I loved that night in the back of the truck when you slept in my arms. I've dreamed about you being there all week, and when I wake up and find I'm holding a pillow, I want to kick something." He pulled her close to his side.

With his arm around her and her head resting on his chest, suddenly wild sex didn't seem as important as listening to him talk about his dreams of her. If nothing more came of their relationship, tonight was a fairy tale that she'd tell her granddaughters about someday.

CHAPTER SIXTEEN

Lizzy's nose twitched and she brushed at it without opening her eyes. She didn't want to wake up. Just a few more minutes to enjoy Toby's arms around her, to be curled up inside the curve of his strong body, and to feel the warmth of his breath on her neck as he slept.

She must have been dreaming about something that smelled horrible because her nose felt as if it were frozen into a snarl. She inhaled, expecting to get nothing but a lungful of fresh night air, but the scent left no doubt that there was a skunk in the area. Both eyes flew open and there he was, not three feet from her face, butt toward her as he dug around in the picnic basket.

"Don't move a muscle," Toby whispered.

Her nod was slight but the skunk's head popped up out of the basket and whipped around to glare at her. She stared back, afraid to blink for fear even that movement would scare him and he'd flip that tail up and spray her right in the face. Finally, he went back to enjoying what was left of the apple pie.

Lizzy had never been able to sneeze like a lady. She could give a four-hundred-pound trucker a run for his money when it came to sneezing, and no matter how hard she tried, she'd never been able to hold one inside. With the skunk aiming something worse than a machine gun at her, she did her best for as long as she could.

Then suddenly, she was moving, strong arms around her as Toby rolled her to his other side, picked her up, and ran toward the well. He dropped down behind it and covered as much of her as he could with his body.

And then the smell hit their noses. The skunk had let go and the stink was everywhere. In the grass. On the quilt. All around them in the air. Lizzy grabbed her nose and tried breathing through her nose, but that made her gag.

Toby pulled a white handkerchief from his pocket and handed it to her. "Put it over your nose and hold my hand. We'll leave everything and come back to clean it up later."

Toby buried his nose in the crook of his shirt and led her toward home. "Holy shit, Lizzy, that's the sun coming up. How long did we sleep? You've got to get that smell off you and get to work in a couple of hours. I'd planned on making breakfast for you, but it won't happen now."

"My morning-after getting-lucky breakfast?" she asked.

"No, your morning-after-our-first-date breakfast," he answered. "It was going to be very different than those others. I make a mean crunchy French toast served up with blueberries soaked in wine overnight."

"Can we have it on our morning after our second date?"

"If we don't sleep late and get awakened by a skunk."

When they were halfway back to the house she stopped. "We should go back and throw out all that uneaten food. It will draw all kinds of wild animals."

"I'll take care of all that after I do chores this morning. You've got to get the stink out of your hair and go to work, darlin'," he told her.

"Bet you never said that to a woman before," she said with a smile.

"You are one of a kind." He chuckled.

Lizzy lathered up her whole body with soap three times and washed her hair twice. After two cups of coffee she could still taste the smell of the skunk in her mouth. She'd squirted saline mist up her nose every fifteen minutes, but it wasn't doing much to clear out the eau de skunk from her nostrils.

It didn't matter how she and Toby approached a relationship, something always happened. First it was the bar scene and she'd gotten so drunk that he had to carry her into the house. Then the tornado hit and they were trapped in the cellar until a rescue team arrived. Third was the wreck. And now they had a perfect date right up until the skunk woke them from a dead sleep. Would Mama Fate ever stop punishing them for those three weeks of hot sex?

"If I'm going to have the correction, then I should have the game, right?" she said as she rinsed the soap from her body and the shampoo from her hair one more time. It didn't do a bit of good to sniff anything, not when her nose wouldn't let go of the smell.

"Enough is enough!" She shook her fist at the ceiling.

She stepped out and wrapped a towel around her head. Picking a thick terry robe from the hook on the back of the door and shoving her arm into it, she padded to her bedroom where she dressed for work that Saturday morning. Jeans, untucked shirt, hair in a ponytail that would dry by noon, boots, and the stinky skunk smell still in her nose.

Stormy met her at the door that morning when she opened the shop. Lizzy flipped on the lights, adjusted the thermostat, and bent to pick up the cat, but she hissed and ran back to the laundry basket with her kittens. The cowbell rang before she even got to the counter to see what had Stormy's tail in a twist that morning. Fate wasn't done with Lizzy yet, not when she sent Dora June and Ruby into the store before she even had time to get the cash register opened.

"Good morning. You ladies are out early. What can I do for you?" Lizzy said cheerfully.

Ruby sniffed the air. "Must've been a skunk around here. I'm getting a faint smell of him."

"In summertime they come with the territory," Lizzy said with a straight face.

The cowbell rang again, and all three women turned to see who was coming through the door. Toby flashed his brightest smile and said, "Mornin', ladies. How are y'all this mornin'? If you'll open the back door, there's a string of pickup trucks comin' to town to bring the rest of the supplies from the ranch. Deke's got another bunch of kids workin' for him this weekend, and he offered to haul it all to your new storage place before they got busy tightening fence over at his ranch."

Dora June raised her nose and inhaled. "Skunk smell got stronger."

"Must be blowback from the four I saw on the road. It's mating season so they're all over the place. Flat out opened my sinuses up when I passed them, and poor old Blue, who was riding beside me, whined like a puppy. He hates skunks," Toby said. "Give me the new remote to the door and I'll get it opened up so you can wait on these ladies, Lizzy. And one more thing, I do realize that going with me to haul two donkeys home doesn't sound like much of a Saturday-night date, but…"

"I'd love to," she butted in before he could go on.

"Then I'll pick you up at six. We can have supper in Olney."

Dora June's big bosom expanded, putting a strain on the buttons on her shirt. Her chins looked somewhat like a bullfrog down by the river right before he started croaking. Ruby made a noise with her tongue that sounded like an old hen gathering her chickens before a storm.

If either one or both dropped with a heart attack, would it be a sin to wait ten minutes to call 911?

"If you..." Dora June shook a chubby finger at Lizzy, "had been the woman we all thought you were, Mitch wouldn't have needed to find someone else. It's those demons on the Lucky Penny that's causing you to misbehave, but we're prayin' hard that you overcome them."

Ruby pursed her lips together so tightly it was a miracle that words could get past them, but she managed. "Yes, it is. Never thought I'd see the day that Katy would fly off to that city of pure sin for a weekend, either. Gambling and drinking and who knows what else?"

Lizzy shook her head sympathetically. "It is a cryin' shame, ain't it? She might even get laid while she's there."

Dora June gasped. "Don't you get sassy with me. I don't know why I keep tryin' to set you on the right path."

"It's for Irene's sake. She's lost her mind so we have to step up." Ruby sighed.

"Please step down," Lizzy said.

"What did you say?" Ruby asked.

"I don't need or want your advice. I've made that clear. I'm old enough to make my own decisions and live with the consequences. Y'all need something in my store, you are welcome to come in here and buy it. If you're comin' in to fuss at me, then stay out there on the sidewalk," Lizzy said seriously.

"Well, I never!" Dora June huffed.

Ruby stuck her bony nose into the air. "You can't help some people."

"I'll make a deal with you. When I want advice, I will ask for it," Lizzy said. "But today I don't need or want any, so can I help you with anything from the store?"

They marched out of the store without a backward glance. The cowbell announced their departure at the same time she heard the new garage door sliding up. She left Stormy protecting her kittens from the smell of skunk and went to check on what supplies she had left.

It took the guys fifteen minutes to unload the stock and be on their way to Deke's place. Toby hit the button and the garage door slid into place, then he picked Lizzy up and kissed her long, hot, hard, and passionately.

Panting, giggling, and quivering with desire when he set her feet on the concrete floor, she wasn't sure her knees would support her so she held on to him.

"Wow! Just wow!" she said.

"I know. Ain't life wonderful, even when skunks are involved?" he said, and grinned.

Toby whistled as he drove up to the front of Audrey's Place. Lizzy made him happy, plain and simple. There she was on the porch swing as usual. The night breeze picked up strands of her hair and blew it across her face. It was cute the way she tucked it behind her ear.

She waved, picked up her purse, and didn't give him time to get out of the truck and open the door for her. "What song was playing on the radio? It looked like you knew every word."

"Oh?" he asked.

"You were singing something. I could see your mouth moving with the words," she said, then changed the subject. "At least we're finally rid of the skunk smell. Did you go back out there and take care of the food?"

He leaned over the console separating them and kissed her on the cheek. "I sure did and brought the quilt back to the house. It went through three washings before I put it in the dryer. But I think all the skunk smell is gone. At least all we got was his passing-by aroma and not a full-fledged dose of what could have happened if he raised that tail."

"Hangover. Tornado. Wreck. Skunk. What's going to happen tonight?" she asked.

"Not one thing. It's going to go smooth because we've eaten our toad frog and it's time for us to get good luck on our side from now on." He straightened the truck up and started down the lane.

"Toad frog?" she snarled.

"Ever seen a dog froth at the mouth when they eat a frog?"

She nodded. "That's why I can't imagine eating one."

"My grandpa said that you get up every morning and eat a toad frog and nothing can faze you the rest of the day. I reckon what we've been through is our toad frog and now it's happy sailing from here on in." He turned right at the end of the lane and drove through town.

Lizzy hoped that Toby was right and that Madam Fate was through testing her. She felt as if the old witch had picked her up, set her on a spindly tree limb, and then stood back and hurled rocks at her from a catapult. She'd managed to hang on but enough was enough, especially after the skunk.

Riding on a road that she'd traveled so many times that she knew every single landmark from the church in Elbert where they turned on Highway 79 to the old rotting log at the corner edge of the bridge crossing over the Brazos, things went past in a blur that evening. She didn't remember shifting positions to get the setting sun out of her eyes or the time when Toby adjusted the sun visor to keep it from pouring into the truck cab.

"You are awfully quiet." Toby picked up her hand and held it on top of the console separating them.

"I like that we are comfortable enough with each other that we don't have to fill the space with lots of words," she said.

He squeezed her hand. "Me, too."

Lizzy recognized the place when Toby made a left-hand turn, crossed over a cattle guard and under a big sign welcoming them to the Dickson Ranch. The red

barn's doors were open on both ends with several stalls
on each side of the concrete center aisle. Lizzy had
been in that barn before. She'd ridden one of those
horses when she dated Terry Dickson a couple of years
ago.

A very pregnant woman with red hair must've heard
the vehicle approaching because she left a horse stall
and waved. Toby rolled down the window and stuck
a hand out, but Lizzy let herself out of the truck and
started toward the woman.

"Hey, Lizzy Logan." Melanie Dickson smiled.
"What are you buying donkeys for?"

"Not me," Lizzy said. "The buyer is Toby Dawson
from the Lucky Penny."

"And you are with him?" Melanie's green eyes
widened. "I thought you were about to marry a
preacher."

"That's old history. I didn't know about the baby.
Congratulations." Maybe baby talk would steer the
conversation away from Toby.

"I heard that the ranch over there had sold to some
really sexy cowboys." Her eyes got even bigger and
she didn't blink. "They weren't exaggerating," Melanie
whispered. "I wouldn't blame you for throwing out a
preacher and taking him on."

"It didn't happen like that," Lizzy said.

"Hello," Melanie said. "I'm Melanie Dickson. Terry
isn't here but I've got your donkeys in a couple of
stalls, and I know what the deal was between y'all."

Toby stuck out his hand. "I'm pleased to meet you,

Mrs. Dickson. I've got the check ready right here in my pocket. Could I look at the animals before I give it over to you?"

"Why, sure. Right this way," she answered.

Toby tucked Lizzy's hand inside his own and followed Melanie into the barn. The donkeys were housed in the first two stalls. One was a little plain old gray fellow, and the other one reminded Lizzy of a Dalmatian dog with his multiple black spots. Toby petted both and neither offered to take a chunk out of his hand.

"They look like good stock," he said.

"We probably wouldn't sell them, but we're thinning the herd this summer. The gray one is a real pet, but he can get noisy when he doesn't get breakfast on time. The spotted one is bashful and likes his apple in the evening. He's not real partial to the tart kind, though," Melanie said.

Toby handed her the check and opened the first stall door. "Come on, feller." The donkey lowered his head and followed Toby like a puppy.

"He's got a way with animals," Melanie said. "I bet he's got a way with the women, too? What can you tell me?"

"That the stories are probably right," Lizzy whispered.

The donkey hopped up into the trailer without a bit of a problem, and Toby came back for the second one. That time was a different story. The plain donkey had to be coaxed all the way to the trailer where he sat down and refused to get inside. No sir, he was not going to do one thing but sit there on his butt and bray like he was being slaughtered by coyotes.

Lizzy bit back a giggle.

That scene was symbolic of Toby's life up to that time. The fancy donkey was like the bar bunnies who couldn't wait to go home with Toby, to jump through hoops to do what he wanted and do anything to please the hot cowboy. The plain donkey was Lizzy. She knew who he was, what he was, and worried that what he had been would never change. She was the one sitting on the ground fretting that he could never really stay with someone as plain as Lizzy Logan.

Finally, Toby pulled the donkey's ear straight up and whispered something in it. The little gray feller got to his feet and without another peep, hopped up into the trailer beside the spotted one.

"What did he say?" Melanie asked.

"I'm not sure I want to know. Do they have names?"

Melanie shook her head. "Terry won't let me name them. If I do, then I get attached and cry when he sells them. It's worse since I got pregnant, the weeping that is."

"That's what Allie tells me."

"She's pregnant?"

Lizzy nodded. "And so happy. She thought she couldn't have children."

"I've got to get back over to Dry Creek and catch up on everything."

"Nadine has a café between my store and Mama's.

Come on over and we'll have lunch. I might even get Allie to join us." Lizzy smiled.

"And you'll tell me more about Mr. Sexy out there?" Melanie grinned.

"Never know. Did you hear about the town reunion? It's next week, the Saturday before Independence Day. Some folks call it a big town reunion; others are sayin' it's a festival. You should come over then," Lizzy said.

Melanie laid a hand on Lizzy's shoulder. "I was so glad to move from Dry Creek to Wichita Falls when I was in the seventh grade that I never wanted to see that town again. But lately, I miss the folks, so I just might come over part of the day."

Toby fastened the doors of the cattle trailer and swaggered over to the barn. "Thank you so much. If you're ready, Lizzy, I reckon we'd best get these fellers on home before dark. Thank goodness I've got a couple of apples so they won't hate me for uprooting them too badly."

"I'm ready. Nice seeing you again, Melanie. Let me know if you are coming over for the festival," Lizzy said.

"I sure will." Melanie waved until they were out of sight.

"So you know her?" Toby asked.

"Went to school with her until we were in the seventh grade. Then her folks moved to Wichita Falls. She and Terry have been married about a year," Lizzy answered.

"What are you going to name the new livestock?" Toby asked.

"They're your donkeys, not mine."

"If they were yours what would you name them?"

"Hey, I've got four kittens without names," she reminded him.

"I'll help you name them if you'll help me with the donkeys."

"Do you name all your cows?" she asked.

"No, but that's different. Cattle might stay with me for years but it might go to the sale barn or eventually when we get things running good, we might have our own ranch sale. But the donkeys will be with us until they die, and they can live a long time so they need names." They crossed the river bridge, entered Throckmorton County, and left Young County behind.

"I'll have to think about it. We could each make a list of kitten names and donkey names and choose from it."

"Deal!" he said.

An hour later the donkeys were in the pasture, had been given an apple each, and were checking out their new abode. The spotted one stayed close to the cattle, but the gray one circled the fence line, his ears perking up every time a coyote howled in the distance.

What would she name those critters? Their personalities were so different, but she had no doubt they would protect the herd.

Toby slipped an arm around her waist and drew her close to his side. "Some folks get a dog when they begin a serious relationship. Do you think it says something about us that we got two donkeys?"

Serious relationship?

First her blood ran cold and then it hit a simmering boil. The knee-jerk reaction was to hop over that fence, tear out across the pasture, and not stop until she was behind locked doors at her house. Once that settled, the next thought was that if this was serious, then what the hell were they doing watching a herd of cows and two donkeys when his trailer had a really nice bed?

Toby had studied women. He'd learned from the time he'd had his first sexual experience what it took to make a woman happy. He could read their faces and their body language and knew when they were faking and when they were truly satisfied.

But that night, standing there by an old barbed wire fence with sounds of a late spring night around him, he knew true fear. He'd proven that he and Lizzy could make each other very, very happy. But that was sex, and what he wanted now was to make love to this woman. To figure out what drove two people into a place that they wanted to never leave; that was the goal, and he had no idea where to start.

"Got any beer in that trailer?" she asked.

"The four that we left out at the well are in the fridge. I don't think they smell much like skunk," he answered.

She slipped her hand in his. "Let's go talk baby names and find out."

"Baby names? Are you telling me something?" If any other woman had said that to him, he would have cleared the fence in one leap and been halfway to Muenster before he stopped for breath.

"I've already named Stormy's quadruplets. They are Fefe, Duke, Raylan, and Hoss after mine and Allie's favorite cowboys, past and present. But the twins out there in the pasture need names if we're going to keep them," she said. "I'm not pregnant. I'm on the pill and I told you before I wouldn't do that to you, Toby."

She entered the trailer before him, went straight to the refrigerator, and started pulling things out. "We were going to eat in Olney but we were so wound up talking about the donkeys that we forgot so I'm making omelets. What do you want on yours?"

"All of it." He reached around her and removed two beers, twisted the caps off both, and set hers on the cabinet. "I'll make the toast while you whip up the eggs. I'm sorry that I didn't make the turn and go on into town and get us something to eat."

"No need to be sorry. I know how to cook and omelets are my specialty."

The kitchen area was tiny so all he had to do was take two steps and he was behind her with his hands around her waist. She flipped around, slung her hip against the refrigerator door to shut it, and rolled up on her toes. Her hands cupped his face and then her lips were on his in a steamy kiss.

* * *

Pretty, brilliant sparks danced around the trailer and Lizzy's knees went weak. She leaned into him and the second kiss was even more sensational. Hormones whined. Her heart thumped so hard that her chest hurt. Her hands were clammy and his hands on her back were like fire. She wanted him and nothing was going to fill the aching void but Toby.

He pushed back, questions in his blue eyes as they bored into hers.

"Omelets now or later?" she panted.

"Later than what?" he asked huskily.

"How hungry are you?"

"For what?"

She started unbuttoning his shirt at the top, stopping to admire and touch the soft hair on his chest on the way to the bottom. When she reached the last one, she tugged the tail out from behind his belt, slipped her arms around his body, and laid her cheek against his chest.

"Let's make love and only use words when necessary," she whispered.

"Is that a pickup line?" he asked hoarsely.

"I don't know. I've never said it before but it's what I want to do right now. Is the door shut so Blue can't disturb us?"

Little gold flecks sparkled in her brown eyes. How was it that he'd never noticed that before when they were having sex almost every night?

"You are so beautiful." His tone said that he wanted her to believe him.

With a hop, her legs were suddenly wrapped around his waist, her body pressing against his zipper from the outside that made his erection ache. And yet, he couldn't rush this. It had to be different from the sex they'd had before. Tonight had to be special, and tomorrow morning when she awoke, she had to realize the difference.

Their lips met again. The excitement of their tongues touching, the feel of her body heat, the tightness of her thighs against his side; the heat was hotter than anything he'd ever experienced.

"I've wanted to touch you all evening, but this is only our second official date. Is this the way normal people do this?" He buried his face in her hair and carried her to the bedroom.

"We're not normal, Toby. Face it. You are wild and hot and sexy and I almost married a preacher." The kisses grew in heat from a campfire to a blazing wildfire sweeping across the state, devouring everything in its path.

"A match made in heaven?" He chuckled.

"Probably not heaven but right now you can take me there and we'll check it out." She smiled. "Do I really make you hot?"

"Can't you tell?" he groaned.

"I bet I can get out of my clothes faster than you can," she teased.

It was a tie but they were both breathless when they fell back on the bed. He rolled on his right side and she flipped over on her left one, their faces only inches apart. He ran a hand down her back from her neck to cup her butt cheek.

"I like the way your eyes go all dreamy when you touch me," she said.

"No words," he reminded her.

She nodded and traced his lips with her fingers, letting them roam from there down his chest to his erection. Then suddenly she pushed him backward and flipped over on top of him. In an instant, ready or not, he was inside her and she'd taken over the whole game. They rocked together until she was panting so hard that she could scarcely breathe. He pulled her closer to him and with a fast roll he was on top, and the tempo increased until there was an explosion like he'd never felt before. The look in his eyes said that he was every bit as satisfied as she was. He tried to say her name, but a guttural moan was all he could force from his lungs.

He rolled to the side, taking her with him and when he could speak he said, "Oh, Lizzy, I'm so sorry."

"For what?" she panted.

"That didn't last nearly long enough."

"If it had lasted one more second there wouldn't be anything left of this trailer but ashes and dead bodies." She inched over close enough to cup his face in her hands and kiss him hard and lingering on the lips. "Besides who says it's the only time we'll play tonight. But before round two I will need food."

"And beer." He grinned.

CHAPTER SEVENTEEN

Lizzy opened her eyes slowly, expecting to see the sun coming up through her bedroom window. Sunday meant no alarm clock and she got to sleep in until at least eight o'clock. But that morning, not a foot in front of her, were two big round eyes peeking up over the edge of the bed.

Where was she? How did a dog get in her bedroom?

Then reality washed away the questions. She was in bed with Toby in his trailer, and Blue had every right to be there. It was his home, not hers. Holy blazes! She had never spent the night with a man in her life. There had been the night in the back of Toby's pickup, but that didn't count. It wasn't want-to but necessity, and no sex had been involved.

"Good mornin', beautiful," Toby said.

She turned away from Blue's eyes and perky ears to

find Toby propped on an elbow. His blue eyes fluttered shut and he brushed a soft kiss across her lips.

"I fell asleep," she mumbled.

"I like waking up next to you. Has anyone ever told you that you are downright cute with droopy bedroom eyes and your hair all messy?" He pushed a few strands back away from her face and planted another kiss on her nose.

"I'm not sure I like waking up to Blue's eyes staring at me. Gave me a bit of a startle," she said.

"Where?" He peered over her body and chuckled. "I thought I had his door locked. Guess I didn't. Good morning, Blue. Do you think she's as beautiful as I do?"

"He says the tall blondes that he wakes up with those big eyes are more to his liking," Lizzy teased.

Toby's body went stiff and he swung his legs off the bed, sat up, and reached for his jeans. "For your information, there's never been a woman in this bed with me."

The tone in his voice left no doubt that she'd hit a sore spot. "It's too early for someone to have pissed in your coffee this morning, so what's the matter? Regretting that you didn't wake me up and send me home last night?"

He jerked his jeans up over a fine, firm-looking butt. "No, it's not that. I want a fresh start at something new and real with you, Lizzy. I don't want to talk about the past."

"The past is part of who we both are, Toby." She pulled the sheet up over her naked breasts when she sat up. "You can't erase all those women any more than I can hit a button and delete Mitch."

"But we don't have to talk about either of them, do we?" He pulled a T-shirt over his head. "I've got chores to do. Will you be here when I get back?"

"Do you want me to be here?" she asked. "Before you answer that, you should know something about me. I let Mitch lead me about with an imaginary chain around my neck for more than a year. He told me how to dress, what to eat, and how to spend my time. I won't do that again, Toby. I will speak my mind and be myself. I expect you to be the same. This is new territory for us both, but we won't conquer it by walking on eggshells."

He shut the door to the tiny bathroom without saying a word. She heard water running and the toilet flushing as she found her scattered clothing and dressed. She was facing the bed, back to the bathroom, when he stepped out and wrapped his arms around her waist.

"I'm glad you are here, Lizzy, and you are right. I've been in there fighting with myself. Can we start the morning all over again?"

She whipped around and smiled up at him. "Good morning, you sexy cowboy. I think Blue is hungry. He's sitting in front of the kitchen sink staring at it, waiting for you to open up a can of food for him."

Looking at her in the mirror above the built-in dresser, he smiled back. "He can wait a few minutes while I hug my lovely girlfriend. Last night was amazing. I never realized that there's more to sex than sex until you came along."

"I never realized that there was a difference in sex and making love." She wrapped her arms around him and hugged him tightly. "If you'll get the morning chores done, I'll walk across the pasture to my house. Come on over there when you are finished and we can have breakfast together before church."

"Church?" He frowned.

"Yes, darlin'." She kissed him on the chin. "We need to go pray for a crop failure."

The frown deepened.

"We've sown our wild oats on Saturday night." She wiggled out of his embrace. "And now it's time to do some praying that the seed didn't take."

"I thought you were on birth control," he said.

Lizzy stomped her feet down in her boots and headed for the door. "God works in mysterious ways, and I'm not taking any chances. I'll see you by nine, right?"

"Yes, ma'am. I'll bring a healthy appetite and have my boots shined up and ready to sit on our regular pew in church. Wouldn't want our crops to take root."

She glanced over her shoulder at him. "How do you feel about kids, Toby?"

He leaned against the end of the kitchen cabinets. "Love 'em. Plan on spoilin' Allie and Blake's. Don't know how I feel about any of my own because I never figured on settling down until I met you. What about you?"

"I've always wanted a houseful or at least three," she answered honestly.

"Guess we'll worry with that bridge later on down the road," he said.

"If we ever get to it." She smiled again. "One day at a time."

"Sweet Jesus," he sang the first words to the old song.

Maybe Toby was right.

They managed to slip into the back pew five minutes before church started, which meant Dora June and her righteous friends were already seated. And since they were on the last pew, when the services ended and Truman delivered a lengthy benediction in which he made sure God knew how much he appreciated the service, the community, and every blade of grass that had sprung up that spring, they were the first ones out of the church.

They'd paid their dues and everything was going to be smooth sailing for them from now on. Lizzy's confidence mounted even higher when they made it to a steak house in Wichita Falls and didn't have to wait for a table. That was unheard of on Sunday. The church crowd most usually beat everyone to the best eating places.

Toby threw an arm around Lizzy's shoulders as the waitress led them to a booth. "I told you our luck had changed."

"What are y'all havin' to drink?" The waitress eyed

Toby like he was a five-course dinner and she was really, really hungry.

"Sweet tea." Lizzy didn't like that blast of jealousy that shot through her body, but he was a good-looking cowboy and he did throw off come-hither vibes.

"Same." Toby smiled.

"Appetizers?" she asked.

Why don't you slide in between him and the table and give him a little lap dance. I'll study the menu while you do your thing? Lizzy said to herself. *Why am I letting a waitress get to me? I'm not a jealous person.*

"Appetizers, Lizzy?" Toby asked.

"I'm sorry. I was thinking about food not appetizers, but I would like some fried green tomatoes," she answered quickly.

The waitress's eyes were on the little scar on Toby's cheek. "With our special dip or another dressing?"

"I stabbed him," Lizzy said bluntly. "That's how he got that scar."

"Why? I'm sorry. That's personal. I shouldn't ask that." She blushed.

Why not? You've been undressing him with your eyes for the past three minutes and needed a drooling bib when you got to his belt buckle.

"It's okay." Lizzy laid a hand on the woman's arm. "I was mad at a woman for flirting with him and he tried to take the knife away from me. It was an accident."

"I'll be right back with your drinks and appetizer." She turned so fast that she ran into a bus boy with a tray of dirty glasses and he had to do some fancy foot-work to keep it all from hitting the floor.

"Lying on Sunday?" Toby chuckled. "The preacher will make you deliver the benediction next week as penance."

She picked up the menu. "It was worth it. And our preacher only calls on a woman to pray at the end of the service on Mother's Day."

"Little jealous were you?" he asked.

"Right then I was a whole lot jealous, not a little," she answered honestly.

He pushed the menu to the side and covered her hands with his, his gaze captivating her eyes. The whole world disappeared and they were the only two people in a tiny space with no sound except the beating of their hearts. "I couldn't even see that woman be-cause I have blinders on when you are around, and every single thought in my head is about you." His voice was low, seductive, and mesmerizing. "I've never felt like this before and it scares the hell out of me."

"Me, too, Toby," she whispered.

"It's too hot to last, isn't it?"

"Won't know until we try," she answered.

"It didn't last before."

A presence at their table disturbed their private world. Whatever it was, skunk, tornado, hailstorm, or the waitress bringing their drinks, Lizzy wished they'd vanish into thin air and leave her and Toby alone. She sighed as she looked up at Dora June's condescending expression.

"Well, hello, Lizzy. I had no idea that you knew Toby and Blake before they bought the Lucky Penny. My niece, Lacy, works here and she just now told me how Toby got that scar. I bet he's the real reason you broke up with that dear boy, Mitch, isn't he?" Dora June asked tersely.

So much for the bad luck finally playing out. Madam Fate had only given them a slight reprieve before the big storm hit full force.

"Good morning, Miz Dora June." Toby flashed his brightest smile her way. "Wasn't that church service uplifting this morning? And the hymns were sung with such gusto that I bet the angels in heaven are still smiling. Would you and Truman like to sit with us? I'd be glad to buy your lunch or dinner or whatever you folks call it. In my world, it's always been dinner and supper but I wouldn't want to offend you."

"Hell, no!" Truman said as he joined them. "I wouldn't even sit with Deke today. He probably knows that Lizzy broke up with Mitch because of you. Was she the one who told you about the Lucky Penny?"

Toby smiled. "Deke is our good friend and for your information Lizzy was making a joke when she told the waitress that story. Don't punish Deke because you don't like us."

"Guilty by association," Dora June said.

"We'll take him in anytime. Y'all sure I can't buy you dinner?" Toby asked.

"Come on, Dora June. I don't want folks to see us talking to these people," Truman said.

They left in a huff and Toby chuckled.

"What?" Lizzy asked.

"Small world, isn't it? The waitress is her niece. Reminds me of the lyrics in that old song that says he's everywhere and he's watching you."

"I believe that was Santa Claus, not Dora June." Lizzy pulled her hands free so the waitress could set the fried green tomatoes and sweet tea on the table. "Thank goodness there's only a handful of people in Dry Creek who are hoping that the Lucky Penny fails again. The rest of the folks are really great."

"Ain't that the truth? What is it about four women and Truman who've got a burr up their butts?"

Lizzy smiled. "Five out of a whole town isn't a bad number. I imagine they're upset because Truman wanted to buy the ranch and waited too long."

"Waited?" Toby dipped a fried green tomato into the sauce and popped it in his mouth.

"Folks didn't think it would ever sell with the reputation it has, so those who were interested sat back and waited for the price to hit rock bottom. Y'all swooped in before that happened and bought it. Truman was most likely the top dog on that list and now he thinks if he can make life miserable for y'all, then you'll leave and he'll buy it with all y'all's improvements already made on it."

"Is that rumor or truth?"

"Neither. It's my own theory. He wasn't ever a happy person, but he turned really sour when he found out the Lucky Penny had sold to y'all. He's fighting a losing battle, Toby. Folks love you and Blake and what you are doing to the ranch."

"Truman nor his posse of self-righteous women are going to run us off." Toby picked up a slice of fried tomato, dipped it in the sauce, and fed it to her.

"Good. I don't want you to leave."

CHAPTER EIGHTEEN

Dark clouds had begun to gather when they left the restaurant. Lightning streaked through the sky in long spiky strips with thunder following on its heels. The wind whipped around from the south to the north and blasted and shook the tree limbs as the temperature dropped ten degrees in as many minutes. The first big drops of rain sizzled against the hot sidewalk as Lizzy and Toby ran from the truck to the care facility where her grandmother lived.

"Looks like we beat it," Toby said as they rushed inside.

She shook the rainwater from her dark brown knee-length skirt. "Just when I was beginning to think that our luck had run out."

Toby ran a hand over her shoulders, brushing the few drops that had settled on her light tan lacy blouse.

"Have I told you that you look beautiful in shades of brown? Or that I'm real partial to lace?"

"Well, well, well! Look what I found, Laney." A tall blonde with steely blue eyes glued herself to Toby and locked lips with him in a kiss that lasted only three days short of eternity.

"I'll be damned. I thought you went back to the hinterlands. We ain't seen you or Deke since last winter." Another one, just like the one with her body still stuck to Toby's, rounded the corner of the hallway. God must have surely had a sense of humor when he made two just alike.

"Hey, did I hear someone call my name?" Deke stepped in out of the rain and removed his cowboy hat.

"It's a party!" The second woman clapped her hands.

Toby wiped a hand across his lips. "Laney and Lisa, please meet my girlfriend, Lizzy Logan."

Deke poked her on the arm. "Nobody will ever know, Lizzy. You're not going to hold him back are you?"

What in the hell was happening?

It was pretty evident that Deke and Toby knew those two bimbos dressed in shorts so tight that nothing was left to the imagination. Lizzy's eyes traveled upward from the hooker shorts to halter tops that showed cute little belly button rings with a pink arrow pointing downward. They had to be twins and they were six feet tall in those bright red high-heeled shoes. So this was his type—the women that he partied with. No wonder he had second thoughts about a mousey woman with dirty blond hair and brown eyes.

"Not today, Deke," Toby said.

Deke already had an arm around Lisa. "Why not? I thought I'd drop by to see Irene since Katy is gone this weekend, but I can come back anytime. Let's go grab a six-pack."

Laney ran a forefinger down Toby's jawline. "We'll take you to our house. It's not far from here and we can pick up where we left off last time."

Toby stepped away from Laney and tucked Lizzy's arm into his, patting her hand the whole time. "Lizzy and I are going to see her grandmother. Y'all have a wonderful time and I'll see you tomorrow, Deke."

"You ain't no fun at all," Laney said with a pout.

"You were at one time. I remember that morning-after breakfast. Whoa! You look familiar." Lisa eyed Lizzy like she was checking her for head lice or warts. "She looks like that woman that had Blake buffaloed. Remember that morning, Laney, when the grand-mother showed up wearing that crazy outfit?"

"I'm her sister," Lizzy said. "And she and Blake are married."

"Well, shit! I wanted a chance at that cowboy." Lisa sighed.

Laney giggled. "It was one wild weekend, wasn't it? So Deke, you want to go home with us?"

"Naw, if Toby isn't going, I'll take a rain check. Y'all have fun. Y'all visitin' someone here?" Deke asked.

Lizzy could have cut his tongue out with a rusty butter knife. She wanted to get away from the twins, not stand there and catch up with them.

"Our great aunt Myrtle is in here and it was our Sunday to drop by. Thank God she was sleeping so we didn't have to stay. We came. We saw. We are going shopping if we can't talk you two handsome cowboys into going home with us," Lisa said.

"Didn't you hear him? I am his girlfriend," Lizzy finally said.

"Who cares? You can come along, too, and we'll make it an orgy." Laney winked.

"What did you mean, Deke? When you first came in from the rain you said this woman would hold him to something? What's going on here?" Lisa asked.

"Nothing," Deke answered. "I reckon we'd better get on down the hall to see Lizzy's granny."

"If you change your mind anytime between now and midnight." A pen appeared out of nowhere and Laney wrote on Deke's hand. "That is my cell number and we are always ready to party with you cowboys. Give me an hour after you call and I'll be sure the ingredients are in the house for tomorrow morning's breakfast."

Lisa pushed a button above the light switch and an attendant came around the corner to poke in the exit code for that day. The fact that they could run through the rain on slick concrete in those high-heeled shoes left Lizzy completely speechless.

"I'm sorry," Toby said.

"For what? Y'all ain't really dating. Lizzy is a good sport and no one would have even known…Oh. My. God!" Deke slumped down into an overstuffed chair in the lobby. "Pretend is over and you are dating, aren't you? That's the only thing that would keep you from taking those two up on an afternoon of fun and games."

"Yes, we are," Toby said.

"And if you tell anyone, especially Allie, I will make sure they never find your body or bones," Lizzy said.

"Dammit! I lost a good bar buddy." Deke stood up, shoulders slumped in a grown-man pout. "Let's go see your granny, Lizzy. You know she wouldn't like this idea one bit. She wasn't a bit happy with Allie for marryin' Blake."

"I'm dating him, not marrying him," Lizzy said.

Black garbage sacks were stacked up at the foot of Irene's bed. She was sitting in the middle of a bare mattress encased in a plastic protective cover. "It's about damn time y'all got here. I called the moving company hours ago. You just can't get good help this day and age. I swear to God, I'd send you on your way if I didn't need you to take me home so bad."

"Granny, I'm Lizzy, not the moving company." Lizzy moved to the side of the bed and tried to hug her grandmother.

"Don't you touch me, woman. I'll scream and the prison guards will come and throw you in a dungeon," Irene yelled. "You are here to take me home, not hugging me and trying to talk me into staying. I've served my time for falling in love with Walter and it's time to get out of this prison."

"Granny, let's visit for a little while first." Lizzy bit her lip to keep from weeping. Life was so unfair. Her grandmother had been such a force before the dementia. Walter had lived on the Lucky Penny more than thirty years ago, and evidently she'd fallen in love with him. Whether it went beyond a crush and flirtation, no one knew. But today her granny thought she'd been sentenced to prison for whatever happened.

"Take me home, please." Irene's blank eyes captured Lizzy's as she begged.

"Lizzy, it's not possible," Deke whispered.

"Only for a day or two so she won't feel like this," Lizzy said softly.

"Talk where I can hear you," Irene demanded.

"Let's talk about this outside," Toby said.

"Irene, do you remember me?" Deke pulled up a chair and sat down beside the bed. "I'm Deke. I help Allie with her construction jobs and own a little spread in Dry Creek and do some rodeo touring. Remember?"

Toby looped his arm through Lizzy's and led her out into the hallway.

"Hell, no, I have never met any of you. You are here to take me home. Where is Dry Creek? I live at Audrey's Place," Irene said.

Tears streamed down Lizzy's face and Toby held her close to his chest. "Your mama told you that this happens. Is this the first time you've seen it?"

She nodded.

"Lizzy, you can't take her home. She doesn't even know where home is. Tomorrow she won't even remember this," Toby said.

Toby was only trying to console her, but something rebelled right there in the hallway outside her grandmother's room. Maybe it was the flirty waitress or those two hussies who'd met them in the lobby. Or the fact that the brazen twins made her feel so dowdy and ugly. But something triggered a bomb in her heart and it exploded.

"Don't tell me what I can or cannot do with my own grandmother." She pushed away from him and folded her arms over her chest. "You can't begin to understand how helpless I feel. She took care of me. She wiped my nose when I had a cold. She cooked for me, cleaned my room so I wouldn't get in trouble, and I can't do a thing for her. She wants to go home, Toby."

The light above her grandmother's door flashed on and two nurses jogged down the hall. They entered the room with Lizzy and Toby right behind them. Deke was in the corner with his hands up like a villain in an old western movie. Irene had made a gun out of her thumb and forefinger and had it pointed right at his crotch.

"Look what he's done to my room. He's trying to kidnap me. He even took the sheets off my bed." Irene holstered her imaginary pistol and looked past Lizzy at Toby. "He was with him. They were going to rob me."

"You two get on out of here and we'll deal with you

later," the older nurse said with authority in her voice. "You'll probably do jail time over this. What about this young lady? Was she in on it? Who put all your stuff in these bags, Miz Irene?"

"No, they did it all. She's my granddaughter, Allie." Irene sat down in a rocker and frowned. "Or is it Fiona. Yes, this one is Fiona. I haven't seen her in ten years and she looks like her sister. I'll sit right here while y'all put all my stuff away. Fiona, you make up that bed so I can have a nap."

"We'll take care of it," the nurse said.

Irene cocked her head to one side and then the lights went out. She'd been frantic one second and now the muscles in her face were slack and her eyes dull. "Who are all you people?"

"We are the cleaning crew. We'll have everything put to rights in just a few minutes," the older lady said.

"I wanted to take her home for a couple of days," Lizzy whispered.

The younger one shook her head. "Not a good idea."

Irene stared blankly out the window, a smile tickling the corners of her mouth. "When you girls get this room in order, you should go out there and hoe the weeds from the garden."

"Yes, ma'am, we will get right on that," the nurse said.

"Who are you, again? And why aren't you helping taking care of this mess you made?" Irene looked straight at Lizzy and the smile disappeared.

"She's our supervisor," the younger nurse answered.

"I see. I'm sleepy. You can go now. You trained these two pretty good," Irene told her.

"Thank you." Lizzy bit back the tears as she left the room.

Deke and Toby were in the lobby, sitting on the sofa and talking so low she couldn't hear them. Could it be they were regretting not going with those women? All the anger inside her at not being able to do a blessed thing rose to the top, and she marched right up to Deke and held out her hand.

"What?" he asked.

"Give me your truck keys. I'm going home. You can ride back to Dry Creek with Toby or the two of you can do what you wanted to do all along."

"And what did we want to do?" Toby asked.

"Just go. Have a great time with the booty bitches. I'll leave the keys under the floor mat so you don't even have to come in the house," she said.

Deke handed her the keys and she nodded toward a nurse's aide who rushed over and hit the code to let her out. It was like a jail. Granny couldn't come and go when she wanted. The windows were locked so she couldn't raise them to get a breath of fresh air. No wonder she was losing the last thread of her memories and life.

By the time Lizzy had adjusted the driver's seat to fit her small frame, tears streamed down her face. One look in the rearview let her know she was a complete mess with long streaks of dark mascara and light blue eyeliner running down her cheeks and dripping onto the ecru lace top. It was probably ruined but Lizzy didn't give a damn. At least she could walk out of that place and inhale the wonderful aroma of the air after a summer rain.

She was still sniffling when she pulled into the driveway at Audrey's Place. Sitting in the truck with the window rolled down, she imagined the original ladies who lived in the house sprawled out on the porch steps with fans. The madam of those women would be her ancestor.

Granny's great-grandmother had built the place for a hotel with her husband. Then he died and the Depression hit and the rest was history. When she shut down the brothel, she married the local deputy and they had a daughter who lived in the house until she died. It had been passed down from one generation to the next and someday Lizzy might inherit it.

Her mind and heart were at war with each other as her thoughts went from one subject to another. She could have been like those two women in the nursing home if Audrey's Place had been a brothel for a few more generations, so what right did she have to judge them? They'd had a good time with Deke and Toby in the past. So much for forgetting the past like she'd preached about to Toby.

Lizzy groaned when she remembered where she'd heard those two bimbos' names. They'd been the cause of a major fight between Allie and Blake. Allie had gone over to the Lucky Penny to work and found those two women in the house.

"But there it is. Poor old gals didn't have any idea that the playboy they'd had so much fun with was trying to force himself up out of the mold," she said.

She got out of the truck and put the keys under the mat, walked up on the porch, and sat down in the swing. Five minutes later the sound of a truck engine got louder and louder until finally it was sitting in her front yard.

Both doors opened. Deke waved, went to his vehicle, and drove down the lane. Toby leaned against the fender of Blake's truck. Arms folded tightly across that broad expanse of chest, he stared out across the pasture and didn't even glance toward the porch. That he was angry was an understatement. That he had a right to be madder than a wet hen after a tornado hit was a guaranteed fact.

She'd had no right to turn on him in her fit of anger. Even less to demand that Deke hand over the keys to his truck so she could drive home alone. No doubt, he was trying to form the words to tell her to go straight to hell because he didn't need to be in a relationship with anyone as immature as Lizzy Logan.

Planting her feet on the porch, she inhaled deeply and stopped. This was not Toby's fault and he deserved an apology. The longest journey she'd ever made in her life was from the front porch, across the yard, and to the big black truck. Toby drew her to him like a magnet with his clear blue eyes.

With her eyes locked with his, she stopped three feet away. "I'm sorry. None of what happened today was your fault. I was upset about my grandmother, and I took it all out on you and that was unfair."

He opened his arms and she walked into them. "Deke says that a fight doesn't mean that the relationship is over."

"I hope not." She listened to his heartbeat. It represented something steady, true, and dependable.

"Then we are good?" he asked.

She nodded. "Yes, we are."

He ran his knuckles down her jawline and tipped her face up. She barely had time to moisten her lips before his mouth closed over hers. The kiss was different from any they'd shared before. Words could never describe the raw hunger in it. She leaned into it, losing her heart and soul to him.

"After that kiss," he said when he drew back, "this is about as unromantic as anything can be. But would you like to go with me to do chores and then we could fire up the grill and make some burgers?"

He could have asked her to go face off with the skunk again and she would have agreed. "Yes," she said. "But I do need to go inside and change clothes."

"I'll be waiting on the swing." He smiled.

That simple smile said they'd taken another baby step in their relationship.

CHAPTER NINETEEN

Lizzy stripped out of her Sunday best and tossed it on the rocking chair. She pulled a faded army green tank top from the clean laundry basket and jerked it down over her head. When she opened the closet door to find a pair of faded jeans, she caught sight of her reflection and moaned.

White cotton panties looked downright dowdy.

She opened her underwear drawer to find another dozen pair of soft white hip huggers mixed up with bras and a slip that she hadn't worn in years. After she'd tossed every one of them out one by one into the clean laundry basket she found one pair of silky bikini panties hiding in the back of the drawer. They were hot pink with black lace trim, and she had no idea how they got there or if they even belonged to her. Maybe Fiona had left them behind when she moved away from Dry Creek and Allie put them there as a joke. It didn't matter where, what, or who. They were a helluva lot better than white cotton.

It was an important night that warranted something more than plain panties. She'd never had makeup sex before and she wanted it to be special. She removed her underpants and pulled on the sexier ones.

She flipped her hair up into a ponytail and sprayed a bit of perfume on her wrists. Her heart raced as she made her way down the stairs and out onto the porch. What if he wasn't there? What if he changed his mind? What if that kiss had not affected him like it did her?

Her fears and questions disappeared when he smiled at her from the swing. "You should model for country magazines."

"You are full of shit, Toby Dawson."

"Not me, darlin'. I'm speakin' the pure unadulterated truth here. Put you up next to a brand-new John Deere tractor in an advertisement and I bet the sales for that month would triple. You ready to go check on cows and then do some grillin'?" He settled his hat on his head and crooked his arm.

She slipped hers through it and was only slightly amazed at the quiver in her hormones. It was Toby Dawson, for God's sake! If she didn't feel a little something, it would mean she had died and this was a dream.

* * *

At dusk they were sitting in two old green folding lawn chairs behind the trailer. Blue had taken up the space between them, content if either or both of them scratched his ears every few minutes.

Toby was in the process of moving the hot dogs and burgers from the grill to a platter when Deke rounded the end of the trailer. He pulled a third chair along behind him, popped it open, and sat down with a sigh.

"We're okay, Deke," Toby said.

"I know that. If you weren't you wouldn't be sitting here making eyes at each other," he answered.

"Then what's your problem?" Toby asked.

"I've got the opportunity of a lifetime right in front of me and I can't do it unless I sell my ranch," he said. "Don't suppose you want to buy it do you?"

"No!" Lizzy said so loud that Blue yipped and scampered up under the trailer. "You can't sell out and move. Allie would be devastated and so would I. You are the pesky brother we never had."

"I didn't say anything about leaving. The ranch across the road is going up for sale in sixty days. The one that belongs to my cousin, Lake, and his wife, Gloria. He should have realized that she was a city girl when he married her, but then he never much liked ranchin', either." Deke eyed the grill. "I hope you made enough for an extra mouth at the table tonight. I'm hungry."

"Always," Toby said. "Keep tellin' us about this big opportunity."

"I've always wanted that ranch, but my grandparents

left that to him and the one I have to me. He's let it run down in the past five years so I could buy it for what I could get out of mine if I could find a buyer in sixty days," Deke answered.

"Let's take this food inside so we don't have to fight the ants and flies for it." Toby closed the lid to the grill and picked up the platter. He led the way and Lizzy and Deke followed him.

Lizzy set about getting the rest of the food out of the refrigerator and the cabinets while Toby filled three glasses with ice and sweet tea. "Why would you buy a rundown ranch when yours is in good condition?"

"It's the place that actually belonged to my grandparents. It's got more land than mine, and I could run more cattle and I've always wanted to have rodeo stock. I could start small with only a few wild bulls and a half dozen good broncs and build up from there. I'm never going to be a world-class rider on either one, but if I had some good stock I could enjoy the rodeos and make some money with it right up until I was too damned old to get around without a walker," he said.

Toby motioned for Deke to make himself a burger or a hot dog. "I'd love to buy it since it adjoins this ranch, but we're stretched as thin as we can go. If it was five years down the road, I'd snap it up in a minute."

"So exactly how big is your spread? I don't think I ever asked." Lizzy set about making a hot dog with chili, cheese, mustard, and relish. She would have loved to have a big spoonful of chopped onions on it, but those low-riding bikini underpants reminded her that there could be something special later on that evening. And onions should not be a part of it. Still when Deke spread a full inch-thick layer of onions on his burger, she envied him.

"It's a section of land. Butts right up to the Lucky Penny, acre for acre. Runs from the road back as far as this place. Guess I'll fix up a flyer and put it in your store and down at your mama's place. If it's meant to be, then it will sell. If not, then someone else will get the one I've always wanted." Deke bit into the burger. "Man, this is good. I'm glad I came over here."

Lizzy's mind ran in circles as she ate her hot dog. What with Fiona divorced and barely getting by, maybe she could talk her into moving back to Dry Creek. Fiona could be the one who inherited Audrey's Place and kept it in the family name. True, Deke's ranch was not built around the old well, but it already had a house on it and lots of property. If Lizzy couldn't find time to run cattle, she could lease it back to Deke or even to Toby.

That is the most asinine thing you've ever let play out in your head. Think about makeup sex. Think about anything but buying a damn ranch that will make you old before your time. You are a feed store woman, not a ranchin' woman.

"Hush!" she said.

"Which one of us," Toby asked.

"She's fighting with voices in her head. I know these Logan women. I only hope they don't end up like

Granny Irene. So who are you thinkin' might be interested in my place?" Deke talked between bites.

"I heard that Dora June and Truman's oldest daughter was hunting a place," Lizzy answered.

"Hell, no! I wouldn't put that hussy next to my worst enemy. She's just like her mama and they'd both be stickin' their noses in where it don't belong over here on the Lucky Penny," Deke said tersely. "It's damn sure not for sale to them."

"Bring your flyer into the store tomorrow and we'll see what happens," she said.

"Okay." He sighed.

There was something about a pouting friend, be it male or female, that put Lizzy into her fix-it mode. Middle children were doomed to be blessed with that problem and it couldn't be helped.

"It'll sell," she said.

"From your lips to a buyer's ears."

"Trouble is that no one wants to buy something right next to the Lucky Penny, right?" Toby asked.

"There is that and the fact that Dry Creek might have a café and a school and there's a possibility of a day care place and a beauty shop, but there's not much more here to draw new folks. Thanks for supper. What time do Allie and Blake get home?"

"Probably in the next thirty minutes. He texted me a little while ago," Toby answered.

Well, crap! She'd worn those damn uncomfortable silk underpants that kept crawling up her butt all evening for nothing. Allie would want to talk about the trip. Blake would drag Toby off to discuss cows and hay and clearing more land for the cows he'd seen in Muenster. And there would be no makeup sex.

Unless you do some manipulating in a hurry. Surely to God you picked up a few lessons from Mitch in that area.

"I've got to get home. I should be there when Mama arrives so she can talk about her trip," Lizzy said.

"I'm going to wait over at the house for Blake and Allie," Deke said. "Maybe Blake has a friend down in Muenster who's interested in starting small and building up."

"I don't think so, but you can wait. I'll take Lizzy home and be back after a while," Toby said.

Like a gentleman, Toby walked her to the door.

Like a descendent of a hooker, Lizzy took his hand after the good night kiss and led him straight up the stairs.

"I thought your mother was coming home soon," he whispered.

"I didn't say that. I said I should be here when she arrives, but their flight doesn't get in until after eleven tonight and then it will be another couple of hours before they get home. I won't see her until breakfast." She smiled over her shoulder at him. "But I will listen to her talk about her trip then, and all day tomorrow she will pop in and out of the store and tell me tidbits."

"You are a player," he said, and grinned.

She swung open her bedroom door and led him inside. "I do not pretend that I'm a neat person, but this room is probably at its best right now."

"I'm not here to pass judgment on your housekeeping." He turned her slowly and placed her arms around his neck. "I've heard that makeup sex is pretty awesome."

"I wouldn't know from experience but I've heard the same thing." She tiptoed and kissed him. Sparks flashed around the room, bouncing off the walls and landing on the floor, reminding her of Fourth of July fireworks. When she broke the kiss she was already breathless.

"Really, no makeup sex in your history book?" He backed her up several feet, sat down in the rocking chair, and pulled her onto his lap.

The next kiss was even hotter. Maybe it was because he ran his hands up under her tank top. Skin on skin. Blistering steam. Melting hormones whining for more. Mind-blowing kisses.

"No makeup sex in my history book," she muttered. "Yours?"

He bent his head to nuzzle the inside of her neck. "Not a single time. If you don't get involved, you don't break up."

Lord, why had no one ever kissed her on that sensitive part of her neck before? Every nerve in her body was singing in anticipation. Every hormone was gearing up for one hot cowboy night.

"How is it that you never fought with Mitch?" he asked.

She didn't want to talk about Mitch, think about him, or hear his name. Not when Toby had unfastened her bra and now had one of her breasts cupped in his hand.

"We never fought. I let him have his way every time," she groaned. "God, Toby, I don't want to talk about him when every inch of my body is crying your name."

"Want to talk about Laney or Lisa or the girl at the café?" he asked.

"Hush!" She pulled his T-shirt up over his head and ran her fingers through the soft hair on his chest. "I could sleep on this every night for the rest of my life."

"I could let you." He stood up.

She wrapped her legs around his body and he carried her to the bed, but she wiggled out of his embrace before he could put her head on the pillow. In an instant she'd shimmied out of all her clothes and stood before him wearing nothing but her brightest smile.

"I liked the white panties better," he said.

"Oh?" she asked.

"They are you. Those aren't." He pointed at the bikini underwear on the floor. "Don't be something you aren't."

"You, either," she answered.

He shucked out of his jeans and boots, leaving them in the same pile as her things. "Which means?"

"You are more than a one-night-stand cowboy."

He smiled as he picked up her naked body and fell

onto the bed with her in his arms. "You really see that in me?"

"That and so much more," she said breathlessly as she pulled his face to hers.

She could feel the steel hard erection against her belly as his hands explored her body, and his lips scarcely finished a kiss before another began. Every nerve in her body stood at attention, ready to be touched, to be satisfied, to feel his hands touching and exploring. Her fingertips were so sensitive that every part of his body she touched sent shock waves through her own nervous system.

Did he get the same thing when he touched her? Was that what made his blue eyes go all dreamy and soft?

The questions faded quickly because she couldn't think of anything but touching him more, feeling his muscles ripple and then tense at her touch, his erection throb against her bare skin as he ached to be inside her.

"Please take me," she begged. "I'm going to explode any minute."

She wrapped her legs around him as he kissed her one more time, and then with a firm thrust they began to rock in unison. When they reached the very top of the climax together, she couldn't even say his name because she had no more breath in her lungs.

"Oh. My. God," he murmured as it all ended in a crescendo complete with beautiful sparks and all the bells and whistles of fantastic makeup sex.

Five full minutes later he propped up on an elbow and kissed the tip of her nose. "Can we fight again tomorrow?"

She smiled up at him. "I was thinking of starting an argument right now."

CHAPTER TWENTY

Katy breezed into the feed shop, looking happier than Lizzy had seen her in years. Over breakfast, she'd given Lizzy a general play-by-play of her weekend. Then she'd called every half hour all morning as she remembered details.

"I put a sign on the door and thought you could do the same. Nadine has chicken fried steaks on her blue plate special today," Katy said.

"Sounds good to me." Lizzy picked up a sign with a ragged edge from taping it to the window so often. In her handwriting it said, *Gone to Lunch. Be Back at 1:00.*

"Were you bored to tears all weekend or did you and Toby go out?" The wooden sidewalk sounded hollow beneath Katy's cowboy boots. "I've been so wound up in my story and good time, I haven't let you talk."

"We had a nice dinner on Friday." Lizzy wasn't ready to share the story of the well and the skunk. "Then on Saturday after work, we went up to Olney to get two donkeys that he bought. Do you remember Melanie Robinson?"

"Name sounds familiar. Didn't her parents live here for a little while?" Katy went into Nadine's with Lizzy right behind her. She located an empty table in the back corner and made her way to it.

"They left when Melanie and I were pretty young. She's married to Terry Dickson and that's where we went to get the donkeys. She says she might come over here for the festival." Lizzy pulled out a chair and sat down.

"Hey, you two. Y'all want the special?" Sharlene asked.

"Yes." Katy nodded. "With two sweet teas."

"Right on it. And Katy, any time you need me to run the store, just holler. I enjoyed it a lot."

"I'll remember that and might be calling on you pretty often."

Sharlene gave her a thumbs-up sign and headed back to the kitchen to give Nadine the order.

"And yesterday?" Katy asked.

"What about yesterday?" Lizzy frowned.

"What did y'all do yesterday?"

"Church. Dinner. To see Granny where we had a big fight and I drove Deke's truck home and then we made up," Lizzy said.

"That sounds like real dating, not fake."

Lizzy could feel her mother's eyes boring into Lizzy, but she wasn't about to look up from the menu. Even though she'd already given Sharlene her order, it gave her something to stare at. From youth, she'd figured out that if Katy or Granny ever looked into her eyes, they could see all the way to her soul and knew everything she'd done.

"So?" Katy pressed.

"It was a real fight. I wanted to bring Granny home. She had shoved everything she owns into black garbage bags and she thought we were the moving people. She didn't even know where Dry Creek was but she wanted to move home. She thought she was in jail. Toby said I couldn't do that and we had words about it." That much was solid truth so she could glance away from the menu and into her mother's eyes.

"Lizzy, we talked about this before we moved her there. The doctor warned us that things like this would happen and we'd have to stay strong," Katy said.

"But she was so pitiful, Mama. I wanted to protect her like she did us girls when we were little. It's not fair that life dealt this to her. She won't even know Allie's baby, and the times when she is lucid are getting fewer and farther between."

Katy laid a hand on Lizzy's. "I know that but this is best for her, not us. What if she ran away in the night and couldn't find her way back to the house? She could die out in the weather, summer or winter. Did you talk things out with Toby?"

"Yes. He grilled some burgers and hot dogs and we

had supper together with Deke who is in the market for a buyer for his ranch. He wants to sell his and buy the place that his cousin owns across the road." Lizzy gave herself a mental pat on the back for changing the subject.

"It's better property, has two good spring-fed ponds on it, and the house is in better repair. Don't know anyone who wants to buy right now, but he could put up a flyer in my store and in yours, maybe run an ad in the newspaper in Wichita Falls. Trouble is…" Katy paused.

Lizzy pulled her hand free so Sharlene could set two tea glasses on the table.

"I've given up on taking Toby away from you. Now I'm waiting on Jud. I hear he's the lucky cowboy, so I'm going to change my techniques and take a lesson from your playbook and Allie's of course. You have to sneak upon a Dawson cowboy's blind side and I'm going to come off as the sweet little woman who owns and operates a day care center," Sharlene whispered.

"Well, thank you for that. I wouldn't stand a chance if you were serious about Toby." Lizzy smiled.

"No, you would not," Sharlene said seriously. "Your steaks are nearly done. Nadine don't cook nothing ahead of time. Might make it easier to throw it in the microwave to reheat, but she says it softens the crispy outside. Y'all hear that Deke is lookin' for a buyer for his place?"

"We did. I'm surprised that you haven't gone after Deke," Lizzy said.

Sharlene giggled. "Honey, that boy is fun for a night

or two, but it'll take someone hotter'n me to run him to ground and I'm pretty damn spicy. Far as the ranch goes…" She lowered her voice. "He might as well wish in one hand and spit in the other. Nobody in town can afford to buy a ranch but Truman. He might buy it, and then if the Lucky Penny fails again he could swoop in and get it for a song and have a nice big place. But if the Lucky Penny doesn't fail, then there he'd be with a section of land in the middle of two places he can't stand. You know he and Herman Hudson are on the outs, don't you? I hear the bell, which means your dinner is ready. Be back in a second."

"She put it about right," Lizzy said.

"Toby and Blake don't want to make the Lucky Penny another section bigger?" Katy asked.

Sharlene set the plates in front of them. "I heard Toby would love to have the place, but the Dawsons have tied up all their money in the Lucky Penny. Of course, that's fodder for the gossip mill. Folks are saying that if they don't have the capital to keep things going at least five years that they'll throw up their hands and move within a year. Truman is just waiting for his turn to latch on to it and yell 'I told you so.' Oh, crap, there's Dora June and Ruby. Don't worry, I'll head them off at the pass and make them sit somewhere else."

"Now tell me more about your trip. I thought you might come home saying that you were sick of Janie and Trudy and you were never going anywhere with them again," Lizzy said.

Katy picked up her knife and fork, cut into the steak, and popped a bite into her mouth. "Not in the least," she said when she'd swallowed and taken a drink of her tea. "We're planning a trip to Florida after Thanksgiving if I can find someone to mind the store. I wish I had the nerve to move to Wichita Falls to be closer to them and your grandmother, both. But as long as I have a store to run, it will have to be a retirement dream."

Deke was leaning on the door to the feed store when Lizzy returned. He held up a flyer but his expression didn't have much hope.

"Come on in." Lizzy stuck the key in the lock and gave it a twist. "Let's talk about this deal before you put up the flyer."

Deke flipped on the lights and stopped to pet Stormy when she came to meet them. "Why? Do you have someone who is interested in buying my place?"

"I do but they need a couple of days to think about it. Think you could hold off that long?" she asked.

He picked up the cat and held her close to his chest. "Darlin', Lizzy, you've given me some light on a moonless midnight."

"Don't get too excited. They don't know for sure but they did want a few days to think things through. It's a big decision." She picked up the little black kitten from the basket. "Oh, look, Deke, his eyes are open. The other three have all been open for a couple of days."

"It's an omen, Lizzy. His eyes are open so my potential buyers will come at this with an open mind. They won't care if the ranch is in Dry Creek or right next door to the Lucky Penny." Deke set Stormy on the floor and hopped up to sit on the counter. "I've told everyone I could get to stand still about this, Lizzy. I suppose it's all right to say that I have a prospect and that I'm holding off for a few days until they make up their minds."

"I don't see why not. That might even help if there are others who are sitting on the fence about it," she said. "So how quick can you be moved if it does sell?"

"Three days. My cousin and his wife are champing at the bit to get moved to Dallas. He's going to be sorry as hell. He might not like the ranch, but the culture shock from going from Dry Creek to Dallas is going to turn his world upside down. He says they are packed and they can be gone in three days when a buyer shows up with the money," Deke answered.

"Wow! That's fast." She put her black kitten in the basket with Stormy.

"Three days is how long the moving company said it would take to get a truck in here and get them loaded up and gone. He's selling the equipment and cattle with his ranch."

"And you?"

"No way. I'm taking my stuff with me. All I got to do is move it across the road, and I can do that in the three days they're waiting to get out of the house," he answered.

"But what about paper signing and deeds and all that?"

"He says they'll come back up here and take care of

the paperwork later. I'm going to Nadine's for a piece of pie. Want to join me?" he asked.

She shook her head. "Just came from there. Had Nadine's special for dinner. I don't need anything else until supper."

Lizzy turned up the radio when the DJ said that the next song was "Wild Child." She tapped her thumb on the steering wheel to the beat. Like the lyrics said, Toby was a wild child and Lizzy wouldn't ever be the same since he came into her life.

The song was about a woman, but in her mind Kenny was singing about Toby. He had the same rebel soul that the song talked about.

She parked her truck in front of Audrey's Place as the song ended and agreed with the end of the song when it said that he was born to dance to the beat of his own heart. Everything the lady said about staying wild had Lizzy nodding in agreement.

"He brings out the wild in me and makes me shed all my inhibitions and be me. And that's why I'm falling in love with him," she said.

She could hear cows bawling across the pasture fence over on the Lucky Penny along with a few crickets and other summer noises. But mostly she could hear her heart doing double time.

"What in the hell did I just say? Did those words really come out of my mouth?" she whispered.

CHAPTER TWENTY-ONE

Lizzy worried with the idea of buying Deke's ranch for two long days and nights. She stared at the ceiling at night, arguing with herself about such a fool notion. She cleaned her room—again. But not even a tidy bedroom brought about a decision. The only one she could talk to about the crazy idea was her cat, Stormy, and somehow purring didn't bring any satisfaction.

She opened the feed store that morning and Deke was the first person to come through the doors. It had been seven weeks since Toby moved to Dry Creek. It had been four weeks since they started fake dating and one week since they'd been dating seriously. It was too damn early to be thinking about buying a ranch at this point in the relationship.

Deke looked around the store to be sure no one was hiding between the shelves or behind a round rack of new summer clothing. "So what did my potential buyer decide?"

"That they will buy your ranch and give you your asking price," Lizzy said.

Had she really, honest-to-God, said those words out loud? She'd decided buying Deke's place would be a big mistake not two minutes ago, so why in the hell had she changed her mind? But then maybe it wasn't her mind doing the talking but her heart. If so, how could she possibly argue with that? The heart would have what it wanted or else it was almighty difficult to live with it.

Deke threw his hat into the air and shouted, scared Stormy, and sent four little kittens scampering for cover. He picked Lizzy up and swung her around in circles, kissed her on the forehead, and told her that he loved her a dozen times before he set her back on her feet.

"You get the lawyer to draw up the papers and Friday my friend will be there to sign everything and bring you a check. Do you need escrow money right now?" Lizzy panted between words.

"Hell, no! If you say they are good for the money, then I trust you. I'm going to tell my cousin that he can call the movers." Deke started for the door and went back to pick up his hat from the floor. "Lizzy, they won't back out will they? Tell me who they are. I've gone over every single person in town and those that we both know, trying to figure out who they are, and it is driving me crazy."

"Do you trust me?" Lizzy asked.

Fefe, the little black kitten, ventured back out and Deke picked her up.

"With my life." In seconds Fefe was curled up next to his big, broad chest, her eyes shut.

"Then please let this be a secret just for a couple more days. I promise this buyer is not going to back out."

Deke raked his hands through his dark hair and settled his old straw hat back into place. "Then the movers will be here on Friday, but I can start moving my stuff over to the new place today. Tell the buyers that they can move in any time they want to after the weekend. I'll start moving out as soon as I can pack. You are my new hero, Lizzy Logan."

"You don't have to rush. The buyer won't move in for a while," Lizzy said.

"But I do because there's a ton of stuff I want to do at the new place before fall. I'm glad Allie has slowed down taking on new jobs because I won't have any time to give her until after Christmas." Deke fairly well danced out of the store on a cloud of air with his feet six inches off the floor.

"Well, Stormy, we made him happy and cut my bank account into half." Lizzy sank down into the chair behind the counter and shut her eyes tightly.

"Hello, beautiful," Toby said softly.

At first she thought it was a figment of her imagination, but then she got a whiff of his shaving lotion and her eyes popped open. "I didn't hear the bell ring."

He propped his elbows on the counter and supported his chin in his hands. "I came in through the back to tell you that we need a few more fence posts out on the ranch. Did I hear Deke in here?"

"You did."

"What'd you hear about his ranch? He told me that you had a potential buyer on the hook for him. Did it pan out?"

Lizzy pushed up out of the chair and brushed a kiss across Toby's lips. "It did. They're closing the deal Friday. The buyer has cash so they don't have to wait on the bank to finance things."

"Care to share who my new neighbor might be?" Toby whispered as he traced her lip line with the tip of his finger.

"I'm sworn to secrecy until the papers are signed," she said.

"Please tell me it's not Truman." Toby toyed with a strand of her hair, twisting it around his finger and drawing her nearer with it.

"It's not Truman. I would never do that to Deke or to you. Besides I don't think Truman wants land that sets between Herman Hudson and your ranch." She leaned in for another kiss.

"Will I like this new buyer? Will they be good neighbors?" He nibbled on her earlobe.

"I hope you'll like them, and I guarantee they will be good neighbors." She shivered. Talking about a ranch, even if it was the one she'd just agreed to buy, wasn't at all what she wanted to think about right then.

The cowbell above the door sounded loudly and he stood up straight. "So if you will ring up about ten fence posts, I'll be on my way."

She poked buttons on the cash register, ran his credit card, and he signed it before she ever looked toward the door. "Hey, Mary Jo, what can I do for you today?"

"I need some advice. I want to buy a store building to put in a beauty shop and I don't even know where to start." Mary Jo pushed her red hair behind her ears and stooped down to pet Stormy and the kittens.

"Nice seeing you, Mary Jo," Toby drawled. "See you later, Lizzy. Allie says that you are having supper with us tonight. Deke is coming, too, so don't be late. You know how cranky he can get when he's hungry."

"I'll be early but don't worry about Deke. He's running on adrenaline today," Lizzy said.

"Did he sell his ranch?" Mary Jo asked.

"Yes, he did, and he's starting to move things across the road today." Lizzy smiled.

"Who's the buyer? I heard you had a hand in telling someone about it."

"I'm sworn to secrecy until the deal is closed. Now about a building for you." Lizzy quickly changed the subject. "There's lots of empty places. Which one do you have your eye on?"

"I wouldn't mind having the one next door to you on this side of the street, but that won't happen since Truman owns it. Please tell me that you didn't help him buy Deke's place. Allie don't need that old fart next door to her," Mary Jo said.

"It's not Truman, I swear. Besides like I just told Toby he wouldn't want to be sandwiched between Herman and the Dawsons. I thought you were looking at one of the two across the street that Mama has for sale."

"I am but I'd really like to be on this side of the street."

"Good luck with that. Sharlene is looking at the old clothing store, and the old barber shop is right next door to it, so you wouldn't be the only one over there."

"I didn't think of that," Mary Jo said, and smiled. "At one time she thought about the old hotel."

"She wouldn't want the old hotel because it's two stories and the stairs could make the insurance go sky high with little kids around," Lizzy said. "How many kids do you think she'll keep and what ages?"

"She's already got a couple of women interested in helping her run the place and says she'll keep the number to whatever the rules say she can keep. She really likes kids and she's so tired of that job at the bank."

Store buildings. Ranches. Lizzy would rather talk about Toby but that wasn't possible. "I think that would be a great place. Lots of parking since there's nothing else over there right now, and even if Sharlene does put in her day care center, not that many women at one time will be parking out front."

"I really want to do this. I'm so tired of driving to Wichita Falls every day and I have saved a little since I first started to work," Mary Jo said.

"Mama would be glad to rent, sell, or even give you

a deal like she gave Nadine with the café, and you can lease to own," Lizzy answered.

Mary Jo pumped her fist in the air. "You've talked me into it. I'm off to talk to Katy."

Lizzy waved as Mary Jo hurried from the building.

Everyone had thought the Logans were downright stupid to buy the buildings as they came up for sale, but few realized that Katy owned all of them except for the one Truman held the deed to. Lizzy's mother and father had bought them one by one with hopes that someday Dry Creek would be more than a ghost town. Maybe that dream would become a reality even yet.

Thinking of owning land and buildings brought Lizzy back to the situation she'd just gotten herself into that morning. On Friday she would own six hundred and forty acres of land complete with a crop of hay in the field, a couple of barns, two ponds, and an old house that had a decent roof but needed lots of repair. What had she been thinking when she let her heart do the talking instead of her mind?

Supper plans changed for the evening. Allie took a pot of soup and a pan of cornbread to Deke's place and the guys moved tractors, four-wheelers, and cattle across the road all evening. Allie, Katy, and Lizzy sat on the porch after supper, swatted at the flies, and drank a half-gallon jug of iced sweet tea.

Katy slapped the red plastic swatter on the table and two flies were eliminated from the Sullivan ranch forever, amen. "I'm ahead of y'all. That makes forty-three for me."

"Mama is the superwoman fly killer in the whole state of Texas." Allie laughed.

"Yes, I am, and next week I expect a cape for all my efforts. Lizzy, you could whisper the name of the new owner real quiet and we promise we won't tell," Katy said.

Lizzy shook her head. Her sister and mother would both fall off the porch if she told them that she'd bought the ranch. Hell's bells! They might even have her committed or put into the same room with Granny at that place in Wichita Falls.

The decision to buy the property had not been impulsive. When Deke first mentioned selling it, the thought had gone through her head that she should buy the place to help him out, and then she could sell it and make a slim profit maybe. Then she remembered telling Toby about her dreams of having her own place someday. Maybe if she wasn't living at Audrey's, then Fiona would come home permanently. She'd written out pros and cons in a notebook, and even if Fiona never came back to Dry Creek, the pros outweighed the cons. She wanted her own house close to her mother and sister, and the land was an added bonus because it could be leased out.

"Well, they've got a job cut out for them." Allie picked up her glass of tea. "The ranch is in good condition. Hay ready for a second cutting and barns in great repair. But the house. Great God almighty! It needs a hell of a lot of work. As you can see, kitchen hasn't been updated in decades, with those avocado green appliances, and don't even get me started on that Pepto-pink bathroom. I'm surprised that Deke even brought women home with him."

Lizzy swallowed hard. She hadn't thought about that ugly pink bathroom and the green kitchen. It was going to take the rest of her life savings to remodel the place, but everything did work even if it was butt ugly, so maybe she wouldn't start spending money right away. However, that hay in the field would have to be cut in the next two weeks, so that meant telling someone what she'd done before then.

She owned her bed, dresser, chest of drawers, and an old beat-up rocking chair that would look right at home in her new place. But she didn't have dishes, cookware, or even a single towel to call her own since she'd lived in her mother's house her whole life.

There was still a chance to back out. She could always be an anonymous buyer and put the ranch up on the market through a real estate agent out of Wichita Falls, and no one would even know she'd bought it.

No, that would never work.

Sitting there on the porch with her sister and mother, she already felt like she belonged on the ranch, so selling it would not be an option. She thought she'd found peace with Mitch. Peace in knowing who she would spend the rest of her life with. Peace in submitting to her station in life as a preacher's wife. But that was only her mind talking. As she sipped her tea on the porch of an old house that needed so much work something settled into her heart, and she recognized it as true harmony with heart, mind, soul, and the world. No, sir, this place would not go on the market again.

Telling her mother that she now owned a ranch and would be moving onto it would not be easy. Not that long ago she'd planned to move completely away from Dry Creek, and this was only a mile, as the crow flies, from Audrey's Place. The nice thing was that she didn't have to tell anyone until Friday and then she could swear Deke to secrecy for at least a couple of weeks.

Katy set her red plastic cup on the porch. "Mosquitoes are tryin' to carry me off and it's getting late, so I'm going home. Y'all want a ride? I don't reckon these guys will keep after it much longer tonight."

Allie stood up. "I'll go with you. When Deke gets ready to pack up the stuff in the house we'll be a lot more help. Whoever bought this place got a fine chunk of property. I hope they like ranchin' and that they're good neighbors."

Lizzy smiled up at her sister. "I'm still not sayin' a word."

"You are wicked and evil and I will find a way to get even. I should know before all the gossipmongers in town, and believe me, they will find out even if they have to go to the courthouse on Monday and look at the books," Allie said.

"They wouldn't do that," Lizzy gasped.

"They will if they don't have a snitch in the courthouse that will do it for them. Dora June probably has the whole staff on standby. By Friday night the news of the new buyer will be bigger than Mitch coming to the festival on Saturday." Allie wiped beads of sweat from her forehead with the tail of her shirt.

"Hot, ain't it?" Lizzy smiled.

"Come on, Mama." Allie sighed. "She's not going to give up a damn thing. You could make her sleep on the porch until she tells us."

"I could but then I'd have to live with her bitchin', so I'm not going to." Katy laughed. "See you at home or at breakfast if you come in after I'm asleep."

"Good night," Lizzy said.

CHAPTER TWENTY-TWO

Toby eased down on the porch beside Lizzy and laid a hand on her knee. He'd removed his chambray work shirt, and his white undershirt was dirty and sweaty. A line across his forehead gave testimony that he'd only taken his beat-up, old straw hat off a few minutes ago.

She passed him the red plastic cup that she'd been drinking from, and he gulped down the rest of the iced tea. When he handed it back, she refilled it and offered it to him again.

He drank down a third of it before he came up for air. "Thank you. I made a mistake when I didn't go to the bank and get a loan for this place, Lizzy. But we didn't want to be in debt while we're trying to make the Lucky Penny work."

Lizzy swallowed hard. "It is peaceful here, isn't it?"

He nodded. "Reminds me of my grandparents'

place. They raised a pretty good-size family in a little house like this. When things got better, Grandpa offered to build my grandmother a new house but she refused. She said that there were too many memories in her house to leave it behind."

"I'm sure that's one of the reasons that Deke wants the other place. That's where his grandparents made their home. This one belonged to their daughter, Deke's mama, but he was back and forth between the two places," Lizzy said.

"Good land and already cleared. Someone got a bargain. Maybe in a few years they'll want to sell and I'll pick it up then." Toby drained the rest of the tea. "Can I take you home?"

She smiled. "I'd rather you took me to the trailer."

His blue eyes twinkled. "We'd have to get pretty up close and personal to take a shower together in the trailer."

"Who said anything about a shower?" she teased.

"Darlin', I'm not going to bed with you without a shower."

"Who said anything about a bed?"

He grabbed her and pulled her toward him, tipped her chin up with his knuckles and kissed her, long and lingering, leaving her whole body limp and begging for more.

"That answer your question?" he asked.

"Let's forget the shower and go skinny-dippin' in the creek at the back of this place," she whispered. "It's not far from the barn where Deke keeps his hay, so we might watch the moon from the hayloft once we cool off."

He took her hand in his. "Lead the way."

It took twenty minutes, crawling over two fences and shooing a dozen cows out of the way, to get to the creek but when they did, Toby moaned. "Now I'm really mad at myself for not buying this place. I had no idea a creek ran through here."

"Don't kick yourself too hard." She unbuttoned her shirt and tossed it over the top of a low-growing mesquite tree. "This is Dry Creek, and it's running good right now, but we've had an unusual spring and summer. It will be completely dried up by mid-July and there won't be a drop of water in it until next spring. Sometimes it never has water in it. Won't be nothing but a gravel and sandpit, and darlin', the water might be clear but it's only knee-deep, so callin' it skinny-dippin' is for real. It's sure not skinny-dunkin'."

He shucked out of his dirty shirt and jeans, stuffed his socks down into his boots, and waded out into the cool clear water. His back against a rock, the water cut around his naked body, rippling past him, flowing over him. The moonlight defined the angles in his face and lit up his muscles.

She was so involved in watching him and trying to remember to breathe that she almost took the first step into the water without removing her shorts and sandals. In a few swift movements, the rest of her clothing lay on the grassy bank of the creek and the cool creek water was up to her knees.

"Would you lay with me in a tiny creek?" Toby opened his arms.

"I recognize that song, only I think the lyrics said a field of stone, and yes I would." She curled up in his arms, her head on his chest, a blanket of clear water covering them.

Hot night air has a scent all of its own. Add that to the smell of the water, the remnants of Toby's aftershave, mixed with the sweat of hard work and the musty aroma of green grass. Lizzy wished she could bottle it and take it home with her.

With a wet forefinger, Toby started at her forehead and traced the outline of her face, then went lower, barely touching her neck and arm until he reached her hand. Lacing his fingers in hers he brought her hand to his lips and kissed each dripping knuckle.

"You are beautiful, Lizzy Logan," he drawled.

His warm breath on her neck sent a shiver down her spine.

"Cold?" He pulled her closer to his side, wrapping both arms around her, their naked bodies pressed against each other.

"Not at all. It's desire," she said honestly.

"I love that about you." He buried his face into her hair.

"That I'm not cold?"

"No, that you say what you are feeling and aren't dishonest with me."

"We agreed that we'd talk about everything," she said.

A pang of guilt hit her square in the heart because she was keeping a secret from Toby. But this wasn't the time or the place to tell him she was his new neighbor. Tonight was one of those special moments that only came along once in a lifetime, and she would not take a chance of ruining it by talking about a ranch.

She raised her head and caught him staring at her, looking straight into the bottom of her soul, seeing the past, understanding the present, and looking forward to the future without fear. She could get lost in those blue eyes and never surface, not for food or air, just spend eternity in the peace she found that night curled up in the creek water on her ranch with the love of her life.

The words, *the love of her life,* echoed in her heart, but they didn't scare her or put her in flight or fight mode. Instead she embraced them with open arms and decided in that moment that she'd give Toby all the time he needed. If he never fell for her, then she'd have all these fantastic memories to curl up with every night for the rest of her life.

She slung a leg over him and with one swift movement guided his rock-hard erection into her body. It was totally amazing how easy it was in the water. One of his hands cupped her bottom as they moved together, the buoyancy of the water making it effortless. The other hand tangled into her wet hair and pulled her lips to his.

The cool water against her skin, Toby's hot lips on hers as the kisses deepened setting her whole body on fire, and the two of them working together made her forget everything but satisfying the deep need in her body.

With his hand on her bare butt, he controlled the speed, bringing her to the edge of the climactic cliff time after time and then slowing down the pace, only to speed up until she could see the height and depth of what lay before her. When she could take no more, she pulled her lips from his, dug her hands into his chest, and groaned.

"Now?" he asked.

"Thirty minutes ago," she moaned.

With one final thrust everything disappeared into a bright array of brilliant-colored fireworks. Her head, her heart, her soul exploded, and only the golden rays of afterglow followed the sparkling lights as they faded into the sky.

"So that's where stars come from," she panted.

"You are so right."

He flipped her to one side and in one fell swoop, she was in his arms and he was standing, water dripping from their bodies as he carried her to the grassy bank. He laid her down under the drooping branches of a willow tree and stretched out beside her, only their hands touching.

"That was..." He paused.

"Intense. Amazing. Over the moon."

"Doesn't begin to describe it." He rolled over on an elbow and brushed a sweet kiss across her lips.

The reason it was all of the words and more was

because they'd made love, not had sex, on Lizzy's ranch. It was her land even if she hadn't signed the papers yet. The creek water was hers. The soft grass beneath them was hers. Even the willow tree creating a hideaway with its drooping branches belonged to her. She and Toby had christened the land that night. Maybe someday they would christen the house.

"I could spend the whole night here, but I suppose we should get dressed and go home before someone discovers us," she said, and snuggled closer to him.

"It's my turn this time," he said softly.

She didn't have to ask what he meant as his hand skimmed its way down her rib cage, sending delicious shivers all through her body in spite of the hot night breeze fluttering the willow tree's leaves.

Lizzy had never been skinny-dipping before that night. She'd never made love with creek water brushing against her naked butt. But that was only the tip of the iceberg compared to the way Toby turned her on beneath the willow tree that hot summer night.

The clock flashed two a.m. when Toby finally crawled beneath the sheets. He'd taken a shower and wished the whole time that he was crammed into the tiny space with Lizzy's body pressed against his. Worn out, he finally stretched out beneath cool sheets with cold air-conditioned air flowing down on him from a unit above his head.

In four hours he had to crawl out of the bed and have breakfast with Allie and Blake, possibly with Deke there, too. He sighed as he sunk his face into the pillow and shut his eyes. He didn't want the feeling to end, but it would when the alarm sounded.

His eyes popped open and refused to shut. It was only two days until the festival on Saturday. Mitch wasn't married yet and he would be in Dry Creek that day. When he and Lizzy saw each other, would the old flame fire up again? He'd heard it said time and time again that first loves were never forgotten. If Mitch had been her first serious love, would she take a look at him and forget about all the hot nights she'd shared with Toby?

He sat straight up in bed, slung his legs over the side, and had full intentions of going to Audrey's Place to tell Lizzy that he loved her. To propose if necessary so that things would be signed, sealed, and delivered when Mitch rolled into Dry Creek. But the voices in his head said that was crazy.

He could not rope Lizzy down like a calf. He couldn't brand her to make her his property. He had to let these next few days play out the way they would and hope like hell that when she saw Mitch, she would realize that man was part of her past and had nothing to do with her future. He hated that old adage about letting something go and if it came back to you, then it was yours.

For the first time, his heart ached for something he possibly could not have. He wanted Lizzy Logan in his life, but she had to want to be there for it to work.

And this is the cowboy who wasn't sure he could

live five weeks without the excitement of a chase every single weekend? What happened to that wild Dawson? Is this a passing fancy because of what he sees in his brother's newfound love? Or is it really happening to him? The voice inside his head asked a lot of questions.

"His heart found something that it doesn't want to live without," he whispered.

When he shut his eyes the next time, sleep came and with it the sweetest dreams of Lizzy and a hot summer night with cool creek water surrounding them.

The moment the alarm went off he bounded out of bed and jerked on a fresh pair of faded jeans, a tank top, and his socks and boots. The scent of bacon got stronger with every step toward the house. Work hard. Get through today and then tomorrow. Hope like hell that Lizzy didn't fall into Mitch's arms.

The buzz of conversation, the sizzle of frying bacon, the aroma of hot bread in the oven, all met him when he opened the kitchen door. But it all disappeared in the blink of an eye when he saw Lizzy at the counter, helping her sister make breakfast. She wore a pair of skinny jeans and a sleeveless shirt hanging down past her butt, no shoes, and her hair was in a ponytail. His mouth went dry and he couldn't force himself to blink for fear she would disappear. Never, not once, had he seen a woman anywhere in the world as cute as the one standing before him that morning.

"Good mornin'," he said hoarsely.

Lizzy whipped around and smiled, lighting up the entire kitchen. Hell, maybe even the whole world. The twinkle in her eye sure put the rising sun to shame that morning.

"Good mornin' to you," Lizzy and Allie said at the same time.

Toby only heard Lizzy's voice and he nodded. He wanted to hug her, kiss her, maybe even throw her over his shoulder and forget about breakfast. He could take her back to the trailer, lock the world outside, and make wild passionate love to her all day. But for all intents and purposes they were fake dating and he could do absolutely nothing except wink.

Lizzy had no illusions about why her sister left a text message on her phone the night before saying that she expected her to join them for breakfast. It had nothing to do with Toby and their fake/real relationship. It had everything to do with who was buying Deke's ranch. Allie was good at finding out things. That had always been her job as oldest child, and she took it seriously.

"Smells good in here." Toby brushed past her and squeezed her hand on the way.

"Bacon, fried eggs, hot biscuits, and hash browns with pancakes on the side." Lizzy poured a cup of coffee and handed it to him, their hands brushing in the transfer.

"Where's Deke? I thought he'd be here." Toby carried the coffee to the table and sat down.

"He sent a text an hour ago to tell me that he was packing and was eating at home. I guess we are all going over there after work today to help move whatever he gets ready. His cousin has cleaned out a place in a bedroom for him to put his boxes until the end of the week," Allie answered.

"He's avoiding these women," Blake said from the doorway. "He knows that Allie will pester the hell out of him until he tells who is buying the ranch if he knows and I'll bet he does. I sure wish we would have had the finances to take on that place. We could haul half of the cattle we've still got down around Comfort up here if we had all that cleared land and good grazing pastures."

Lizzy vowed that she would tell the whole world after the festival on Saturday but not until then. On that day she planned to tell Toby first and ask him to move in with her. If she'd read him wrong, he could bolt and run right out of their relationship. If he did, then she'd take her broken heart into her new house and get over it. She could live without Toby, but each day would only be breathing, working, eating, sleeping, and starting all over again the next morning. Toby gave her that breathless energy that made it all worth living, and she wanted him beside her through every moment of the rest of her life.

Today was the last Thursday in June. The festival was Saturday. She could hold out against Allie that long. It would break her record for keeping secrets from her sister because she'd only managed to hang on to something for three days in the past.

Oh, no! That voice in her head that sounded so much like Fiona's came through loud and clear. *You've had*

*a real dating thing going on with Toby for longer than
three days and she still thinks it's a fake relationship.
So you are getting stronger. It's Toby who's giving you
so much strength. You'd better hang on to him.*

Lizzy stole a glance across the room at Toby, only
to find him staring at her again. If they didn't get
control of the sparks dancing around the room, Allie
and Blake would realize that they'd gone from fake
to real. She winked and turned around, but the heat of
his gaze on her back only made the sparks even more
brilliant.

"If I guess who bought the ranch will you at least
nod?" Allie asked.

That much she could do because there was no way
Lizzy would ever think to say her name. "I guess I
wouldn't be tellin' then, would I?"

"It's not Truman for sure?"

Lizzy nodded. "It is definitely not Truman. Deke
said that he would never sell to any member of that
family because it wouldn't be right to put them next to
the Lucky Penny."

"Is it Herman Hudson or any of his family?" Allie
put the last of the bacon on a platter with the eggs and
carried them to the table.

Lizzy lined a bowl with a cloth napkin and filled it
with hot biscuits straight from the oven. "That is more
than one name."

Blake picked up the plate of hash brown potatoes
and carried them to the table. "Okay, then is it
Herman?"

Lizzy shook her head.

"Sweet Jesus! He's got half a dozen kids. Do we have to guess each one by name? I might have forgotten a couple of the ones that's older than we are," Allie said.

"Then is the game over?" Lizzy asked.

"You are wicked. I shouldn't even let you eat breakfast with us since you won't tell," Allie said with a pout.

"Suck in that lower lip. It won't work with me anymore." Lizzy picked up a biscuit and filled it with eggs and bacon. "And if you don't say the exact name, then I don't have to nod."

"That's not fair, Lizzy Logan!" Allie said.

Lizzy came close to dropping her biscuit, but then she remembered that she'd said her sister had to come up with the exact name. It might be splitting hairs but the name on the deed would be Elizabeth Jane Logan, so she rationalized that she did not have to nod.

"Maybe not, but you made up the rules." She slid a hash brown onto her plate and reached for another biscuit.

"Okay, Deke will have to know who the buyer is, so I'll get him to either tell me when we go over there to help him pack," Allie said. "And if he doesn't I'm not helping."

"And I'll tell Deke he doesn't need you to help when he's got me to pack for him. Besides, you've got that big old baby bump and it'll get in the way," Lizzy countered with a smile.

Toby squeezed her knee under the table and sparks danced across the table like gypsies around a bonfire. She placed her hand on his and squeezed, but that did not mean she was spilling the news to him, either, not even in the midst of a night of scorching sex.

CHAPTER TWENTY-THREE

Lizzy leaned on the broom and looked around at the house she'd bought that Thursday evening. The hardwood floors had a few scuff marks but nothing that would have to be dealt with right away. The bathroom fixtures were that pink used back in the seventies, but they were in good shape. Built like so many ranch homes in those days, the house had a front door that opened right up into the living room with the big square country kitchen through an archway straight ahead. A hallway led to three bedrooms, a couple of closets, and ended with a door into the bathroom. It was basically the same layout that Allie and Blake had except that the living room was smaller and the kitchen bigger.

"Deke, I have to tell you something but I don't want my family to know until after the festival," Lizzy said.

He crossed his heart with his finger and held up his palm. "I can keep a secret."

"I'm the buyer. I'm the one buying your ranch. You won't back out will you?" she blurted out.

Deke threw an arm around her shoulders. "I already figured that out and I'd never back out on you, Lizzy. I couldn't be happier. Just knowin' who's going to be takin' care of this makes me happy."

"How did you know?" Lizzy asked.

"I know you," Deke chuckled. "This means you aren't going to let Mitch talk you into a second chance, doesn't it?"

Lizzy stepped out of his embrace and thought about smacking him with the broom. "What in the devil made you say that?"

"I heard it through the gossip vine that he's not happy in Mexico after all and that his woman is having second thoughts," Deke answered.

"It's a little late for that," Lizzy said.

"Who knows about that? They might be but there's been so many stories that it could go either way. You didn't answer my question though. If he's not married and wants a second shot, what does that do about this ranch? Will you sell it and go with him and turn into that Lizzy that I don't like?"

She slowly shook her head. "That ship sailed."

"Are you sure?" Deke pressed.

Allie peeked around the corner of the hallway at the other end. "Sure about what? The person buying this place better not back out at this late date. I've got your kitchen cabinets all packed up and cleaned out. Whoever moves in here will have a spotless kitchen. And what ship sailed?"

"The one with Mitch at the helm. Deke heard that he's not real happy with his new woman now and she's got cold feet," Lizzy answered.

Allie's big brown eyes widened. "Promise me you won't give him the time of day."

Lizzy held up two fingers and then crossed her heart. "Too much water has run under the bridge at this time to go back to that pain."

"Give me a match and I'll set the bridge on fire for you," Deke said. "Thanks for all y'all's help. We'll load it and take it over to the new place. Y'all are the best friends ever." He slid a sly wink toward Lizzy.

Blake hollered at Allie and she disappeared into the kitchen. Deke followed her, leaving Lizzy alone with her broom and the trash left in one of the spare bedrooms. She took a swipe at it and leaned on the broom again.

Lizzy would own this place for less than twenty-four hours when Mitch came to town. She played out two scenarios in her mind. One involved Mitch apologizing and admitting he'd made a mistake when he broke their engagement back in February. In the other he would be aloof and more than a little self-righteous with that look that was so very familiar. The one that said the man ruled the roost and the woman was only there to scrape the shit off his boots in the evening.

Neither one weighed down her heart or made it leap

around in her chest. If he apologized, she would accept it. If he was high and mighty, that was okay, too. He'd ceased to matter in her world.

"Hey, gorgeous." Toby broke into her thoughts but it didn't startle her.

She set the broom in the corner and walked into his open arms. They belonged in this house. It might take a while to convince him, but she wasn't in a hurry.

"I've got a blanket, a six-pack of cold beer, and a paper sack with sandwiches and cookies. Want to see what's going on at the willow tree when we get done here?" he whispered as he buried his face in her hair.

"You sure know how to woo a woman," she said, and laughed. "I'll meet you there."

He tipped her chin up with his fist and their lips met in a blaze of heat like always. She leaned into the kiss, hands splayed on his broad chest, fire building from a spark into a raging wildfire in seconds.

He wrapped her tighter into his arms. "I could get used to coming home to kisses like that."

"How about leaving in the morning?" she mumbled.

"Are you asking me to run away with you, Lizzy Logan?"

"No, I'm asking how would you like to have a kiss like that in the morning and have to walk out the door and work all day?" she answered.

"In my line of work I can always sneak away for a break any time of the day."

"Hey, Toby, it's wagons-ho time. Got the last pickup loaded and we're ready," Blake yelled.

Toby stayed long enough to brush another sweet, brief kiss across Lizzy's lips and then she heard the back door slam and the sound of Allie's boots coming her way. She quickly began to sweep again, shoving the dust, stray bits of paper, and other things that accumulate in a guest room toward the door.

"My job is done. I'm going home. Need a ride?" Allie asked.

"No, I want to get this room and the one across the hall completely swept and clean so I'll catch a ride with Toby or Blake," Lizzy answered.

"Be careful," Allie said softly.

"About dust bunnies?" Lizzy giggled.

"No, about a hot cowboy named Toby. I'm not blind. I see the way he looks at you," Allie answered. "And be careful about Mitch, too. He's real good at manipulation. Oh, and one more thing, who bought this place?"

Lizzy pointed at Allie and shook her head. "You are pretty slick, but I'm still not telling."

"Good night then. You sure have gotten sassy since Mitch broke it off with you."

"It was either that or curl up and die, and there's a lot of livin' in me yet." Lizzy hugged Allie. "Good night to you."

"I'll tell you what we're going to name the baby if you will tell me who bought the ranch."

"Not unless you are going to name her after me," Lizzy teased.

"On that note, I'm going home for real now. See you tomorrow."

Allie was going toward the door when Lizzy's phone buzzed in her hip pocket. The text was from Toby saying that five of Deke's cows were on the road. He was helping get them back in the pasture and then they'd have to fix the fence before they could unload the packed boxes. They'd have to take a rain check on the willow tree date.

She threw the broom on the floor and raced out the door, caught Allie as she was settling into the seat of her old work van, and hitched a ride home with her.

Toby awoke on Friday morning before the alarm sounded. He rolled over to gather Lizzy into his arms but all he got was an armful of air and pillow.

"Dammit! I was dreaming again."

Blue whimpered at the side of the bed and Toby rolled over to see two big dog eyes staring at him over the edge of the mattress. He scratched the dog's ears and wished he could go back to sleep because in the dream he and Lizzy were together. They were sitting under the willow tree and watching a bunch of kids play in the shallow creek water. Whether those children belonged to him or to Blake and Allie or even to Deke, he didn't know, but there was something peaceful in the dream.

Blue yipped once, wagged his tail, and meandered toward the kitchen.

The reflection in the small mirror above the sink said that it was still Toby Dawson staring back at him. The scar where the bull gored him was faint but still there. His hair was still dark and his eyes hadn't changed from blue to brown. His dark whiskers said he needed to shave. Nothing had changed and yet his world had been turned upside down by a fireball of a woman with brown eyes and dishwater blond hair.

He ran a razor over his face, got dressed, fed Blue, and opened the trailer door to the sounds of cattle, crickets, and a soft breeze rattling the wind chimes out in his backyard.

Tomorrow night the festival would be over and he and Lizzy would have no reason to go on pretending they were having a relationship. He'd know where he really stood with her. He pushed open the kitchen door to the ranch house and found Blake making breakfast. Pure unadulterated disappointment shot through his veins.

"Where's Allie?" he asked.

"She's been working pretty hard so I told her to sleep this morning and I'd make breakfast for the two of us. I worry about her, Toby."

Toby poured a cup of coffee and sipped at it while he set the table. "She is a force. Must be in the Logans' genes."

Deke stopped in the door and sniffed the air. "I don't have a kitchen anymore, not even a coffeepot. I'm used to setting the timer on the pot the night before so the coffee is ready."

Toby filled a cup and handed it to him. "Tomorrow you'll be unpacked and have a coffeepot."

"I plan to wake up over there tomorrow morning in

my brand-new place." He sipped the coffee and rolled his eyes. "Never miss something until it's gone."

"Amen to that," Toby said.

"What are you missing? Hand me that platter so I can stack up the pancakes as they get done," Blake asked.

"He's missing his wild and woolly days. I swear, I've lived here my whole life and no one has lassoed me. Y'all come to town and Blake gets a rope around his neck within six weeks and I believe I see stars in Toby's eyes these days." Deke opened the pantry door and pulled out two bottles of syrup.

Blake whipped around, flapjack turner in one hand and platter in the other. "So that's the way it is for real?"

"Don't tell Allie. Let Lizzy tell her when she's ready," Toby said.

"Wouldn't think of it. She'd just fret and worry," Blake said. "So what are you going to do about it?"

Toby finished setting the table. "Today I'm going to eat a big stack of pancakes and a bunch of bacon, plow some land, check on some cattle."

"And about Lizzy?"

"What can I do? Mitch is coming to town. If she's not over him, then things could go sideways in a hurry. I'm learning patience but it's not easy," Toby answered.

"Okay, then. Let's eat breakfast and get on with what we have to do. We don't need to worry about what we have no control over," Blake said.

"Spoken like three wise cowboys." Deke laughed. "Ever think about how we just face things and go on and women talk every single thing to death?"

"Oh, yeah." Blake grinned. "So who bought your ranch, Deke?"

Deke scooted five pancakes over onto his plate. "I will tell you one thing about that and then I'm not sayin' another word. When the buyer gets ready to tell you, you are going to be two surprised brothers. You might want to be sitting down. I'm sworn to secrecy until after the weekend. If it hasn't been discovered by Monday morning, then I will tell you, but right now all I'm going to talk about is how damn fine this breakfast is."

CHAPTER TWENTY-FOUR

The energy in Dry Creek that Saturday morning was electrifying. Nadine had opened her café but she was only serving as a hostess, talking to people, providing headquarters for the festival along with platter after platter of cookies and gallon after gallon of sweet tea to the folks.

Banners stretched across both ends of Main Street and God bless Lucy Hudson's heart because she'd taken it upon herself to invite vendors to the festival. Since it was the first year, they could set up their tables and booths on the sidewalks on both sides of the street at no charge. Folks sold hand-tied horse halters, purses, and blinged-out western jewelry, artwork, woodcrafts, and handmade items along with Indian tacos, baked goods, chili pies, and hot dogs.

A bouncy house and pony ride for the kids and a me-

chanical bull for the bravehearted took up a chunk of
the blocked-off Main Street. People had parked up and
down the road for a mile on either end of town, and by
midmorning Dry Creek was buzzing with excitement.

At noon folks began to meander down to the church
to eat a free lunch provided by the churchwomen and
then came back with their lawn chairs to sit and visit
until time for fireworks.

Lizzy and Fiona were busy helping Nadine in the
café that afternoon. Lizzy was jealous of every single
person who stopped to talk to Fiona that day. Not
because she was getting attention, but because Lizzy
didn't want to share her sister. She would have rather
spent the whole day just the two of them in her feed
store with the door locked. Then she and Fiona could
play with the kittens and talk about the new twists in
both of their lives.

"So do you see Mitch anywhere yet?" Fiona asked.

"I hope I don't see him at all. I hope he and his new
wife are so swamped with events that they can't find
time to get down here," Lizzy answered as they carried
two empty platters to the kitchen to refill with cookies.

"You probably need to see him one more time just
for closure." Fiona piled chocolate chip cookies on one
platter and peanut butter brownies on the other. She
handed one to Lizzy and nodded toward the dining
room. "Folks are going through these so fast I'm wondering if we'll make it to the end of the day."

"If we don't, there's about twenty bags of store-
bought cookies in the pantry. Nadine said they aren't as

good as these but latecomers can't be choosers," Lizzy said.

"Elizabeth?" The voice was familiar.

Lizzy set the platter down and turned slowly to find Myra Turner, Mitch's fiancée/wife/whatever, at her elbow. The woman hadn't changed much in the past five months. Long brown hair flowed down her back to her waist. Hazel eyes were set in a round baby face with full lips and a perky little nose. That day she wore a multicolored skirt that skimmed her ankles and a lovely little Victorian lacy blouse.

"Myra." She nodded.

"Could we talk?" Myra's eyes darted around the full café. Folks had been taking advantage of the tables and the air-conditioning as well as the refreshments all day.

"It's pretty quiet in the kitchen. Come on. Fiona, folks can help themselves to cookies," Lizzy said.

"Are you sure?" Fiona asked.

"Very sure." Lizzy led the way and didn't have to motion toward the chairs pulled up to an old yellow chrome table for Myra to slide into one. The poor woman looked pale and absolutely miserable.

"I've made a big mistake and it's too late to get out of it," Myra said. "But before I unload on you because I know you will understand, I need to apologize for what Mitch and I did to you. That was cruel and ugly, and I'm sorry."

"That's in the past but thank you and apology accepted," Lizzy said.

"I'm pregnant and I don't want to marry Mitch,"

Myra spit out as if she had to get the words out in a hurry. "What do I do?"

Fiona went to the refrigerator and brought back a bottle of water. "Here, drink this. You look like you are about to faint."

"Thank you," Myra said softly. She twisted the top off the cold water and took a tiny sip. "I'm miserable and I'm about to marry a man I don't love, and I don't know how to change things."

"I barely know you. I met you at the church, shared a few potlucks with you, and sang in the choir together a couple of times. All I can tell you is to follow your heart," Lizzy said.

Myra wrung her hands and looked like she might break into tears any minute. "I thought it was cute the way he was so possessive at first. It made me feel protected and loved, but that's changed to controlled and smothered. We're supposed to get married tonight in a small ceremony at my parents' house with just family there. Everyone thinks we are already married, even our church in Mexico. We did say vows to each other before we…" She paused and blushed. "Well, you know."

Myra looked over Lizzy's shoulder and gasped. Her face registered fear, shock, and disgust all at the same time. Lizzy followed her gaze to see Mitch pushing through the swinging doors from the dining room to the kitchen. "Hello, Lizzy. Nadine said I'd find you back here."

His cold gaze started at her head, hair thrown up in

a ponytail with errant strands sticking to her sweaty neck. It dropped down to the hot pink tank top that hugged her body like a glove, then on to the skinny jeans held up with a blinged-out cowboy belt with a diamond-studded four-leaf clover on the belt buckle. His lip curled in a sneer like she'd seen it do a million times when he didn't like what she was wearing.

"Mitch," she acknowledged. Mentally, she stood at the end of a bridge with Mitch on the other side with a raging river below them. She held a flaming torch in her hand ready to set the brittle wood on fire.

"Myra, darlin'." He crossed the room and laid his hands on her shoulders. "We must be going. It's only three hours until wedding time, and you still have to do your hair and get into your dress. Lizzy, I hear you are seeing one of those cowboys who bought the Lucky Penny."

"I am." She nodded. "You should remember Toby. I sat between you two at Sunday dinner when he came to visit one time."

"Oh, I remember him well. I'm sure with your background, you are pretty well suited," Mitch said with a sneer.

"I hope so." She smiled. "Y'all been in town all day?"

Myra nodded. "We watched the parade, prowled around the vendors, talked to some of Mitch's friends, and ate at the potluck. Where were you all day?"

"Enough chitchat, Myra. We have to go." Mitch let go of her shoulders and took her hand, pulling her up to her feet.

She broke free of his death grip and took two steps backward. "I need to go to the ladies' room. I will meet you out front."

His jaw worked in anger. "Don't take more than five minutes."

Her smile was forced as she waved and pushed through the doors toward the hallway to the restroom area. Poor thing had a tough decision to make and very little time to do it in. But it sure wasn't Lizzy's problem.

"It would have never worked between us." Mitch kept an eye through the window where the orders were passed rather than looking at Lizzy.

"Probably not," she said.

"Myra and I will be happy."

Who was he trying to convince? Himself? Her? God?

Hopefully, it was himself because Lizzy didn't give a damn and she didn't think God was taking time out of his schedule to attend the Dry Creek Festival.

"I hope you are very happy." In that mental picture of the bridge, she tossed the torch and immediately there was nothing but a gaping hole between her and Mitch.

Fiona had been right. Complete and utter closure was a beautiful thing.

Fiona! Dammit! Where were her manners?

"I'm so sorry. Mitch, this is my sister, Fiona. You heard me talk about her a lot but I don't think you two ever actually met each other."

Fiona stretched out a hand. "Pleased to meet you. How are you enjoying Mexico?"

Mitch had no choice but to shake hands with her. "It's God's work and that brings happiness."

"I see. Well, I do hope you and your new bride are happy." Fiona held on to his hand a moment longer than necessary.

Lizzy had closure and she'd expected her fiery-tempered sister to cuss Mitch out at the least, maybe send him to the wedding with a black eye at the worst. It was over now so why was her sister continuing to engage this sorry bastard in polite conversation? She tilted her head to one side and caught Fiona's very slight wink. Her sister, bless her heart, was thinking about Myra. She was trying to give the woman a few more minutes in the bathroom to figure out a way to get out of a doomed marriage.

"We will be." He jerked his hand free. "Tell her I'm waiting beside the car for her when she returns."

Fiona nodded. "I'll do that. I'm sure she won't be much longer."

He was all the way at the swinging doors when he turned around. "You would have never gone to Mexico with me, would you?"

Lizzy shook her head. "My store is in Dry Creek. Going to Wichita Falls was a stretch."

"Then you would not have followed me wherever God led me?"

What was he trying to do? Find closure for his heart and mind or justification for what he'd done?

Another shake of the head. "Mitch, what we had is over. What I might or might not have done isn't important. What is crucial right now is that you learn to let Myra be a partner and not a slave to your every whim."

"God says a wife will be submissive, and Myra will learn in good time. Good-bye, Lizzy."

She waited until he was gone and then she and Fiona hurried to the ladies' room.

Lizzy opened the ladies' room door and found a pale Myra sitting in the corner, her head in her hands. Fiona went straight to her, slid down the wall to sit beside the girl, and hugged her. Myra looked up, misery written in her eyes. Lizzy remembered the day that Allie had found her huddled in the bathroom, weeping because Mitch had dumped her to be with this woman. She should be gloating with glee because the *other woman* had gotten her comeuppance, but she only felt pity for Myra. The poor darlin' didn't have a Logan backbone like Lizzy, and she damn sure didn't have two sisters to help her fight her way out of the misery.

"Where is Mitch? Is he mad at me?"

"He's waiting beside your car," Fiona said.

"I cannot do this, not today, probably not ever. I just need a place to go for a couple of weeks to get my head on straight." Tears streamed down Myra's face as she looked up into Lizzy's eyes. "Help me, please, Lizzy. I'm not as strong as you and I need help and there's no one to ask."

"If you had a way to get out of town, do you have a friend or money to stay in a hotel?" Lizzy asked.

Myra nodded. "My very best friend in college lives in Olney. He would let me stay with him."

"He?" Lizzy asked.

"Rowdy Williams and he lives up to his name. We were as different as night and day. He was the wild child. I was the preacher's daughter in every sense of the word, but we were good friends. I can stay with him and no one will even know where I am. God knows, I couldn't ever bring him home to meet Mama and Daddy or even talk about him back in those days," Myra said.

"Lizzy, you don't have to get tangled up in this," Fiona said.

"She needs our help. Where's your car parked, Myra?" Lizzy asked.

"Across the street. In front of that old hotel," Myra answered.

"My truck is parked out behind my store. Go through the dining room and kitchen and out the back door. Fiona is going to drive you up to the Dairy Queen in Olney where your friend is going to pick you up. She'll drive my truck home." Lizzy fished in her purse for a set of keys and handed them to Fiona. "And, Myra, let your mama and daddy know that you are okay. They'll worry."

"I'll text them and Mitch. I can't call him or he'll talk me into the marriage. He's real good at manipulation." She peeked out the door and turned around. "Thank you, Lizzy. If you ever need anything at all, I owe you big time."

"What are you going to do, Lizzy?" Fiona asked as she extended her hand to Myra.

"I'm going to keep Mitch in town as long as I can so y'all can get away," Lizzy answered. "Good luck, Myra."

"Thank you." Myra took Fiona's hand and stood up.

Lizzy marched out of the café and then across the street. Mitch was sitting on the sidewalk right beside the car, feet extended down the three steps, crossed at the ankles and a smug expression on his face.

"Where's Myra?" he asked.

Lizzy sat down beside him. "I've got some more that I need to get off my chest so I told her to sit down and have a cookie or two while we have a private talk."

"I'm going to be her husband in less than three hours. She needs to listen to me, not to you, and I told her that it was time to leave," Mitch said coldly.

"If you truly love that woman you need to treat her as an equal, not as property. She's fragile." Lizzy saw the tail end of her truck make a left-hand turn at the end of the road. She caught a glimpse of Fiona's flaming red hair, but no one was in the passenger's seat. Either Myra was lying low or she'd backed out. If it was the latter, she'd show up at the car in the next few minutes.

"She's submissive, which is what a good wife is supposed to be. You wouldn't know anything about that, Lizzy," he said.

"You should at least give me points for trying." Lizzy smiled up at him.

"Regretting your decision?" he whispered as he leaned over toward her.

"You left me, Mitch, and broke my heart with that phone call." She fluttered her eyelids in mock flirtation. Anything to keep him in Dry Creek until Fiona got a good head start.

"But you fought me and God about doing my bidding," he said.

"I was doing my best to change," she said softly.

Toby and Blake had been on the other end of town sitting on the tailgate of Blake's truck when Herman Hudson showed up. Toby talked to him a few minutes, then realized it had been a while since he'd seen Lizzy.

"Y'all excuse me. I need to go find my girlfriend before some other feller makes off with her." Toby grinned.

"Last I saw her, she was sitting across the street in front of the old hotel, talking to Mitch. You might want to head on up that way to protect your interests or keep her from killin' him. Sorry sumbitch has balls showin' his face in town after the way he hurt her." Herman laughed.

A heavy stone replaced Toby's heart. What if seeing Mitch had stirred all Lizzy's old feelings for him? As much as she said she was over him, Toby knew the man had broken her heart. She'd been so looking forward to planning their wedding. What if Mitch was right now offering Lizzy the family she wanted so much?

Toby managed to laugh at Herman's joke but it was

hollow. "See you guys later," he said as he waved over his shoulder. Every step was like one of those horrible dreams when a person needs to run but their feet feel like they are encased in concrete. People were everywhere, sitting in lawns up against the buildings. Roaming in and out of Nadine's and the convenience store. It wasn't until he reached the end of the block that he could get a view of the old hotel, and sure enough there was Mitch leaning down to whisper something in Lizzy's ear and she was smiling back up at him.

Toby rounded the end of the building, got into Blake's truck, and headed out to the willow tree. He needed air. He had to think. He loved her with his whole heart. He wanted to spend his life with her. But not if she still had feelings for Mitch.

He parked at Deke's old place and walked down the pathway to the creek and the tree, leaving pieces of his heart behind the whole way. This is why he didn't want a relationship. The pain was even greater than the day the bull had gored him. That was a wound that would heal.

His phone buzzed and dreading what the text might say, he still whipped it out of his pocket and checked the message. It was one of his former women asking if he was coming to the bar in Abilene that Saturday night. Was that an omen that he should have never let go of his previous life and should go back to it?

The next time his phone buzzed, he didn't even bother looking at it. He sat down at the edge of the creek, took off his boots, rolled up the legs of his jeans, and put his feet in the water. Then his phone rang and Lizzy's smiling face popped up on the screen.

"Hello," he said hoarsely, waiting for the dreaded news.

"Where are you? I've looked everywhere and I can't find you," she said.

"By the creek and the willow tree."

"Don't leave. I'll be right there," she said, and the screen went blank.

He lay back on the green grass and waited even though he wanted to get up and run away. Pulling his hat down over his face, he shut his eyes and a thousand pictures of her flitted through his mind. There she was that first day sitting between him and Mitch, as nervous as the old proverbial long-tailed cat in a room full of rocking chairs. Then there she was at Allie's wedding in that pretty dress dancing with him at the reception. She'd looked so fragile and hurt that afternoon, and it wasn't until later that he'd found out that Mitch had broken up with her. One picture after another flashed, leaving the last one of her sitting on the curb, flirting with her old flame, polishing off the whole display.

He felt her presence but with that vision still in his mind, he didn't want to look at her or hear what she had to say, and he damn sure hoped that Mitch wasn't with her. Something touched his arm and he picked the hat off his face to see her slinging her clothing every which way.

"God, I feel so dirty. I have to get in the water and get what just happened off me," she said.

"What?" Toby sat up so fast that the water swirled around in circles and the willow tree leaned toward the sun.

"That damned Mitch. It was the only way to keep him in town a few more minutes, but just being that close to him made my skin crawl."

She was naked except for her panties and she peeled those down over her curvy hips and tossed them toward the willow tree. Wading out into the water, she crooked her finger toward him. "Come on in, the water is nice and cool, but you might want to shed more than your boots and socks."

"Talk first. Skinny-dip next," he said, hardly believing the words came out of his mouth. Since when was he not in a rush to get naked and horizontal?

She lay down in the water, letting it flow over her entire body, face and all, and came up like a goddess, the sunlight sparkling on the water as it dripped from her hair. "I feel like I've been baptized and all the past is now gone. Oh, Toby, it was horrible."

"Keep talking," he said as he peeled his T-shirt over his head.

She told the story, only pausing for breath a couple of times. "And now Myra has been delivered to her friend Rowdy. Fiona is back in town and after helping out at Nadine's earlier is with Allie at Mama's store," she said at the end. "I'm happy for Myra, but I'm sad for Mitch a little bit. Don't get me wrong. He's a son of a bitch in every sense of the word, but he'll never know true happiness like I've found with you."

Toby finished undressing and joined her in the water. "You didn't have to help her, you know."

"My sister was there for me when I fell apart in the bathroom. Myra needed someone to help her, so I did. It's not a big deal, and it's not to get back at Mitch. She's a woman in trouble. I'd like to think that if Fiona ever needed help that some other woman would step up to the plate," Lizzy said.

"What about Allie? What if she needed help?" Toby asked.

"I'd take care of her, too, but Fiona is down there in south Texas where she has no family so she came to mind," Lizzy answered.

He heard a tinkling piano playing "Amazing Grace" and cocked his head to one side. Even if they were playing that at the church, there was no way the sound could carry a whole mile. Lizzy looked up at him quizzically, her head cocked to one side and her eyebrows drawn together.

"It's no one on my list." He shrugged and shook his head.

"Dammit! I'd forgotten. That is the ring tone for Mitch." It had stopped by the time she fished the thing out of her purse but the phone buzzed in her hand.

"Text message?" Toby asked.

"He wants to know what I said to Myra. I don't have to answer it." She turned the phone off, deleted his number, and blocked any texts from him. "His drama is not part of my world. Neither is Myra's from this point on. Or those hussy twins we met in Granny's new place or the waitress who fawned over you. We are in a bubble where only you and I are allowed. No past can come inside with us."

"Well, I damn sure like that idea." Toby chuckled. "Now tell me who bought Deke's ranch."

"That's tomorrow's business. No future can come inside our bubble, either."

"I can live with that."

"Do you think someone from the gossip squad is watching or are they all at the festival gathering even juicier rumors to spread?" She giggled.

"Who cares? Have I told you that I like you all wet and naked?" He grinned.

"I like naked cowboys." Lizzy nipped at his earlobe.

"Your mouth anywhere on my body drives me crazy," Toby gasped.

"Then prepare for an afternoon of pure insanity." Lizzy laughed.

"Confession, Lizzy. I saw you talking to Mitch and I was scared out of my wits that you were going to give him a second chance." Toby picked her up and set her in his lap.

"Every time that phone of yours buzzes and it's a text from one of your past women, I get that same feeling," she said.

"I'll get a new number next week."

"Not necessary, Toby. I trust you."

"And I love you, Lizzy Logan," Toby said as his lips found hers in a long, hard kiss.

* * *

Dusk was settling over the countryside around Dry Creek when the fireworks display started. With the red blanket from his truck wrapped around their naked bodies, they watched the brilliant colors lighting up the sky a mile away. He was not sure when he would ask her, but he made up his mind when a bright array of bright red sparkled in the sky that he was going to marry Lizzy Logan. He wanted to spend the rest of his life with her, produce that yard full of kids that she'd talked about, and when they were old and gray, he wanted to look back on their lives with lots of stories and no regrets.

CHAPTER TWENTY-FIVE

It was time.

Plain and simple. No skirting the issue any longer. No teasing or squirming her way out of the truth. Lizzy's hands grew clammy and her heart slipped in an extra beat. A hot summer breeze ruffled the willow tree's green leaves, but that wasn't what caused her hands to sweat.

Ahead of her, Dry Creek still had water running in it on Sunday afternoon, the second day of July, which was a miracle. To her right was Deke's old house, cleaned out and empty, waiting for her to move into it, which was another miracle. Pretty red roses tangled themselves in the barbed wire fence to her left and the whole pasture was filled with white daisies and purple wild flowers, making a third miracle because usually the blooms had dried up because of the summer heat by now.

That was three. Could she hope for a fourth? Hope that Toby would understand why she bought the ranch, that he wouldn't have his pride all shattered because she now owned the land he so desperately coveted.

"Don't go away," he drawled beside her.

Instantly he was on his feet and in a few long strides he reached the fence. She rolled onto one side on their red blanket and watched him choose several of the prettiest blooms. When he returned he kneeled before her and laced them into her hair, creating a halo.

Sitting with their knees together, he took her hands in his. Now was the time to tell him, but the moment was so special and so electrified with sparks dancing around them even brighter than the ones from the night in this very same spot that she could not spoil it with words.

"I'm scared to death to say these words, Lizzy Logan." He paused.

Dear lord, was he going to break up with her? Had he found out about the ranch and thought she was being underhanded? Or maybe since the festival was over, he'd figured out that he really wanted to be free to chase the bar bimbos like those twins who'd showed up at Granny's residence.

He inhaled deeply and cupped her chin in his hand.

He was going to kiss her good-bye. Lizzy's heart cracked and tears formed on the back side of her eyes.

She wouldn't let him see her weep and she wouldn't try to hold him if he wanted to go.

"I was afraid to start a real relationship, but I've fallen in love with you, Lizzy. I cannot imagine life without you and..." Another pause.

"Me, too," she mumbled.

"Me, too, what?" His lips were like fire on hers.

"I love you, Toby Dawson," she managed to get out in a whoosh before she lost her nerve.

"I've thought about a dozen scenarios for this moment, but I cannot hold it in another minute." Toby moved a few inches closer.

That old song came to her mind and she hummed it without thinking.

"I remember 'Would You Lay With Me?' and the answer is yes, I would walk a thousand miles through the burning sand if you'll give yourself to me."

"And I would lay with you in a field of stone," she whispered.

The moment was corny, but it was their time as the sun shimmered over the tops of the mesquite trees. It was so sweet that it made her heart swell with love. She got lost in his blue eyes, forgetting that he had been talking about scenarios when she'd started humming Tanya Tucker's old song.

"Will you marry me?" Toby drawled.

Lizzy blinked a dozen times. Had she heard him right? Did he just propose to her? Sweet Jesus in heaven! Now what in the hell did she do?

"No," she whispered.

* * *

Toby had envisioned all kinds of answers when he thought about proposing to Lizzy, but downright refusal wasn't even in the top one thousand. His heart tumbled out onto the green grass and rolled into the creek to drown.

"I cannot marry you until you hear me out," she said.

He grabbed his heart and shoved it back into his chest. The no wasn't final; there was a glimmer of hope.

She removed her hands from his and scooted back until they weren't touching anymore. "I did something on impulse, but now it feels right and you should be the first one to hear. Then I'll tell Mama, Allie, and Fiona."

"Is it Mitch after all?" Toby could feel and hear the pain in his voice.

"No," she said quickly. "God, no!"

"Okay, anything else we can work through. At least I know I haven't lost you to him," Toby said.

"You Dawsons have a lot of pride and…" She paused and sucked in a lungful of air. "I bought Deke's ranch and…"

"That's why you said no?" Toby asked incredulously. She nodded.

"You thought I'd let pride get in the way of love?"

Another brief nod. "Fear of losing you, Toby. I want to incorporate Deke's place into the Lucky Penny. I want to live in that ugly house with you. I want Allie to remodel it a little at a time. But…"

Toby's mouth turned up in a grin. "I was thinking that we'd have to live in that travel trailer until we could get a house built, and that could be five years."

"Then..." she mumbled. "You are okay with it?"

"If that's the only thing standing in our way, then I'm going to ask you the question one more time, Lizzy. I'm amazed that we can add Deke's property to the Lucky Penny, grateful that you bought it, and I love you for doing that for us. I don't have a ring today but will you marry me?"

"Yes!" she squealed, and landed in his lap, knocking him backward and covering his face with kisses.

Toby wanted to hang on to the love he felt right then forever, never letting it out of his reach. Not for a single second, now that he'd found it.

She pushed away from him but kept her hands on his chest. "Are you sure you want to marry me? I will keep working at the feed store and I'm not a neat person."

"I reckon we can put up a baby bed in the office and, darlin', you do the cookin' and I'll make sure the house is semi-clean," he said.

"Deke's house isn't a mansion but it's all paid for, lock, stock, and barrel," she said.

Toby gasped. "You paid cash?"

"The feed store does well and I had a little inheritance from my grandpa. You aren't going to have a problem with me helping with finances are you?"

Toby shook his head. "I love you, not your bank account. But I'm not arguing if you want to buy a pound of bacon. Having Deke's land is going to put us ahead by three years."

"I reckon we can stop calling it Deke's place as of right now. It's all part of the Lucky Penny, so it makes it our place." Her lips found his in a tender kiss that said volumes. His Lizzy could be wild and hot or she could be vulnerable and soft. He loved all her many moods and ways and hoped there were even more to discover in the next sixty or more years they'd have together.

"Well, now that the shock of being told no has worn off and finding out that the Lucky Penny has grown by about thirty percent, let's go take a look at our new house," Toby said.

Walking hand-in-hand, they were halfway to the house when Lizzy's cell phone rang. She let go of his hand, worked it up out of the hip pocket of her skinny jeans, and answered it.

Lizzy did not recognize the phone number but she answered it. When she heard nothing but weeping on the other end, the mesquite trees started to spin around her and the ground was coming up to meet her face when suddenly strong arms circled around her waist.

"Lizzy, are you all right? Look at me?" His voice was husky with concern.

"Allie, are you all right? Is it the baby?" she whispered.

"No, it's Myra," the woman on the other end sobbed.

Lizzy slid out of Toby's arms and sat down in the

grass. The dizziness did not disappear in a minute, but things slowly stood still and she found her voice. "What's wrong, Myra?"

"I need you, Lizzy. I don't have anyone else and Rowdy doesn't know what to do with me, and please, Lizzy, I caused this because of yesterday and now God is punishing me and…"

"Where are you?"

"At the little hospital in Olney," she answered between violent sobs.

"I'll be there in thirty minutes or less. Tell them at the front desk to let me come in," Lizzy said.

"What's wrong?" Toby asked.

"I thought it was Allie. Something terrible has happened to Myra and she wants me to come to Olney. I'm so sorry, Toby. This is our engagement day but I feel like I need to go. She sounds horrible and she has no one."

Toby extended a hand. "Then we'll go together. Marriage is more than hot nights between the sheets, darlin'. It's teamwork and from right now on, we are a team. I'll drive if you'll tell me where to go."

"Thank you," Lizzy said.

Toby was a keeper for sure. A man who would give up his wild women for her, who didn't bat an eye when it came to helping someone that she damn sure didn't owe jack shit to, and who loved Lizzy the way she was without a single word about changing anything.

When they reached the hospital, Lizzy headed for the front desk but a scrawny little fellow stepped in front of her. He had a scraggly blond mustache and his thick hair braided in two ropes that hung down his back. He wore cargo shorts, sandals, and a wrinkled plaid shirt over a tank top.

"I'm Rowdy. Are you Lizzy?" His deep voice did not match his size.

Lizzy nodded. "I am and this is…"

Toby extended his hand. "I'm her fiancé as of an hour ago. I'm Toby Dawson."

"God, I'm glad you are here. I can't call her parents. They're so mad at her they're about to disown her, and she don't want Mitch to know where she is. The only person she said she'd talk to is you, and she's blaming herself for losing the baby even after the doctor said it wasn't anything that she did or didn't do and…" He stopped to catch his breath. "She's right down this way. I'll show you the way."

Lizzy could hear the weeping before she reached the room, and her heart went out to poor Myra. Toby said they were a team and this was their first job as such, so she laced her fingers in his and pushed open the door into the hospital room.

"Lizzy, thank you," she whispered. "God hates me."

Lizzy thought about what her grandmother, her mother, and/or both her sisters would say at that moment and drew on their strength as well as her own. She let go of Toby's hand and crossed the room to stand beside Myra's bed.

"God does not hate you. This is not God's fault or yours. It's an act of nature that happens sometimes.

Don't take the blame on yourself because you feel guilty about Mitch. He's not worth it."

Myra wiped her eyes on the edge of the bedsheet. "Thank you."

Lizzy patted Myra on the shoulder. "This would have happened no matter where you were. You can grieve but you shouldn't punish yourself."

"That's what I've been telling her," Rowdy said. "She's got spunk. I saw it in college. And she can live with me as long as she wants. I've got a nice little house with two bedrooms."

"Okay, then. Are we all good here?" Lizzy asked.

Myra nodded. "Thank you. Rowdy is my friend but..."

"I understand." Lizzy patted her one more time and circled back around the bed to lace her fingers in Toby's. "I'd like you to meet my fiancé, Toby Dawson."

"Congratulations. I wondered why you had roses in your hair."

Lizzy touched them and smiled. "They are pretty, aren't they? Toby gathered them from the fence and the pasture of our new ranch. And now we're going home to tell my mama and sister that I'm engaged," Lizzy said.

"Thank you one more time," Myra said. "You are an angel."

Lizzy giggled all the way out of the room.

"What's so funny?" Toby said when they were well out of hearing distance.

"You know what they say about angels?" she asked.

"That they have wings and a halo?"

"No, that they are just wild women who've had the hell screwed out of them," she said with another giggle.

"Maybe that's what turned my life around. I got the hell knocked out of me during those hot nights with you," he said.

"We really are a team, aren't we?"

"You got it, darlin'."

CHAPTER TWENTY-SIX

Good grief! What are you doing with roses in your hair?" Allie asked when Lizzy and Toby reached the house that evening.

"What are y'all doin' here? No, don't answer that. I'm glad you are here because now I won't have to make two announcements," Lizzy said.

"Deke is here, too, and he says he ain't sayin' a word until you get here. This has been the best-kept secret Dry Creek has ever had. Everyone is sitting beside their phones waiting to hear who bought Deke's ranch and..." Allie stopped for breath. "And we're all in the kitchen around the table. Mama made chocolate cake and home-made ice cream, but she won't let me have any until you tell us."

Allie led the way to the kitchen with Lizzy and Toby behind her and talked the whole way. The heat of

Toby's hand on Lizzy's back made her wish they were back under the willow tree or even in his tiny trailer. She could think of all kinds of ways that this teamwork could play out.

"Where have you been? I called and it went to voice mail." Katy looked up from the head of the table. Deke was at the other end. Blake was to her right and Allie's chair was still pushed out from where she got up to meet them at the door.

Fiona looked up from the chair closest to Deke. "I tried to call you a dozen times."

"Had to turn off the phone in the hospital," Toby said.

"Hospital! What happened?" The chair made a loud scraping noise as Katy got to her feet. "Are you all right?"

"I'm fine. It wasn't me. It was Myra. I'll help dip ice cream and tell you what happened." Lizzy headed for the cabinets and took a stack of bowls from the cabinet. While she and Katy filled the bowls and cut into the double layer chocolate cake, she told them the story of what had happened that evening. "And you all have to swear that Myra's new residence does not leave this kitchen because she needs to get a hell of a lot stronger before she has to face Mitch or her parents."

"You are a good woman to do that for her," Deke said. "But then we always knew there was a heart hiding down inside that stubborn streak. How'd she get away from Mitch anyway?"

Fiona raised her hand. "I helped with that. Poor girl

was scared out of her mind and wouldn't even sit up straight in the seat until I parked in front of her friend's house. He seemed like a good person and he didn't ask a bunch of questions. Just took her right into the house and I turned around and came home. And now I've got to hurry up and eat ice cream and then get on the road so I don't miss my flight. Tomorrow it's going to be back at the work grind."

Lizzy carried the bowls of ice cream and dessert plates of chocolate cake to the table. "I wish you could stay longer, but I'm so glad for this weekend and I'm really happy that you are here for my two announcements. This evening can be our celebration."

"Do the roses in your hair have something to do with one of them?" Allie asked.

"The roses came from the barbed wire fence down by that little section of Dry Creek that still has enough water in it to…" She paused and blushed. "To go wading in. It'll dry up in a couple of weeks. I can't remember a time when it had water in it this late in the summer."

"I picked them and wound them into her pretty hair," Toby said.

"Who bought Deke's ranch? Mary Jo and Nadine are on pins for me to call them and deliver the news. Money will pass hands on bets that have been made," Allie said.

"And I've got a five-dollar bill on a name, too, with four-to-one odds, so I stand to make twenty bucks if I'm right," Fiona said.

"I did," Lizzy said. "Deke and I closed the deal on Friday. What's left on the ranch belongs to me or rather to the Lucky Penny Ranch because I'm incorporating my land into the ranch."

Fiona let out a whoop. "I knew it and everyone said I was crazy as hell, but you would have told me if it had been anyone else but you! I'll make Lucy Hudson send me every bit of that money."

Allie's spoon stopped midway between the bowl and her mouth, and she looked at Lizzy as if she'd grown another eye right in the middle of her forehead.

Poor old Blake was so stunned that his eyes wouldn't blink. And Katy popped the side of her head, as if trying to make her ears work.

The silence was deafening until Deke chuckled. "I told you that you'd be surprised." He took a bite of his ice cream as if nothing had just happened.

"You are shittin' me," Blake whispered.

"No, she's not," Toby said. "Shocked the hell out of me, too, brother."

"Are you going to move into the house?" Allie asked.

"I am," Lizzy answered.

Blake's expression testified that he was still in shock. "And you really want to add that to the Lucky Penny?"

"I do."

"Why?" Allie asked.

"Because I want my own place and I had the money saved up, and Toby's trailer is too damn small for two people," she answered.

"We're engaged," Toby blurted.

"Bullshit!" Allie said.

Fiona dropped her spoon. "I'll be damned. You did sneak that one in on me."

"And this halo of roses is my engagement ring. Isn't it pretty?"

"Congratulations!" Deke said. "I knew it was going to happen. I just didn't know when. I'm damn sure glad you bought that house and ranch, Lizzy. Jesus couldn't live with you in that cramped-up trailer of Toby's. You might have done a good deed tonight, but there's still a lot of Logan stubborn hiding in that body of yours."

Toby drew her close to his side. "I'm a lucky man."

"Yes, you are," Katy said. "I'll add my congratulations to Deke's, but there's sadness in my heart because my last baby girl is leaving Audrey's Place."

"Maybe someday Fiona will come back to Dry Creek." Lizzy looked across the room at her sister.

"Hell will freeze over before that happens." Fiona smiled. "But congratulations, sister. I thought this might happen on down the road, but I did not see this coming this quickly."

Allie groaned. "Please tell me we aren't going to have to endure the wedding book again."

Lizzy laughed and leaned her head on Toby's shoulder. "No, ma'am. No wedding book. No big wedding. Friday night y'all come over to my new house and we'll have a preacher there. Blake and Allie can stand up with us. Mama, you and Deke can be the witnesses. Or we can go to the courthouse one afternoon and it will all be done. You sure you can't stay until then, Fiona?"

"No, darlin'. As much as I'd love to be here, I've got to get back to work or I won't have a job, and I do like to eat so I have to make money," Fiona said.

"Friday night sounds good to me," Blake said. "Whew! My mind is still reeling. Have you told our mama, Toby?"

"Not yet but I will," Toby said.

"No more bars and chasin' women?" Deke sighed. "I've lost the best bar buddy I ever had."

"Yep, you sure did." Toby nodded. "But Jud will be here in the fall and I'm sure he will be ready to take on that role."

"I'm not complainin'. I got my sassy sister back," Allie said.

"Yep, you sure did." Lizzy grinned.

On Friday night, after work, Lizzy hurried home to Audrey's Place for the last time. She dressed in a white eyelet lace sundress that skimmed the tops of her new bright blue cowboy boots with lace insets on the tops. Sitting still while her mother wove fresh white daisies and a few wild flowers into her hair was not easy.

"Stop fidgeting," Katy said.

"She's more nervous than I was," Allie said.

"You were marrying a wild cowboy and you'd tamed him. I'm marryin' the hot cowboy in the Dawson family and I'm not even his type," Lizzy smarted off.

"Oh, honey, the way he eats you up with those blue

eyes, I'd say his type changed drastically when he came to this part of Texas," Katy said. "I'm going to miss you, baby girl."

"I'm not the baby girl. Fiona is and I'm tellin' you she'll get tired of that big city shit someday and show up here in Dry Creek," Lizzy told them. "It's perfect, Mama. Just what I wanted. We've got fifteen minutes until we need to be at the house. Have you got any last-minute advice for me?"

"Never go to bed angry. Always talk to each other. Never talk about each other behind the other one's back, unless it's to your sister or to me. We can still love Toby even when he makes you mad as hell, and we'll listen to you vent without judging either of you. But remember if you vent, then we have the right to tell you if it's you who's wrong in the fight."

"How about you, Allie? You got anything to say?"

"I'm still worried that this is too fast, but like Mama says, he looks at you like Blake does me and I believe with all my heart and soul that Dawson men can be trusted. So go get 'em, sister. I'm just glad that you'll be living right next door to me and you aren't moving off to Wichita Falls or Mexico," Allie answered. "And I wish Fiona could be here."

Toby plowed all day, took a quick shower, and dressed in creased jeans, shined black boots, and a white pearl snap shirt. That's as fancy as Lizzy wanted him to be and he was fine with her decision. He'd picked a huge bouquet of roses that day, and with Allie's help they'd wrapped blue satin ribbon around the stems to hold it together for Lizzy.

He'd never been so nervous in his entire life. He combed his dark hair back, looked at the reflection in the mirror above the sink, and told the man staring back at him that he was the luckiest son of a gun in the whole world. Tonight he and Lizzy would start their married life in their new house.

Their ugly house as she called it but there wasn't one thing ugly about it to Toby. The walls might need some paint and they had very little furniture, but it was their home, the place where they'd love, argue, make up, hopefully raise kids, and someday even see grandkids coming around to visit. Nothing with that much potential could be ugly.

"Been where you are and know how you are feelin'." Blake leaned against the doorjamb into the pink bathroom.

"I want it to be done with so I know she's mine," Toby said.

"Never thought I'd hear those words out of your mouth."

"Me, either. I hear a vehicle. Is it the preacher or the ladies?"

"One. Two. Three. Four." Blake counted off the doors as they slammed. "I'd say it's both. If you are going to change your mind, now is the time to run."

"Hell, no! I've never wanted anything more in my life," Toby said.

"Then get married and get on with living."

Someone knocked on the door and Blake opened it. The preacher stood there with a Bible in one hand and the marriage license in the other.

"Come right in," Blake said.

Blue looked up from the corner of the living room and growled.

"Does that dog bite?" the preacher asked.

"No, he's only protecting his new harem of kittens. The mama cat is somewhere in the house, but he's adopted those babies and thinks they are his. Long as you don't try to take one of them, he's fine," Toby explained.

"Katy says we are to stand in front of that fireplace right there. Deke is to sit on the..."

"I'm right here." Deke rushed into the house through the kitchen door. "Cow got out so I'm a little bit late, but I'm cleaned up and ready to do my part. I see Lizzy brought the cats home."

"She wanted Blue and the cats to be in the house for the wedding." Toby grinned.

"You are to sit on one of the folding chairs and Katy will sit in the other one," the preacher pointed. "I hear them on the porch. So gentlemen, take your places."

Katy came in first, crossed over to her chair and sat down. Then Allie arrived wearing a sweet little blue sundress and carrying a bouquet of wildflowers from the pasture. Right behind her was Lizzy, Toby's Lizzy, in a white dress, carrying the roses he'd picked for her. He was afraid to blink for fear she would disappear.

She handed her mother her bouquet, took his hands

in hers, and looked up into his eyes. "Toby Dawson, I never meant to fall in love with you, but I did and it was the right thing to do because my heart is at peace with it. I'm not arguing with myself. I'm not changing myself and I don't want to change you. God sent you to me at the right time, and I'm damn sure not going to argue with God. So tonight I'm going to vow to love, honor, and respect you. I'm going to vow to protect this love with all my strength and soul, and if you die before I do, promise me you'll drag your feet a little when you start up the stairs to the Pearly Gates because I swear I'll be with you in a day or two. Because I can live without you Toby, but I don't want to."

Toby swallowed hard and forgot every single thing he'd planned to say to her. He'd practiced it all week and now it was gone. The only thing he could do was speak straight from his heart and hope to hell it made sense. "Lizzy Logan, I love you. I didn't think you were my type and thank God you weren't or this day wouldn't be here. My type wasn't what I needed to make me happy, and I was drifting in a swirling pool of muddy water. I needed you in my life and although we both fought what our hearts knew long before we did, I'm glad that we are here and that you are going to be my wife for all eternity. I vow to honor, respect, be true to you, and love you, not until my dying day but way past that. And if you die before I do, just sit down on the nearest hay bale and wait. I'll be along real quick because my heart would break without you in my life."

"Well, it looks like all I need to do is ask for the

rings and bless his marriage." The preacher removed a white hanky from his pocket and handed it to Allie, who wiped her eyes and passed it off to her mother. Deke snatched it before it made its way back to the preacher.

Ten minutes later, a bright shiny gold band was on Toby's finger and Lizzy wore the matching one. The marriage license had been witnessed and hugs given. Toby and Lizzy were officially married.

"You have today and tomorrow and I'll even put the Do Not Disturb sign on your door," Katy said. "But you will be in church on Sunday morning because the ladies are planning a potluck dinner complete with a wedding cake reception. And all of Toby's family will be there, just like they were at Blake and Allie's wedding."

"Yes, Mama Katy." Toby grinned.

"I like that title just fine." She hugged him tightly. "Welcome to our crazy family."

"Thank you."

Deke slung open the door. "The honeymoon is going to be short enough. Out everyone."

When the last vehicle was gone, Toby scooped Lizzy up into his arms and carried her to the master bedroom. He kicked the door shut with his boot and laid her on a brand-new bed that had been delivered that day. A wedding gift from her mother, it was a four-poster made of oak.

"I reckon she knew we'd need something sturdy for a lifetime of hot cowboy nights." Lizzy laughed.

Toby slowly started to undress her, kissing each inch of bare skin that he uncovered. "And they start right now, Mrs. Dawson."

"No, darlin', they started months ago but they'll go on for the rest of our lives." She grabbed the top of his shirt and with one fell swoop, undid every pearl snap.

Stranded by the side of the road, Fiona Logan eagerly accepts a ride from the most handsome cowboy she has ever seen. And when they both wind up staying at the same place for the holidays, well, Christmas suddenly gets very cozy...

Please see the next page
for a preview of

Merry Cowboy Christmas,

Available now.

Jud Dawson tapped the brakes and slid a few feet before his big black truck came to a stop. The rusted out old bucket of bolts he'd been following on the slick road wasn't quite so lucky, though. It kept going right through a barbed wire fence. The whole scene played out in the blink of an eye and yet it felt like an eternity for the old truck to come to a complete halt, kissing a big scrub oak tree about fifteen feet from the fence line.

Jud barely scrambled from the cab of his truck to see if the other driver was unhurt when a redheaded woman dressed in tight jeans, boots, and a sweater hopped out of the run-down vehicle, kicked the shit out of her blown-out tire, and tangled both her fists in her hair in anger.

"Are you okay?" he yelled as he ran toward her, phone in hand ready to call 911 if he needed to.

"Hell, no! My truck is a wreck. I'm going to be late to dinner, and I'm so mad I could spit tacks," she screamed, and shook her fist at the gray skies. "Damn tires only needed to run for another half a mile. Now I'll have to walk, and I didn't even bring a decent coat. Since when does Dry Creek get snow in November?"

"I can take you wherever you need to go," Jud offered.

"No, thank you. It's not that far and I can walk." She stopped ranting and shivered. "Do you know where Audrey's Place is?"

He nodded. "Yes, ma'am, that is where I was headed. You must be..." He hesitated, trying to remember her name. Faith. Fancy. Something that started with an F or was it a V? If she was headed to Audrey's, then she had to be the youngest Logan sister, the red-headed one who was married, doing very well, and on her way to giving Midas a run when it came to money. So what the hell was she doing driving a ratty old truck?

"I'm Fiona Logan and thank you. I'll get my purse. The suitcase and box can wait," she said.

Evidently she'd decided he wasn't an ax murderer or a crazy ex-con because she smiled. "Just so you know." She opened the passenger's door of the truck and fished around in the glove compartment. "I do carry a weapon and I have a concealed permit and I can take the eyes out of a rattlesnake at twenty yards."

Damn, but she was cute with that curly red hair, a faint sprinkling of freckles across a pert little nose, and all those curves. "I'm not a rattlesnake, ma'am." Jud grinned. "And since we're already here, why don't we throw your things into the backseat of my truck and take them now? It'll save a trip back."

"Thank you. I appreciate that." She nodded toward the fence. "Looks like I've done some major property damage to the Lucky Penny. My sisters and their husbands own this place. I hope they're not mad at me for tearing up the fence."

"Pleased to meet you, Fiona Logan. And your sisters will be so glad you aren't hurt that they won't care about a few feet of fence. And I'm Jud Dawson, cousin to your new brothers-in-law, but you already know that. Turns out, I'm staying at Audrey's. Your mama didn't want me to live in the travel trailer with winter coming on." Jud removed an expensive, mono-grammed suitcase from the passenger seat. It looked as out of place in that old vehicle as a cowboy at an opera.

"Maybe if I don't have to ask them to come out here and get my stuff they won't make me fix the fence," she answered.

The stories he'd heard did not match up with a truck that looked like it was ready to cross the bridge into that great junkyard in the sky. The suitcase was one of those fancy four-wheeled jobs, but there was no way it would travel across the rough ground, so Jud hefted it up on his broad shoulder.

"What did you pack in this thing? Rocks?" he asked.

"Everything I could. What wouldn't fit in there is in the box."

"Lot to bring home for a four-day holiday," he said.

She ignored his remark with a shrug and a shiver.

He whipped off his Sherpa-lined leather coat and handed it to her. "You're freezing. Get inside the truck and warm up. This won't take but a minute."

The box was only slightly lighter than that monster suitcase. As he was walking away from her vehicle, he heard a hiss and turned back to see steam escaping from under the hood. Either the steel fence post had punctured the radiator or barbed wire had ripped away hoses and belts.

He shoved the box in the backseat beside the suitcase and slammed the door, circled around the front of the truck, and crawled inside. "Looks like you've made your last voyage in that thing." He started the engine and eased down on the gas. Ice and gravel crunched under the truck's tires as they eased on ahead.

"I was hoping that it would get me all the way home."

A little shorter than either of her sisters, she was definitely built with curves in all the right places. He started the engine, eased forward on the slippery road, and stole a glance toward her. She sat ramrod straight in the seat in a no-nonsense, take-control posture, but her dark green eyes and the way she kept biting at her lower lip said that Fiona Logan wasn't real sure of herself that Thanksgiving.

Her obvious insecurity didn't jibe with the stories he'd been told about the third Logan sister, either. It was shaping up to be an interesting day.

"So what are you doing out on these roads today?" she asked.

"I was sent on an errand. It appears that giblet gravy cannot be made until there is a can of evaporated milk in the house, and since Thanksgiving dinner can't be put upon the table unless there is giblet gravy, then someone had to go for milk," he drawled.

She nodded and looked even more nervous when the old brothel known as Audrey's Place came into view.

Fiona cut her eyes around at the cowboy. So this was Jud, the cowboy in the Dawson family that everyone said was the lucky one. His blond hair was a little shaggy, hanging down to the collar of his pearl snap shirt in the back. An errant strand or two peeked out from under his black cowboy hat and inched down his forehead toward his dark chocolate brown eyes. His face would make a sculptor swoon with all those perfect planes and contours, and the way his muscles bulged under his shirt when he'd picked up her suitcase and box could turn a holy woman into a hooker.

She was glad that he'd been close by when that damn tire decided to blow out. But sitting with him in the truck, traveling at a snail's pace? The air in the cab of the black, club-cab truck was way too thin. She inhaled deeply and let it out slowly and was glad it was only half a mile to her home because his coat around her shoulders suddenly made her hotter than blue blazes.

That he didn't seem to be in a hurry was fine with

her. She needed a few minutes to get a grip on her hormones and her racing heart before she arrived. It couldn't be Jud Dawson with those sexy eyes and dreamy body causing her to sweat in the middle of a damn blizzard. It was the fact that she was back in Dry Creek, starting all over from scratch. But she'd had two choices when the groceries and rent played out at the same time. She could either go home or go homeless, and the former, even though she'd have to eat all of her pride, was better than living in a cardboard box and eating from Dumpsters.

He parked beside another big fancy truck, and she sat there, staring at the house, unable to open the door. She wanted to go into the house and surprise her family, so why couldn't she make herself open the damn door? Lights shining out through the windows threw rays of yellow onto the snow-covered yard and beckoned her to come on inside where there was comfort and unconditional love. But first, she needed something, anything, to calm her shaky nerves. She clasped her hands tightly in her lap and waited.

"You going to get out or sit here and watch it snow all day?" the cowboy asked.

She frowned, a smartass remark on her lips. But that little voice inside her head reminded her that Jud had helped her out. She swung the truck door open, stepped out into the blowing snow, and grabbed the suitcase from the backseat. It thumped along like a miniature snowplow all the way to the porch where she tugged it up the three steps with both hands. She parked it beside the door and reached for the cold handle, but she could not turn it.

"Go on inside and I'll bring the suitcase and the box," Jud said.

Every step took her a foot closer to the porch and he was right behind her, box in hand, with two cans of milk sitting on the top of the cardboard box.

With the driving force of a north wind behind them, the snowflakes felt more like hard sleet pellets when they hit her face, so she walked a little faster—until she reached the porch and opened the storm door.

This was it! She'd made a full circle. Left home to go to college right out of high school. Got a fantastic job with the law firm in Houston when she graduated. Married the son of the firm's senior partner a year later. He divorced her last year and made sure her name was ruined when it came to getting another job. She'd worked at a coffee shop until a week ago when the whole business closed down. And now she was back home, right where she said she would never, ever return to, not even if she had to stand on a street corner to make a living.

"You'll freeze if you don't go inside," Jud said. "And this milk will have to be thawed before it can be used."

She looked over her shoulder. His warm smile melted a few snowflakes but didn't do jack shit when it came to easing her nerves.

"Please open the door...please. This damn box is heavy." He chuckled.

What was so damn funny? Matter of fact, what could be humorous right now in anyone's world? There was a freaking blizzard going on in Texas. That should wipe the smile off anyone's face. She wanted to weep because she'd made it home. She quickly gave thanks that the old bald tires had gotten her that close and there was someone who'd brought her the rest of the way. But there was still enough anger over the way fate had treated her that she'd like to kick a few more tires. She brushed away a single tear and inhaled deeply as raw emotions raced through her body, leaving her with still another case of jitters. Finally, she slung the door open into the foyer.

"Fiona!! Oh. My. God! Allie! Mama! Fiona is home," Lizzy squealed, and turned into a bright red blur as she ran from the kitchen. Fiona's eyes barely had time to focus when she was engulfed in a hug that came close to knocking her square on her butt. And then her mother and Allie were both there and it became a big group hug that kept them all steady and on their feet.

"Surprise," she said weakly.

Jud stood inside the door, that wickedly sexy smile on his face as if he was Santa Claus and had just shimmied down the chimney with a big bag of toys. He sat the box on the floor and then effortlessly pulled the suitcase in from the porch.

"Jud, where's the milk?" A tall dark-haired cowboy carrying a pink bundle stepped from the kitchen out into the foyer.

"Right here along with the store keys." He headed to the kitchen with both in his hand.

Sweet Jesus!

He'd told her that he lived at Audrey's and that he was Jud Dawson. But it didn't sink in until that moment that she would be sharing a house with him.

Carolyn Brown is a *New York Times* and *USA Today* bestselling romance author and RITA® finalist who has published more than seventy-five books. Presently writing both women's fiction and cowboy romance, Brown has also written historical single title, historical series, contemporary single title, and contemporary series. She lives in southern Oklahoma with her husband, a former English teacher, who is not allowed to read her books until they are published. They have three children and enough grandchildren to keep them young.

You can learn more at:
CarolynLBrown.com

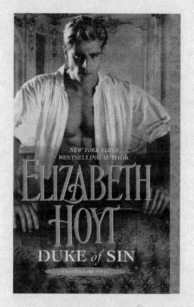

DUKE OF SIN
By Elizabeth Hoyt

Valentine Napier, the Duke of Montgomery, is the man London whispers about in boudoirs and back alleys. A notorious rake and blackmailer, Montgomery has returned from exile, intent on seeking revenge on those who have wronged him. But what he finds in his own bedroom may lay waste to all his plans.

Fall in Love with Forever Romance

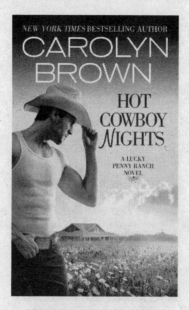

HOT COWBOY NIGHTS
By Carolyn Brown

New York Times and *USA Today* bestselling author Carolyn
Brown brings us back to the Lucky Penny Ranch for some
HOT COWBOY NIGHTS. Toby Dawson never was and
never will be the settling-down type. But what harm could
there be in agreeing to be Lizzy Logan's pretend boyfriend?
They'll put on a show so all of Dry Creek knows Lizzy's
over her ex, then be done. Yet the more Toby gets to know
Lizzy—really know her—the harder it is for him to keep his
hands off her in private.

Fall in Love with Forever Romance

PRIMAL INSTINCT
By Tara Wyatt

When Taylor's record label hires a bodyguard for her, she's less than thrilled to find it's her one-night stand, ex-army ranger Colt, who shows up for the job. But as danger from an obsessed stalker mounts, crossing the line between business and pleasure could get them both killed. Perfect for fans of Suzanne Brockmann, Pamela Clare, and Julie Ann Walker.